Red Queen

Red Queen

WITCH WORLD, VOL. 1

CHRISTOPHER PIKE

Previously titled *Witch World*

SIMON PULSE

NEW YORK   LONDON   TORONTO   SYDNEY   NEW DELHI

SIMON PULSE

An imprint of Simon & Schuster Children's Publishing Division
1230 Avenue of the Americas, New York, NY 10020
First Simon Pulse paperback edition August 2014
Text copyright © 2012 by Christopher Pike
Previously titled *Witch World*
Cover photographs copyright © 2014 by Marta Bevacqua/Trevillion Images
All rights reserved, including the right of reproduction in whole or in part in any form.
SIMON PULSE and colophon are registered trademarks of Simon & Schuster, Inc.
Also available in a Simon Pulse hardcover edition, titled *Witch World*.
For information about special discounts for bulk purchases, please contact
Simon & Schuster Special Sales at 1-866-506-1949 or business@simonandschuster.com.
The Simon & Schuster Speakers Bureau can bring authors to your live event.
For more information or to book an event contact the Simon & Schuster Speakers Bureau
at 1-866-248-3049 or visit our website at www.simonspeakers.com.
Cover designed by Regina Flath
The text of this book was set in Garamond.
Manufactured in the United States of America
2 4 6 8 10 9 7 5 3 1
Library of Congress Control Number 2013944712
ISBN 978-1-4424-3028-0 (*Witch World* hc)
ISBN 978-1-4424-3029-7 (pbk)
ISBN 978-1-4814-2502-5 (eBook)

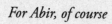

For Abir, of course

CHAPTER ONE

ONCE I BELIEVED THAT I WANTED NOTHING MORE THAN love. Someone who would care for me more than he cared for himself. A guy who would never betray me, never lie to me, and most of all never leave me. Yeah, that was what I desired most, what people usually call true love.

I don't know if that has really changed.

Yet I have to wonder now if I want something else just as badly.

What is it? You must wonder . . .

Magic. I want my life filled with the mystery of magic.

Silly, huh? Most people would say there's no such thing.

Then again, most people are not witches.

Not like me.

I discovered what I was when I was eighteen years old, two days after I graduated high school. Before then I was your typical teenager. I got up in the morning, went to school, stared at my ex-boyfriend across the campus courtyard and imagined what it would be like to have him back in my life, went to the local library and sorted books for four hours, went home, watched TV, read a little, lay in bed and thought some more about Jimmy Kelter, then fell asleep and dreamed.

But I feel, somewhere in my dreams, I sensed I was different from other girls my age. Often it seemed, as I wandered the twilight realms of my unconscious, that I existed in another world, a world like our own and yet different, too. A place where I had powers my normal, everyday self could hardly imagine.

I believe it was these dreams that made me crave that elusive thing that is as great as true love. It's hard to be sure, I only know that I seldom awakened without feeling a terrible sense of loss. As though my very soul had been chopped into pieces and tossed back into the world. The sensation of being on the "outside" is difficult to describe. All I can say is that, deep inside, a part of me always hurt.

I used to tell myself it was because of Jimmy. He had dumped me, all of a sudden, for no reason. He had broken my heart, dug it out of my chest, and squashed it when he said I really like you, Jessie, we can still be friends, but I've got to go now. I blamed him for the pain. Yet it had been there before I had fallen in love with him, so there had to be another reason why it existed.

Now I know Jimmy was only a part of the equation.

But I get ahead of myself. Let me begin, somewhere near the beginning.

Like I said, I first became aware I was a witch the same weekend I graduated high school. At the time I lived in Apple Valley, which is off Interstate 15 between Los Angeles and Las Vegas. How that hick town got that name was beyond me. Apple Valley was smack in the middle of the desert. I wouldn't be exaggerating if I said it's easier to believe in witches than in apple trees growing in that godforsaken place.

Still, it was home, the only home I had known since I was six. That was when my father the doctor had decided that Nurse Betty—that was what my mom called her—was more sympathetic to his needs than my mother. From birth to six I lived in a mansion overlooking the Pacific, in a Malibu enclave loaded with movie stars and the studio executives who had made them famous. My mom, she must have had a lousy divorce lawyer, because even though she had worked her butt off to put my father through medical school and a six-year residency that trained him to be one of the finest heart surgeons on the West Coast, she was kicked out of the marriage with barely enough money to buy a two-bedroom home in Apple Valley. And with summer temperatures averaging above a hundred, real estate was never a hot item in our town.

I was lucky I had skin that gladly suffered the sun. It was soft, and I tanned deeply without peeling. My coloring probably helped. My family tree is mostly European, but there was an American Indian in the mix back before the Civil War.

Chief Proud Feather. You might wonder how I know his name, and that's good—wonder away, you'll find out, it's part of my story. He was 100 percent Hopi, but since he was sort of a distant relative, he gave me only a small portion of my features. My hair is brown with a hint of red. At dawn and sunset it is more maroon than anything else. I have freckles and green eyes, but not the green of a true redhead. My freckles are few, often lost in my tan, and my eyes are so dark the green seems to come and go, depending on my mood.

There wasn't much green where I grew up. The starved branches on the trees on our campus looked as if they were always reaching for the sky, praying for rain.

I was pretty; for that matter, I still am pretty. Understand, I turned eighteen a long time ago. Yet I still look much the same. I'm not immortal, I'm just very hard to kill. Of course, I could die tonight, who's to say.

It was odd, as a bright and attractive senior in high school, I wasn't especially popular. Apple Valley High was small—our graduating class barely topped two hundred. I knew all the seniors. I had memorized the first and last name of every cute boy in my class, but I was seldom asked out. I used to puzzle over that fact. I especially wondered why James Kelter had dumped me after only ten weeks of what, to me, had felt like the greatest relationship in the world. I was to find out when our class took that ill-fated trip to Las Vegas.

Our weekend in Sin City was supposed to be the equivalent of our Senior All-Night Party. I know, on the surface that sounds silly. A party usually lasts one night, and our parents believed we were spending the night at the local Hilton. However, the plan was for all two hundred of us to privately call our parents in the morning and say we had just been invited by friends to go camping in the mountains that separated our desert from the LA Basin.

The scheme was pitifully weak. Before the weekend was over, most of our parents would know we'd been nowhere near the mountains. That didn't matter. In fact, that was the whole point of the trip. We had decided, as a class, to throw all caution to the wind and break all the rules.

The reason such a large group was able to come to such a wild decision was easy to understand if you considered our unusual location. Apple Valley was nothing more than a road stop stuck between the second largest city in the nation—LA—and its most fun city—Las Vegas. For most of our lives, especially on Friday and Saturday evenings, we watched as thousands of cars flew northeast along Interstate 15 toward good times, while we remained trapped in a fruit town that didn't even have fruit trees.

So when the question arose of where we wanted to celebrate

our graduation, all our years of frustration exploded. No one cared that you had to be twenty-one to gamble in the casinos. Not all of us were into gambling and those who were simply paid Ted Pollack to make them fake IDs.

Ted made my ID for free. He was an old friend. He lived a block over from my house. He had a terrible crush on me, one I wasn't supposed to know about. Poor Ted, he confided everything in his heart to his sister, Pam, who kept secrets about as well as the fifty-year-old gray parrot that lived in their kitchen. It was dangerous to talk in front of that bird, just as it was the height of foolishness to confide in Pam.

I wasn't sure why Ted cared so deeply about me. Of course, I didn't understand why I cared so much about Jimmy. At eighteen I understood very little about love, and it's a shame I wasn't given a chance to know more about it before I was changed. That's something I'll always regret.

That particular Friday ended up being a wasteland of regrets. After a two-hour graduation ceremony that set a dismal record for scorching heat and crippling boredom, I learned from my best friend, Alex Simms, that both Ted and Jimmy would be driving with us to Las Vegas. Alex told me precisely ten seconds after I collected my blue-and-gold cap off the football field—after our class collectively threw them in the air—and exactly one minute after our school principal had pronounced us full-fledged graduates.

"You're joking, right?" I said.

Alex brushed her short blond hair from her bright blues. She wasn't as pretty as me but that didn't stop her from acting like she was. The weird thing is, it worked for her. Even though she didn't have a steady boyfriend, she dated plenty, and there wasn't a guy in school who would have said no to her if she'd so much as said hi. A natural flirt, she could touch a guy's hand and make him feel like his fingers were caressing her breasts.

Alex was a rare specimen, a compulsive talker who knew when to shut up and listen. She had a quick wit—some would say it was biting—and her self-confidence was legendary. She had applied to UCLA with a B-plus average and a slightly above-average SAT score and they had accepted her—supposedly—on the strength of her interview. While Debbie Pernal, a close friend of ours, had been turned down by the same school despite a straight-A average and a very high SAT score.

It was Debbie's belief that Alex had seduced one of the interviewing deans. In Debbie's mind, there was no other explanation for how Alex had gotten accepted. Debbie said as much to anyone who would listen, which just happened to be the entire student body. Her remarks started a tidal wave of a rumor: "ALEX IS A TOTAL SLUT!" Of course, the fact that Alex never bothered to deny the slur didn't help matters. If anything, she took great delight in it.

And these two were friends.

Debbie was also driving with us to Las Vegas.

"There was a mix-up," Alex said without much conviction,

trying to explain why Jimmy was going to ride in the car with us. "We didn't plan for both of them to come."

"Why would anyone in their right mind put Jimmy and me together in the same car?" I demanded.

Alex dropped all pretense. "Could it be that I'm sick and tired of you whining about how he dumped you when everything was going so perfect between you two?"

I glared at her. "We're best friends! You're required to listen to my whining. It doesn't give you the right to invite the one person in the whole world who ripped my heart out to go on a road trip with us."

"What road trip? We're just giving him a three-hour ride. You don't have to talk to him if you don't want to."

"Right. The five of us are going to be crammed into your car half the afternoon and it will be perfectly normal if I don't say a word to the first and last guy I ever had sex with."

Alex was suddenly interested. "I didn't know Jimmy was your first. You always acted like you slept with Clyde Barker."

Clyde Barker was our football quarterback and so good-looking that none of the girls who went to the games—myself included—cared that he couldn't throw a pass to save his ass. He had the IQ of a cracked helmet. "It was just an act," I said with a sigh.

"Look, it might work out better than you think. My sources tell me Jimmy has hardly been seeing Kari at all. They may even be broken up."

Kari Rider had been Jimmy's girlfriend before me, and after me, which gave me plenty of reason to hate the bitch.

"Why don't we be absolutely sure and invite Kari as well," I said. "She can sit on my lap."

Alex laughed. "Admit it, you're a tiny bit happy I did all this behind your back."

"I'm a tiny bit considering not going at all."

"Don't you dare. Ted would be devastated."

"Ted's going to be devastated when he sees Jimmy get in your car!"

Alex frowned. "You have a point. Debbie invited him, not me."

On top of everything else, Debbie had a crush on Ted, the same Ted who had a crush on me. It was going to be a long three hours to Las Vegas.

"Did Debbie think it was a good idea for Jimmy to ride with us?" I asked.

"Sure."

I was aghast. "I can't believe it. That bitch."

"Well, actually, she didn't think there was a chance in hell he'd come."

That hurt. "Love the vote of confidence. What you mean is Debbie didn't think there was a chance in hell Jimmy was still interested in me."

"I didn't say that."

"No. But you both thought it."

"Come on, Jessie. It's obvious Jimmy's coming with us so he can spend time with you." Alex patted me on the back. "Be happy."

"Why did you wait until now to tell me this?"

"Because now it's too late to change my devious plan."

I dusted off my blue-and-gold cap and put it back on. "I suppose this is your graduation present to me?" I asked.

"Sure. Where's mine?"

"You'll get it when we get to Las Vegas."

"Really?"

"Yeah. You'll see." I already had a feeling I was going to pay her back, I just didn't know how.

CHAPTER TWO

I WAS AN IDIOT TO GET IN ALEX'S CAR. BUT I WAS NOT fool enough to sit in the backseat between Ted and Jimmy. Debbie ended up sandwiched between the boys, where she looked quite content.

It was two in the afternoon by the time we hit the road. Our parents had insisted on taking us three girls to lunch, but it was only fun as long as our appetites lasted. We were anxious to get to Vegas. Also, there was tension between Alex's and Debbie's parents.

It was rooted in the UCLA fiasco and the ugly talk surrounding it. The truth was Debbie had only been accepted by the University of Santa Barbara—an incredibly beautiful campus, in my humble opinion—and she had graduated second in our class, while Alex had finished thirty-eighth. Alex made no effort to soften the tension, wearing a UCLA T-shirt to lunch.

Out of the five parents present, my mom was the only one who did much talking.

No one was jealous of me. I had finished tenth in our class and my SAT scores equaled Debbie's, but I hadn't bothered to apply to college. It was a money thing, I didn't have any. And I couldn't apply for financial aid because my father was rich.

Silly me, I kept hoping my father would suddenly remember he had a daughter who had just graduated high school and who needed six figures just to get an undergraduate degree. But so far he had not called, or written, or e-mailed me.

My mom didn't appreciate his silent rejection. She bitched about it whenever she had a chance. But I took the rejection in stride. I only cried about it when I was alone in my bed at night.

I hardly knew my dad but it was weird—I missed him.

"I enjoyed your speech," Jimmy said to Debbie as he and Ted climbed aboard in a deserted parking lot far away from any stray parental eyes.

"Thank you," Debbie said. "I was afraid it was too long. The last thing I wanted to do was bore people."

Christ, I thought. Her thirty-minute speech had been twenty minutes too long. I knew because neither Alex nor I could remember the last twenty minutes.

Debbie had spoken on the environment, of all things. What did she know about that? She had grown up in a goddamn desert.

We didn't have an environment, not really, just a bunch of sand and dirt.

"Your point on the impact of methane versus carbon-dioxide gases on global warming was important," Ted said. "It's a pity the tundra's melting so fast. I wouldn't be surprised if the world's temperature increases by ten degrees in our lifetimes."

"Won't happen," Alex said, swinging onto the interstate and jacking our speed up to an even ninety. She always sped and often got stopped by the cops. But so far she had yet to get a ticket. Go figure.

"Why do you say that?" Ted asked.

"We'll never live that long. We'll die of something else," Alex said.

"Like what?" Jimmy asked.

Alex shrugged. "That's my point. Here we're worrying about carbon dioxide raising the temperature and now it turns out methane is the real culprit. That's the way of the world, and the future. You can't predict nothing."

"Anything," Debbie muttered.

"Whatever," Alex said.

"What are you majoring in at UCLA?" Jimmy asked Alex.

"Psychology. I figure there's going to be a lot of depressed people pretty soon."

"You plan to cash in on their sorrows?" Debbie asked.

"Why not?" Alex replied.

"You're so altruistic," Debbie said sarcastically.

Alex laughed. That was one of her great qualities—she was almost impossible to insult. "I'm a realist, that's all." She added, "Jessie thinks the same way I do."

"Not true," I said. "No one thinks the same way you do."

Alex glanced over. "You have the same attitude. Don't deny it."

"My attitude changes from day to day." Ever so slightly I shifted my head to the left, to where I could see Jimmy. I added, "Today I feel totally optimistic."

Jimmy was dressed simply, in jeans and a red short-sleeved shirt. His brown hair was a little long, a little messy, but to me it had been a source of endless thrills. It might have been because it was thick and fine at the same time, but when I used to run my fingers through it, I always got a rush. Especially when he would groan with pleasure. One night, I swear, I did nothing but play with his hair.

His eyes matched his hair color, yet there was a softness to them, a kindness. People might think "kind" an odd word to apply to a guy but with Jimmy it fit. He was careful to make the people around him feel comfortable, and he didn't have to say much to put others at ease.

When we had dated, the one thing I had loved most about him was how he could sit across from me and stare into my eyes as I rambled on about my day. It didn't matter what I said, he always made me feel like the most important person in the world.

It had been early October when he asked me out. He came into the city library where I worked and we struck up a conversation in the back aisles. I knew he was dating Kari so I kept up a wall of sorts. I did it automatically, perhaps because I had liked him since our freshman year.

He must have sensed it but he didn't say anything about being broken up with Kari. It was possible they were not formally divorced at that exact moment. He kept the banter light. He wanted to know what I was going to do after graduation. He was in the same boat as me. Good grades, no money.

He left the library without hitting on me for my number. But a week later he magically called and asked if I'd like to go to a movie. I said sure, even before he explained that he was free and single. He picked me up early on a Friday and asked if I felt like going to Hollywood. Great, I said, anything to get out of Apple Valley. We ended up having dinner and watching three movies at the Universal CityWalk. We didn't get home until near dawn and when he kissed me good night, I was a total goner.

First love—I still feel it's the one that matters the most.

We spent the next ten weeks together and it was perfect. I was in a constant state of joy. It didn't matter if I ate or drank or slept. I just had to see him, think of him, and I'd feel happy.

We made love after a month, or I should say after thirty dates. He swung by on a Saturday after work. He was a mechanic at the local Sears. My mother was at work at the nearby Denny's, where she was the manager, and I was in the shower. I didn't know he was coming. Later, he said he'd tried knocking but got no answer. That was his excuse for peeking inside my bedroom. But my excuse, for inviting him into my shower, I can't remember what it was. I don't think I had one.

It didn't matter—once again, it was perfect.

I felt something profound lying in his arms that I had never imagined a human being could feel. I was absolutely, totally complete, as if I had spent my entire life fragmented. Just a collection of cracked pieces that his touch, his love, was able to thrust together and make whole. I knew I was with the one person in the world who could allow me to experience peace.

Later, when I tried to explain my feelings to Alex, she looked at me like I was crazy, but I sensed she was jealous. Despite her many lovers, I knew that she had never felt anything close to what I had with Jimmy.

Six weeks after our shower, he was gone.

No, that would have been easier, had he just vanished. Had he died, I think it would have been simpler to bear. But no, I had to see him every day at school, Monday through Friday, with Kari—until she graduated early, at the end of January. He told me he had to go back to her. He didn't say why. But watching them holding hands across the courtyard, I couldn't help but feel the smiles and laughter he shared with her were all fake.

But Alex said they looked real to her.

And she was my best friend. I had to believe her.

"Jessie," Jimmy said, startling me. It was possible my discreet peek out of the corner of my eye had accidentally lengthened into a long, lost stare. Had he caught me looking at him? He was too polite to say. He quickly added, "Do you guys know where you're staying?"

"At the MGM. Aren't you? That's where our class got the group rate." I paused. "Don't tell me you don't have a reservation."

He hesitated. "I wasn't sure I could get off work this weekend. By the time my boss finally said okay, I tried calling every hotel on the Strip but they were booked. I thought when we got there I'd see if there were any cancellations."

"That will be tricky on the weekend," Debbie warned.

"No biggie—you can always stay with us," Alex said.

A tense silence ensued. Ted must have immediately shorted out at the thought of Jimmy sleeping in the same suite as me. The idea drove me nuts as well, but for radically different reasons. Debbie was annoyed that a guy might be staying with us period. Despite her lust for Ted, she was a prude. She glared at Alex and spoke in a deadly tone.

"Nice of you to volunteer our accommodations."

Alex ignored the sarcasm. "Hey, the more the merrier." I knew what was coming next. Alex was never going to let me get away without putting me on the spot. She glanced my way and smiled wickedly. "Let's vote on it. Jessie, you okay with Jimmy sleeping in our suite?"

I had to act cool, I thought, it was my only escape.

"As long as we get to use his body in whatever way we see fit."

Alex offered me five. "Amen to that, sister!"

I gave her five while the three in the backseat squirmed. Ted turned to Jimmy. "If you get stuck, stay with me and Neil. We can always call down for a cot."

"You're rooming with Neil Sedak?" Alex asked, stunned. "That guy's never stepped out of Apple Valley in his life. Plus he was our class valedictorian, which means he's got to be a nerd."

"You have something against nerds?" I asked.

"I love nerds!" Alex said. "You know me, I'm never ashamed to admit my best friend works at the library. But I'm talking about Ted's rep here. Ted, if you spend a night with Neil, everyone will assume you're unfuckable."

"Hardly," I said. "I know two girls who've slept with Neil."

"Who?" Alex demanded, getting out the first half of the word before suddenly grinding to a halt. I smiled at her knowingly.

"Is someone forgetting a certain confession?" I asked.

Alex acted cool. "Confession is private."

"Oh, my God, Alex. You didn't," Debbie squealed with pleasure. Screwing Neil the Nerd went above and beyond the UCLA admission-man rumor. This one would be all over Las Vegas before the weekend was done. Alex cast me a dirty look.

"Tell her it ain't so," she ordered.

"It's possible it ain't so," I said. There was more truth to

Alex's remark than I let on. I *was* a bit of a nerd. The reason I worked at the library was because I loved to read. I was addicted. I read everything: fiction, nonfiction, mysteries, sci-fi, horror, thrillers, biographies, romance novels, all the genres, even magazines and newspapers. It was probably why my brain was stuffed with so much arcane information.

"Explain that I was only joking about Neil," Alex insisted.

The sex secrets of Alex and Neil could have gone on another hour if Jimmy hadn't interrupted. He was not a big one for gossip.

"I don't give a damn about Neil's sex life," Jimmy said. "But I do appreciate your offer, Ted. If I get stuck for a place to stay, I'll give you a call."

"No problem," Ted said, a note of relief in his voice. He reached in his pocket and pulled out a card. "Here's a fake ID if you plan to gamble."

"Great." Jimmy studied it. "This license looks real."

"It's not," Ted warned. "Don't use it at the MGM's front desk to check in. It'll fail if it's scanned. But don't worry about gambling at the other hotels. I haven't seen them scan IDs on the casino floors."

"How do you know?" Jimmy asked.

"He's been to Vegas tons," Alex said. "He's a master card counter."

"Wow." Jimmy was impressed. "Is it hard to learn?"

Ted shrugged, although it was obvious he enjoyed the

attention. "It takes a good memory and hard work. But you don't have to be a genius to do it."

"You should teach us all this weekend," Debbie said, a bold comment coming from her. Ted shrugged.

"I can teach you the basics. But it takes hours of practice to make money at it. And the casinos keep changing the rules, making it harder to get an edge."

"The bastards," Alex muttered.

We reached Las Vegas before sunset so we weren't treated to the famous colorful glow suddenly rising out of the desert night. It was a curious phenomenon, I thought, but during the day Las Vegas looked far from imposing. Just a bunch of gaudy buildings sticking out of the sand. But I knew when night fell, the magic would emerge, and the town would transform itself into one gigantic adult ride.

Alex drove straight to the MGM, where we checked in to our room, a decent-sized suite with a view of the Strip and three separate bedrooms—plus a central living area that came equipped not only with a sofa but a love seat. The price wasn't bad, one hundred and fifty bucks: fifty bucks when split three ways. Still, the weekend was ruining my savings. The library was not exactly a high-paying place to work.

With the sofa and love seat, we had room for another two people. But Jimmy, damn him, was too much of a gentleman to impose. He also seemed reluctant to take Ted up on his offer. He tried his best to find his own room, using our hotel-room phone to call several hotlines that supposedly could find you a suite on New Year's Eve. But it was all hype; it was Friday evening at the start of summer and Las Vegas was bursting at the seams. Jimmy struck out.

"This couch is softer than my bed," Alex said, sitting not far from where Jimmy had just finished dialing. I was glad we had temporarily left Ted—who had gone off to find his own room. Alex, it seemed, was determined that Jimmy stay with us.

"We settled the sleeping arrangements in the car," Debbie said, studying the minibar. Because it was filled with tiny bottles of liquor, and we had checked in to the room using our real IDs, the bar should have been off-limits. But Ted had managed to bypass the locking mechanism before departing for his quarters. I was glad, I loved minibars. The snacks tasted ten times better to me, probably because they cost ten times as much as they were supposed to.

"When we talked about it in the car, we didn't know this suite would be so large," Alex said.

"We only have one bathroom," Debbie growled.

"Do you plan on spending the weekend throwing up?" Alex asked.

Jimmy interrupted. "Hey, it's okay—remember, I've got Ted's room as a backup. Don't worry about me."

Alex went to reply, but then her eyes slipped from Jimmy to me. Her unspoken message couldn't have been clearer. She wasn't worried about Jimmy, she was worried about me. Or else she was trying to force the two of us back together, which, in her bizarre mind, was the same thing.

It didn't matter. The elephant standing in the room had just quietly roared. It could no longer be ignored. Jimmy and I had to talk—soon, and alone. But I felt too nervous to say it aloud. I stood and caught his eye, and headed toward my room. Jimmy understood, he followed me and shut the door behind him.

Before I could figure out where to sit, or what I should say, he hugged me. The gesture caught me by surprise. I didn't hug him back, not at first, but when he didn't let go, I found my arms creep up and around his broad shoulders. It felt so perfect to stand there and listen to his heartbeat. Yes, that word again, I could not be free of it when I was around Jimmy.

The hug was warm but chaste; he didn't try to kiss me. He didn't even move his arms once he had ahold of me. Although we were standing up, we could have been lying down together, asleep in each other's arms. I don't know how long the hug lasted but it felt like forever . . . compressed into a moment.

Finally, we sat on the bed together. He was holding my hands, or trying to, but I had to keep taking them back to wipe away the silly tears that kept running over my cheeks. He didn't rush me to speak. But he never took his eyes off me, and I felt he was searching my face for the answer to a question he had carried with him a long time.

Of course, I had my own question.

"Why?" I said. The word startled me more than him. It felt so blunt after our tender moment. The question didn't offend him, but he let go of me and sat back on the bed, propping himself up with a pillow.

"Do you remember the day we drove to Newport Beach?" he asked.

"Yes." It had been during Christmas break, a few days before the holiday. I wasn't likely to forget because it was to turn out to be the worst Christmas of my life. He dumped me December 22. Then I hadn't known what to do with the presents I had bought, or the ones I had made for him. In the end, I hadn't done anything. I still had them in my bedroom closet. They were still wrapped.

"When we got back to Apple Valley, Kari was waiting at my house." Jimmy paused. "She said she was ten weeks pregnant."

I froze. "We were together ten weeks."

Jimmy held up a hand. "I never slept with her once I was with you. I never even kissed her."

"I believe you." And I did—he didn't have to swear. Jimmy was incredibly rare; he didn't lie. I added, "Did you believe her?"

"She had an ultrasound with her."

"That doesn't mean it was yours."

"Jessie . . ."

"Saying, 'I'm pregnant, Jimmy, you have to come back to me.' That's like the oldest trick in the book."

"I know that. I know Kari's not always a hundred percent

23

straight. But I just had to look in her eyes. She was telling the truth."

I crossed my arms over my chest. "I don't know."

"And she was showing a little bit."

"At ten weeks?" I asked.

"It might have been twelve."

"And it might have been a folded-up pillowcase."

He hesitated. "No. She lifted her shirt. It was for real."

"And she wanted to keep it."

"Yes. That wasn't an issue."

"She wanted you back. That was *the* issue."

He lowered his head. "I don't know. Maybe."

It was a lot to digest. It was a minute before I could speak.

"You should have told me," I said.

"I'm sorry. I wanted to, but I felt it would hurt you more to know she was having my baby."

I shook my head. "You've been good so far, real good, but that, what you just said, is nuts. Nothing could hurt worse than that call I got. Do you remember it? 'Hello, Jessie, how are you doing? Good? That's good. Hey, I've got some bad news. I don't know exactly how to tell you this. But Kari and I are getting back together. I know this is sort of sudden, and the last thing I want to do is hurt you, but Kari and I . . . we're not done yet. We have stuff we have to work out. Are you there, Jessie?'"

He stared at me. "God."

"What?"

24

"You remember it word for word."

"I'll remember it till the day I die."

"I'm sorry."

"Don't say that word again. Tell me why."

"I just told you why. She was pregnant. I felt I had to do the right thing and go back to her."

"Why didn't you tell me the truth?"

"I was ashamed, it's true, but I honestly thought the truth would hurt you more."

"That's so lame. Didn't you stop to imagine how I felt? You left me hanging. Hanging above nothing 'cause I knew nothing. One moment I'm the love of your life and the next a cheerleader has taken my place."

He nodded. "It was dumb, I made a mistake. I should have explained everything to you. Please forgive me."

"No."

"Jessie?"

"I don't forgive you. I can't. I suffered too much. You say you felt you had to do the right thing so you went back to her. Let me ask you this—were you still in love with her?"

"I was never in love with Kari."

"Were you in love with me?"

"Yes."

"Then what you did was wrong. So she was pregnant. So she wept and begged you to come back for the sake of your child. That doesn't matter. I was more important to you, I should have been more important. You should have said no to her."

"I couldn't."

"Why not?" I demanded.

"Because when she rolled up her shirt and I saw that growing bump, and realized that it was true, that it was mine, my flesh and blood, I knew I had to take care of that baby."

"Bullshit."

"You're wrong, Jessie. At that moment, nothing mattered more to me than that child. And yes, forgive me, but it mattered even more than us."

I stood. "Get out."

He stood. "We should talk more."

"No, leave. This was all a . . . mistake. Go stay with Ted."

Jimmy stepped toward the door, put his hand on the knob. He was going to leave, he wasn't going to fight me. That's what I liked about him, how reasonable he could be. And that's what I hated about him, that he hadn't fought for me. I was the one who had to stop him.

"Where's the baby now?" I asked. Kari had graduated at the end of January and left campus early. I assumed she'd had the child.

But Jimmy lowered his head. He staggered.

"We lost him," he said.

"She had a miscarriage?"

"No." The word came out so small. I put my hand to my mouth.

"Don't tell me she had the baby and it died?" I gasped.

He turned and looked at me, pale as plaster. So frail, so hollow. I felt if I said the wrong word, he'd shatter.

"His name was Huck. He lived for three days."

"Why did he die?" I asked.

The wrong words. Jimmy turned, opened the door, spoke over his shoulder. "You're right, I should go. We can talk later."

He left; it was amazing how much it hurt. It was like he was breaking up with me all over again. It was then I wished I hadn't said the "why" word. We should have left it at the hug.

CHAPTER THREE

I DID NOT LEAVE MY ROOM FOR SOME TIME, AND WHEN I did, I found a note from Debbie and Alex. They had left to find the kids from our class and plan the night's festivities. That's the word Alex chose—"festivities." I doubted she had seen Jimmy's face when he had left our suite.

I was tired and knew we'd be up late. I tried napping but had trouble falling asleep. Huck haunted me, perhaps the way he haunted Jimmy. I didn't fool myself. Jimmy had won our fight—if it could be called that. And here I had been positive I would humiliate him when we finally spoke. I was sure I owned the moral high ground. But Jimmy was right, the child was his own flesh and blood; it transcended infatuation, even our love, never mind that the infant had died.

I kept wondering what had killed Huck.

A part of me sensed Jimmy did not know the whole story.

At some point I must have blacked out. The next thing I knew, Alex was sitting beside me on my bed. "You all right, Jessie?" she asked softly.

She had seen Jimmy's face after all. She was concerned about me.

I sat up quickly. "I'm fine. What time is it?"

"Five."

"Five! Why did you let me sleep so long?"

"You looked exhausted. Besides, the gang's not getting together until six."

"Who exactly is the gang?"

Alex continued to study me. "Not sure, whoever comes. But I've got some good news. You know how you said you wanted to see *O*?"

"Don't tell me you got tickets?"

"Six seats. Ted got them from a scalper. He says he doesn't care who comes with us. He's even volunteered not to go, in case you want to bring a date."

"Bullshit. He never said that."

Alex shrugged. "All right, I made that up. But he's not stupid. He saw the way you and Jimmy were looking at each other." She paused. "Can you tell me what happened?"

"Later," I said.

I took a quick shower and put on the only dress I had brought—something short, black and sexy that Debbie had sewn for me for my birthday. She had designed it after a dress we had seen on *Project Runway*—we were all addicted to the show. Debbie's dress was even more inspired than the one on TV. She was a woman of many talents. A pity she kept most of them hidden.

Our class was staying at the MGM, but our celebratory dinner was to take place at the Bellagio. It was supposed to have the best restaurants. Our reservations were for a high-priced Italian bistro but our class was no sooner gathered in the Bellagio lobby than an argument broke out. Half our gang didn't like Italian—they wanted to eat elsewhere. On the surface that didn't seem like a major problem. Unfortunately, as Debbie shouted over the bedlam, we had already promised the hotel a minimum of two hundred guests.

"If we don't all eat here, we lose our discount," Debbie said.

"How much is that?" someone demanded.

"Forty percent," Debbie replied.

About fifty percent of our class didn't give a damn. They split for other hotels. When we finally made it to the restaurant, the manager looked like he'd have a nervous breakdown when we told him we were missing half our entourage. He screamed at us in Italian, but since none of us spoke the language, it didn't do much good.

He had no choice, he had to seat us immediately. We were taking up the entire waiting area. Jimmy didn't show, which hurt. I had told him where we were eating. Of course I had also told him to get out of my room.

Ted sat beside me. He said he had not seen or heard from Jimmy. "He didn't stop at your room?" I asked.

"No," Ted said.

"Did you try calling his cell?"

Ted looked annoyed. "I'm not his babysitter. I offered him a place to crash. If he doesn't want it, that's his business."

I touched Ted's arm. "You're right. Sorry."

Ted tried to act casual, and would have succeeded if he didn't sound like he was choking on his next question. "You two back together?"

"Absolutely not," I said.

The food was excellent. I had a pasta dish with shrimp. The cook had seasoned it with a fantastic mix of herbs. The incredible taste quickly improved my mood. By the end of the meal I was laughing with the rest of my class. It might have been the alcohol. Alex had flashed her fake ID and convinced our waiter we were teachers from Apple Valley High. He brought us two bottles of chilled wine that the outside heat caused us to polish off way too quickly.

I cannot hold my liquor. Two glasses of anything above ten proof and I fall in love with the universe. Worse, the love created by my inebriated state usually wants to flow in a direction. And since kindhearted Ted was sitting beside me, I couldn't stop thinking how he had gotten us O tickets and fake IDs, offered Jimmy a room, and broken into our minibar. . . . Why, I felt I just had to express my undying gratitude to him.

I suddenly leaned over and kissed him on the lips.

It took me maybe two seconds to realize what I had done.

Shit! Oh, shit!

Talk about sending wrong signals. His face broke into an expression of pure delight. But Debbie—who sat to his right—cast me a look so dirty I felt like our friendship wouldn't survive the blow. Plus Ted grabbed me after the kiss, probably hoping our brief oral contact was the beginning of something extraordinary.

"Have I ever told you how wonderful you are?" he said with feeling.

"Maybe once or twice," I muttered, trying to extricate myself from his arms without being too obvious.

Alex was as drunk as I was. She studied her empty wine glass and waxed philosophical. "Why is it we always say such emotional crap at times like this? The truth is the feelings you two share are as obvious as a one-way street."

"Huh?" Ted said, blinking. He'd had some of our wine.

"Don't be so cold," I said quickly, diplomatically, still trying to slip from his bear hug. "Ted is a dear old friend."

"Friends," Alex said, practically spitting the word. "What good are friends? You can't f—"

"Why did you just kiss me?" Ted interrupted, his joy slowly fading.

"Because I care," I said.

"And she's drunk," Alex added.

"Is that true?" Ted asked, his expression darkening.

"Well," I said.

"Ignore her," Debbie said, reaching over and taking one of his hands, which gave me one less hand to escape from. "When Jessie gets drunk, she always acts like a whore. We were at this party once where she downed a six-pack and got up and started dancing on the tabletop. She stripped down to her panties."

Ted released me all of a sudden. He practically shoved me away. He looked upset, confused. "What's going on here?" he mumbled.

"Knock it off, Debbie, would ya? You know damn well that was me," Alex said. "And the panties didn't stay on."

"I really am grateful for all you've done for us," I told Ted.

"For us?" he snapped, beginning to sober up.

I searched inside for the perfect remark that would completely repair the damage I had caused. The only problem was I was working with an IQ of around fifty.

"For all of us," I told Ted. "For me, for Alex, and especially for Debbie. You may not know this but Debbie has a major crush on you. She's had it for years but she's too much of a coward to tell you. So I'm telling you now."

My words didn't go over as well as I hoped. Debbie threw down her napkin and got up and ran from the restaurant. Ted watched her go, then turned to me, probably hoping I would clarify my remark. The best I could do was belch, which sent Alex into an uncontrollable fit of laughter. Ted had finally had enough. He shook his head and stood and handed me two tickets.

"I got you great seats," he said in a bitter voice. "Enjoy the show."

He left, chasing after Debbie, or so we assumed. The rest of our long table fell silent and stared at me, making me feel like a total ass. But Alex was quick to reassure me.

"Although your drunken stupor is obvious to all," she told me, "your words were positively brilliant. Your remarks may even change the course of those two mediocre lives."

"Don't call them mediocre," I said.

"Their lives will be if they get married two years from now. All because of what you said here tonight."

I sighed, and studied the tickets in my hand. "I just hope we're not sitting beside them during the show."

"When does it start?" Alex asked.

My eyes slowly focused on the tiny print on the tickets.

I gasped. "In ten minutes!"

We paid our share of the bill, in theory, although we probably cheated our classmates since we were the only ones who had ordered wine. But we didn't have time to hang around and haggle over an exact figure.

We were lucky *O* took place in the Bellagio. A hotel employee was kind enough to lead us to the appropriate hall. He could tell we were stinking drunk. We kept giggling and bumping into each other.

I had read so much about the show, I worried my high expectations could never be met. But the truth was, it blew me away. The stage was supposed to have cost fifty million to build. The money had not been wasted. It kept changing shape. One minute it was filled with water, like a small lake, and the next it had shallow streams running down the center. Then all the water would disappear and it would be covered with gravel.

The performers were close to superhuman. They could bend and twist their bodies into positions that would have challenged Gumby. Several times Alex and I gasped and grabbed hands. One of the leads did high-wire stunts a hundred feet above the stage and then dived into a square pond less than three feet across. What nerve! The exotic colors, the brilliant lighting, the hypnotic music, the songs, the dancing—I felt like I'd been transported into another dimension.

For a time I forgot about Jimmy and the others. It was a relief, in a way, we didn't see another person from our school.

Alex and I were sober by the time the show finished, but neither of us had any desire to return to our suite. Alex wanted to gamble. She was keen to play twenty-one, blackjack. But I was worried we'd lose too much money and suffer for it the rest of the weekend. I pointed to the small signs on the sides of the tables.

"Look, the minimum bet's twenty bucks! We can't afford that!"

"The Bellagio's for high rollers," Alex said. "Come on, we'll find a place with a five-buck minimum."

"Where?"

Alex nodded toward the hotel exit. "Let's hit the Strip, there's a hundred hotels out there. We'll find what we're looking for."

Alex strode toward the door. I had to struggle to keep up. "Why blackjack? We'll get creamed without Ted's help. Why don't we play the slots?"

"Blackjack's the best game to meet guys," Alex said, pulling a small plastic card from her purse. "You get to sit at a table and talk to the other players. It's the only game where you really get to know them. Plus I got this cheat card—it tells you exactly when to hit and when to stand. It was designed by a computer, it gives you the best possible odds. We won't lose too much."

"I don't want to lose anything. I want to win. We need Ted."

Alex put an arm around me. "Sorry, sister, but that kiss you planted on his lips has made him radioactive for the rest of the summer. At least when it comes to you."

"I was drunk. He'll forgive me."

"The only way he'll forgive you is if he ends up having sex with Debbie, and I don't think they've made a cheat card that could compute such lousy odds."

"I don't know. He ran after her pretty fast."

"Whatever. The point is, we don't need Ted. There will be plenty of cute guys at the tables to help us play."

I studied Alex. "Are you planning on having a one-night stand?"

"You say that like I'm some kind of slut."

"Well, it would be a pretty slutty thing to do."

"This is Vegas! People come here for three reasons: to drink, to gamble, and to get laid. Those are the only reasons this place exists."

I sighed. "All right. But if I give him a thumbs-down, you can't bring him back to our room."

Alex took my hand and pulled me out the door. "Jessie, you can be sure whoever has the good luck to end up with me is going to have his own luxurious suite."

"You'd sleep with a guy just because he has money?"

"Money and a dick."

"Whore."

"There are no whores in this town. Only givers and takers."

Outside was the real Las Vegas. The sun had set and the town glowed with a million electric rainbows. Not to mention the fantastic fountains in front of the Bellagio. We stared at them, mesmerized, as we crossed the long entrance. The entire Strip looked surreal. Paris was across the street, New York was to our right. There was a pyramid and a castle down the road. I loved how so many of the hotels had adopted exotic themes. The sidewalks were jammed, with most of the people laughing and carrying on. The smell of booze was all-pervasive.

The night air was hotter than at home, in the high nineties.

I knew it would take all night for the temperature to drop another ten degrees. Then the sun would rise and another scorcher would begin. As we walked, our thirst quickly returned. We had barely reached the Tropicana when Alex pulled me inside.

"This is an old hotel but it has class," she said. "Plus they have low minimums. We should be able to find a five-buck table."

"How about a dollar table?"

"Sure. Hop on down to Mississippi and catch a steamboat on the river."

It being a Friday night, the place was jammed. We didn't have our choice of blackjack tables. Indeed, it took a long wait before we found a table that could seat us both. Fortunately, they barely looked at our IDs.

We ordered drinks before trading our cash for chips: four large Cuba libres—the name translates as "free Cuba," in English—Coke, rum, and lime. The table drinks were supposed to be watered down but these babies packed a punch. I had barely finished my first when I began having trouble counting to twenty-one.

The minimum was five bucks, the maximum ten thousand. Alex and I each bought a hundred bucks' worth of five-dollar chips and prayed we didn't lose it all in the first twenty minutes, which I had done before. I was not a total novice—I had played the game before in Las Vegas with my mom and knew the basic rules. Of course, when I had played with her, I'd had to dress up and wear plenty of makeup so I looked older.

To start, we relied on Alex's card. The hardest thing for me was when to split and when to double down. The card made it simple. It had three color-coded columns. If the dealer is showing this, and you have that, then do this . . .

We were at the table maybe half an hour, and I was down fifty bucks and Alex was ahead a hundred, when a guy showed up. He caught my eye instantly. It wasn't just because he was handsome. Las Vegas had no shortage of beautiful men.

Nor was it the fact that he set down a fat roll of hundreds and asked for thirty thousand in chips. Again, the town was loaded with high rollers. It was more his calm expression, his quiet confidence, that drew me in. As he casually stacked his chips and lit a cigarette, he looked neither happy nor sad. He was just there to win.

A man a few seats over—he was a truck driver out of Chicago, and he had hit on me and Alex the second we had sat down—called to the new guy. "Hey, dude, can't you read? This is a no-smoking table."

The guy stared at him with large, steady eyes. They were blue, but so close to black they looked as if they had never seen the sun. "No," he said, and blew smoke in the man's face.

Trucky got annoyed. "No what?"

"I can't read."

"Listen, put out the cigarette or find another table."

"Go find your own table."

Trucky stood. "Looking for a fight, bud?"

39

The guy smiled easily, still calm and cool. He was six-two, muscular, probably in his mid-twenties. He could have been a cop, someone who worked in a dangerous field. He had that kind of vibe. Although he looked at ease, I had the feeling Las Vegas was not home. He had closely cropped blond hair and a slight accent I couldn't place.

Facing the dealer, I was on the far left. Alex was to my right and the new guy was next, followed by Trucky and a young Japanese couple who could not stop staring at the newcomer's mountain of chips.

I hoped the threat didn't scare him off. I doubted it would. From the moment I saw him, I felt I knew him, like he was a piece of my past I could no longer remember clearly. I wanted him to stay.

"Not afraid of one," he told Trucky.

Trucky went to snap at him, then suddenly seemed allergic to our newcomer's stare. He lowered his head and spoke in a meek tone. "I don't smoke. I shouldn't have to inhale your crap."

Alex spoke. "You heard the guy, he can't read. It's not his fault."

The guy turned and smiled at her. "Thank you." He offered his hand. "I'm Russ."

"Alex." She shook his hand and added hastily, "This is my friend Jessie."

"Jessica." His eyes lingered on my face, long enough to where I ended up blushing. There was power in his gaze. "Love that name."

"Bets down," the dealer snapped. He was frail, three times our age, and already showing signs of the disease that would probably kill him. His face was not merely pale but pasty. He could have washed it with bacteria-friendly soap. The few gray hairs he had left looked like they were glued on. I had tried joking with him earlier but he only responded to tips. He was a smoker, though; it was obvious he liked when Russ exhaled in his direction.

We laid down our bets. Twenty bucks for the truck driver. Five for me. Twenty for Alex, who was feeling bold with her extra hundred in her pocket. Russ put down a grand, which caused the Japanese couple to gasp. They talked excitedly in their native tongue before they each put down twenty. The dealer dealt us our cards.

"Damn," I swore when I saw mine. A powerful ten, followed by a feeble six. Sixteen, worst hand in the book, especially against a dealer who was showing a ten. The computer card said I had to hit, but it also said I was probably already going to lose. Trucky was in the same boat as me. I could tell from his disgusted expression he was going to stand.

The Japanese couple each had nineteen, which meant, of course, they were going to hold tight. Alex had eleven—the perfect hand to double down on. Russ also had eleven. I assumed he would play the odds and double his bet.

Nevertheless, I watched him closely. There were two reasons why he might choose to ignore the odds: the size of his bet and the dealer's powerful ten. Myself, I would have simply hit. But I suspected Russ had more guts than I did. And money.

Alex turned to Russ and acted like she knew nothing about the game. It was Alex's firm belief that there had never been a male born who did not enjoy telling a female what to do. "Should I double?" she asked.

He shrugged. "The book says you should."

"You're going to double, right?"

"Nope."

Alex was surprised. So was I. Russ looked like an experienced player but his choice indicated he was not—at least, according to our card.

Alex doubled, shoving out four more chips. Russ left his grand alone.

Russ hit and got three. Now he was looking at fourteen—a shit hand. He hit again, which he couldn't have done if he had doubled down. He got a seven, twenty-one, sweet.

Alex had forty bucks riding on one hand. The dealer hit her and she got two, the worst possible card on a double down. She cursed her cards and the dealer. The latter didn't blink. Against my better judgment I took one and got an eight and bust. Alex lost as well.

Russ was the only one who won.

Then, the nerve of the guy, he let his two grand ride. It was such a ridiculous amount to bet on one hand, the rest of us didn't pay attention to our own hands. Except for Alex.

She was pissed she had lost the forty and was trying to make it back in a hurry. She put down a stack of eight five-dollar chips.

"You're throwing away your winnings," I warned her.

"Hush!" she snapped.

I stayed at five bucks. Trucky and the Japanese couple played twenty. Our dealer hit me with another sixteen, which made me feel cursed. Trucky got twelve. The Japanese couple got nineteen again. Russ got ten. Unfortunately, the dealer also showed ten.

Alex got a miserable fifteen.

"Do I hit?" Trucky asked Russ. A few minutes ago the man had wanted to punch Russ. Only in Vegas.

"Don't ask me for advice," Russ said.

"Come on," Trucky insisted.

"Well, you can't sit at twelve."

"Maybe the dealer will bust," Trucky said.

Russ shrugged. "You decide."

Alex appealed to Russ. "How do I get out of this mess?"

Russ didn't hesitate. "Hit."

It was decision time. The Japanese couple stood. Trucky hit and got nine—twenty-one. He patted Russ on the back, called him a good man. Russ drew another ten for an even twenty. Alex also drew ten, which caused her to bust. She slammed her fist down in disgust.

"You told me to hit!" she complained to Russ.

"I also said not to ask me for advice," he said.

I hit and got six and bust again. I was down to forty in chips and only had another hundred in my purse to last me all weekend. The dealer turned his hole card over. He had only seventeen. The Japanese couple had won, as well as Russ, who was already three grand ahead. Wow.

The smart thing for me to do was leave. Alex was already packing up to go. She was annoyed at Russ, at his attitude, although she should have accepted it had been her decision to bet so much at once.

"Come on, Jessie," she grumbled.

I hesitated. "I want to keep playing."

"You're getting shit hands every time. Let's try somewhere else."

I glanced at Russ—who lit another cigarette—and turned back to Alex. "Go ahead, I'll catch up with you later."

"Right."

I nodded toward Russ. "I promise. I'll call you on my cell."

Alex got the message. "Remember, most cells don't work inside these places. Go outside if you can't reach me." She leaned over and whispered in my ear. "Watch out for this guy, he looks like trouble."

I just nodded. Hadn't we come to Vegas for trouble?

We played another hour, together, and no one left the table except the dealer. The breaks he took were short. With our original dealer back at the helm, my meager bankroll began to dwindle again. Actually, the situation got serious. I dipped into my purse and took out the hundred I'd sworn I was going to save for the next two days. I was playing with money I couldn't afford to lose. True, my room was paid for but I needed the cash to buy food and drinks.

Why was I being so reckless?

It made no sense but I felt my luck had to change. Plus I wanted to stay near Russ. I had moved closer to him, taking Alex's vacant chair. For the first time in a long time, Russ looked over at me.

"How much are you in the hole?" he asked.

"Close to two hundred."

"Can you afford that?"

"Hell, no." I had been watching him play. He was easily a hundred grand ahead. I thought maybe he was going to offer me a loan, not that I would have taken it. I had too much pride. He surprised me when he told me to bet everything I had left on my next hand.

I shook my head. "Are you nuts?"

He stared at me. "I'm serious, Jessica."

"It's Jessie."

"Bet it all, Jessie."

I gestured to his stacks of chips. "That's easy for you to say, you're winning like a fiend. How much are you ahead?"

"I don't know, I can't count."

"You can't count and you can't read. What a winning combination."

"It hasn't hurt me tonight."

"Should I bet everything I've got?" Trucky interrupted.

Russ ignored him. He was focused on me. The dealer was demanding we place our bets. "Decision time," Russ said.

There was something in his confidence that made me reach into my pocket and pull out my final forty. There was no point in asking him again how he knew it was time to go all out. He had said what he had to say and that was that. I could trust him or forget it. Taking a deep breath, I shoved the red chips into the white circle painted on the green velvet.

"No guts, no glory," I said.

Russ smiled and put down ten grand. "True."

I shook my head at the size of his bet. "You're crazy."

"Gambling's crazy."

"True. But you're ahead. You should quit while you're ahead."

"Why?"

"Duh. You're playing against the odds. In the long run, you can't win."

"I'm not playing against the odds."

"Really?"

"I'm playing against myself."

His remark should have been sufficiently cryptic to ignore. Except for the fact that I had watched him for more than an hour and he had won over eighty percent of his bets. A person who could play at such a high level and consistently win either knew something the rest of the world didn't or was one lucky bastard. Hell, look at me, I was trusting him with my last few chips.

The dealer dealt once more. My first card was an ace. God in heaven, I prayed. If only my next card were a ten . . .

I got a queen of diamonds. Blackjack, which paid one and a half times my original bet. Suddenly I was sixty bucks richer and back up to a hundred. I should walk, I thought. Walk away with enough cash to maybe rent a boat on Lake Mead and go waterskiing with Jimmy, or else return to that Italian restaurant at the Bellagio with him. Jimmy loved pasta; he loved food.

But Russ was watching me with his navy blues. The sea behind them was too deep, too calm, to say no to. He wanted me to let it ride.

I left the hundred bucks on the table.

The dealer made up a new shoe and dealt. I got seventeen, an awful hand, especially when the dealer was showing a ten. I could only wait and see if he bust. I wasn't Alex, I didn't snap at Russ. I had made my own decision and I'd have to live with it.

"Hit," Russ said when the dealer got to me. He had won his last hand and with another twenty sitting in front of him it looked like he was going to win again. His ten-grand maximum bets kept piling up.

I snickered at his suggestion. "Right. And pray for a four, a three, or a two. Those are the only cards that can help me."

"You need a four," he said.

None of the original players had left. For the first time, they were focused on me. They knew the hundred was all I had left.

"But the odds . . . ," I began.

"Screw the odds," Russ said.

"That's not what you told Alex."

"That's because I wanted you all to myself," he replied.

He was saying he had given her bad advice on purpose. To piss her off so she would leave. Who was this guy?

"Hit me," I told the dealer.

I got a four—twenty-one. The table cheered loudly. Trucky wanted to hug me. The dealer turned over his card. Russ had been right, I had needed the four. The dealer had twenty.

I had won my money back. I shoved my loot toward the dealer so he could give me two black hundred-dollar chips to take to the cashier's window. But Russ stopped me.

"Change them into greens and play some more," he said.

Greens were twenty-five-dollar chips. A person could win or lose awfully fast at that rate.

"I need to find my friend. I think she's mad at me," I said.

"This is Vegas. No one stays mad for long here," Russ said.

I tried arguing with him but my heart was not in it. Especially when he offered to tell me when to bet heavily. I was no fool, I could see what he was capable of. If I could make money and flirt with a cute guy at the same time, then to hell with Alex.

I asked for another Cuba libre and gulped it down. Russ ordered us both more drinks and we lined up our chips and prepared to do some serious gambling. He had finally stopped to count his chips. He was up a hundred and fifty thousand. He told me with a straight face he wanted to win half a million. He tipped our dealer ten grand—the guy finally smiled—and then he appeared to change our strategy and instructed me to bet low for a few bets. That meant I had to cash in two greens for ten five-dollar chips.

I lost the next five bets. Naturally, I was relieved I was playing at the casino minimum. But as soon as the dealer whipped up a fresh shoe—there were actually six decks of cards in the shoe, all mixed together—Russ told me to bet a hundred. That was more than half what I had left, but there was no saying no to him. Especially with Trucky begging for help on the far side.

"Why are you helping her and not me?" he demanded when I won the next hand.

Russ turned to him. "You want some advice? Leave the casino now and don't come back."

Poor Trucky, Russ had hurt his feelings. "What did I do to you? I stopped complaining about your smoking."

Russ ignored him and focused on the game. The dealer tossed out the cards with practiced ease. I bet another hundred and got a twenty, which made my heart skip. Especially when the dealer ended up with nineteen.

Suddenly I was up two hundred. Ten minutes later I was

a thousand ahead. It was just the start. Russ varied his bets between one thousand and ten thousand, nothing in between. After I had won more than three thousand, he told me to vary my bets—either five hundred or fifty.

Of course, Russ told me when to place the big bet. But that didn't stop my hands from shaking every time I pushed it out.

I assumed he was counting the cards, but based on what Ted had told us, he was winning far too often for an ordinary counter. No, I thought, he must be using another kind of system. But what?

I wasn't the only one who was stumped. His winning streak naturally attracted the pit bosses. We had at least two standing over us from the time Russ passed a hundred grand in winnings. Eventually the floor manager appeared, a big burly guy with a neck as thick as his thighs. He had "mob" written all over him.

The manager occasionally glanced up and signaled with his hands. I realized he was communicating with the "eye in the sky" that Ted had told me about. All the casinos had people watching the tables from above with special cameras, searching for cheaters, for counters in particular. Yet none of them seemed to feel Russ was counting. They let him play, even though he kept winning. I assumed they hoped his luck would change and he'd lose it all back, and then some.

I leaned over and whispered in Russ's ear.

"Does it bother you, all this attention?" I asked.

"Nah. They're like everyone else. They hate parting with their money."

"What if they ask us to leave?" I asked.

"These are private clubs. We'd have to leave."

The alcohol went to my brain and danced. I suspected the bar had upped the juice in our drinks so Russ would play recklessly, although to be honest, I was drinking more than he was. I was playing like a robot that had an internal happy switch broken in the on position. The money we were making made me want to sing. It felt unreal. I stared at the stacks of chips piling up in front of me and I told myself that they had not given me real chips. That I was playing with Monopoly money. The idea did not disturb me because, well, in real life no broke eighteen-year-old chick from Apple Valley ever went to Las Vegas and won huge sums of money.

Our dealer went for a break and never returned. It seemed we had a new dealer—a hard-looking fifty-year-old female who wore her makeup so thick it looked like it held her nose on her face. Russ instructed me to keep my bets low. Ten minutes later he leaned over and spoke in my ear.

"We're leaving. This woman is what's called a mechanic. Her hand and eye coordination are extraordinary. She's the best I've ever seen. She's hitting us with cards that are two, three, or four deep in the deck. Trust me, if we stay, we'll keep getting losing hands."

I nodded. "Okay."

The woman, along with the floor manager and pit bosses, waited for us to make our next bet. Russ pushed all our stacks of chips forward and told the dealer to count us out.

"Excuse me, sir?" the woman said, clearly unhappy.

Russ stayed cool. "Do you want to count us out here, or should we do it at the cashier's window?"

The floor manager stepped forward. He offered his hand to Russ and they exchanged names and other pleasantries. He ignored me completely. He seemed concerned that Russ didn't want to leave his winnings in the hotel vault, so he could play again at a later date. From my side, I would have brought up the fact that they were trying to cheat us with a mechanic. But Russ apparently knew better.

He told them we wanted checks for the amounts we had won, and insisted the chips be counted in front of us so that they never left our sight.

Our chips were loaded into two glass racks: one for Russ, one for me. We followed the loot and the floor manager to a cashier's window. The manager wanted to take us in the back but Russ insisted he count the chips right there on the counter. He seemed reluctant to pass through any door that could be locked behind us.

The manager agreed to Russ's terms. He called for two women who grouped the chips in stacks of twenties, after first separating them by color. Russ had won so many gold chips— worth a thousand dollars a pop—it made my head swim. Yet

Russ seemed to take it all in stride. It was just another night at the casinos to him.

The women completed my count first. $57,800.

"You've got to be shitting me," I gasped.

"Would you like a check or cash?" the manager asked me.

"A check," Russ replied. "Jessie, is your legal name Jessica?"

"Yeah. Jessica Ralle. Do you need my middle name?"

"It's not necessary unless your bank prefers it," the manager said.

"Hell. My bank has probably never seen a check that large."

The women finished with Russ's count. $642,450.

"My full name is Russell Devon," Russ said.

"We need to see both your IDs," the manager said. "And as I'm sure you're aware, we'll automatically be withdrawing the sum you'll owe the IRS for these winnings."

I suddenly felt faint. Of course, I had been playing with a fake ID. I had never planned on winning an amount where they would need to see my ID, never mind withdraw money for the IRS. I leaned against Russ and buried the side of my face in his ear.

"I need to talk to you alone," I said.

Russ asked if we could be excused for a few minutes and the manager was agreeable. We went around the corner, out of earshot, and even before I could explain what the problem was, I burst out crying.

"Shit, shit, shit," I kept saying through my tears. Luck like this really didn't happen in the real world. I wasn't going to get the money.

Russ stared at me with a faint smile on his lips.

"Let me guess," he said. "You're not twenty-one."

"I'm so sorry, Russ."

"Relax. Did they ask for ID when you two first sat down?"

"We showed them something our friend whipped up on his computer. These guys will know it's fake."

"I'm sure they will, since they'll want your Social Security number as well. But it's not as big a problem as you think. You're going to leave here, now, and walk across the street to the Mandalay Bay. It's only two hundred yards up the Strip. That's where I'm staying and that's where I planned to take you for coffee when we were done here. Go through the front door and take a sharp right. You'll find a coffee shop that's always open." He checked his watch. "I'll meet you there in fifteen minutes."

"What are you going to do?"

He shrugged. "Tell them that you were obviously playing with my money and under my direction and that we changed our minds and want it all under my name. But I'll take out sixty grand in cash so you get your share tonight."

"Will they give you that much cash?"

"They won't want to. But I'll tell them if they can handle this whole matter quietly, I'll promise to return tomorrow night to gamble. They'll go for it. At this point, all they care about is getting a chance to win their money back."

I wiped at my teary eyes. "I feel like such an idiot."

He leaned over and kissed me on the forehead.

"Not at all. Anyone else would have gotten hysterical if they thought they had lost so much money." He paused and glanced around. A pit boss watched us from a distance. "It's important you leave before they stop and check your ID. If they see it's fake, they'll deny your winnings."

Just then a faint doubt stirred deep inside me.

What if I went to the coffee shop and sat there for thirty minutes and I started to get nervous with him taking so long? And what if another half hour went by and he still didn't show up? Then, finally, what if I went to the front desk and asked them to ring Russell Devon's room and, lo and behold, he wasn't registered at the Mandalay Bay?

What would happen?

I'd realize I was the biggest fool on the whole damn Strip.

"Shouldn't we meet in your room?" I asked casually.

He didn't hesitate. He pulled a room card from his pocket. "First tower. Room four-three-one-four. Be careful, that's the only key I have on me. I'll knock four times."

I suddenly felt much better. "Great." I went to leave.

"Jessie?" he called.

I paused. "What?"

"What's my room number?"

"Four-three . . . Ahh . . . damn, I'm drunk."

"Four-three-one-four. Say it aloud three times."

"Four-three-one-four. Four-three-one-four. Four-three-one-four."

"Once you're in the room, call down for coffee and dessert."

"What kind of dessert do you want?"

"I'll have what you're having. Now get out of here."

The moment I stepped out of the casino and onto the busy Strip, I felt a wave of relief wash over me. The night was still warm but I felt embraced by a delicious joy that cooled my brain. I had just won an impossible sum of money, I realized, but it seemed as if my happiness came from another source. Russ was not an ordinary guy, he was a magic man. I had a strange feeling that if I stayed close to him, really got to know him, I'd discover the source of his magic.

CHAPTER FOUR

RUSS'S PLACE WAS PHENOMENAL. ON THE TOP FLOOR of the Mandalay Bay, he had the corner suite facing the Strip. It had a huge bedroom, a dining area, a kitchen, and a posh living room that I believed only the rich could truly be comfortable in. I mean, I hesitated to sit on the sofa. The light brown material was so soft, so luxurious, I could drown in it. To keep from dozing, I ended up sitting in a black leather chair that overlooked the endless hotels.

Fortunately, I could reach the phone from where I was sitting. The guy down in room service referred to me as Mrs. Devon. I found the name amusing until I realized he might have spoken to a real Mrs. Devon earlier in the day. It was possible. How well did I really know Russ? The truth was, all I knew was that he was a genius at blackjack.

After placing an order for a pot of coffee and an assortment of cakes and ice cream, I jumped out of the chair and did a hasty search of the suite. As a rule, I hated snoops, but caution told me to learn what I could about the mysterious Russell Devon while he was out of sight.

There were only male clothes hanging in the closets. He had brought two large suitcases to town; he had three full suits, and plenty of ties and shirts to choose from, not to mention four pairs of shoes, all made of rich leather. Clearly, he planned to be around for a while.

He had left a laptop running on the table in the dining area, beside a pile of flyers that were stamped with two bright red letters: *WW*. A closer look revealed that the initials stood for West World.

I assumed it was a company he worked for. I didn't study any of the brochures in detail, but read enough to learn the firm dealt with some kind of genome project—in other words, the study of human genes.

His laptop posed a real temptation. His files were open and available to be read; he had already entered his password. He had obviously left it on with the confidence he would be the first one to return to his room. I could read his private mail if I wanted to. He must have forgotten about the laptop when he had given me the key to his room.

Nevertheless, I found it odd he had left the computer on. I wasn't a privacy freak but I never left my laptop in a position where even my mother could read it.

Two things kept me from checking out his mail: the fact that I would hate it if he did the same to me, and the chance he would later discover I had done so. Russ was obviously smart; he wasn't someone to miss that kind of detail.

I returned to the comfort of the leather chair. It was a quarter past midnight. It had been a long day, an eventful day, and with the alcohol in my bloodstream, I began to yawn and closed my eyes. The next thing I knew there was someone knocking at the door; the noise woke me with a start. But the person hadn't knocked four times. Of course I had just called room service. Carefully, quietly, I crept to the door.

"Hello?" I called.

"Room service."

"Great." I opened the door. The guy—he was young, but quick on his feet—wheeled in a tray loaded with enough desserts for a party. What the hell, I thought. Russ couldn't be worried about the bill. After writing in a big tip for the waiter, I signed the check using Russ's name. The waiter smiled and left and I poured myself a large cup of coffee, topping it off with cream and sugar. One sip told me I was drinking coffee I had never been able to afford in my life.

Ten minutes later there were four light knocks on the door. I opened it and smiled when I saw Russ's grin and the bag of cash he was carrying. I assumed it was cash. He tossed me the leather sack, and it had that "money" feel to it.

"Did they let you take sixty grand?" I asked.

"A hundred." He walked in and saw the tray of desserts. "Jesus, Jessie. You must be someone who doesn't easily gain weight."

It's funny but it was only then that I took the time to size up his body. I wondered if the inspiration came from the sack of cash I held. Why did money and sex go so well together? Without a blackjack table in his way, I could see just how well-built he was. He must have worked out regularly. With such a great ass, and those blue eyes of his, he was going to be hard to resist.

However, it wasn't as if I decided to sleep with him right then. But yes, I began to think about it.

"You're wrong," I said. "I count every calorie I eat."

He gestured to the desserts. "How much is here?"

"About sixty thousand."

He cocked an eyebrow. "Is that a hint?"

"What do you mean?"

"Are you afraid I'm not going to give you your money?"

I shrugged, trying to act cool. "I had a good time winning it. I don't care if you keep it."

"Bullshit!" He laughed. "You should have seen the look on your face when I asked that question. It was priceless."

"Great. Then I just earned my money."

"Touché." He paused. "You can let go of it, you know."

"What?"

"The bag of money. You're holding on to it for dear life."

I wanted to snap at him that I didn't give a damn about the money, but he had me. I was hugging the bag so tightly to my chest I had to make a conscious effort to set it down. The bag was hard not to stare at. It represented a whole new future for me.

"How old are you?" I asked.

"How old do I look?"

"You're a tough one," I admitted. "Your body language puts you past thirty. That's a compliment, by the way. You have a commanding presence. But if I just saw your picture, I'd say you could be as young as twenty-five."

"Interesting."

I picked up the bag of cash and threw it at him. "Interesting? Is that all I get? How old are you?"

"How old are you?"

"I'm legal."

"Legal for what? Not gambling, that's for sure." He paused. "You must be between eighteen and twenty."

"True. Now you give me an in between for your age. As long as it's only two years apart."

He shook his head. "No can do."

"Why not?"

"Because then I'd have to lie to you. And I don't want to do that." He held up the bag of cash. "You know what? You're a first."

"A first at what?"

"I threw a bag of cash at you and you threw it back. I've never seen a woman do that before. Once they have their hands on it, they usually don't let go."

I was flattered. "I trust you. Besides, it's not really my money, and now I'm being serious. I did nothing to earn it. You're under no obligation to share it with me."

"You trusted me. That's enough." He set the cash down on a nearby table. "By the way, you can keep the whole hundred if you want."

I almost fell over. I shook my head firmly. "No, absolutely not. That wouldn't be fair. After taxes, at most I should get thirty-five grand. You can't give me three times that amount."

"I can give you whatever I want. It's up to you to accept it. You saw how much I won. The extra money won't make any difference to me. But it can help you. At the table, you mentioned how you wished you could go to the same school as Alex." He gestured to the bag. "Well, there's your ticket."

"Like I could walk into UCLA and pay for my tuition with cash."

"Believe me, they would take it and not ask a single question. All the campuses in California are hurting for money. They'll be happy to let a bright young woman like you in, especially if you're not asking for financial aid."

"It's too late to apply for the fall semester."

"Show them the money and see what they say."

My head spun. I retreated to my chair and my cup of coffee

and swallowed a big gulp of caffeine. The waiter had brought six different dishes of ice cream—all of which rested on ice cubes—and six varieties of cake. The dishes looked divine but my stomach was spinning along with my brain and I didn't know if could eat. Russ sat on a nearby sofa and poured himself some coffee. He took it black.

The funny thing was, I knew he was going to take it black.

"Was the floor manager upset I left?" I asked.

"If he was he didn't show it. Remember, the money you won pales compared to what I won. At this point, his job is to treat me nice so I'll feel at home in his casino and return to play some more."

"He figures if you keep playing, you're bound to lose."

"Sure."

I studied him. "But it doesn't matter how long you play, you'd keep on winning, right?"

Russ met my gaze. "Yes."

"How?"

"No offense, Jessie, but we just met. Isn't that sort of a big secret to share so soon?"

"You spent hours flaunting your ability in front of me. I think I deserve some explanation."

"All right, in exchange for a hundred thousand, I'll tell you my secret."

He was bluffing; it was a favorite pastime of his. I decided to call him on it. "Fine. I'll trade the cash for your technique."

He leaned over and spoke in a confidential tone. "I cheat."

"Be more specific."

"I know when to bet high or low because I know what kind of cards I'm going to get next."

"How?"

He smiled. "That's twice you've asked that. No matter what I say, you're going to keep asking it."

"That's not true. You're not telling me anything. That's not fair."

"Fair? Is it fair I should have to tell you all my secrets on the first date?"

"Is that what this is? A date?"

He drank more of his coffee. "I hope so."

He said the line so sweetly, I was touched. And it was true, he had a point, I was being too demanding. I settled down and sipped my coffee, while he began to dig into a piece of German chocolate cake. He took man-size bites.

"Are you going to play there again?" I asked.

"I've drawn too much attention. At most I can play at one or two other hotels on the Strip before I'll have to get out of town."

"Are you saying your life would be in danger?"

"You act surprised—don't be. If I continue to win, the people who own these glittering towers will get annoyed. They're used to taking people's money, they don't like handing it out in suitcases." He paused and drank some more coffee. "Someone, at some point, would take action."

"You're talking about the Mob, right? I've heard it still controls Las Vegas from behind the scenes. That people just don't realize it."

He surprised me when he shook his head. "The Mob has no power here."

"Then who, exactly, would take action against you?"

"That's a story for another night. The main thing is you have enough money to go to school."

"If I accept the hundred grand."

"You'll take it. You may be a nice kid but you're not stupid."

"I'm not a kid."

He bowed his head. "My apologies."

I nodded toward the dining area. "You left your laptop on. You should be thankful I'm not a spy. I could have gone through your mail."

He was unconcerned. "I just use it to access the Internet and keep up with a few friends."

"I noticed the brochures beside the computer. You work for West World?" I asked.

"Yes."

"I glanced at the brochure. They're a genetics company?"

"They've developed a technology whereby they can take a three-dimensional picture of your entire genome in a matter of seconds."

"A real picture? One that shows where you might have a defect?"

"An extremely detailed picture. When our product hits the market, it will explode. It will allow any doctor to take a picture of you the instant you're born and predict—with a high degree of accuracy—what diseases you're likely to catch during your life."

"The insurance companies will love that."

"You're quick. A few years from now the insurance companies will probably demand to see such a photograph before they agree to insure you."

"That's terrible. Just because someone has a predisposition to catch a disease, they shouldn't be denied insurance."

Russ wasn't offended. "You won't get an argument from me. The potential for abuse with this device—we call it the scanner—is frightening. WW is having a convention in town this weekend to address these precise issues. Tons of insurance company CEOs, deans of medical schools, presidents of hospitals—just about everyone who's a major player in the medical field is in Las Vegas to hear about our technology. There are politicians here as well. Next to defense, the health industry is the largest industry in the world. Everyone who knows about the scanner wants some say in how it's to be used."

"It shows how clueless I am. I didn't even know this convention was taking place."

"Don't be embarrassed. The convention is large but West World has gone out of its way to keep the media away. There hasn't been a single article in the papers about our meetings."

"I'm amazed you can keep anything a secret nowadays."

"It's not a problem if you have enough money. West World is heavily capitalized, to the tune of twenty billion, and it's not even a public company. They know how controversial their project is. They want the scanner in widespread use before it gets major publicity."

"Wait. You said 'how controversial their project is.' Did you mean 'product'?"

Russ put down his coffee and stared at me. "You don't miss much, do you? West World didn't just develop the scanner so it can pass them out to whoever can afford one. They're in the middle of a project where they're trying to scan the genetic code of every person on earth."

"You're joking."

"I wish I were."

"How many people has your company scanned so far?"

"That information is proprietary."

"Private?"

"Yes."

I fidgeted uneasily. "Have I been scanned?"

I assumed he would say no, that I would know if I had been. But he stood and headed for his bedroom. He spoke louder as he disappeared from view.

"I don't know—I'll have to scan you and compare you to everyone we have in our database," he said, as I heard him going through his drawers.

"You're going to do this now?"

"It only takes a few seconds. It doesn't hurt."

"All right." It was hard to say no to a guy who wanted to give me a hundred grand.

Russ reappeared a minute later with what appeared to be a narrow flashlight. Six inches long, it had a black metal exterior and a red tinted lens at one end. But the lens looked more like crystal than glass, and the thing hummed when he sat beside me and flipped on a side switch.

"We are now being recorded," he said.

"Really?"

"This is an official reading." He paused and continued in a businesslike tone. "Jessica Ralle, do I have your permission to scan your genetic code into the data banks of West World?"

I hesitated. "I guess so."

"You need to say yes or no."

"Yes."

"Hold out your arm, please, and roll up your sleeve." I did as I was told. He continued, "Rest your elbow on the arm of the chair. It will make it easier to keep still."

"Okay." I discovered I was shaking a bit.

He flipped another switch and a red beam emanated from the top of the scanner. The beam was narrow. There was no question in my mind it was a laser beam. I felt its warmth as it struck my arm. The sensation was pleasant but short-lived. The laser was on a total of three seconds. The device beeped faintly, the humming stopped, and the laser vanished.

"Got it," Russ said, as he stood and walked toward his laptop. I rubbed the spot he had zapped. It felt warm.

"How does this device work?" I asked.

"It uses a laser to create a holographic image of your genes. Once your information is downloaded into the company's database, it's used to create a picture of your DNA."

I stood and walked over to where he was using a cable to connect the scanner and laptop. The screen flashed a wave of binary code, at incredible speed, before it settled on a picture of what I knew from basic biology to be an image of a double helix.

It was so rich in color and detail, it literally took my breath away.

"God," I whispered.

"Not quite. It's you."

"Me?"

"Your essence. Because the image is recorded in holographic form, I can rotate it in any direction I wish, focus on any gene I want to."

"Was I already in your database or not?"

He hesitated. "No."

"Do you see any problems with my genes?"

"I'm not looking." He glanced up. "I know you hear the reluctance in my voice when I talk about West World's project. There's a reason for that. What I just did to you isn't like taking your fingerprints or even your blood. It's much more intimate. I now have the ability to know a tremendous amount about you—more than you would probably want me to know. For example, say I saw that you have a fault in your M5H2 gene. That would mean your chances of developing colon cancer are ten times greater than normal."

I put my hand to my mouth. "Is that gene damaged?"

"I don't know."

"But you just said—"

"I told you, I don't know anything about you because I chose not to look. However, if I change my mind and do look, I might discover your M5H2 gene is defective. Then I'll probably feel compelled to tell you to start having regular colonoscopies for the rest of your life."

"Is that where they stick a rubber tube up your butt?"

"That's a sound scientific explanation of the process."

I found myself fidgeting. "It's weird—I want you to look and I'm afraid for you to look."

"Your reaction is normal. Most people feel the same way. They say knowledge is power but too much knowledge can be a curse. Especially if it falls into the wrong hands. Besides learning about your physical health, I can study your mental health as well by studying this hologram. I can even estimate your IQ. I can do all this in a few seconds, without asking your permission."

"But you did ask my permission," I said.

"True. I told you, it was an official reading."

"As opposed to an unofficial one." I paused. "Does West World have the resources to scan everyone in the world without their knowledge?"

"They act like they do. But in the developing world, it's hard. Too many people and not enough roads to reach them all. But West World might go for it."

"That seems to scare you."

"A lot of things about this technology scare me."

"Russ, if you don't like this company, if you don't trust them, why do you work for them?"

He reached over and turned off the picture of my DNA. He took his time answering. "Because by working for them, I remain in a position where I might be able to stop them from abusing the scanner."

"Are you high up in the company?"

He glanced out the window. "You think I'm too young, I can't be very high up. Unless I happen to be related to the founder."

He had read my mind exactly. "Are you?" I asked.

He shrugged. "Let's just say I'm deeply involved in the firm. But I don't want you sharing that info with your friends from school."

"Why tell me if you don't want me to share it? How do you know you can trust me?"

"Because I know they won't give a damn who I work for. Not when they see your bag of money. All they'll care about is how I win at twenty-two."

"Twenty-one."

"Huh?"

"You said twenty-two. The game is twenty-one."

He stopped smiling and stood in front of me, placing his hands on my shoulders. For a moment I was sure he was going to kiss me. I had already decided I would let him. He was cute enough and I owed Jimmy nothing.

Nothing except months of pain.

"How would you like to learn to play twenty-two?" he asked.

"Don't be silly—there's no such game."

"My friends and I play it all the time. It's the same game, really, it just has a few extra rules." He added, "It might help you understand how I win at twenty-one."

"You're joking."

"I'm not."

"Aren't you tired of playing cards?"

He checked his watch. "It's just after one. I have an early meeting. I have to be in bed by two. But we could play for a little while." He added, "I'd enjoy it."

Once again, who was I to argue with a man who wanted to pay for my college education?

Russ, to my surprise, had six decks of cards handy. They were new decks, still wrapped in plastic. He opened them and spread them out on the dining-room table. He shuffled them as quickly and smoothly as any dealer; he was a regular pro.

He took twelve packets of cash from the bag. Each one contained fifty one hundred dollar bills—five grand. Looking at the money, touching it, made my heart pound. It was mine, I kept thinking, all mine.

Unless I lost it playing twenty-two. Russ wanted to use the cash to play. He told me so in a serious tone. He kept thirty grand and gave me thirty.

"Since there's only two of us and you don't know all the rules, I'll play the part of the dealer," he said.

"What do you mean, all the rules? I don't know any of the rules."

"I told you, they're almost identical to blackjack. The big difference is the winning hand is twenty-two, not twenty-one. And the value of two cards is slightly different. In twenty-two, the queen of diamonds and the queen of hearts are worth eleven points rather than ten. In this game, if you get both those cards at the start, you have the equivalent of blackjack, or a natural. You immediately get paid twice your bet."

"Not one and a half times your bet?"

"No. The reason is it's a harder hand to get than twenty-one."

"Because all the picture cards aren't worth eleven?"

"Exactly. In blackjack, the best card to get at the start is an ace—that's how you get blackjack. But in twenty-two, an ace is no longer an important card."

"Is an ace still worth one or eleven?"

"An ace is only worth one point, nothing else." Russ paused. "By the way, twenty-two isn't called blackjack. It's known as the red queen."

"Because the queen of diamonds and the queen of hearts are the easiest way to get winning hands?"

"Yes. And if you get two of each it pays double."

"With that kind of payout, the game seems to favor the player over the dealer."

"It only seems that way on the surface. Besides the fact that the ace is no longer helpful to the player, the dealer only has to hit up to sixteen, even though we've raised the winning number to twenty-two. That gives him an edge."

"He busts less often."

"You got it. I knew you'd catch on fast." He slipped the six decks into a shoe he had taken from a nearby drawer. It looked as if he'd come ready to play. "Place your bet."

I put down a hundred dollar bill. All I had were hundreds.

Russ dealt a card facedown, to himself, then dealt me a card faceup. The next two cards he dealt faceup, one to me and one to himself. I got a ten and a queen of hearts. I had twenty-one, by the new rules. He was showing a queen of diamonds. Naturally, I couldn't see his hole card.

"Do you wish to stand?" he asked.

"Yes, Mr. Dealer."

He flipped over his hole card. He had a nine, twenty altogether, which meant I had won. He paid me a hundred and we continued to play. Frankly, I was feeling my fatigue but I strained to focus. Yet I saw no point in playing a game that was virtually identical to blackjack, especially after such a long night at the casino tables.

While we played, my curiosity over how he had won so much money continued to plague me. How had he done it? Once again, I tried prodding him gently.

"I know you weren't counting at the casino because I have a friend who explained how it works. The shoe gets favorable only when there are plenty of tens and aces left in it. But even when it swings in favor of the player, the advantage is only two or three percent. Five percent if the counter is real lucky."

"I can't argue with your friend," Russ said.

"So you weren't counting. And I have to assume you're not psychic, because I don't believe in that crap. So all I'm left with is that you're another *Rain Man*."

"What's that?"

"It's an old movie that starred Tom Cruise and Dustin Hoffman. In the film, Tom and Dustin are brothers, but Dustin's a lot older and really messed up. He's mentally retarded and needs constant care. Only toward the end of the film does Tom discover that he's a savant. I assume you know what that is?"

"It's a rare condition found in mentally disabled people. Their mental disabilities allow them to use parts of the brain that most people never use. That gives them special abilities."

"Are you one of them?" I asked.

He smiled. "Do I seem retarded to you?"

"No. But not all savants are."

"The vast majority are."

"You still haven't answered my question," I said.

"I told you, this is only our first date."

I persisted. "I remember at the casino, every time the dealer prepared a fresh shoe, he spread the cards out on the table for everyone to see. You would study them right then. Also, when he shuffled the cards, you would watch him closely. It was like you were memorizing their sequence. I don't know how you did it. I would assume it would take a special ability, like a savant would have. But *if* you were a savant, then it would explain how you were able to predict whether your next hand would be strong or weak. It would also explain how you knew when the dealer was going to bust."

Russ nodded as we continued to play twenty-two. "It's true I did well at the table. But if I could remember everything you're saying I could, then I should never have lost."

"That's not true. It was inevitable you'd be dealt weak hands from time to time. Not only that, you're smart enough not to win every hand that was strong. I think you occasionally put a big bet on a bad hand just to throw off the casino employees."

"So you have me all figured out?" he asked.

"I can't help but notice you're not denying any of it."

"There's no point. You believe what you want to believe."

I thought I had figured out his secret but his quiet mystery disarmed me. My theory was all talk. I could feel him laughing at me inside.

No, not laughing, but smiling. Yes, I knew he liked me.

Russ looked down at the last cards he had dealt. I was showing a queen of diamonds and a king of jacks—twenty-one, another strong hand. Even against the queen of hearts he was showing. I told him that I'd stand. He turned his hole card over. He had a queen of diamonds, which gave him twenty-two, or what he called a red queen.

He went to take my money. I had grown careless, winning the last few hands in a row, and had let my cash pile up on the table. I had just lost a grand, or so I thought. Then he explained that in red queen, when the dealer got a natural, the player had to fork over an additional 100 percent.

"You didn't explain that rule before," I complained.

"I figured you'd learn it as we played." He had already taken the grand.

"So I have to give you another thousand dollars?" I asked.

"Yes."

"But we're just playing for fun, right?"

"No. I told you, red queen is a serious game. What you win or lose here is for real."

I snorted. "You have got to be joking!"

He didn't blink. "No."

I reluctantly peeled off ten hundreds and threw them at him. "Any other rules I should know about?"

"Yes. This one is important. After the dealer gets a natural, the player must immediately try to win his or her money back."

"You're saying on my next hand I have to bet two thousand dollars?"

"Yes."

"That's a crazy rule. What if I didn't have it?"

"Then you shouldn't be playing red queen. The game's older than blackjack. It has a rich tradition. It's never played just for fun and no one is ever supposed to break the rules."

"That's silly."

"It's a fact. You have to bet me two thousand dollars right now."

I yawned loudly in his face. "Forget it, I'm tired. Let's call it a night."

He nodded. "Fine. As soon as we complete this hand."

"Forget the hand. Let's just quit."

"We can't quit in the middle of this kind of situation. I'm the dealer, I just got twenty-two. As the player, you're required to try to win your money back."

"I told you, I'm tired."

"And I told you, in red queen every bet counts."

"So the money I've just lost—you're going to keep that?"

"Yes."

"Then why did you give it to me in the first place?"

"I gave it to you so you could afford your college tuition. But as a dealer, playing red queen, I'm required to keep the money and give it to . . . I mean, I just have to keep it. Those are the rules."

I acted bored. "Fine. Deal."

"Place your bet on the table first."

"All right." I slapped down two grand. "Deal, Mr. Dealer."

He dealt. I got seventeen. He was showing a queen of diamonds.

"I'm screwed," I muttered.

"Not necessarily. Remember, taking a hit at seventeen in this game is like hitting sixteen in blackjack." He paused. "The book says you should do it."

"Barely." I paused, convinced he knew what card was coming next. "Are you telling me to hit?"

"I can't give you any advice."

"You did before."

"Not in this game."

He was acting awfully weird, I thought.

"Hit me," I said impatiently.

He hit me with a five—twenty-two. He turned over his hole card. He had a king of jacks—twenty-one. He had lost and I had won. I got my two grand back plus an extra two thousand.

"Who do you have to give it to?" I asked as we began to clean up. The ice cream was melting and the cakes had begun to look sad. I hated to send them back, though. Then I remembered he had a full-size fridge.

"What do you mean?" he asked.

"You began to say you were required to give the money to someone. Then you stopped and said something else."

"I'm sorry, I don't remember."

I touched his arm. "Russ."

"What?"

"You've been great tonight. The perfect gentleman. Please don't ruin it now by lying to me."

He stared at me. "I'm sorry, I can't tell you who I would have given the money to. But it's not an issue because you won back what you lost. So can we just leave it at that?"

I smiled. "You don't play fair. You know it's impossible for a girl to get mad at a guy who just gave her a hundred grand."

He stood and came around the table and gently put his hands on my shoulders. I say gently because his approach was totally nonthreatening. He didn't try to kiss me until I gave him the hint by tilting my head back. He turned his own head slightly to the side, so I didn't have to strain my neck to match his height. Then his lips were on mine and they were not normal lips. They were perfect lips, and only Jimmy was supposed to have those.

I felt myself falling as he kissed me harder, and I fought to keep from going off the ledge, but it was no use. By some strange magic we were in the dining room one moment and in his bedroom the next. The lights were off but the window curtains were pulled back and the kaleidoscope of colors from the Strip played through the open glass and into my brain.

It seemed as if his eyes turned purple, orange, and green, while his skin—I must have pulled off his shirt—remained a burning red. His strong hands were on my breasts, outside my dress, and then we both began to undo my buttons, so fast, so furiously, that I started to hyperventilate.

I was light-years beyond turned on. We fell on the bed and I felt I would explode. All thoughts of safe sex were washed away. My body wanted his body so bad I honestly felt I would die if he didn't make love to me.

He took off my dress. I tore off his pants.

He removed my underwear. I ripped off his.

I pulled off his watch and threw it away. I wanted nothing in my way. But then something surreal happened. I was about to climb on top of him. He raised his head and backed up to give me room, and I looked into his face from inches away and felt his hot breath on my cheeks.

Then I saw Jimmy's face. I swear, it had taken the place of Russ's.

The image was more real than our bodies, more powerful than my lust. Maybe it was love that caused me to see it. Love or pain, if the two were even separate things. The love of my life, Jimmy, was the only one who had ever made me cry.

Maybe that's why I burst out crying.

The sound caused my Jimmy hallucination to crumble. It was replaced by Russ's confused expression. Not that I was confused. I realized that the months had not mattered. That I loved Jimmy as much as the first day I had made love to him, and the last day. I knew then that my mind kept track of time, but not my heart, and that I had to give him another chance or else I would regret it for the rest of my life.

I stood from the bed and walked naked to the tall windows. Behind me, I heard Russ sigh. "There's someone else," he said.

"Yes." I stared down at the throngs of people still partying beneath the lights. "I'm sorry."

"Why are you sorry?"

I looked at him. He was partway under the blankets, covered at the waist but still beautiful. "I feel like I led you on," I said.

"I'm sure you didn't mean to."

"How do you know that?"

"You're a good person." He paused. "You don't have to apologize for crying over someone you love."

"Why are you taking this so well?"

"Because I doubt anyone's ever cried over me." He lit a cigarette and stared at the ceiling. "Is he here? He must be or you wouldn't be so upset."

"He's here."

"Is he with someone else?"

"I honestly don't know."

Russ found his watch and checked the time. He took one last hit of his cigarette and put it out. "It's late, I better sleep. Grab your clothes and the money and get a taxi downstairs. Don't even think of leaving the crowd at the door unless you're in a cab. I left some smaller bills on the living room table. Don't share a cab no matter how much someone begs you to. Remember, in this town, always take your own taxi."

"I understand." I began to pick up my clothes. "Will I see you again?"

"That's up to you. Take the key I gave you. I can always call down to the front desk for another. Come by whenever you want." He added quietly, "Or else come by when you don't know what else to do."

"Russ?"

"Just do what I say." He turned away, wrapping himself in a blanket. "I really have to sleep," he whispered.

His breathing had altered by the time I was dressed. He was out cold—not snoring, but far from this world. I collected my purse, his key, the cash he had left on the table, and the leather bag crammed with a hundred thousand dollars. Swinging it over my shoulders by its straps, I felt as if I discovered golden wings that could fly me to a new destiny. Only I knew this was Las Vegas, the City of Sin, and that the gold here was really colored green.

There was a line for taxis at the door. I was tempted to

set off for the MGM on foot. But I remembered Russ's warning, and there were a few dark spots between the two hotels, areas where someone wicked who had been spying on me earlier, and knew what I had won, could stage a surprise attack. I forced myself to wait for a taxi. Finally, when my turn came, the driver was annoyed I was only going a few blocks. He wanted to pick up the couple behind me as well.

"No," I said. "Take me alone."

He was old, grouchy, burned-out from too many years under the desert sun. "I've waited thirty minutes. I can't make any money off your fare."

"Hey, babe, we don't mind riding with ya," the guy behind me said.

His girl kissed him. "We like threesomes."

I ignored them, spoke to the driver. "You have to take me alone, those are the city rules. But I promise to give you a big tip."

"How big?" the taxi driver demanded.

I opened the door and jumped in. "Shut up and drive," I said.

We arrived at the MGM in fifteen minutes. The traffic caused the delay. Plus I refused to get out of the cab until the driver took me to the front entrance. Then I opened my purse, not the bag Russ had given me, and gave the driver ten bucks for the fare and another twenty dollars for a tip. He seemed satisfied, although he didn't thank me. He had no idea the kind of tip he would have received if he'd been the least bit polite.

Inside, I checked at the front desk and asked if they had a vault with private lockers where I could store an important bag. Of course they had just the place; they were used to people with valuables. A guard led me to a room lined with lockers and handed me a key. I opened the locker and put the bag inside and relocked it.

"Does anyone come down here without an escort?" I asked.

"No, ma'am. They need a key and have to be with me or one of the other guards to get in here."

"What if I lose the key and someone else finds it?"

"You have to show ID to get in this room. Don't worry, ma'am, your bag is completely safe."

"Thank you," I said.

Upstairs I found Jimmy sitting outside my door on the hallway floor. He was dozing, with his head on his knees, but he heard me approach and stood quickly. He looked happy to see me. Of course the reverse—times a thousand—was also true.

"How long have you been waiting here?" I asked.

"I don't know. A while."

"You couldn't share a room with Ted?"

"No. I mean, yes, he loaned me his key." Jimmy added, nodding toward my suite, "He's inside, with Debbie."

"With Debbie?" I had to laugh. "How long have they . . . oh, never mind. Do you know where Alex is?"

"I haven't seen her. Wasn't she with you?"

"We were together but she got annoyed and ran off. You know her."

"Yeah."

"What brings you here?"

Jimmy took a breath. He went to answer but then his pain got in the way of the words and his face crumpled. He stopped breathing; the air around him seemed to go numb.

"I don't know why Huck died," he said finally. "He was small and frail. He had come early, a few weeks, but the doctors said that wasn't the reason he died. They wanted to do an autopsy but I didn't want them cutting him up. Kari felt the same way. We wrapped him in a blanket and took him away and had a private funeral for him and that was that."

"How long ago was this?"

Jimmy looked dazed. He counted on his fingers. "A month ago, I'm not sure." He added as a tear ran over his cheek, "I'm sorry, I should have told you earlier."

"Oh, Jimmy, don't say that. You did nothing wrong." I hugged him and held him for what seemed like forever. Then he kissed me and I kissed him and it was okay that I had been with another man less than an hour ago. Because Russ had been a dream, I realized, while Jimmy was the only real thing in my life. I loved him, God how I loved him.

CHAPTER FIVE

TWO SURPRISES GREETED JIMMY AND ME THE FOLLOWING morning.

First, Debbie and Ted joined us for room service in our suite and neither of them said a harsh word to me about my drunken behavior the night before. Indeed, they were both glowing so brightly I wouldn't have been surprised if they thanked me. They were barely dressed and it was clear Ted had spent the night.

So much for Ted's undying love for me.

The second surprise, which should have been no surprise at all, was that Alex didn't return to our suite until we were halfway through our pancakes. She didn't act embarrassed or ashamed, but it was obvious she was exhausted. However, just before she went to bed, she yanked me into her room and closed the door.

"What happened after I left?" she asked as we sat together on her bed.

I shrugged. "Nothing."

"Bullshit. I tried calling you ten times and got no answer."

"I didn't get your calls. You said it yourself, cells don't work very well on the casino floors."

"So you stayed and played with Russ?"

"We played twenty-one."

"Anything else?"

"A few hands of twenty-two."

"Huh?"

"Never mind. Look, nothing happened between us, nothing sexual."

Alex studied me. "You're lying."

Damn, I hated how she could read me.

"We made out, that's all," I said. "Then I thought of Jimmy and I stopped."

"If you made out, you must have gone back to his room."

"We went to his room to split our winnings."

She saw I was serious. "How much?"

"A lot. I'll tell you about it later. The main thing is Jimmy was waiting for me when I got back. And he spent the night."

"So you're back together?"

"Yes."

"You sound confident. Need I remind you this is the same guy who dumped you for no reason."

"You're the one who put us in the same car. I thought you wanted us to get back together."

"Maybe. But I wanted you to make him beg a little."

"Plus he had a reason why he went back to Kari, a good one."

"What?"

"We can talk about that later as well. Now I'm tired of your questions, and you look like you're ready to collapse. Where were you all night?"

"The Mirage. The top floor, corner suite."

"Russ has a suite on the top floor of the Mandalay Bay. We could have waved to each other. So what's his name, how old is he, is he rich, and what's his favorite position?"

"Alfred Summon, but I call him Al. He's younger than Russ and older than Jimmy. He has money, he sells drugs to doctors who in turn sell them to their patients. I don't know if I'd call him rich. He told me he doesn't have a favorite position, only a favorite girl, and last night I was her."

"Was it a one-night thing?"

The question gave Alex reason to pause. "I hope not."

"You say that like you care."

Again, she hesitated. "I know this will sound totally lame but I think I do. There's something about this guy. He's not like anyone I ever met before."

I could have said exactly the same thing about Russ.

"How did you meet?" I asked.

"In a bar. Downstairs."

"Who approached who?"

"I don't know, I was drunk. Does it matter?"

"Is he here on a medical convention?"

"How did you know that?"

"It's why Russ is here."

"Well, maybe they're friends. Are you going to see Russ again?"

"I'd like to, he's a fascinating guy, but I don't want to risk anything with Jimmy." I paused. "That reminds me. Can I borrow your car? Jimmy and I want to take a ride out to Lake Mead and rent a boat."

Alex held out her keys. "Sure. But I think you're risking more by not seeing Russ again. Jimmy's let you down before. He can do it again. He might take you more seriously if he knows he has competition."

"You know I'm not into mind games. I love Jimmy, I'm not going to do anything to hurt him." I stood. "And before you start on another lecture, try sleeping for eight hours. You look like shit."

Alex plopped back on the bed, closed her eyes, and sighed. "I don't care, it was worth it. Al, it's hard to explain . . . it's like he's got some kind of magic."

Just like Russ. I gave Alex a quick kiss on the forehead and left her to rest. She was snoring before I closed her door.

While the others were finishing breakfast, I ran downstairs

and withdrew twenty-five hundred bucks from my bag. I felt guilty not telling Jimmy about the money but I didn't want to have to explain how I got it.

At the same time, I *needed* clothes. When we had checked in to the hotel the day before, we had passed a row of stores that had made my eyes bug out of my head. That was, until I saw the prices.

I was beyond happy to be back with Jimmy and was desperate to look my best. But the sad truth was my wardrobe sucked. My bimonthly checks from the Apple Valley Library averaged eighty bucks after taxes, which left no room for buying sexy clothes. It was no joke—the swimsuit I had brought to Las Vegas was the same suit I had worn to try out for our high-school freshman swim team.

There was this white bikini, though, that had caught my eye the day before, and now I didn't care what it cost. I just marched into the store and pointed to it and asked them to check in the back for my size. While I was waiting for the saleswoman to return, I spotted a mannequin wearing a red silk blouse and a short black skirt. I didn't stop to ask the dummy's permission, I pulled the clothes right off her. When the woman finally did return with the bikini, I was dancing around the dressing room. I had never been so excited about something I had bought.

The three items took the bulk of my cash. $1,874.56. God, normal people couldn't even walk into such stores.

* * *

Two hours later I was floating in sunshine, water, and bliss. After driving to Lake Mead, Jimmy had rented a fast-enough boat that we were able to water-ski behind it—by trading off places, of course. But I wasn't nearly as physically fit as Jimmy and my arm and chest muscles quickly tired. Taking mercy on me, Jimmy anchored our boat near the Hoover Dam, where the water was at its deepest, and I inflated a raft and floated around on my back with a book in hand while Jimmy snorkeled in circles around me.

The warm water lapped peacefully at my sides. The dam was less than a quarter mile to my right. Jimmy had already snuck up and dunked me once, but under the threat of no sex for a year, I had managed to convince him it would be a bad idea to repeat the trick. Besides not wanting to ruin my paperback, I was covered in SPF 100 sunscreen and was wearing a new pair of sunglasses I had purchased on the way out of the hotel. The price had turned Jimmy's head—they had cost a hundred bucks. I explained the splurge by saying I had lucked out at the tables the night before.

However, I had to be more careful. The casual remark did not satisfy Jimmy, especially when I unveiled my new bikini. He wasn't into fashion but he knew money when he saw it. He flipped over how I looked, and in the same breath asked who'd bought it for me.

"My dad. It's a graduation present," I said.

"I thought you said he didn't even call?"

"He didn't. He just sent the gift."

"Your father the famous doctor sent you a piece of clothing that has but one purpose, and that is to make every guy in our class want to have sex with you? Sorry, I don't think so."

I smiled sweetly. "Okay. I lied. Someone else gave it to me. You don't need to know who."

The remark shut him up. Maybe Alex was right, maybe it was better if there was competition he had to worry about.

He surfaced close to where I floated, after being underwater God knew how long. Jimmy had amazing endurance. Up until his senior year, he'd run long distance for the track team and won every race. His coach had said he had Olympic potential. Yet he had quit the team the last year. Now, with what had happened with Kari, I understood why.

"How's your book?" he asked.

"The mystery part is excellent but it feels like the author wrote it in a month. All the paragraphs are short and jumpy."

"If it holds your interest, that's all that matters."

"I suppose." I frowned as I studied the cover. A black snake tooth dripping red venom, or else human blood. I had picked it up because I was sure I had seen the cover before, only I didn't know where. I continued. "What bugs me is the author is talented. She can turn it on when she wants to, but it's like she can't be bothered because she knows she's only writing for a set amount of money and it doesn't matter how good the book turns out."

"Don't authors get royalties? The more a book sells, the more money they make?"

I waved the book. "You haven't read about the new trend in publishing. This author pumps out too many books a year to write them all. She just sticks her name on stories that have been ghostwritten."

"So the ghostwriter could be a he for all you know."

"That's right. But I read in a magazine that they never get royalties. They're just out-of-work writers who need the cash."

"It sounds like it bugs you."

"I take back what I said a moment ago. I do respect the ghostwriter. He or she has to live. It's the woman on the cover I dislike. She's the one who is whoring her name."

"Most successful people whore their names. It's why they're successful."

Jimmy swam closer, treading water, his brown hair plastered back by the water. He pushed back his snorkel mask. He had a tan, I was not surprised. When he worked on cars out back of Sears, he often took his shirt off. He looked good—he always looked good. It was ridiculous how nice it was to have him near.

"A penny for your thoughts," he said when I fell silent.

I smiled faintly. "I was just thinking of the first time we made love."

"Damn. And I was hoping you were thinking about last night."

"Why?"

"I like to think that I've improved with practice."

"Us girls are silly. The first time is always the best time." I paused. "Do you remember how I didn't answer the door? I knew it was you. But I knew you'd hear the water running and come in."

Jimmy rubbed at the water in his eyes. "What are you talking about?"

"Do you need a blow-by-blow? That Saturday afternoon. You came over after work. My mother was out and I was in the shower. You said you knocked but I didn't answer. You stuck your head in my bedroom and called out. You must have known I was in the shower." I leaned over and kissed him. "You must have known I'd invite you in."

He didn't smile like I assumed he would. Instead, he looked puzzled. "No offense, Jessie, but that's not what happened. I never had sex with you right after work. The first time we did it was at night after we went to the movies. It was late. Your mother was asleep in the next room."

"Excuse me. We only went to two movies. On our first date and our last." I pushed him away. "You bastard, you're thinking of Kari."

"No. I swear, I'm not."

"I don't care. I'm right and you're wrong."

"Hold on a second, don't get mad. Remember back to that afternoon you're talking about. I came over and asked if I could take a shower in your bathroom. I'd just gotten off work. I'm a mechanic, my hands were covered in oil. Whenever I leave work, I have to soak my hands in a solvent to loosen the oil. Then I have to scrub them with a harsh soap. But you didn't have all that stuff so my hands were still pretty grimy even after the shower. Think, Jessie, I would never have taken you to bed—especially for the first time—with dirty fingers."

"Are you saying you didn't take a shower with me?"

"I did. But it wasn't after I got off work."

"Jimmy, this is ridiculous. You can't be getting senile already. We didn't jump straight into bed. You joined me in the shower and we washed each other for a long time. I cleaned your hands. You shampooed my hair. That's what made it so romantic. That's why it's such a special memory to me." My voice cracked, I was getting emotional. "It upsets me you can't even remember it."

He raised a hand. "Hold on, let me give you another clue that might help jog your memory. Let's go back to that afternoon you're talking about, or you think you're talking about. When we got into bed and were lying there, facing each other, were you lying on your right side or your left side?"

"I was lying on my left side most of the time. Standing at the foot and facing the bed, I was on the left side."

"That's impossible."

"Why?"

"Because that means I would have had to be lying on my right side. And two weeks after we started dating I broke three ribs on that side and it was still tender when we first made love. I couldn't lie on my right side, it was too painful."

"How were you able to make love to me?"

"It was a month after the injury and it was less painful. But I was still careful to lie on my left side, not my right."

"Wrong. Wrong. We made love four weeks after we started dating, not six weeks. And you lay on your right side plenty."

"Only later. Only during the weeks before Christmas."

"That's bullshit. That day was precious to me. Everything that happened that day—I've played it over and over again in my memory. How could I be so wrong?"

I had even had what many would call a mystical experience after we made love. I saw a white light, and heard a sound that was unlike anything I'd ever heard before. It was more like a pure vibration, something no musical instrument could make. It sent a thrill through my whole body.

"The stuff about my oily hands and my broken ribs are facts. I didn't make them up." He paused. "I didn't mean to upset you. I just . . . I don't know."

"What? Say it."

He shook his head. "It's not important."

"But it is important! That's what I'm trying to tell you. That's why I'm upset. The most important day of my life seems to have meant nothing to you."

"Jessie."

"My diary! I wrote down everything that happened in my diary! When we get back to the hotel, I can show it to you."

"You told me you don't keep a diary."

"I lied."

"Why did you bring it to Las Vegas?"

"I couldn't leave it at home. My mother might find it."

"Oh."

"I'll let you read the pages about that afternoon. I wrote them down that same night. You'll see, it's all there, and it's not like I would have written down stuff that didn't happen. I don't lie to myself."

Jimmy continued to look troubled. "I'm not saying you do. I'm sorry."

My anger left as quickly as it had come. I reached out and touched his face. "I'm the one who should apologize for snapping at you. I'm sorry."

"It's all right. It's just our minds playing tricks on us."

A cold, eerie feeling swept over me right then at his remark, even though the sun was blazing down on us and the water was as warm as a bathtub. Suddenly, when I thought back to that day we were discussing, I couldn't remember exactly what had happened. Yet the memory had been so clear a few minutes ago. Now, it was weird, it was like a part of me was starting to remember it the way he was describing it.

"When was your first entry about me?" Jimmy asked.

"It was when we were freshmen," I said.

"Why did you write about me then?"

Because I got a crush on him the moment I met him. But I couldn't tell him that. "We had just met. You seemed like an interesting person," I said.

"Oh." I could tell he was still preoccupied.

"Do you get déjà vu much?" I asked.

"All the time."

"How come you never told me?"

"Why should I have?"

"Because I get it all the time, too." I paused. "But déjà vu doesn't relate to memory, not directly."

He stared at me. "Now you sound like you are trying to convince yourself. What's wrong, Jessie?"

I hesitated. "This argument sort of scares me. I sometimes wonder if I do have a problem with my memory. My mom often complains that she's told me to do an errand—like pick up some milk or bread at the store—and I'll have no recollection of it. Or else I'll remember it slightly different. I'll pick up eggs and butter instead. Does that ever happen to you?"

"Since my dad never talks to me, I'd have to say no." He paused. "Can I ask where you were last night?"

"I was just out, goofing off."

"But you weren't with Alex?"

"No."

"It's none of my business. The only reason I ask is because

the whole night I was searching for you, it felt like one long déjà vu."

My chill deepened. Because hanging out with Russ had been like one long déjà vu. The whole time I had been with him, I had felt like I knew him from somewhere. It had not helped that he had treated me like an old friend.

I still could not believe he had given me so much money.

I still had the key to his room.

But what was the room number? Four-three-four-one? That was not right. It didn't matter, it had been the corner suite on the top floor. I would always be able to find it.

"I know what you mean," I whispered.

Jimmy forced a smile. "Meet some hot guy?"

"What if I did?"

He shrugged. "Like I said, it's none of my business."

"Good."

"As long as you didn't sleep with him."

"You're the only one I've ever slept with," I replied.

I wished the same were true for him. Especially when we returned to shore, two hours later, and he left to return the boat while I went for the car. Kari met me in the parking lot, not far from the edge of the lake. She was sitting in the sand by the shore and only glanced up at my approach. To say I was shocked would be putting it mildly. Jimmy had been certain Kari hadn't come to Las Vegas.

"Fancy meeting you here," she said before turning back to

stare at the water. I had to remind myself the girl had just lost a child. Otherwise, I'd have wrung her neck.

"I didn't know you were here," I said.

She had on blue shorts, a white T-shirt. Her feet were bare. She stretched her legs over the sand, still looking out at the water.

"I'm not in the habit of sharing my itinerary with you."

"Are you in the habit of following me?" I asked.

"No." She finally looked at me. "I'm not stalking you."

I nodded to Alex's Camry. "But you recognized the car."

"Yeah." She stood and took a step toward me. Kari was a head shorter than me, a blond beauty. Except for her height, she could have been a natural model. Indeed, she'd worked with a few magazines. Her smile was the brightest in the school. It looked like she had lost most of her pregnancy weight. I felt disgusted at myself that she intimidated me.

"Where's Jimmy?" she asked.

"He'll be here in a few minutes."

"Did you have fun on the lake?"

"A blast." I paused. "Why are you here, Kari?"

She shrugged. "It's our graduation party. One long weekend of thrills and chills. Why shouldn't I be here?"

"Jimmy told me what happened." She didn't respond and I added, "I want to tell you how sorry I am."

She smiled right then, it was spooky. "Why are you sorry? It wasn't your fault."

"You must be going through hell."

"You have no idea what I'm going through."

I wanted to be compassionate. "Do you want to speak to Jimmy? I can go for a walk if you need time alone with him."

She shook her head. "I'm not here to see him."

"Why are you here?" I repeated.

"To warn you."

"Warn me? About what?"

"The same thing is going to happen to you."

"What are you talking about?"

"Huck. Jimmy told you his name, didn't he? I see that he did. It's good, you should know. At least that way you can't say I didn't warn you."

"Huh?"

"They never take just one, Jessie. They always take both."

"Kari, I'm sorry. I haven't a clue what you're talking about."

She smiled again, faintly, and casually walked past me. For an instant I was sure she was going to attack. I held my breath, prepared to respond. But all she did was brush my side.

"Good luck," she said.

Jimmy arrived minutes later. By that time Kari was long gone. He knew I was upset. I had to tell him what had happened. We spoke in the car in the lake parking lot, then he reached for his cell.

"What are you doing?" I asked.

"Calling her. She has no right to stalk us like that."

"Please don't. Let her be."

Jimmy hesitated, then put the phone away. It was clear he didn't want to talk to her. "The loss of Huck was hard on her. I think she's having a nervous breakdown. What else did she say?"

"I told you everything," I said. Except how deeply her weird remarks had shaken me. I felt as if I needed help, protection even, but I didn't know who to turn to.

"Come by when you don't know what else to do."

Why had Russ told me that? It was almost like he had foreseen this moment and understood how confused I would feel. A sudden strong desire to see him again swept over me.

I knew then that my theory on how he had beaten the casino was seriously flawed. He had won using magic. He really was the magic man. If I could see him again, he would know what I should do next. At least, like with cards, he would know whether I should act or hold.

"Take me back to the hotel," I told Jimmy.

Our suite was deserted when we reached the MGM. There was a note from Alex that said to call her on her cell but that was it. I told Jimmy I was tired and wanted to take a nap—alone. He was sensitive to my moods. He said he would go out for a walk, come back in an hour or so. I told him to make it two hours. He kissed me before he left but my mind was elsewhere and he sensed that as well.

"Are we okay?" he asked.

I forced a smile. "We're fine."

"She told me she wasn't coming. She swore it."

"Swear too much and it loses all meaning."

He hesitated. "Good-bye, Jessie."

"Good-bye, Jimmy."

There was something frightening in the sound of our fare-wells. Like they had the potential of being permanent.

With Jimmy gone, I took a quick shower and dressed in the new clothes I had purchased, the short black skirt and the red silk blouse. I picked up the phone to warn Russ I was coming over. I had to go through a switchboard. I asked for him by name, not by room number. He answered on the second ring.

"Hello?"

"Russ. It's Jessie."

"Jessie." He sounded pleased. "I wasn't sure if I'd hear from you again."

"Don't be silly, I had a great time last night."

"So did I."

"Hey, would it be okay if I stopped by and said hello?"

"Right now?"

"Yeah. There's some stuff that's going on and, well, I guess I could use your opinion on what to do about it." I added, "But I can come later if that would be better."

"Now is fine. But come right away. I have to go out later."

"I'll be there in ten minutes."

"Take a taxi, don't walk. It's a thousand degrees outside."

"Don't I know it," I said.

I went downstairs and exited through the main entrance and got in line for a taxi. His hotel was only a quarter of a mile from mine. It seemed silly to waste money on a cab. Yet I was tired from our hours on the water, and although the sun was heading toward the horizon, the temperature was still over a hundred. I was lucky the line for the taxis was short.

My driver didn't even look at me when I climbed in his cab.

"The Mandalay Bay," I said.

He nodded, started the meter, still silent. He was squat, dark-skinned, foreign, with a heavy beard. I searched for an ID and a license, which were usually pinned where a passenger could see them, but I saw nothing. We pulled away from the MGM onto the Strip.

He went the wrong way. That didn't trouble me. The exit left the MGM at an angle that made it difficult to drive directly to the Mandalay Bay. I assumed he was circling the block so he could come at our destination more easily. But when he had driven three blocks away from the Strip, I began to worry.

"Hey, where are we going?" I demanded. "I told you to take me to the Mandalay Bay."

He nodded. "Mandalay Bay."

I tapped on the plastic window that separated us. "It's back there."

He nodded, pointed in front of us. "Mandalay Bay."

"No. Turn around. Go back to the Strip."

He shook his head. "No Strip."

"God, don't you speak English?"

Apparently my question offended him. He stopped talking but kept driving farther and farther from the Strip. He turned onto another road that appeared to lead into an industrial section. There wasn't a hotel in sight, and that was rare in Las Vegas. I continued to bang on his window but he ignored me. I was pissed I had forgotten my cell. I would have called 911.

But I was more annoyed than afraid.

All right, I thought, two can play this game. I'd wait until he had to stop at a light. Then I'd leap out the door and run like hell and he could chase me on foot if he wanted to get his fare.

The problem with my plan, though, was that it seemed to take forever until we reached a red light.

Finally, he had to stop. My door was unlocked.

I was out of the taxi in a second.

He cursed and leaped out his side of the cab but I was already running down the street. For a moment I was afraid he would jump back in his taxi and try to run me down. But out the corner of my eye I saw him drive off.

I stopped running and took stock of my surroundings. It was definitely an area of town that didn't appear in any travel brochures. Besides rows of warehouses, there were numerous factories. Dusty buildings with peeling paint—they looked as if they had been built during World War II. It was Saturday, so unfortunately, they were all closed.

Nevertheless, it was eerie. There wasn't a single car in any of the parking lots. It was almost as if this section of town was under quarantine. The idea had no sooner occurred to me when I noticed a smell of decay. The bloated sun burned on the horizon like the mushroom cloud of an exploded nuke. It was still unbearably hot but the stench seemed immune to the dry air.

The concrete sidewalk was broken and uneven. It was easier to walk down the center of the asphalt road. But when I stepped over a sewer cover, I thought I heard faint moans. It sounded like a large group of people in horrible pain.

It was real, it wasn't my imagination. I returned to the sewer cover and went down on my hands and knees on the hot ground. The moaning grew louder. I could hear the voices of women and children mixed together. I tried to envision who could be trapped down there but I just made myself sick thinking about it.

Whoever they were, they were in pain.

A red sports car approached. It was a Porsche. The driver, a woman, had the roof down. Because she was obviously dressed for a night on the Strip, I assumed she, too, was lost. She slowed as she came near and halted when I waved for help. All around us, the shadows lengthened. It would be dark soon.

"What are you doing here, dear?" she asked, checking me

out. I did likewise. Besides wearing a rich black evening gown, she had on jewelry: an expensive pearl necklace, ruby earrings that matched her red hair, gold and diamond rings on both hands. She looked like a fifty-year-old who was trying to be forty.

"I think I'm lost," I said.

"That makes two of us. Hop in, maybe we can figure out a way back to the Strip."

Had it been a guy, I would have continued on foot. But I was anxious to get out of this section of town and she looked safe. I climbed in the front seat, closed the door. She put the car in gear and we rolled forward.

"I take it you're not from around here?" she asked.

"Is anyone from around here?"

She smiled. "I hear ya. How long have you been lost?"

"Not long. I caught this crazy taxi driver and told him to take me to the Mandalay Bay and he drove me out here. I don't think he was ever going to stop. He just kept driving and driving."

"How did you get away?"

"I bolted when he stopped at a light."

"Did you get his name?" she asked.

"No. He didn't have his license posted."

The woman nodded. "Bad sign. It means his vehicle's not registered. He could have been anybody."

"How did you end up out here? If you don't mind me asking."

"Got in a fight with my boyfriend. Jumped in his car and took off. I didn't think where I was going, and before I knew it, I had no idea how to get back." She nodded to the road in front of us as she slowed back down. "What do you think? Should we go left or right?"

I twisted both ways in the front seat, trying to peer between the buildings, hoping to get even a glimpse of one of the taller hotels. But the dirty monoliths had us surrounded. I struggled to remember how many turns the taxi driver had taken.

"I think we should go left," I said.

The woman turned to the right. "I disagree," she said.

"Really? You just said you had no idea where you were headed."

"That's true. But you see, I'm not in a hurry to get back to the Strip."

"I thought you were."

"No."

"Is it because of your boyfriend?"

"No." She glanced at me, and it was only then I noticed how dark her eyes were, how cold. "It's because of you, Jessie."

In that instant my blood turned to water, to ice; it seemed to freeze in place. I felt a pain in my heart and wondered if it had stopped beating. My fear transformed into terror. I reached for the door but the woman accelerated sharply.

"Jump out of the car now and your friends won't recognize you at the hospital," she said.

I struggled for calm, failed. "How do you know my name?"

"I know everything about you."

"What do you want?"

"Everything." Suddenly she had a gun in her hand, but it was no ordinary weapon. I had seen enough cop shows. It was a Taser. She was going to knock me out.

There was nowhere to run. Our speed was more than sixty miles an hour. I could face the impact of the asphalt or her lightning. Neither choice was very appealing. As she activated the Taser and green sparks crackled between twin coils, I slashed at her right arm with my left. I hit her hard and I had a good angle but still her arm didn't budge an inch.

Steadily, she moved the Taser toward my head, the burning green light glowing in her cold green eyes. Again I tried to strike but my hand caught the sparks and an unforgiving current shot up my arm and into my brain.

For an instant, I felt as if my mind was on fire.

Then everything went black.

CHAPTER SIX

I AWOKE IN THE DARK AND COLD.

I was lying on the floor. I felt the ice with my fingertips and the skin on the back of my skull before I opened my eyes. After the oppressive heat of Las Vegas, cold was the last thing I expected. But this freeze went deeper than a change in the weather. I knew in an instant it could be fatal.

Opening my eyes, I saw a dull orange light shielded by a band of small steel bars. It was high up, on a metal ceiling twenty feet from the frosty floor. It was one of a series of lights; they gave off a faint glow. Nevertheless, there was enough light to see that the room was large and filled with a grisly cargo.

I was in an industrial-size meat locker. Dozens of rows of beef hung from hundreds of steel hooks. The meat slabs were red and white, thick with muscle and fat. A huge slab hung inches to my left. I touched it; the meat was hard as stone.

I knew what that meant. The beef was not being kept cool to sell in the near future. It was frozen solid, which in turn meant the room temperature was below freezing.

How far below, I didn't know. I didn't know how long I had been unconscious, but the fact that I was still alive indicated it had not been long. I was still dressed in my red silk blouse and black skirt, and losing body heat at a terrifying rate. As I briefly fingered the slab of beef, the tips of my fingers got even colder. Soon my hands and feet would be numb. I knew I had to act quickly.

Sitting up, I groaned in pain. Whoever had handled me while I had been unconscious had been rough. I felt as if my entire spine was bruised. The bastards had probably thrown me from one place to the next, until they had finally dumped me on this floor.

It made me wonder why they had chosen this place. Obviously they meant to kill me, but they could have done that while I was unconscious. I wondered—it was more of a hope, actually—if this was part of an elaborate ritual. Was it possible someone was trying to scare me into . . . what?

It didn't take long to come up with a possibility.

I stood and called out loudly, hoping someone was listening.

"Hey! I'm awake! If it's money you want, you can have it! It's in a safe at the MGM! The key's in my purse! Let me go and I'll take you to it!" Not that I knew where my purse was.

Silence. No one answered.

"I've got a hundred grand in cash!" I yelled.

Complete silence. My disappointment was crushing.

I couldn't be sure but it felt like no one was there. It was probably their plan—whoever they were—to let the cold do its work and then return later for my corpse. Then they could dump me anywhere: in a shallow grave in the desert; on the street where that bitch had picked me up. I didn't know if an autopsy would reveal if I had frozen to death, especially if they gave me time to thaw out before disposing of my remains.

It was hard to think of being a corpse.

I circled the freezer, searching for a way out. There were no windows, only one exit, located at the far end of the long building. The door was a thick steel monster. I tugged on the handle but I might as well have been yanking on a boulder. It didn't budge a fraction of an inch.

There were straps mounted on the back of the door, where I assumed an ax was supposed to be fixed in case of emergency—such as mine—but my captors had been alert enough to remove it. Bless their hearts, they had thought of everything.

But why? Why me?

The only one I knew who hated me was Kari, and she had mysteriously appeared at Lake Mead. She had tried to warn me, it was true, that I was in danger, but her warning had been vague and rambling. She'd made no sense. She had been acting like a crazy person and crazy people did crazy things.

Yet to arrange a kidnapping as elaborate as this was way

beyond her scope. She was a blond cheerleader, for God's sakes. How could she have managed to hire the taxi driver—I had no doubt he was part of the plan—and the woman in the Porsche? Kari might have been pissed I had stolen Jimmy away but she simply wasn't smart enough to have arranged such a complex scheme.

Few people on earth could have arranged such a scheme.

Yet I had met such a man the previous night. The one person in the whole world who had known I was about to run downstairs and catch a cab.

"Take a taxi, don't walk. It's a thousand degrees outside."

If I had to create a short list of who was behind my abduction, Russ's name would be at the top. His sitting at our blackjack table couldn't have been by chance. It was all so clear now. When I had tried to leave, he had done everything in his power to keep me there. Indeed he had suckered me with the oldest bait in the world. The promise of free money. And he had delivered, he had won a hundred grand for me as casually as I had ordered room service afterward. On top of that, he had won more than six hundred grand for himself.

But had he really won any money at all?

No one in the world could beat the casinos. Was it possible the people at the Tropicana were part of this scam? It was difficult to believe. The more people I added to my list, the more complex the crime became. Yet if Russ was acting alone, with only a few hired thugs to help with the dirty work, then

I was still left with the mystery of how he had beaten the casinos.

Hell, I was left with a much more pressing mystery.

Why he wanted me dead.

My fingers were freezing, I couldn't stop shivering, and my feet were going numb. I stomped on the floor to stimulate the circulation, but it only worked as long as I kept it up. The moment I stopped, the cold returned to my toes.

The numbness in my feet scared me more than my freezing fingers. I knew if my feet failed, I wouldn't be able to stand, to move around, and that was the only thing that was keeping me warm. I would be forced to sit down, beside the dead steers, and I'd probably black out fast. I wasn't exactly a candidate for Jenny Craig. I weighed at best a hundred and ten pounds.

I jumped up and down, sang to myself, tried to keep my spirits up. Most of all, I struggled to figure out a way through that damn door. It was made of steel; I was flesh and blood. Okay, I told myself, I had to level the playing field. How did I do that? I needed tools, steel tools.

I searched the locker again, more closely this time. The only things that remotely resembled instruments were the hooks holding up the meat. Their points were extremely sharp. I wondered if I could get one free, if I could use it to rip the hinges off the door. It was worth a try. The chances someone would burst through the door in the next thirty minutes and rescue me were pretty remote.

I thought of Jimmy then. He must be looking for me by now, worried where I had disappeared to. He had probably spoken to Alex and she might have gotten spooked and told him about the man we had met the night before. Yet Alex wasn't someone who panicked. She might wait before saying a word. Her virtue might be my curse. She might wait to talk about Russ until long after I was dead.

I ran into problems getting a slab of beef off the hook. I didn't know where these steers had been raised but there must have been plenty to graze upon. The meat was heavier than I could lift.

Yet my fear gave me added strength, and trial and error taught me to use more of my leg strength to lift rather than just my arms. I finally managed to free one of the smaller steers and drop it on the floor. Immediately I set to work trying to unscrew its hook.

Unfortunately, by now I could feel only two fingers on each hand, and none of them was a thumb. I couldn't get a grip on the hook. Plus the hook had either been screwed in place by a machine or else it was frozen in place. Whatever, it refused to budge.

"Damn!" I screamed. "God damn you!"

A minute later I got a brilliant idea.

I prayed to God it would work.

Yeah, so I was a hypocrite, so what. I was dying.

I had made a mistake removing the meat before the hook.

The reason was simple. The hooks were deeply ingrained in the meat. The beef had bulk and weight. If I could get my arms around one of the smaller steers and rotate it, I should be able to multiply my leverage tenfold.

I had already bumped off the smallest steer. I tackled the next one in size; it was substantially larger. But I managed to get a solid grip on its ribs and hindquarters. Looking up, I assumed the hooks had been screwed in clockwise. I began to twist counterclockwise.

I talked to the steer as I worked, like it was my partner in escape.

"Don't let that hook rip you apart inside. You were born for better things than to help fatten a bunch of fat tourists. Even in death you can save a life. You can be a hero. You and I, we're a team. Just hold together and help me tear your hook out of the ceiling."

Wrestling with the steer, trying to get it to spin around, proved exhausting. I was just about to quit when suddenly the hook screeched. It did more than that; it twisted more than a half circle around. After that it was easy to unscrew the hook, I just had to give the steer a shove every now and then.

Two minutes later the meat fell to the floor, and the impact helped shake the hook free of the beef. Grabbing it by its pointed end, I hurried to the door, finally ready to try out my plan.

I discovered I had another problem.

While struggling with the meat and the hooks, I had managed to keep my fingers warm. But I had forgotten about my feet. I had spent too long standing in basically the same spot.

Now, I couldn't feel my toes. Worse, the soles of my feet had gone numb. It was weird, the instant I realized how bad they were, I began to have trouble standing. I shot out an arm to keep from falling. I was tempted to sit down, to rest and rub them and try to restore circulation that way. But it was a fool's temptation. If I sat down I knew I would never get back up.

The door waited for me but I had to turn my back on it and try walking away. Jumping was no longer an option, but I felt if I could just keep using my feet, they would return to me. My walk looked more like a side shuffle. I had to keep both hands planted on the wall to maintain my balance.

I ended up circling the meat locker before I began to feel a tingling in my feet. A second lap restored feeling to my soles and I even began to feel a few of my toes again. At last I was able to stand without having to use the wall for support. I swore to myself that, while working on the door, I would take a break every two minutes and walk around. Stomping my feet was still an effective method of stimulating my circulation, but it had begun to hurt. I wondered if that meant I was getting frostbite.

The door, the steel door, the damn door. It was so thick and strong! It was like the thing had been built to withstand an atomic blast, when all it was really doing was keeping a bunch of dead cows cold.

But there was good news. The tip of the hook was sharp enough to slip in behind the door hinges. Also, the handle of the hook was long, which provided me with plenty of leverage.

I started work on the lower hinges, figuring they would be easier to break because I could use the power in my legs to press on the hook. Now that I was finally using my feet for more than support, they began to wake up even more, and I was able to jump on the end of the hook. Once more I heard a reassuring screeching sound as the screws in the hinges began to tear free. Pressing my palms against the door for balance, I leaped again and again onto the flat end of the hook.

The lower hinge broke, snapping free of the wall.

Unfortunately, I fell on my last leap onto the hook, and ended up twisting my right ankle as I went down. Sorry, no mild sprain for you, babe. I heard a pop just before I hit the floor. Granted, it might have been the hinge snapping free, except the sound came from deep inside my ankle and a thunderbolt of agony shot up my right leg. The agony was both numbing and burning. I couldn't decide which was worse. All I knew was that I had hurt myself at the worst possible time.

Rolling on the floor, cursing, I tried to stand by clawing at the wall, but the second I was up and put my foot down, I screamed. The bone was broken. There was no doubt. The pain throbbed with my heartbeat. It pounded in my skull, in my mind, as waves of dizziness and nausea swept over me. I bent over and vomited but nothing came up. It had been a long time since I had eaten. I felt as if I had been in the freezing locker forever.

I had no choice—I had to sit, to rest a few minutes and try to recover. I hoped that my ankle had simply popped out of its socket and would somehow magically pop back in. There was nowhere to place my butt except on the icy floor, and I sat with my back to the door, my spine pressed against the frozen steel.

I tried focusing on the busted hinge, which lay beside me. I had come far, I told myself, I was halfway to safety. All I had to do was break the top hinge and I would be free. I promised myself the instant the pain in my ankle stopped pounding I would stand and go at it. There was no way a little hinge was going to end my life. Not when my friend the steer had given up his life to free the hook so I could use it to snap the hinge . . .

"My friend the steer?" I said aloud. What was I thinking? What the hell was I doing? The broken hinge had vanished from view. Why? Because my mind had wandered off and I had closed my eyes. The danger of my predicament hit me like a boxer's blow. I was sitting with my eyes closed in a meat locker where the temperature was in the twenties. I was setting myself up to pass out.

To die. I was going to die unless I got off my butt.

Forcing my eyes open, I sucked in a series of fast breaths and tried pushing myself up with my good ankle. It seemed to work, at first, I started to slide up. But then I slipped and fell back down. The reason was horribly clear. Even with my unin-jured foot, I couldn't get a grip on the floor because the sole of my left foot was numb. The pain in my ankle was decreasing because my right foot was also going numb.

I had broken my promise to myself. That I would not sit down under any circumstances. I had broken it because the cold was playing tricks with my head. It had convinced me I had to sit down because I was injured. But the cold was not my friend, it was my enemy. It was trying to kill me. It would kill me unless I got moving.

Rolling onto my knees, I pressed the top of my head against the door and tried to stand, reaching up for the door handle. For a few seconds I was able to pull myself up to where I swayed on what seemed to be invisible legs, when I suddenly slipped and smashed face-first into the door. My fall to my knees was not far, not as far as when I had twisted my ankle, but a dark trail followed me back to the floor. My nose had struck the door and I bled all over it.

"Damn!" I screamed at no one. "God damn you!"

I raised a hand to my nose and felt the warm blood oozing over my face, but then it was like someone threw a switch and the blood stopped. At least that was what I thought happened. Then I realized my fingers had gone numb. My hands and feet were now both numb, both useless.

"I have to get up, I have to get up," I kept repeating as I rolled over once more onto my butt. I had come too far to quit.

The hook was right there. The top hinge was a mere five feet above the floor. If I could get off the floor, slip the hook behind the hinge, and hang on it with all my weight, it would probably bust. If only I could stand up. If only I had not hurt my ankle.

If only I had not trusted Russ.

"Goddamn bastard, Russ. You'll pay for this. I'll make you pay."

That's the last thing I recall saying aloud. At some point I must have closed my eyes again, although I don't remember doing so. My thoughts drifted back to the previous night at the blackjack table, when I realized that Russ had offended Alex on purpose. He had caused her to lose money so she would get pissed off and leave. He had admitted as much. Yet he had been confident I wouldn't leave with her. Strange how sure he was of himself. She was, after all, my best friend, and I didn't know him.

Why would he assume I'd stay with him?

Why had he seemed so familiar?

This guy I had never met before.

I noticed I was no longer shivering. That was a relief. If anything, I felt as if warm liquid were being pumped through my veins. Yet a part of me worried if that was a good thing. I seemed to recall that when people froze to death, they started to feel warm first.

Yeah, I had read an article about this high-school girl who

had gone skating on a lake that was supposed to be frozen over, but which had broken and swallowed her up for like ten minutes before a fireman had rescued her. The girl had been my age, we could have been friends . . .

She had been dead for more than ten minutes. More like fifteen.

But the fireman had brought her back to life. It was a miracle.

I tried focusing on what else the article had said but my brain got bored with the subject and wandered to Jimmy, to the one place where it had spent the better part of the last six months. Jimmy, my poor boyfriend, he must be real worried about me now. He was probably calling the police, maybe even filling out a missing-persons report. But I knew what the police would tell him. All the cops always said the same thing on TV. "Sorry, but we have to wait at least twenty-four hours before your friend's disappearance is official."

They would look at Jimmy with pity but secretly they'd probably think the chick had run off with some older guy with money. Especially if Alex told them about Russ.

"Are you saying you didn't take a shower with me?"

"I did. But it wasn't after I got off work."

That had been a strange discussion we'd had up at the lake. How could Jimmy forget the first time we'd had sex? Why, that was like him forgetting when my birthday was. Of course, he had forgotten my birthday. It was in November,

November twelfth, and I had told him it was coming up but it had come and gone before he remembered. I hadn't yelled at him or anything. We had just started dating and I didn't want to annoy him and come across as a bitch, and besides, it didn't really matter when I had been born, the date. What was more important was the date I died, which was going to be today, unless I got my butt in gear and . . .

And what? I couldn't remember, it must not be important.

Anyway, the first time we had sex, that was important. It had been in the shower, like I had told him, or rather, just after we took a shower. But he was right about one thing—he had not spent time in the shower washing the oil off his hands because he had not just come from work. I realized I had gotten part of the story right and part of it wrong. He had come from home and I was in the shower getting ready for our date. I had known he was coming over. He had called before coming. We were supposed to go to dinner and then a movie.

I had jumped in the shower because I was hot and sweaty. It was the middle of summer, it had been a hot day. And I had gone in the shower because I thought it might be a cool way of seducing him. He was kind of shy when it came to sex. I mean, I was too, since technically I was still a virgin. But I was getting kind of tired of waiting for him to make the first move so I figured I'd make it for him. In other words, the shower was just an excuse.

A nice cool excuse on a hot summer day.

Only I hadn't started dating Jimmy until October.

Wow, that was weird. Now my memory of that day was getting worse than his. But I could have sworn, right now, that we had made love in the middle of summer, or else late summer. Yeah, it must have been real late because it wasn't until after Halloween when I started to worry if I might be pregnant . . .

Pregnant? Whoa, hold on, I was never pregnant.

Yet I remembered . . . something. My swelling belly.

It was strange. It was like a mystery.

I don't know why it bothered me so much. I had much more serious matters to worry about. My nose was bleeding, my ankle was injured, and I was freezing to death. Still, it bugged me that I couldn't recall Jimmy washing his hands in the shower, which would have settled the argument once and for all of when we first had sex.

I had to admit, though, I was beginning to remember the situation a lot more the way he did. The day had definitely been hot, a real cooker, and he had not come over in the day-time, after work, but in the evening, to go out on a date. Yeah, his argument had a few facts in its favor, I would have to tell him that when I saw him again.

If I ever saw him again.

My last coherent thought.

Once more, everything went black.

Only it was a lot blacker than before.

CHAPTER SEVEN

I AWOKE TO LIGHT AND COLD.

It was a fact, even though I was no longer in the meat locker, I felt just as cold. In some ways I felt even worse, strange, like I was a piece of meat hanging from a steel hook. But that was not true because I was staring up at a hospital ceiling. A faint female voice spoke over an unseen speaker.

"Dr. List to emergency. Dr. Michael List to the emergency ward, please."

I was safe, that was good, I could relax. Someone had found me and taken me to a hospital. The doctors were probably trying to warm me up as I lay there.

Yet I didn't see any doctors and I didn't feel any heaters. I felt . . . well, I couldn't feel anything. I would have said I felt nothing below my neck but I couldn't feel my face, either.

My vision of the green tile ceiling didn't waver, even for an instant, which led me to believe I wasn't even blinking.

That worried me. Blinking was a reflex. I had read somewhere that if a person went as little as an hour without blinking, their pupils began to suffer damage. That was why it was important to tape shut the affected eye of people who had strokes or other conditions that often paralyzed one half of the face. I made a conscious effort to close my eyes and they didn't budge. The green ceiling refused to go away.

I disliked this particular shade of green. I was surprised the hospital staff had gone with such a blah color, even if I was stuffed somewhere in a cheap emergency cubicle. The green had a faint yellow tinge to it that reminded me of vomit. Perhaps my nose was influencing my eyes. There was an odor in the air that was making me nauseous. Not rubbing alcohol, something else I couldn't pinpoint, although I was sure I had smelled it before.

Without thinking, I reached up to close my eyelids and discovered my arm wouldn't move. Even though I couldn't feel anything, I had assumed I had the use of my limbs, that I wasn't frozen. But it was beginning to look like I was numb all over.

I had never heard of such a thing. I wondered if that meant my condition was serious. Yet the fact that no doctors or nurses were hovering over me reassured me somewhat. If I were truly in danger, the hospital staff would be working on me this minute. They had probably left me to slowly thaw out. I was sure I was going to be okay.

I wished I could turn my head, get a better look at my surroundings. The green tiles were getting on my nerves. I tried glancing out the corners of my eyes but discovered my field of view did not alter. What the hell? Were my eyeballs frozen, too? Now that was getting ridiculous. I wished someone would stop by and check on me so I could ask what was going on. Nothing about this hospital felt right, except for the occasional page.

"Dr. William Jacob to X-ray. Dr. William Jacob to X-ray, please."

Lying there, my thoughts drifted back to my captivity in the meat locker. I remembered how I had tried to break through the metal door, how close I had come to escaping. If only I hadn't fallen and broken my ankle. Wait! I had hurt my ankle. I had hurt my nose as well. Why didn't I feel any pain? I mean, yes, I knew I was still thawing out and all that but I would have expected those two sore spots to be the first to wake up and start complaining. Yet I continued to feel nothing.

Just strange, very strange.

I heard footsteps, two people talking, a man and a woman. They were definitely approaching—their voices were steadily getting louder. What a relief, I thought, finally someone to talk to. Someone to answer my questions.

The man and the woman entered my room. I tried turning

my head to look at them but it refused to budge. I could hear them but I couldn't see them. Yet I was aware the man was off to my right, while the woman was closer, on my left.

"Would you believe I had tickets to the championship game and didn't go?" the man said. "I thought to myself, why drive all the way down to Staples Center when I can watch the Lakers on TV."

"But you missed out on the excitement of being there," the woman replied. "I heard the crowd was practically in tears as the final minutes counted down."

"That's true," the man said. "You can get a rush from being in the crowd and yelling your head off, especially if you're drunk. But I had cheap seats, they were way up in the nose-bleed section. That's why I stayed home and watched the game on TV. Staples is a lot bigger than the Forum used to be. Sit in one of the last rows, and I swear you can hardly see the play-ers. They look like cartoon figures. And we're all spoiled with instant replay. On TV, when someone makes a great dunk or an off-balance three-pointer, they replay it ten times. You get to enjoy it over and over again. But live, you blink and you can miss the biggest play of the game."

"Don't they have a screen at Staples where they show instant replays?" she asked.

"They've got several. They're all pointed toward the rich seats. I tell you, the whole arena is designed for those who pay five hundred bucks a seat and up. Peons like us they can't even be bothered with. Even the food they offer in the cheap seats is different from the food you can buy in the high-priced sections."

"Really? It seems there should be a law against that."

"There should be a law against many things," the man said.

The woman seemed to pick up a chart. I heard the fumbling of papers, and the sound came from the left, where she stood. "All right, what do we have here? A twenty-year-old Caucasian female. Discovered by a family who got lost after leaving the Strip, some place in the industrial section of town."

"Poor girl. What a crappy place to get dumped."

The woman continued to read from her chart. "She was brought into emergency an hour ago, not long after midnight. Dr. Palmer and Dr. Kirby tried a lengthy resuscitation. Cardiac massage was immediately applied, while patient was ventilated using a tracheal tube. One milliliter of epinephrine was injected in the internal jugular vein along with ten milliliters of calcium chloride. Defibrillation was repeatedly tried with no response. Dr. Palmer certified her a DOA at twelve fifty-nine." The woman stopped and spoke to her partner. "What do you think we're looking at here, Dave?"

DOA? I thought. Didn't that mean "dead on arrival"?

What the hell were these two talking about?

For a moment thick stubby fingers passed over my eyes.

"It's a strange one, Susan," Dave said. "Look at this blood on the nose. Someone must have roughed her up. Before they . . ."

"Before they what?" Susan asked.

"Feel how cold her skin is. And she's been here over an hour. You would at least think she would be at room temperature."

I heard Susan feeling my left arm, although I couldn't see or feel her doing it.

"God, you're right, she's like an icicle," she said.

"Palmer didn't mention it in his notes?" Dave asked.

"He made a quick note she appeared hypothermic but this is ridiculous. It's like someone had her stored in a freezer before they finally decided to dump her body. You know what that means?"

"What?"

"She could have been dead for a long time," Susan said.

Dead? I thought. That word again. They were talking about me like I was dead. What the hell was wrong with them? They were doctors, for God's sakes, and I was lying right here in front of them. All they had to do was check my pulse or listen to my chest and they would know I was alive.

But what if they weren't real doctors, just interns or even medical students? They might be examining me as part of their studies, in the same way they might dissect a body during gross anatomy in their first year in medical school.

"If she's been dead a long time," Dave said, "then whoever killed her went to a lot of trouble to keep her in good shape. She almost looks alive."

Yes! I tried to scream. *I am alive! What's wrong with you people?*

But I couldn't get my mouth to move. I couldn't make a groaning sound deep inside my throat, or any other sound to let them know they weren't dealing with a corpse.

"True, she looks great," Susan said. "I hope I look that good when I die. But it makes me wonder."

"What?"

"If the cause of death was hypothermia."

"That's a leap," Dave said. "They could have simply frozen her after killing her. For all we know this blow to her nose sent bone fragments into her brain."

"You're right. We won't know until we open her up. But I've been doing a preliminary exam of this arm and I can tell already her blood wasn't pooled in the lower extremities when she was put in the deep freeze."

Open me up!

My horror transcended reason. It came close to shorting out my brain and leaving me in a quivering, mindless corner. What stopped me from cracking up completely was the realization that I was in greater danger than I had been in the meat locker.

Dr. Susan and Dr. Dave were not real doctors who treated living people. They were goddamn coroners. They were the kind of doctors who were only interested in corpses.

Christ, I had to get out of here. Or else I at least had to make some kind of sound before they started cutting. I struggled with all my might to make my lips move, to twitch, but I couldn't move what I couldn't feel.

Dave appeared to examine my right arm. "I see what you mean. The veins on the front and back of her arm and hand are filled with fresh blood. I wouldn't be surprised if your theory turns out to be correct." He paused and then added, "What a horrible way for a cute young thing like this to go. To freeze to death in some dark box."

"I disagree," Susan said. "I can think of a lot worse ways to go."

"Do we have permission to perform a full autopsy?"

Susan studied the chart. "We don't need it. She's been classified an official Jane Doe, and a probable murder victim. Which means the LVPD has been notified and wants answers right away. We can open her up now if you want."

No! Dave, you don't want to open up such a cute young thing like me!

But Dave suddenly sounded excited. "Can I take the lead on the case?" he asked.

"Do you want the headache? A case like this, you'll probably end up in court answering a hundred questions."

"I told you before, I think it's time I stretched my legs. For years I've been working cases no one wants to hear about, other than the immediate family. I've watched you in court, I think I can handle the pressure." He added, "Unless you have an objection?"

Object! He's an idiot! He can't tell a dead girl from a live girl!

But neither could Susan. I was mentally screaming at the

wrong pair. Susan put down her chart and wheeled an overhead light above me. She turned it on, and I was bathed in blinding white light. For several seconds, I couldn't see a thing.

"Be serious, Dave. I've been waiting for the day you would step forward like this and demand your day in court, as the lawyers like to say. It's time you used your talents to the fullest and this looks like the perfect case. You have a beautiful young victim, a mysterious method of murder. I wouldn't be surprised if two months from now we see you on TV three nights a week, giving the locals the latest update on the Fridge Freak Killer."

Dave chuckled. "The Fridge Freak Killer. I like that."

"I thought you would. Now, since we're talking about a possible court case, we have to start recording in the preliminary stages. I know you're not used to that."

"I don't mind. When do you want to turn on the mic?"

"In a couple of minutes. Let's take her clothes off. But no tearing of the material. We have to bag everything and label it and hand it over to the detective in charge of the case."

"But the docs in the ER ripped the buttons off her blouse when they were working on her," Dave said.

"That usually happens. The police won't hassle you about that."

"Gotcha," Dave said.

They were going to strip me naked? I shouldn't have cared, of course, they were going to cut me open. But I did care. Plus their excuse for doing my autopsy without a family member—

or even a friend—signing off on it was bogus. At least I thought it was bogus. The fact was, I didn't know much about the law. But shit, if they simply checked with the police, they would discover that I was missing.

That is if Jimmy had filed a missing-persons report. I was beginning to think Alex had told him about Russ, maybe to calm him down and make him jealous at the same time, and Jimmy had yet to go to the police. Nothing made any sense, I only knew I was trapped in a nightmare. It couldn't get any worse.

Of course it could get a lot worse.

They could start cutting.

As they removed my clothes, my head rolled from side to side and I was able to get a look at Dave and Susan. From their comments, I expected Dave to be younger than Susan. Such was not the case. Susan was an extremely attractive thirty, with dark features that had probably originated with a dash of Middle Eastern genes. Her hair was a dark brown, but because it was tucked behind a surgical cap, I couldn't tell its length. As she turned me, it was as if her eyes caught mine.

"Dave?" she said.

"What?"

"This girl freaks me out. It's almost like she's alive."

Go, Susan! Go, girl! Look into my eyes again! Look and you'll see I'm still here!

"I know how you feel," Dave said. "She's almost perfectly preserved."

Susan sighed. "It's a shame, isn't it? Young, pretty, her whole life in front of her. Then some creep gets hold of her and she ends up on our chopping table."

"Well, we're all going to end up here one day."

"That's true. But I'd rather not think about it."

"I think about it every time I eat another doughnut."

Susan chuckled. "It doesn't stop you from putting another one in your mouth."

My head rolled in Dave's direction. He was older than Susan by ten years, but it looked like twenty because he was obese. He had huge fleshy lips and fingers, and a serious problem with body hair. It was everywhere but where it was supposed to be. His green eyes bugged out of his fat head.

They finished removing and bagging my clothes. Since they had both moved closer to the table, I could see the two of them, especially when they were examining the upper part of my body. Susan reached for a black wire and I heard a loud click. A twitch of nervousness crossed Dave's face.

"How do I start?" he asked.

"Identify yourself and your subject. In this case just refer to her as Jane Doe. Say what you know, don't extrapolate. Here, let me set the digital recorder to zero. Ready?"

"Yeah."

"You're live," Susan said.

"This is Dr. David Leonard, a coroner and pathologist at Las Vegas Memorial. Also attending is Dr. Susan Wheeler.

Today's date is June twelfth; the time is two sixteen a.m. The subject is an unidentified Jane Doe who was dead upon arrival at the hospital approximately two hours ago. The patient is a female, approximate age twenty. She was admitted to the ER with zero respiration and pulse. An EKG showed no brain activity and she was pronounced dead at twelve fifty-nine by Dr. Fred Palmer."

Susan stopped the recording. "You're getting stuck in your introduction. Start describing what you see in the patient."

"Can we go back and erase the rough parts?"

"We can edit it any way you wish. Now continue."

"The subject has two striking characteristics. There's a large quantity of blood around her nose, and her skin and musculature are unusually cold, well below room temperature. Yet the lack of pooling of blood in the lower extremities indicates she was alive when she was put in a freezer. For that reason, it would appear that the cause of death might be hypothermia."

Dave paused and wiped the sweat from his brow and I heard another click on Susan's end. "Boy," he said. "This is a lot harder when you realize jurors might be listening to it one day."

"You get used to the spotlight. You're doing fine, by the way. But it might be time to open her up and see what we've got. To speed things up, I can saw open her skull and remove her brain while you remove her viscera and perform the pericardium cut. Understand, I'll keep my mouth shut and let you describe the condition of the cranium."

"How do we coordinate it so it looks like I'm in charge the whole time?" Dave asked.

"It's easy. I'll just hold the brain out for you to see. If you want to slice it, do a microscopic exam, I can do that while you keep talking."

Dave rubbed his hands together. "Sounds like a plan."

Stop! Oh, please God in heaven, STOP!

They couldn't hear me. They were too busy with their toys. Susan had a handheld band saw that was powered by a tiny motor. She checked to make sure the motor was working, then reached for a scalpel.

Every medical thriller I had ever seen came back to haunt me. I knew precisely what she was about to do. Using the scalpel, she would cut an incision around the entire top of my head. She would cut down the sides of my face. Then, using her gloved hands, she would grip my skin and peel it off. Yeah, just like I was some kind of bloody doll. Next she would peel the flesh on my face all the way down to my chin and let it hang from my jaw.

Finally, she would cut open my skull and yank out my brain.

Dave was holding a pair of scissors large enough to slice open my abdomen, which is precisely what he was going to use them for. He would pull out my guts—my liver, gallbladder, spleen, large and small intestines, stomach—and toss the whole mess into a steel bowl to be weighed and examined later.

Then, using the same pair of Paul Bunyan nail clippers, he would move on to the ever-popular pericardium cut, a favorite of coroners everywhere because they get to snap open the sternum and pretend for a while they're performing heart surgery. When in reality he was just going to cut out my heart and toss it into another bowl.

Dave pressed the tip of his blade in a place I couldn't see.

For the first time I felt something, a dull pressure.

I think he had the blade pointed at the top of my pubic bone.

OH, GOD!

Dave frowned. "Susan, turn off the mic a sec."

Susan did as he requested, her scalpel in hand. "What's the problem?" she asked.

"It's her skin. It's so cold, it's still partially frozen. I'm not sure how easy she'll be to open up."

"You won't know until you try."

"That's just the thing. I think maybe we should wait another hour."

YES! WAIT ANOTHER HOUR! GOD BLESS YOU!

Susan sounded annoyed. "I don't have another hour. Look, if it's too much pressure, let me handle this one. You can always do the next one."

"But you were saying what a special case this is. I don't want to miss out."

"Then start cutting."

Dave sighed. "All right. Turn the recorder back on."

NO! WAIT! GOD DAMN YOU! NO!

A female voice spoke over the hospital intercom.

"Dr. Wheeler to emergency. Dr. Susan Wheeler to emergency, please."

Susan tossed her scalpel down. "I wonder what that's about."

Dave set aside his giant scissors. "You better hurry. I heard they're undermanned tonight. I told you before, Palmer's never going to forget you got your start in ER."

Susan glanced down at me before leaving. Again, I felt as if we connected. The sensation was stronger this time, the certainty. It was almost as if she were inside my head.

It must have been my imagination. Pulling off her gloves, she turned toward the door, calling over her shoulder. "Don't do anything until I return," she said.

"How long do you think you'll be gone?" Dave said.

"If I have to see a patient, at least half an hour."

A half hour is good, I thought. I can live with half an hour.

The moment Susan vanished, I heard Dave walk to the door and close it shut. He might have locked it, I thought I heard a dead bolt being thrown. I assumed that was my imagination as well, until he returned to my side and I saw his face. His pupils were twice the size of a minute before, and he was glowing. He searched me up and down, drinking in the view.

I finally understood why he was sweating so much over me.

Why he hesitated to cut me up right away.

He wanted to enjoy himself first.

Dr. Dave was into necrophilia.

He grinned as his hands reached for places I couldn't see.

"Baby, I've waited a long time for one like you. So young, so sweet, so cold. My cold, cuddly baby. You and I, we're going to make some magic together."

He let go of me. I couldn't see but I thought I heard him undoing his belt, pulling down his zipper. For once the curse of my frozen eyeballs was a blessing. Yet it was only then, as my absolute horror transformed itself into pure disgust, that I felt a wave of fire rush through my icy body. It was as if a trillion cells thawed in an instant and reconnected to my brain.

I suddenly sat up. Every bone in my spine popped.

I stared at him with loathing. "You goddamn pervert!" I said. "Touch me again and I'll cut off your dick!"

Dr. Dave staggered back as I cursed him, a hairy hand flying to his chest. All the color seemed to drain from his face. He was having trouble breathing. His pale sheen changed to a sickly blue. Christ, he was having a heart attack. I watched in disbelief as he collapsed on the floor, gasping for breath, his drool leaking onto the floor of the morgue.

My burst of anger subsided and with it the wave of fire that had reanimated my body. Suddenly my limbs were stuck again and I fell back on the slab beneath the overhead light and beside the skull saw and the heart scissors. I heard a pounding at the door, Susan calling Dave's name. I wondered how she knew he was in pain, and I wondered how she managed to open what appeared to be a locked door.

I saw her stride into the room and kneel beside Dave. I must have been able to move my eyes now. She put a hand on his chest and went very still.

"Is it very bad?" she asked softly, her voice sounding deeper than before, older.

"Pain," he gasped. "Chest. Dying."

"It's true. You feel death approaching," she replied, a weird thing to tell a patient, I thought, even one as perverted as David Leonard. Casually, Susan stood and stepped to an intercom, where she pushed a button and spoke. "This is Dr. Wheeler. I'm in the morgue. I have a code blue. I repeat, I have a code blue. Please send immediate assistance."

Susan returned to where her partner lay gasping on the floor. Picking up his blue hands, she pressed them to her chest and closed her eyes. It was like she was trying to heal him, I thought, comfort him somehow.

Yet I knew I didn't understand this woman any more than I understood what I was doing on an autopsy table in the middle of the night. Because she wore a blissful smile as she held Dave, as if his pain were giving her a rush.

A crash team arrived two minutes later and loaded Dave onto a gurney and vanished out the door. Susan didn't follow

RED QUEEN

them, not right away. She turned and walked back to where I lay helpless. For the third and last time our eyes met, and I knew for a fact that she knew I was alive.

She held my purse in her hand.

She set it down beside my bare leg and spoke.

"You were lucky this time. You managed to invoke the fire. But don't think for a second that you're in control." Susan gestured behind her and to the right, to a spot where there was nothing but empty air. "Remember, you and I, we're watching."

With those weird words she turned and left.

She left me alone on the cold slab. But it was as if her strange remarks had explained that I had the power to get up if only I could stir the fire again. The key was to focus, I realized. The fact that they were going to cut me open had caused me to cower. But Dave's attack had stirred my rage, which had ignited the fire. The fire was the key. Suddenly I was confident that all I had to do was ignite it again and the frost in my limbs would melt.

I'm Jessica Ralle. I'm eighteen years old, and there's no way I'm going to die in this godforsaken dungeon. I'd rather burn first.

I repeated the lines over and over again.

Loud, inside my head, with growing intensity.

Then, suddenly, a wave of heat started in the center of my solar plexus. It was *powerful*. It radiated like a blazing sun. Again I felt the heat flow through my nerves, thawing out my

143

muscles and tendons. The fire appeared to migrate upward toward my heart. Soon my blood was pumping through my veins with wild abandon. My diaphragm snapped up and down like a piston in a racing car and I drew in a series of quick sharp breaths.

Seconds later I was able to bend my arms and legs. In minutes I was able to stand and search for my clothes. They had not gone far. They were in a bag beside the autopsy table, neatly labeled.

Jane Doe. For some reason, I kind of liked the name. It was the name given to the dead, and they, in their own way, were free. At least free of the pain the living could inflict on them.

I washed the blood off my face, dressed quickly, grabbed my purse, and left the hospital.

CHAPTER EIGHT

OUTSIDE, I STRUGGLED TO GET MY BEARINGS.

I soon came to the conclusion that I was downtown, off the Strip, in an old section of town. Yet the area was not free of big hotels. I saw the Golden Nugget and felt somewhat reassured.

The people who had kidnapped me had not robbed me. My purse still held the cash I'd had left over from that morning's shopping spree. Or from yesterday's spree, I corrected myself. It was the middle of the night.

What a dark night it was. The sky was black as spilled ink, and the few visible stars were like hazy blobs rather than sharp points of light. It was like the earth itself had been thrust to the edge of the galaxy, where everything was dark and lonely. The air felt heavy, not polluted, but far from fresh, as if I were locked in a gigantic stuffy room. I assumed it was just me, that I was still recovering from my ordeal.

Since I didn't see any taxis, I decided to take a bus back to the Strip. I was surprised to hear from the people waiting at the stop that bus shuttles ran free twenty-four hours a day.

Yet the bus didn't go all the way to the MGM. It dropped me off on the edge of the Strip. The night was still warm. By now my thirst had become an ache. I searched for signposts and didn't see any. I was in no-man's-land. I hiked toward a medium-size hotel I didn't recognize. To reach the entrance I had to take a dark side street and cross a relatively deserted parking lot.

It was there I ran into three drunk guys in uniform. It might have been because their uniforms were so discombobulated, but I was unable to tell if they were army, navy, air force, or whatever. They had shiny crew cuts and belligerent attitudes. They stopped me as I tried to pass, grinning as they surrounded me, three jocks on steroids. Just what I needed after all the shit I'd been through.

They didn't scare me so much as bugged me.

I decided to go on the offensive, show I wasn't intimidated.

"Get the hell out of my way!" I snapped.

The wolf-pack leader was directly in front, a tall blond with a red scar that ran from his right ear to a bloodshot eye. He took a step closer, he stank of booze. He nodded to my purse.

"What you got there, pretty sister? Some winnings from the tables? Or from some hot loving with your sugar daddy?"

Ordinarily—say, to keep from getting raped—I would have surrendered my purse. But there was something about the night, or my mood—I was tired of being pushed around. I stared at the guy.

"I ain't got no sugar daddy and I ain't got no winnings. Not that I'd share them with a creep like you."

He chuckled, glanced at his friends, who grinned to show their support. "Why, pretty sister has a bark. Couldn't tell by looking at ya." He lost his smile, his tone turning serious. "You ain't connected, are ya?"

The way he said "connected," it was like the word had a special meaning to him. My gut told me to say yeah, I was, but my head said he'd want proof. And since I didn't know what he was talking about, I stood my ground and continued to act unafraid.

"Screw you," I said.

My courage caused them all to hesitate. The leader's partner, on his right, lost his smile. "Maybe we should cook, Wing," he said to his boss.

Wing threw him a hard look. "You want to leave right after telling pretty sister my name? Think that's smart, Moonshine?"

Moonshine lowered his head. "She might be connected. She's got the look. Her eyes, they're kind of spooky. But I don't know."

"She'd say it if she was," the third guy said. He was short and squat, but heavily muscled. He sounded like a moron.

Wing pointed to my purse. "Hand it over or we take it, along with a little of your honey, pretty sister. Ain't that true, Squat?"

"Absolutely," the third guy said.

Suddenly the phlogiston inside my solar plexus began to swell again. I meant the heat—yeah, I didn't know why I thought of it as phlogiston, except that I knew that the word meant heat. I felt the same burning I had experienced in the morgue. Once more it swelled in strength and size until it filled my body. The tips of my fingers felt as if they were on fire. I moved fast, without fear, until I was standing in Wing's face.

"Back off," I swore. "Back off now or you'll regret it the rest of your pathetic life."

Wing's eyes fixed on me, turned a cold blue, then flicked to the side, to his buddy, Squat. Wing gave an imperceptible nod and suddenly Squat came to life. He was fast. He started on my left but an instant later he was trying to grab me from behind. He clawed at my elbows, twisted them backward, lifted me off the ground a few inches.

At the same time Wing reached inside his pocket and brought out something silver, shiny, and sharp. Switchblade.

"Hold still, pretty sister, and it won't hurt so much," Squat whispered in my ear. His words, his paws, his grip—none of that scared me. It was strange, I felt no fear. I *knew* I could handle him and his partners.

"You should have listened to your own advice," I replied, as I shook my right arm free and rammed my elbow backward into Squat's ribs. The sound his ribs made as they snapped was distinct, sort of like a row of chicken bones caving in. Squat screamed and fell to the ground.

Wing gave Moonshine a sign and the guy closed in. A pity he was slower than Squat, and even more scared. Slashing out with my left foot, I struck him deep in the most tender part of his groin. He, too, screamed and dropped to the pavement.

"Enough!" Wing swore as his blade sliced through the air toward my exposed throat. If anything, he was faster than Squat. His blade whistled as he swung his arm, and I knew if it reached its intended target, I'd be squirting a thick red river onto the parking lot ground.

Yet my eyes seemed to switch into high-speed mode and I was able to follow his knife simply by willing it to slow down. Not that his thrust actually slowed. The newfound ability appeared to be strictly a mental trick that allowed me to study the trajectory of the blade so I had time to plan my reaction.

I reached up and grabbed Wing's wrist. My grip was as hard as a steel vise, and I *squeezed*. Again I heard bones breaking and suddenly Wing was crying for me to let go. But, like I said, I was in a bad mood. He had tried to kill me and now I wanted him to suffer.

I could have forced him to drop the switchblade—it was still in his hand—but I brought the tip close to his eyeball instead. He began to pant, to beg.

"Mother, please!" he cried. "We was just playing with you! It was all in good fun. We didn't know you was connected. You heard me ask. You heard me say . . . Oh, Lord, please don't take my eyes! I needs my eyes to see!"

"What do you need to see?" I asked. "More victims to steal from? To rape? Give me one good reason I shouldn't pluck them out?"

"Please, Mother! I have a wife! I have a wife and child!"

I turned to Moonshine, who was barely crawling back to his feet. "Is that true?" I asked. "Does he have a wife and child? You know I'll know if you lie so speak the truth!"

Moonshine nodded weakly. "He has a daughter and wife. But he never talks to—"

"Enough!" Wing cried. "Mother asked the question and you answered it. Now shut up!"

I grinned at Wing, holding the blade a millimeter from his bulging eyeball. "Enough? That's what you shouted before you tried to open my throat. Is that what you shout at your wife when she misbehaves?"

"No, Mother! I'm a good husband, I swear it!"

"Swear too much and it loses all meaning," I said.

My words had a profound effect on me. I suddenly realized I was in a situation that could not be real. When had I ever been mugged by three jerks and then casually fought them off? Never. Yet everything around me looked and felt real. I knew who I was, Jessica Ralle, although I felt like someone else, sort of like a character who was playing a part in a play.

Why did Wing keep calling me *Mother*?

At the same time, I knew I couldn't just release Wing. He

and his buddies were bad. A statement had to be made before they were let go.

I plucked the switchblade from his broken hand.

"I'll do better, Mother! Please give me a chance!"

"Fine, you'll have your chance," I said softly. Just before I slashed downward with his blade, over his left cheek, and opened up two inches of raw flesh. He shuddered from the pain but didn't bolt as I expected. Not even as the blood dripped over his uniform. "Something to remember me by," I said, taking a step back. "Now go."

The three guys split; they practically flew out of the parking lot. Dropping the knife, I turned back toward the hotel. I was still plenty thirsty.

Inside I found a coffee shop with an elevated counter that overlooked the casino floor. The place was hopping. Then again, it was a weekend night.

My waitress was a heavy middle-aged woman, with a sad but knowing expression. I ordered a large Coke. She hesitated as she took the menu back.

"You want ice with your cola?" she asked.

"Sure. But I want Coke, not Pepsi."

"We've got cola, sister. One kind, take it or leave it."

"I'll take it." She was calling me sister the same way Wing had. Just before he'd attacked. Thinking back, I realized it had only been when I had demonstrated that I could fight that he had switched to calling me Mother.

Once he knew I was connected.

Whatever that meant.

My cola came and it tasted enough like Coke that I couldn't complain. Drinking it hungrily, I ordered a second and turned in my chair to study the casino. The coffee shop offered a clear view of the main floor. From where I was sitting, I could see plenty of action: the poker tables, the slots, the dice pit, the blackjack tables. Only the twenty-one tables looked odd. I had to study them a moment before I realized what was wrong.

They were not playing twenty-one.

They were playing twenty-two.

The sign above the tables didn't say BLACKJACK.

It said RED QUEEN.

"Oh, Lord," I whispered, a phrase that sounded funny coming from my own mouth. I had meant to say, "Oh, God." I never said, "Oh, Lord." Of course, I never sat drinking a "cola" in a casino where twenty-two was the most popular game around.

When my waitress returned, I asked her about the twenty-two tables. She looked annoyed. "What's wrong with them?" she said.

"Where are the blackjack tables?"

"The what?" she asked.

"They're playing twenty-two! What happened to twenty-one?"

"You fooling with me, sister?"

"I most certainly am not."

The woman shook her head impatiently. "There ain't none of that played here. We play twenty-two, like we always have."

"That's insane."

"I wouldn't say that so loud if I was you." She nodded as she spoke, sort of as a warning. Yet there was something about my face that puzzled her. Perhaps something in my eyes that made her wonder if she should take me more seriously. But she appeared to shake the fear off. Once again her tone grew brisk. "You going to pay for those drinks?" she asked.

I took two twenty-dollar bills from my purse and handed them to her. "Keep the change," I said as the woman's eyes swelled.

My drink in hand, I headed toward the twenty-two tables. I wanted to see how they played, if the rules matched what Russ had taught me.

That was the first time I had thought of Russ in a long time.

Damn him, I thought, a half hour later, after having observed the dealer work through three shoes worth of cards. There was no denying the bizarre connection. Russ had taught me the identical rules this casino was using.

Twenty-two was the best hand you could get. It paid double. Aces were worth only one, not eleven. The queen of hearts and the queen of diamonds were the most important cards—worth eleven each.

No one talked or joked while sitting at the red-queen tables. It seemed Russ had been right about that as well.

"The game's older than blackjack. It has a rich tradition. It's never played just for fun, and no one is ever supposed to break the rules."

I saw what happened to a player who tried to evade the rules. He was a young man, kind-looking, definitely out of place in the company he was keeping. He was playing with a small amount of chips when the dealer got twenty-two. Like Russ had done to me in his hotel room, the dealer took all the bets off the table and demanded an extra 100 percent of each bet from each player. Everyone paid up quickly, including the guy in question.

But then the dealer got twenty-two again, and he not only gathered all the bets, he demanded that the players pay him another 100 percent of their previous bet. For most of the players that was a lot of money because, as Russ had demonstrated, the rules forced a player to immediately try to win their money back. So their bets were now *four times* what they had originally been.

The shock of two huge increases hit the players hard. The young man not only ran out of chips, he was suddenly in debt to the dealer. He stood as if to leave, but the dealer quickly pushed a button. A pit boss the size of King Kong appeared out of nowhere and stopped the guy.

"Is there a problem?" the pit boss asked.

The dealer nodded to the young man, who stood fidgeting, obviously scared. "I got hit with two naturals," the guy stuttered. "I can't cover it. I mean, I can but I have to go to my room to get the cash."

The pit boss nodded politely but his cold eyes said, *You ain't going nowhere, mister.* "Where are you staying?" he asked.

"The Dunes," the guy replied. I had heard of the Dunes but thought the hotel had been torn down years ago.

"Show me your room key," the pit boss said.

The guy searched his pockets. "I don't have it on me. My wife has it."

"Where is she?"

"Next door. Please, let me go and I'll return in a few minutes."

The pit boss gave him a hard stare. "We'll need insurance that you'll return."

By now the guy was shaking in his shoes. "I have none to offer, sir."

The pit boss stretched out a heavy arm. "Come with me."

The guy took a step back. "No, a moment, sir, please. I can get the money. My woman has it."

I don't know what prompted me to intercede, except for perhaps three small facts: the guy was lying; the pit boss knew he was lying; and the pit boss hated liars but loved to deal with them harshly.

Opening my purse and reaching for my cash, I suddenly stepped between the young man and his assailant. Kissing the guy on the cheek, I glanced at the pit boss out the corner of my eye.

"Hello, honey. Sorry I'm late." My glance at the pit boss shifted to a full-on stare. "What's that look you're giving me? Is there a problem?"

The pit boss studied me closely. He liked what he saw but also feared it. He bowed his head. "You this man's wife?"

I smiled. "I ain't his sister. What can I do for you?"

"Your husband has run up a small debt. We'd like it settled before he leaves."

"How small is small?" I asked, although I knew the number.

The pit boss hesitated. "Five hundred even. But we'll take four hundred in cash."

My grin turned to ice. I thought it odd that he was trying to cheat us when my supposed husband was standing right beside me. It was like he expected a negotiation.

"I think you'll take three hundred in cash, since that's all my man owes you," I said.

The pit boss backed up a step. "I thought you just arrived?"

I stepped toward him. "I've been here long enough. My husband owes you three hundred and not a penny more." I paused. "I do hope you're not thinking of cheating us, are you?"

Now it was the pit boss's chance to fidget. "No, Mother, never. Why don't we make it two hundred and call it even?" He added in a worried tone, "Does that sound fair to you?"

"Mighty fair." I peeled off two hundred-dollar bills. The

cash looked darker than what I was used to; there was more red in the ink than green. But when I studied the bills up close I saw the familiar Benjamin Franklin staring back at me.

I held the cash out for the pit boss to take. But before he could reach the bills I let them go, let them float toward the floor, so he had to bend over to recover them. The move was designed to make him bow to me, and the weird thing was, it felt natural.

The pit boss quickly picked them up. "Thank you, Mother."

"Thank my husband, please. And apologize."

The pit boss bowed. "I apologize for the misunderstanding, sir. Please feel free to play here again, with your room and food comped, of course."

"Of course," the guy said.

"Come along, dear," I said, grabbing the guy's hand and pulling him away from the tables. I didn't let go until we were near the exit. By then the guy was ready to prostrate before me.

"I don't know how to thank you for your help, Mother," he said. "I'm in your debt."

"No problem. There's just one thing I want in return."

"Anything!"

"Don't gamble anymore. You're never going to win."

He seemed to take my advice to heart. He bowed and hurried off. I also felt the urge to flee, to get out of that place and into the night air before I started screaming. I felt trapped in a spell only Russell Devon could have cast.

"Come by when you don't know what else to do."

He was the last person I should go see. He was the only one who knew I had been heading to his hotel in a taxi. Therefore, he must have been behind my kidnapping. The logic was simple and couldn't be denied. I should go to the police, report him, or at the very least talk to Jimmy and Alex and let them know I was all right.

I did neither. That single remark of Russ's continued to haunt me. I had died and been reborn in a hospital morgue. I had slipped and fallen into the Twilight Zone. And it occurred to me that he had told me that weird line because he had known I was going to end up in this exact situation. How did I know this?

Because he had taught me how to play twenty-two.

Plus I was afraid if I told Jimmy and Alex everything that had happened to me, they wouldn't believe me. Had our places been reversed, I wouldn't have believed them. But Russ would believe me. Even if he was a bad guy, even if he tried to kill me again, I knew he wouldn't laugh at me. At that moment, finding a way out of this nightmare seemed almost as important as staying alive.

I walked briskly up the Strip. When I reached the Mandalay Bay, the bright gold letters on top of the casino said THE MANDY. I tried telling myself it wasn't an issue, that a few lights had burned out. Yet the letters didn't add up.

Inside the hotel, on the casino floor, everyone was playing red queen.

I took the elevator to the top floor. Yesterday it had been the forty-third floor. Today it was the forty-fourth, because there was no longer a thirteenth floor. Who wanted to stay on the thirteenth floor anyway? Especially here, in Las Vegas, the most superstitious town on earth.

On the top floor I exited the elevator to the left and marched down to the last room on the right. To the opulent suite that I knew overlooked the entire Strip. I could have used his key to enter—it was still in my purse—but decided to be polite and knock.

He answered immediately. It was four in the morning but he was well dressed. A dark blue suit and a red tie. More formal than the night before. He studied me with his blue eyes, which matched his suit, searching for clues. I don't know if he found what he was looking for but there was no mistaking his relief.

"Jessica! You're okay."

"Why wouldn't I be?"

"Do you want to come inside?" he asked.

"Outside is fine."

He spoke with feeling. "It's good to see you, Jessica."

Jessica. That was my real name, true, but everyone called me Jessie. I had told him that yesterday.

"It's not so good to see you, Russell," I replied.

"Why do you say that?"

"Going to play dumb or can we skip that part?"

"You look like you've had a rough night."

"You could say that. Got picked up by a taxi driver from hell and got dropped off in nowhere's land. Then I got a ride from a middle-aged bitch with a Taser. I never did get her name. Next thing I know I'm cooling off in a meat locker with a thousand dead steer. Spent the next hour trying to break out. But I just ended up breaking my nose and ankle. The cold finally got to me and I blacked out. Then I woke up in a hospital, which looked like a turn for the better until they assumed I was dead and started doing an autopsy on me." I paused. "Yeah, you're right, rough night."

He interrupted. "A hospital?"

"You act surprised, Russell. Don't be. The autopsy with Susan and Dave was the highlight of the night. If she hadn't been called off to treat an ER patient, and if he hadn't had a weak heart and an insatiable lust for teenage corpses, then I'd probably be just another disemboweled stiff in the morgue right now. Can you imagine? My brain in a jar? Hell, if that had happened then we'd have nothing to talk about right now."

Russell looked shocked. "You're serious? They almost cut you open?"

"Why not? According to them I was DOA. Dead on arrival."

"I know what it means."

"Well, that's a huge relief."

"How come they failed to revive you?"

"I don't know, they couldn't get hold of Jesus?"

"But why . . . ?"

"They couldn't revive me because I was dead. Dead!"

"Jessica."

"Quit calling me that! It's Jessie!"

"Why? You keep calling me Russell."

He was right. I hadn't noticed. I was doing it automatically, even in my mind.

"Would you please come in," he said when I didn't answer.

"No."

"Why not?"

"Because you were the only one who knew I was coming over here yesterday afternoon. And when I think about it, I can't help but recall how the first taxi that drove up at the MGM refused to let me in. I had to take the taxi after that. Because that taxi was *waiting* for me. And it was when I got in that cab that my wild ride through hell started." I paused. "Is that enough reason not to come inside?"

He checked his watch. "If you don't want to talk, then why are you here?" he asked.

"You tell me."

"You're here for answers."

"Yes. Give them to me. Why did you have me kidnapped?"

"I had nothing to do with you ending up in that morgue."

"What about the meat locker?"

Russell glanced down, studied my dusty shoes, ignored my question. "You look like you walked here," he said.

"Well, I sure as hell wasn't going to get in another taxi, was I?"

"How did you walk here on a broken ankle?"

His question threw me for a loop. I wasn't sure how badly I had hurt my nose but my ankle was another matter. When I had leaped and missed the meat hook, it had definitely snapped. It was possible it hadn't broken, but at the very least I had sprained it so bad I shouldn't have been able to walk on it.

Yet I had just stormed up the Strip on foot.

Russell could see I was confused, probably because I didn't know what to say. He spoke in my place.

"Who are you going to talk to if you don't talk to me? To James? To Alexis?"

"How do you know about Jimmy?"

"I know him."

"How?" I demanded. "And why do you call Alex Alexis? And Jimmy James?"

"Come inside and I'll explain."

"No! You sent those psychos after me!"

"Those people were interested in you long before we met."

"What's that supposed to mean?"

He opened the door wider. "It's a long story. Come in."

"How do I know you won't try to hurt me again?"

Russell did an odd thing right then. He smiled as if I had said something silly. "How could I possibly hurt you?" he asked.

"You could cut my throat. You could shoot me."

His next question threw me for an even bigger loop. It was almost as if he had witnessed my encounter with Moonshine, Wing, and Squat.

"Wouldn't you be able to protect yourself?"

Again, I was stumped. He had all the answers; I was just a warmed-up corpse with possible brain damage. "They're playing red queen downstairs," I said.

"I know."

"Twenty-two. Not twenty-one."

"I know."

"That doesn't bother you?"

"Nope," he said.

"Why did you teach me that game?"

"So you would know to come here."

"When I didn't know where else to go?"

"Exactly."

I hesitated. "Are you connected?"

"Yes. Now you're connected. Please come in, Jessica."

He had me, I had nowhere else to go. Except into the suite of the man who had arranged my kidnapping. I stepped through the door and he closed it at my back.

CHAPTER NINE

THE SUITE APPEARED THE SAME AS THE PREVIOUS night. His laptop was open and running on the dining room table. A neat pile of his firm's leaflets sat beside it. However, the coloring of the brochures was different. I needed to study one up close to be sure, but the black and red lettering looked like a fresh touch.

I sat on the same leather chair as before. He sat across from me, on the love seat. He took a cell phone out of his pocket.

"May I call some friends of mine and tell them you're here?"

I snorted. "Not!"

"These people are important. You'll want to meet them. They'll be able to answer questions that I can't."

"Are these the people who orchestrated my kidnapping?"

"They wouldn't call it that, but yes."

"Forget it," I said.

"I have to call them at some point."

"Fine. Call them when I'm ten miles from here."

"What if I told you that someone close to you is with these people?"

"I would assume you were lying."

"I have tried hard not to lie to you, Jessica."

"Gee, Russell, why do I have trouble believing that?"

He sighed and put the cell phone away. "All right, what do you want to know?"

"Why are they playing twenty-two downstairs?"

"Instead of twenty-one?"

"Duh. Yeah, instead of twenty-one."

"That's a long story."

"You said that already. I assume we have time." I added, "Or do you need to get to bed early? If that's the case, I'm afraid you're too late. The sun will be coming up in about three hours."

"That doesn't bother me. I just have to be in bed before dawn. So do you."

"Why?"

"That's part of the long story."

"Great. I love stories. Tell me your story."

He pointed to the brochures on the table. "Remember the scanner I told you about? How it was designed to read a person's genetic code?"

"Yes. Was that a lie?"

"No. It does read a normal person's genetic code. Only that's not its main purpose." He paused as if searching for the right words. "It was originally built to identify people who are more than normal."

"More than normal? Like superheroes or something?"

"The scanner is able to identify people who have an extra set of genes. Genes your average person doesn't possess."

"How many people possess these extra genes?"

"It's impossible to answer that question with a simple number. One in ten thousand people might possess one of the genes I'm talking about. But only one in a million would possess three or more."

"How many of these genes exist?"

"So far we've identified ten."

"What do they do for the people who have them?"

"Most people who have them don't even know they exist. They lie dormant and don't do a thing. But once they've been activated, well, they give a person special abilities."

"Let me guess. Like the ability to win at cards?"

"Yes."

"So you're special, Russell."

"Why the sarcasm? You know it's true."

"Forgive me. It's just that I hate it when a guy starts talking about how special he is. Especially when the same guy keeps ignoring my question. Why are people downstairs playing twenty-two?"

He held up a hand. "I warned you, to properly answer your question, I need time."

"I assume, since you say I'm connected, that I have one or more of these genes?" I asked.

"That's right. You have more than I do."

"Gee whiz, that must make me one in a billion."

"Jessica. We're going to get nowhere if you don't drop that snide attitude."

"I might drop it if you called me Jessie instead of Jessica." I paused. "Why do you keep calling me that?"

"It's your name here."

"What do you mean, 'here'? In this suite? In this hotel?"

"Please, if you'd let me continue."

"No. I need you to tell me where 'here' is. If you don't, I might start screaming, and if I start, I'm not sure if I'll be able to stop."

"Just because they're playing twenty-two downstairs instead of twenty-one?"

"Yeah. You see, I have this small problem when one of the cornerstones of the universe suddenly changes. It makes me feel uncomfortable. And since this is supposed to be Las Vegas, and in Las Vegas they play twenty-one, I want to know where I'm at." I paused. "Please."

"All right." He suddenly stood. "Let's go in the bedroom."

I remained seated. "Why?"

"We're not going to get anywhere unless you open up your mind. Come, we need to go in the bedroom."

"What's in the bedroom?"

"A mirror. I want you to look into it."

"Is that all?"

"Yes. Come."

"No."

"Why not?"

"Duh. You helped kidnap me yesterday. Now you want me to trust you to go in your bedroom."

"You're as safe in there as you are out here."

"I'm not going in your bedroom."

"I can't answer your questions without the mirror."

"Try."

He paused. "Don't you feel like you could protect yourself from me if the need arose?"

"What do you mean?" I asked, although I knew exactly what he meant. Just look at what I'd done to Wing, Squat, and Moonshine. Russell was watching me closely.

"Something's happened to you since you awakened in the hospital. Something that's told you the answer to my question is yes. So let's be honest with each other. I know you're not afraid of me."

He was right. Instinctively, if it came to a fight, I knew I would be hard to beat. He didn't scare me.

I followed him into his bedroom. There was a lamp on low by the tall windows that overlooked the Strip, but otherwise the room was mostly shadows. The mirror he was referring to was connected to the main closet. It reached from the floor to the ceiling. He sat on the corner of the bed and told me to stand in front of the mirror and gaze into it.

"What do you see?" he asked.

"Me. The bed. The windows."

"Can you see me?"

"Not unless I turn my head and look at an angle."

"Don't do that. Just stand perfectly still and stare at the mirror and listen to my voice."

"You're not going to hypnotize me, are you?"

"I'm going to help you see something you've forgotten."

"What does that mean?"

"For now, drop all your questions and just go along with me for a few minutes. When we're done, you can ask anything you wish. You can leave if you want, go see your friends. But for now, to get to the heart of your questions, you must cooperate. Okay?"

"Okay. But I'm not taking off my clothes."

"You don't have to take off your clothes. Just stare into the mirror. Focus. Tell me what you see."

"Myself."

"Raise your right arm. Like you're about to wave hi to someone. What do you see?"

I raised my right arm. "My arm in the air."

"Is it your right arm or your left arm?"

"It's my right arm."

"But you're staring at your reflection. Does it look like your right arm or your left arm?"

"It looks like my left arm because in the mirror everything is reversed. But I know it's my right arm."

"Because your intellect tells you it's your right arm?"

"Yes."

"But when you stare at the mirror, innocently, everything in the room appears to be backward?"

"I would say inverted or reversed."

"Those are good words, accurate words. Still, the image of you in the mirror is a reflection of who you are. Now let your right arm drop and raise your left arm. What do you see?"

I obeyed his instructions. "My left arm in the air."

"But you really just see an arm in the air? You have to think about it to know it's your left arm."

"Yes."

"Good. Now we're going to play a little game. You're going to let the analytical part of your brain slowly turn off so you see what you see without questioning it. We're looking for inno-cence here, nothing more. It might take a few minutes to get in this state but we're in no hurry. All your questions, all your doubts, we can save them for later. Okay?"

"Okay."

"Let your arm fall to your side and relax. Stare at the mirror. What do you see?"

"My face."

"Good. You've begun to focus on your face. Now smile, smile brightly, and tell me, what do you see?"

I smiled as best I could, but it was hard to maintain while I answered. "I see my teeth, my gums, my lips curving upward."

"Good. Your reflection responds to what you do. Blink a few times. What do you see?"

"I see myself blinking."

"See. You're in control. It can only do what you do. Why? Because it's only a reflection. You're what's real. Agreed?"

"Yes."

"Wiggle your nose."

I wiggled my nose.

"What do you see?"

"My nose wiggling."

"Take a long last look at your face, and a long last look at your body. Soon you're going to close your eyes. But before you do, you want the image of yourself fixed firmly in your mind. Do you understand?"

"Yes."

"Study yourself closely."

"I am."

"Study your hair, your face, your shoulders and your arms.

Let your gaze slowly travel the length of your body, and when you feel ready, go ahead and shut your eyes."

I started my exam from the top, like he told me to. But I don't remember exactly when I closed my eyes. At some point I just realized they were shut. A part of me suspected he was trying to hypnotize me, but I wasn't worried. I knew no one could be hypnotized against their will.

Also, I found the practice pleasant. He had a soothing voice, and it was relaxing to stare into the mirror. Even standing in front of it, with my eyes shut, was calming.

Russell spoke as if from far away.

"You know you're standing in front of a mirror. You don't need to open your eyes to see your reflection. You know it's there, just a few feet in front of you. And you know your reflection is under your control."

"Yes," I said softly.

"When you move, it moves."

"Yes."

"We're going to continue with our game. It's totally safe and you'll be in control at all times. Now I want you to imagine that your mind is *inside* your reflection. That the control over your body has moved *into* your reflection. This is easy to do. Like I said, your reflection is just a few feet away. To all intents and purposes, it's identical to you. The only difference is everything in the mirror is reversed. Other than that, you are moving your consciousness into an exact replica of yourself." He paused.

"Relax and let your mind drift forward. Let it drift toward your reflection. Don't think too much about it. Don't worry if you're doing it right or wrong. Just let your mind float forward into your reflection and enjoy the sensation of letting go."

I was surprised how easy it was to obey his instruction. The truth is, I think a part of me did something similar every morning when I brushed my teeth in front of my home mirror. I *enjoyed* staring at myself, although I had never told anyone before. I was probably afraid they would think I was vain. For me to let my mind drift inside my reflection seemed like no big deal.

Again, his voice seemed to come from far off.

"Do you feel like you have moved into your reflection?"

"Yes," I heard someone whisper. It was me talking but it sounded like another person, someone nearby.

"Are you comfortable where you are?"

"Yes," I said.

"Even though your eyes are closed, can you imagine your body standing in front of you?"

"Yes."

"Can you imagine if you move your right hand, the right hand of your body will also move?"

"Yes."

"Let's give it a try. Without opening your eyes, raise your right arm."

I wasn't sure, but I felt movement. Yet the movement was effortless. I didn't have to try to lift my arm, it simply lifted.

"Your arm is in the air," he said. "It might be your right arm, it might be your left, it doesn't matter. Did you notice how easily it floated into the air?"

"Yes."

"It happened automatically."

"Yes."

"That's because your mind is inside your reflection."

"Yes."

"Now raise your other arm."

Again, I felt movement, but no effort, and yet in my mind's eye I could see both my arms in the air. In my body and in my reflection.

No, wait, that wasn't exactly true. I saw only one image at a time. It must have been my body I was looking at, since my mind was *inside* my reflection, looking out at my body. That's right.

But what difference did it make? They were carbon copies of each other, or reversed copies of each other, to be more precise.

I decided not to worry about it. Just to go along.

"Both your arms are now in the air," he said.

"Yes."

"Does it tire you to hold them up?"

"No."

"Why not?"

"They're just images."

"Good. And what are you?"

"An image. A reflection."

"Because you have moved your mind inside the mirror."

"Yes."

"How does it feel to be a reflection?"

"Nice."

"Do you have all of Jessica's memories?"

"Yes."

"Perfect. Let's move on to the next stage. Remember back to last night. You were in this bedroom with Russell."

"I remember." And I didn't mind he called himself Russell instead of Russ. Indeed, it felt more natural, like that was what I always called him.

"You were in this bedroom and you were kissing him."

"Yes."

"Then you took off your clothes and kissed him some more on the bed."

"Yes."

"Then you thought of someone else."

"Yes."

"And suddenly you wanted to be with that person."

"Yes."

"What was his name?"

"James."

"You suddenly felt the urge to see James."

"Yes."

"What did you do next?"

"I stood and went to the window."

"Go on."

"I started crying. I told Russell I couldn't do this."

"Did Russell understand?"

"He was very understanding. He didn't pressure me. Even though I know he has a crush on me, he respects my relationship with James."

"How did he demonstrate this respect?"

"He saw I was upset and knew I was thinking of James. He told me to go to him."

"Was it hard to leave Russell?"

"It's always hard. He's attractive and exciting to be near."

"But you love James more?"

"Yes," I replied firmly.

There seemed to be a long pause.

"What did you do next?"

"I dressed and left this suite."

"Let's follow your every act from right there. Are you fully dressed?"

"Yes."

"You're ready to leave Russell's suite and go downstairs."

"Yes."

"Let's go together. You open the door and leave the suite. Do you walk down the hallway to the elevators?"

"Yes."

"Do you get in the elevator?"

"I push a button and wait for one to come."

"Good. What do you do next?"

"When the elevator arrives, I step inside and push the button that takes me down to the casino floor."

"Tell me what you see."

"The doors slide open. I step away from the corridor of elevators and see the casino stretched out beneath me."

"Do you see people gambling?"

"Yes."

"What are they playing?"

"Slots, poker, dice, red queen."

"Red queen?"

"Yes."

"You see them playing twenty-two?"

"Yes."

"Does it bother you?"

"Why should it bother me?"

"What do you do next?"

"I take a taxi back to my room."

"Who do you find in your room?"

"James."

"Where is he?"

"Inside, waiting for me."

"Is he asleep?"

"No."

"Are you sure?"

"Yes."

"Why is he awake?"

"He knew I was going to see Russell."

"How did he know you were going to see Russell?"

"I told him I was going to see you . . . to see him. We discussed it, James and I."

"Is James jealous you're going to see Russell?"

"A little. He knows Russell cares for me."

"But if it makes James jealous, why do you go?"

"We need Russell's help."

"Why?"

"To help us find . . . someone."

"Who?"

I disliked the question. "I don't know."

"You don't know who you're trying to find?"

"No. Wait. Stop."

"Shh. It's all right, we can stop."

"Thank you."

"You're safe. Nothing can harm you."

"I . . . I don't know."

"You think something can harm you?"

"I don't want to talk about it."

"About what?"

"Why I went to Russell for help."

"Are you embarrassed that you started kissing him?"

"Yes. But . . . there's something else."

"What?"

"I can't tell you!" I shouted.

I heard my voice rise in volume. At the same time I felt a sudden constriction in my heart. It appeared to come out of nowhere. The sensation made it hard to breathe. It took me completely by surprise. One minute I was looking forward to returning to my hotel room to see James and the next instant my mind was filled with a terrible burden. I could hardly bear it.

"Stop. I want to stop," I heard myself gasp.

"We can stop in a moment. Why did you go to see Russell?"

"I told you. To get his help."

"Why did you think Russell could help you?"

"He's connected."

"Did he tell you he was connected?"

"No! But he knows people. Powerful people. He can help us."

"Help you with what?"

The crushing pain increased tenfold. I could hardly draw in a breath. The air could have been choked with smoke.

"I can't tell you!"

"Can he help you find someone?"

"Yes! No!"

"You said yes. Can he help you find someone?"

"Yes! Yes! Now please stop!"

"Who are you trying to find?"

"I don't know! I don't want to know!"

"What's her name?"

My chest pain seemed to burst and assume a form of terrible loss. I had just been asked the only question that mattered because *she* was the only thing that mattered—to me. I couldn't bear to think of her, though, to even admit that she existed. I was afraid if I did my pain would become great enough to kill me.

"Lara," I wept.

"Who's Lara?"

"No!" I screamed and my eyes flew open and I ran toward the mirror and hit it with my nose. Blood spurted out my nostrils, on the glass, as I fell to the floor. In an instant Russell was by my side but I pushed him away and leaped to my feet. It was not as if I used my muscles, though. I simply willed myself to stand and I was up. Russell was unable to stop me.

I had to get away. I couldn't face the truth about Lara. The agony was too great and besides, she wasn't real, I couldn't let her become real.

I rushed toward the door and threw it open.

A man stood in the hallway. A handsome man with my eyes. I hadn't seen him in years but he wasn't someone I was likely to forget.

"Daddy," I cried as I collapsed in his arms.

CHAPTER TEN

WHEN I AWOKE, MY FATHER WAS SITTING BESIDE ME ON the bed. I hadn't seen him in years but he didn't *feel* like some distant figure. This man seemed familiar, like we had talked yesterday, although I couldn't recall any recent memories of him. I knew then the bond between a father and daughter never really dies. It was wonderful to see him. I squeezed his hand when he touched mine.

"Dad," I whispered.

"Jessica. It's me. I've been here all the time."

He was talking about *here*, wherever here was.

I had forgotten what a powerful presence he had. He was six-three, taller than Russell and James, and had beautiful green eyes and dark maroon hair, which he wore past his collar. His features were closer to mine than my mother's. They were even sharper, somehow richer, perhaps as a result of time. He had obviously seen a lot in life. His hands were large, even for his size, strong but also nimble. His gestures were so smooth. He looked like a doctor, a healer, and he looked like my dad. He *was* my father, I had to remind myself. I was still recovering from the shock of seeing him.

"How do you feel?" he asked.

"Like an idiot."

"Why?"

"Because of the way I behaved. Russell did an experiment with me and I panicked for no reason."

My father shook his head. "You remembered something extremely painful. It's only natural you would try to run from it."

"But what I remembered never happened. There's no reason it should upset me."

My dad gestured to the closet mirror. "Maybe it did happen."

"Are we talking about Alice and the Looking-glass here?"

He nodded seriously. "There's a reason Lewis Carroll wrote that novel."

"There was a red queen in that book."

"It wasn't a coincidence."

"So you know why they're playing twenty-two downstairs?"

"It's because we're in witch world," he said.

The name sounded too familiar to joke about.

"It's real?" I asked.

"As real as the real world. Maybe more so." He stood. "Let's talk in the living room. We have the place to ourselves. Russell went out to run an errand. But first you might want to wash up. I'm afraid you smashed your nose again."

I grabbed his hand before he could leave. "What about Lara?"

"She's real as well."

I wiped away a sudden tear. "My daughter. I have a daughter."

"I know it must be hard to believe. But you are a mother."

I felt a stab of pain again. "They took her, didn't they?"

My father hesitated. "Yes."

"Is she safe? Will they hurt her?"

"She's fine. They're afraid to hurt her."

"Can we get her back?"

"We're going to get her back." He patted my shoulder. "Go ahead, wash up—we have much to discuss."

Before rejoining my father in the main suite, I took a quick shower. Since I had left my hotel and been kidnapped by the taxi driver, my body and clothes had been put through the wringer. Besides washing off the sweat and dust, I had to scrub to get the dried blood off my face. My nose was bruised but it didn't feel broken.

My father was drinking coffee when I entered the living room wearing a hotel bathrobe. He quickly poured me a cup and I settled into a leather chair while he sat on the main sofa. His company made me feel safe for the first time in what seemed like ages.

He smiled. "I can't imagine what's running through your mind right now."

"You mean you can't read it?" I asked, half teasing. But he replied seriously.

"Your mind would not be an easy one to pry open."

"Why?"

"Because you're unique."

The fact was easier, and at the same time harder, to take coming from my father. I knew it was for real. "Russell said there are ten unusual genes," I said.

"Ten that we know of. Some of the genes overlap to create different abilities. For example, a person could have three extra genes and possess six unusual abilities. However, that would only happen long after a person had mastered their basic three gifts."

"Of these ten genes, how many do you have?"

"Five. James has five too, which is rare. Russell has four. And you, my dear, have a whopping seven, which is even more rare."

"Wow."

"Wow is right. There are only a handful of people in the world who possess that many. Most are a member of what we call the Council. They're an ancient group. One of their members has eight witch genes."

"Witch genes? Why do you call them that?"

"Because most of us discovered our powers long ago, when the world called anyone who was different a witch." My father shrugged. "It's just a name. Saying someone has witch genes is the same as saying someone has reached the next stage in human evolution. Their appearance is a natural event."

"I assume you know what genes give what kind of powers," I said.

"I do. But I'm not going to say what powers your seven genes represent."

"Why not?" I asked.

"It's important the abilities appear spontaneously. That you don't force them to come."

"I won't force them. I just want to know what they are."

"Knowing will spoil your innocence. You have to trust me on this. I have a lot of experience in this area."

"Can you tell me if there is a specific gene for longevity?"

"There's a gene for healing. Many witches are born with it. When you learn the ability to heal others, you'll also discover you can heal yourself, and continue to repair your body and prevent it from growing old." He added, "I can tell you this much. You have that one."

"So if someone slit my throat, I could fix it before I died?"

"No. You'd be dead before you could repair the damage. But you can heal almost anything in your body if you have the time."

"So a bullet between the eyes would kill me?"

"It would kill any witch," my father said.

"Thanks for the heads-up. Now I bet you know what I'm going to ask next."

"How old am I? Are you ready for a shock?"

"This whole day has been nothing but one shock after another. So yes."

"I was born not long before the Elizabethan era began, in the year 1528, in London, England."

"Oh, Lord," I gasped.

He chuckled. "I was lucky I possessed the healing gene. Even before I became connected, I was somewhat psychic. I accidentally exposed my gift and was tried and sentenced to death. But I was fortunate to be hanged instead of burned at the stake. It would have been difficult for a newborn witch to bring himself back after being turned to ashes."

"Who tried you?" I asked.

"The local bishop. He later became a full-time inquisitor. He was a good friend until he discovered I was in league with Satan."

The memory appeared to amuse my dad.

"Is that how you got . . . connected?" I asked. "The hanging?"

"Yes. You're beginning to grasp the mechanics."

I shook my head vigorously. "I'm grasping very little. I just said that because we both went through a death experience, and then woke up here—wherever here is. I have to assume that dying somehow activates the witch genes."

"Exactly. That's the key. You got it."

"I've got nothing. What the hell is witch world? Where is it?"

He smiled faintly. "First off, it's not hell, although to my primitive brain—five centuries ago—it seemed that way at first. At the very least, I felt like I kept living the same day twice over."

"What do you mean?"

"Right now, in witch world, two or three hours ago, it just became early Monday morning. But when you wake up tomorrow, in what you call the real world, it will be Sunday morning."

"How is that possible? Does one of the genes transport us back in time?"

"I wish. Then we could fix all the mistakes we've made in the past. Trust me, Jessica, the answer to your question is both more simple and more complex than anything you're going to have to absorb right now. Especially since I'm going to have to rely on words to explain the paradox."

"Please, try. What is witch world?" I said.

"Witch world is a parallel dimension to what you call the real world. It exists at the same time as the real world, simultaneously. But because human beings cannot experience two time frames at the same time, those who have awakened to the existence of witch world discover they live one day here and then live the same day over again in the real world. Are you with me so far?"

"Are the days identical?"

"They used to be virtually identical. Almost everyone you know in the real world has a counterpart in witch world. They live out their lives the same way people do in the real world. To them, *this* is the real world, the only world. Take James and Alexis, for example. They're your best friends here. They're also your best friends in the real world. But James and Alexis know as little about Jimmy and Alex as Jimmy and Alex know about James and Alexis."

"You said *almost* everyone has a counterpart in both worlds. Why doesn't everyone?"

"Because it's possible their counterpart died in one of the worlds."

I grimaced. "So then that person is only half alive?"

"No. They don't even need to know their counterpart has died."

"Wait a second! How come Lara doesn't have a counterpart in the real world? I know she didn't die there. I mean, I never even had her."

My father hesitated. "Huck is Lara's counterpart."

"Huh?"

"In witch world, James had a daughter. In the real world, Jimmy had a son."

"Why are you talking about Jimmy? What about me? I didn't have anyone in the real world."

My father spoke gently. "I know, it's complicated. Frankly, it's something that's never happened before, not that we know of. I suggest you hold that question until you meet with the Council."

"It's not an easy question to hold."

"I'm sorry, I don't know what else to tell you."

I tried to drop it but continued to fume inside. "All right. You said that James—Jimmy—has five witch genes. Wouldn't that many genes give him a sense of this world?"

"His genes are inactive. Look, you have seven and still you had almost no idea that this world existed."

I pondered his words. "Déjà vu," I muttered.

"Excuse me?"

"When Jimmy and I were up at the lake yesterday, we talked about how we kept having flashes of déjà vu. We even seemed to have two sets of memories that conflicted with each other."

"That's a sign your genes were spontaneously becoming active. You started to get a glimpse of this world. But even though you have become connected to your latent abilities, your memory of the real world will continue to overshadow your memory of witch world for the time being."

"Why?"

"Because it's impossible for a human being to suddenly absorb an entire lifetime of memories overnight. Everything that's happened to you in witch world—for example, the birth of your daughter—will return to you slowly, over the next few months."

"Are you saying I have an entire lifetime of memories I know nothing about?" I asked.

"Yes and no. I warned you, at first the truth will appear contradictory. You know something about the Jessica of witch world. Her life has paralleled yours to a remarkable degree. But it's also been different in a few important details. Those details will return to you in time."

"Why do the memories of the real world dominate at first?"

"They do for you because you went through the death experience in the real world. Had you done it in witch world, then those memories would have been the first to dominate. The point remains the same in both cases. It takes time to absorb our other set of memories. But just yesterday, in witch world, when I spoke to you, you knew all about this place and nothing about the real world."

"How did the memories get wiped out?"

"Forgive me for repeating myself. They didn't get wiped out. They're still inside you, only your brain can't process them right now because it just got overlaid with a lifetime of memories from the real world."

"This is confusing."

"It takes some getting used to. Remember what happened to you when Russell had you focus on the mirror? You remembered your daughter, Lara."

"I did but . . ." I felt embarrassed to continue.

"But the memory of Lara has already begun to fade."

"Yes! It was so vivid for a few minutes. Her birth, holding

her, staring into her eyes. She has beautiful eyes, doesn't she?"

"Yes. Do you recall their color?"

"No! That's what I'm trying to say. The memory has begun to fade. It's weird—how can I forget my own daughter?"

"Because Jessie never gave birth to her. Jessica did."

"But I am Jessica."

"Yes."

"But the way you spoke just now, you said it like we were two different people."

"In a sense, until you get your witch-world memories back, you are two different people. Because you have different pasts. For that reason, I'm going to insist you avoid James for the next few days. You won't know him and he will think there's something wrong with you. But you don't have to worry about hurting his feelings. I saw him before coming here and explained that you were being connected and that the process was going to take a few days to complete."

"But you said it takes months to get back all my memories."

"True. But if I told him it was months he would have freaked out. Besides, the first few days are the most crucial. You'll feel delicate, with so many new experiences bombarding you from every side. While in witch world, the best thing you can do is hang out with friends who are already connected. For that reason, it's a good idea to avoid Alexis and Debra for the time being."

"What about Mom?"

"I don't think she's going to be a problem."

"Why?"

"You're going to be in Las Vegas longer than you planned."

"To get Lara back."

"Exactly. She's here."

"Who took her?"

"Let's deal with that in a few minutes. I want to make sure you understand what's happened to you, and how it's going to affect you over the next few days."

I shook my head. "Intellectually, I understand what you say about two dimensions and living the same day over again twice. But this whole 'getting connected' process sounds bizarre. I mean, on one hand it's an awakening experience and on the other hand an entire lifetime gets erased."

"Once again, your memories of witch world are still intact. Try looking at the temporary amnesia you're experiencing as a natural coping mechanism. Without it, you'd have to be sedated."

"Because I'd suddenly be looking at everything from two different points of view?"

"Exactly."

I frowned. "I just had a flash of memory that's not exactly mine. But I'm not sure if it really happened."

"Tell me about it and I'll let you know."

"I remember going to Russell for help to get Lara back. That memory came back to me while I was standing in front of the mirror. But I also remember something about that Council you mentioned. I went to him because I was hoping he could get in touch with them."

"That's a genuine memory."

"Good," I said. "I suppose it's good."

"What's troubling you?"

"Oh, about ten thousand things."

My father was patient. "What confuses you the most?"

"I can't imagine that for the rest of my life I'm going to have to live the same day over again twice."

"It won't be exactly the same day because the worlds are no longer identical."

"When does this transfer happen? I mean, when does my mind go from the real world to witch world, and back again?" I asked.

"At dawn. Precisely when the sun rises. At this latitude, it takes just under three minutes for it to clear the horizon. During that time—in both worlds—you will suddenly lose consciousness. If you were standing up, you would fall over because all life would appear to leave your body. An outside observer would probably think you had stopped breathing because your respiration almost ceases. That's why it's a good idea to be in bed at dawn."

"What's so special about the sun rising?"

"The sun is the source of all life on Earth. A new day begins when it appears."

"I know that. What I'm asking is—does our spirit or soul suddenly leave one world and fly to the other?"

"In a manner of speaking. The transition is impossible to describe with words. It just happens once you're connected."

"What if I choose to stay awake at dawn?"

"You won't be able to. Not during that three minutes."

"If I'm asleep, do I notice the switch?"

"No. You go to sleep in one world, you wake up in the other."

"That's so fucking freaky." I paused. "Pardon my French."

"It's not a shock to me that my daughter cusses."

"So we're good friends in this world?"

"Yes."

I hesitated. Lara was not my only source of sorrow.

"Why not in the real world?" I asked quietly.

My father sighed. "I stayed away to protect you."

"From who?" I asked.

"The same people who kidnapped Lara," he said.

"How did staying away protect me?"

"In the real world, they know who I am. But they don't know who you are. At least, we didn't think so."

His remark did not surprise me as much as it should have. A part of me had always felt he had stayed away on purpose. He had not protested when I had adopted my mother's last name—Ralle—and written Dr. *Major* off. Indeed, when I was ten and officially changed my name, my mother had told me that my father had been happy I had disowned him.

It had made no sense. Until now.

"Who are *they*?" I asked.

"I promise to answer that question in a few minutes. Just as soon as I know you're no longer confused about how the switch from one world to the other works."

"I'm sorry, I must be dense in this world. I'm still struggling with all the new concepts."

My father was sympathetic. "I know how you feel. On the surface the situation's simple. You live the same day over again in a slightly different world. But when you start to examine it from different angles, you get a headache. Trust me, I've been there, we all have."

"Did you have someone to guide you at the start?"

"No. You're lucky. After my hanging, when I woke up the next day, I felt like I had died and gone to hell. I would go to bed Saturday night and wake up Saturday morning and everyone would do the same thing they had done the day before. This went on for months, until I realized that if I suddenly did something drastic in witch world, out of the norm, then I could change events in the real world."

"What do you mean by drastic?"

My father studied me. "Understand, I was born in what you would consider a barbaric society. Back then life was cheap."

"Don't tell me you killed someone."

"I killed three men in self-defense, and I used my unique abilities to accomplish the deed. They had been sent by a local magistrate to arrest me for, well, getting one of his daughters pregnant. I met them alone, with a sword, in what seemed from the outside to be a fair fight. But one of my abilities is supernormal strength and speed. They didn't stand a chance."

"What happened the next day?" I asked, thinking I had the same ability.

"They came for me again. But I knew they were coming so I fled at dawn. I didn't want to have to kill them again." My father paused. "It was only later that I discovered they had been hijacked on the road and slaughtered."

"By who?"

"I don't know, and it doesn't matter. What matters is that they died anyway, and on the same day."

"But not in the same way," I said.

"Correct," my father agreed.

"Does that mean what happens in this world affects the real world?"

"Yes. But not always in the way you expect. Also, the reverse can happen. What occurs in the real world can change what happens in witch world. The worlds are interconnected. It's wrong to say one is more important than the other."

For some reason, I didn't feel what he said was completely accurate. Not that my father was purposely lying to me, but that his understanding was incomplete. The feeling had a sharp edge to it, a certainty, and I wondered if there was an intuition gene and I had been born with it.

I no sooner thought the question when the word "yes" popped into my mind. I went to tell my father about the experience but something stopped me. Maybe it was my intuition.

"But the days in witch world come first," I said.

"We experience them as occurring first. To someone as old as Cleo, they happen simultaneously."

"Who's Cleo?"

"The head of our Council. The one with the eight genes."

"She must be pretty powerful."

"That's an understatement."

"Are you saying her days overlap?"

"Yes."

"How does her brain cope with that?"

"It's hard to imagine. Over time, she must have gotten used to it."

"How old is Cleo?" I asked.

"She's been around since the beginning."

"Of witch world?"

"Of human civilization. She's never told anyone her exact age but we know she was alive before the pyramids were built. In fact, she helped build them."

"So she runs the Council?" I asked.

"It doesn't work that way. She's not the boss. But when Cleo speaks, everyone listens."

"Are you a member of the Council?"

"No. But I work closely with them."

"Russell wanted me to meet with certain people tonight. I think he was talking about the Council."

My father waved a hand. "He was but it's too late for that now. Besides, security at this hotel is far from foolproof. There's a chance you were followed here."

"Followed by who?"

He hesitated. "The Lapras."

"Finally. I assume those are the bad guys."

"Yes. I'll tell you all about them after I finish the overview of my life story. It'll help you understand the two worlds better."

"It's cool just getting to know you better."

My remark made him smile. "Thank you."

"You're welcome," I said.

"I mentioned the three men I killed. The deed didn't trouble me much and it seemed to have no major effect on witch world or the real world. Actually, my life was pretty carefree in those days, especially when I discovered that I could stop my body from aging. Each of my powers manifested slowly but steadily and it didn't take too many years before I accumulated tremendous wealth. In time I was knighted by Queen Elizabeth herself for my courage and generosity. I was even instrumental in helping my country drive off the Spanish Armada."

"I'm surprised you're not in the history books," I teased.

"I was but the Council had my name erased. It was shortly

after the failed armada that they became aware of me, and sent someone for me. I remember how frightened I was to meet a group of people with powers like mine, only greater. However, as soon as I was introduced to the Council, I knew I was among friends. They were such a loving group. They told me that I wasn't alone in the world, but that it was better if I kept a low profile and didn't call attention to myself."

"I can see the reasons for keeping a low profile. But why doesn't the Council help mankind?"

"Why do you assume it doesn't?"

I shrugged. "I have never read about their good deeds on the Internet."

My father smiled. "They do help, from time to time, but they do so quietly—you might even say reluctantly. They don't like to infringe on people's free will. It's impossible for them to use their powers to help society out of a jam without causing some alteration in the natural course of events."

"When have they helped?" I asked.

"A few times when it looked like civilization might collapse. They were a big help during World War Two, when the Allies defeated the Axis powers. They steered the Nazis away from developing the atomic bomb. For that matter, since those days, they've been instrumental at keeping nuclear weapons under control."

"You call the others the Lapras. Do you have a name for yourselves?"

"The Tar."

"What does that mean?"

"Cleo chose the word. She says it means 'the old ones.'"

"Tell me more about your life."

"I brought up World War Two. After that conflict the Council became aware of two phenomena. Events in the real world were beginning to diverge more and more from events in witch world. And the Lapras had organized themselves into a potent force."

"Had the Tar been aware of the Lapras before then?"

"Yes. But they hadn't paid them much attention. They saw them as a bunch of selfish witches who had accidentally stumbled upon their powers. For example, the Lapras almost all held positions of power in society, even though the Council had warned them that it was a mistake to become well known."

"Did the Council ever use its power to kill the Lapras?"

"Only when they acted totally out of control."

"Are any Lapras historical figures?" I asked.

"Yes. But I'm not at liberty to give out names. Let me continue with my tale. As I mentioned, we began to notice that witch world no longer mirrored the real world the way it used to. The Council knew of only one thing that could cause that. Witches who were behaving badly."

"Because they were awake in both worlds," I said.

"Right. Only people with the extra genes could consciously decide to act in such a way that their behavior in witch world was no longer the same as it was in the real world. Up until World War Two, there had been too few of us to impact society, unless we chose to do so deliberately, which was rare. But suddenly, for seemingly no reason, tons of witches were waking up. And virtually all of them were joining the Lapras."

"Were more people being born with the genes?"

"That was happening. Like I said, their appearance in our race is a natural phenomenon. But that wasn't the real problem. It was the way these people were being found and awakened. The Lapras were finding them. They were seeking them out. And the way they were activating their powers was brutal. We estimate that eighty percent of the people they put through the death experience didn't survive to tell the tale."

"What kind of numbers are we talking about?"

"These are only estimates but we believe the Lapras have identified and tried to activate fifty thousand people. That's worldwide."

"And only ten thousand survived?"

"Yes."

"But forty thousand deaths. How could the Lapras hide such a thing?"

"People disappear all the time. The FBI has thousands of unsolved cases every year. Murder has been epidemic since mankind learned to swing a stick, and in developing countries disease is so rampant, forty thousand deaths is nothing. Hiding their failed experiments has never been a problem for the Lapras."

"Yesterday, Russell showed me the scanner. Do the Lapras use a similar device to identify people with witch genes?"

"They're the ones who invented the scanner."

"I don't understand. Russell works for their company."

My father hesitated. "What I'm going to tell you next is very secret. It's important you tell no one. Not James or Alexis or any of their counterparts in the real world."

"I understand."

"Russell's a double agent. The Lapras believe he's spying on us, when in reality he works very closely with the Council."

"You're absolutely sure he's not a triple agent? Is it possible he really works for the Lapras?" I couldn't help but recall how he had tried to seduce me, when he knew I was with Jimmy. At the same time, I had vague memories of flirting with him in witch world. It was frustrating not being able to remember the details of our relationship. For all I knew, he was a lover.

"When you meet Cleo, you'll realize there's no way he would be able to fool her," my father said. "She has total confidence in Russell."

"Does he work with the scanner company to keep tabs on them?"

"Yes. We have it now but the Lapras had it first and it gave them a tremendous advantage over us. They could get to people with extra genes before we could. And once the Lapras activated someone, they would invariably tell them their way of life was the only way."

"What is the Lapras' way of life?" I asked.

"They see themselves as superior beings, the natural rulers of mankind. Their people inevitably seek out positions of power—in the government, the military, industry. There's hardly a senator or congressman in DC who doesn't have their support, or who's not one themselves."

"Dad, I'm sorry, you're beginning to lose me."

"You don't believe in power-hungry witches?"

"I would expect that. The wrong people always seem to make the most money and get elected to the highest offices. I'm not naive, I know mankind is selfish. It's just hard to imagine a huge conspiracy that's secretly working to take over the world."

My father gestured to the bright lights of the Strip. "You had a chance to stroll around witch world before coming here. What did you think of our alternate dimension?"

"Frankly, what I saw gave me the creeps."

"Why?"

"The people seemed afraid of their own shadows. They were all worried if I was connected or not."

"Did they know what you were connected to?"

"I don't know, I'm not sure."

My father nodded. "Let's take a lesson from history. In Italy, in the years following World War Two, after Mussolini was killed, the criminals gathered together and formed what became known as the Mafia. It existed before the war, of course, but from the mid-forties on, it grew so swiftly it became more powerful than the official government. Think about that for a moment. Italy had a constitution, it was a democratic nation. It had elected officials and laws everyone had voted on. Yet the average man had no faith in these laws. The police and officials who were supposed to enforce them were corrupt. If a person wanted justice, he had to go to the Mafia. But in those days, they didn't even say the word Mafia aloud. They feared to, it was so powerful. But if they needed help in business, or if someone in their family had been harmed, they ran to the Mafia and the Mafia delivered."

"Dad. I've seen *The Godfather*."

"That dealt with the American Mafia, which was only a shadow of its predecessor across the sea. What you felt tonight while walking around witch world was how it felt to live in Italy after the war. Tell me, while you were out tonight, were you accosted?"

"How do you know that?"

"I sensed it. What happened?"

"Three guys tried to mug me. They might have tried to rape me, had I given them the chance."

"What did you do?"

"I fought them off."

"Did that surprise you? That you were able to fight them off?"

"Sure."

"I bet it surprised them as well. Before these guys attacked, did they first try to find out if you were connected?"

"Yes."

"What did you tell them?"

"I didn't know what to say. It happened so fast. But after I beat them to a pulp, I went from being called pretty sister to being addressed as Mother."

"'Mother' refers to a woman who's connected. They would have called me 'Father.' They're Lapra expressions but the public can't tell us apart."

"But they know you exist?" I asked.

"The general population has become sensitive to people with power, and they've learned to fear them. That's the work of the Lapras. In this world, on the surface, our nation has the same constitution as the U.S. government. The identical number of senators and congressmen and Supreme Court justices. Yet something similar to the Mafia has taken over and the average person knows it's more powerful than the government. Few talk about it, they're too afraid. Especially here in Las Vegas."

"What's special about Vegas?"

"The Lapras have a lot of their people here."

I shivered. "I wish I didn't have to spend so much time here."

"Witch world has advantages over the real world. Your powers will develop here much more quickly and they'll help you get around."

"By scaring people?" I asked.

"You won't have to do that. But it must be obvious to you by now that the Lapras have focused on first taking over witch world. That's why this world's become a gloomy place. Yet what they do here also damages the real world."

"Give me an example," I said.

"Let's take my job in the real world as a medical doctor. Did you know that sixty years ago I treated cancer in three ways—with chemotherapy, surgery, and radiation? Now, more than half a century later, if I use anything other than those three methods to cure a patient, I'll lose my license and probably go to jail."

"Really?"

"Frightening, isn't it?"

"Yes. But what does that have to do with the Lapras?"

"They see normal human beings as inferior. They plan to be the next dominant life form on this planet. They don't want mankind to live long and healthy lives."

"So they're messing with our health-care system?"

"They have complete control of the American Medical Association and the Food and Drug Administration."

"Do they plan on wiping out normal people?" I asked.

"Perhaps. At the very least they want humanity under their control. That's why they've taken over witch world. It gives them a head start when it comes to taking over the real world." My father paused. "That's why they have to be stopped."

"Surely you don't blame the Lapras for all of our problems?"

"Not at all. But they're preventing men and women of goodwill from solving the problems facing both worlds. They're poisoning all levels of society."

I shook my head. "I wish you hadn't told me all these things."

"It's important that you know."

"Why?"

"Because you can help us. You might be able to help us more than you realize."

"What are you talking about?" I asked.

"Your daughter. Lara."

"My daughter is an infant. She's not some kind of weapon."

"She was born with ten witch genes."

"I thought nobody had them all."

"Lara is the first," my father said.

I felt anger rise inside. "Then if she was so important to you and your bloody Council, how come you let the Lapras steal her away?"

My father didn't answer right away. He turned and stared out the window at the pageant of colored lights. It seemed right then that I could sense the weight of his age. His body had not grown weary but perhaps his soul had.

"I remember the night Lara came to us," he said finally. "There was a full moon in the sky, straight overhead, and the whole world felt as if it were bathed in a sweet radiance.

The light seemed to come from a celestial realm. There was music, too, not a sound I heard with my ears, but a vibration inside, which filled me with incredible joy. I thought it was my imagination—the dreams of a proud grandfather running wild. But when I spoke to the members of the Council, they said they felt the same thing. When Lara was born, it was as if a great being entered the world."

"You're scaring me, Dad."

"Why?"

"You sound like a religious fanatic."

He smiled. "Maybe I am. But Cleo felt the same way I did and she's not easily moved. She privately named the child Isis, an ancient name for the divine mother. Isis was the primary Egyptian goddess. Legend has it that she bathes her devotees with a healing white light at the time of death."

"Does Cleo believe this light activates the witch genes during the death experience?"

"That's a shrewd insight. Cleo says that's how the death experience pushes us on to the next level in human evolution."

I shook my head. "I don't know. If this Cleo's so wise, why wasn't she able to protect my baby?"

"You were heavily guarded. The Council was watching both of you night and day. But on the seventh night something strange happened, something we had never encountered before. A red cloud seemed to descend on the house where you were staying. It was probably more mental than physical, although it caused the stars to dim and the moon to vanish. Suddenly, we all became confused, and none of us knew exactly where you and Lara were. Our panic grew and we kept searching the house but we couldn't even keep track of each other. When the red cloud finally lifted, at dawn, we realized someone had snuck into the house and taken the child."

I wiped at the tears on my cheeks. The loss had returned with almost the same pain as before. I had to struggle to breathe.

"But your Council's so old, so wise. They must have a theory how this happened," I said.

"Ask them when you meet with them tomorrow."

"I will. How old is Lara now?"

"She must be close to a month."

I nodded sadly. "She was born right around the same time as Jimmy's baby."

"The Lapras took him as well."

I almost jumped from my seat. "What are you talking about? Jimmy's baby is dead."

"They just led Jimmy to think that."

"How?"

"They stole another baby from somewhere else and killed it and gave him the body. At that age, tons of babies look alike. They didn't have to use an elaborate scheme to fool Jimmy and Kari."

"How could they do such a thing?" I gasped.

"The Lapras will do anything to achieve their goals. They appear to be devoid of empathy."

"Why did they take our babies?"

"They took Lara because they somehow scanned her cells and discovered she possesses all ten genes. They see her as a potential ally."

"A one-month-old baby."

"The Lapras think long-term."

"Why did they take Jimmy and Kari's baby?"

"Probably to manipulate Jimmy so he will put pressure on you—when the time is right."

"What does that mean?"

"The Lapras know we're going to try to get Lara back. The more leverage they can exert over Jimmy, the better. Remember, all he knows about is Huck. Only James knows about Lara. Lara will mean nothing to Jimmy."

"But when I explain that she's his daughter . . ."

"We'll see," my father said. He glanced at his watch. "Russell should be back soon."

"What kind of errand did you send him on?"

"It concerns Lara. But let him explain how it went when he returns."

"Russell acted shocked that I ended up in the morgue. But it seems you guys wanted me to get kidnapped and dumped in that meat locker. What went wrong?"

"The Lapras kidnapped you from the meat locker before we could get there."

"I assume you had me heavily guarded?" I said sarcastically.

He lowered his head. "We took every precaution."

"I'm sorry, Dad. I had no right to snap at you like that."

"No. We deserve it." He looked miserable. "I'm a doctor and you're my daughter. The Council put me in charge of reviving you. There were four of us in a van. We knew when you had been placed in the freezer and when you would begin to pass out from hypothermia. We also had two people at the freezer. They had a camera on you and were sending us a live feed of what you were doing."

"You saw me talking to the steer and using the hook to break the hinges?"

"That was very clever. But I'm your father, it was torture to watch you suffering. At the same time, if you had escaped, we would have had to start all over again."

"What happened next?" I asked.

"We lost our live feed. We tried calling the men guarding the meat locker but neither responded. Then the same thing happened the night Lara was taken. A red haze came and we began to have trouble communicating with each other. It was like we were all speaking a foreign language we had never heard before. Then we got lost."

"On your way to the meat locker?"

"I know it sounds impossible. I know every street in this

city. But it didn't matter which way we turned. We kept coming back to the same place."

"Where?"

He shrugged. "Nowhere. We were driving in circles. It went on for hours. Finally, it was as if a veil lifted and we knew which way to go. But when we reached the freezer, you were gone and our partners were dead, their throats slit. They had been murdered."

"Were they friends of yours?"

"Yes."

"I'm so sorry." I paused. "I understand how I froze to death in the real world. But when I woke up here, in witch world, I was frozen as well. Who put me in the meat locker here?"

My father hesitated. "It must have been the Lapras."

"And they froze me in exactly the same place?"

Before he could respond, there was a knock at the door, four quick taps. We both stood. "Hello?" my father called.

"It's me," Russell replied.

My father let him in and immediately asked how things had gone. Russell looked pleased. "Excellent," he said.

"What's this all about?" I asked.

"There's a phone call you have to make," Russell said.

"To who?"

"The Lapras," Russell said.

"Huh?" I thought I would be sick.

My father glanced at his watch. "It's a complex situation.

It's probably better the Council explain it to you tomorrow. For now, the Lapras have contacted Russell, and through him they have made it clear they want to meet with you."

"Why?" I asked.

My father answered. "Lara's upset she's been taken from her mother. And it seems she's upsetting her captors."

"How? Is she crying nonstop?" I asked.

Russell grinned. "I think she's doing a lot worse than that."

My father reached for the phone. "It's getting near dawn. We have to call them soon."

I shook my head. "Please, don't rush me."

"The call doesn't have to be long," Russell said. "All they want you to do is to agree to meet them at a certain time and place. Try to make the meeting near midnight. That's midnight in witch world."

"Why?" I asked.

"So you can meet with the Council first," my father said.

I tried to think fast. "Do you guys know where Lara is?"

"I told you she's in Las Vegas," my father said.

"How can you be sure?" I asked.

"Las Vegas is their main center of power," my father said. "Not so long ago the government used to test atomic weapons in the desert not far from here. These tests were supposed to have been curtailed years ago but they still go on, at least underground. The Lapras have a major interest in man-made radiation because it leads to mutation, and mutation leads to evolution, eventually, although most mutations are of a negative type. The Lapras don't care, they're only interested in creating more people with witch genes. If they have to ruin a hundred to make one, they're happy."

"You mean they deliberately expose normal people to radiation?" I asked.

"Yes," my father said. "It's a long story. We don't have time to go into it now. Just trust that we know they would keep Lara in Las Vegas. Besides, the Council can feel her here, although we don't know exactly where she is."

"Why don't you know?" I persisted.

"They keep moving her around," Russell said.

"Wait," I said, turning to Russell. "Did you contact them about talking to me or did they contact you?"

"They contacted me," Russell said.

"Let's place the call," my father said.

"Wait! What's Lara done to force them to contact me?"

My father shrugged and turned to Russell.

Russell spoke carefully. "It seems Lara is an especially aware child, and she wants her mother back. To keep her happy, the Lapras say they're willing to work with you."

I was confused. "Why should they care if my daughter's miserable? They don't strike me as a sensitive lot."

Russell answered. "We think she's making them pay for what they've done. That's our best guess."

"Pay how?" I asked.

"We don't know," my father said, growing impatient.

I could see I was pushing it. I pointed to the phone. "All right. Go ahead, make the call," I said.

My father handed the phone to Russell, who quickly dialed the number from memory. "The less you talk, the better," Russell said. "Many ears will be listening on the other end. Just agree on the time and place and get off."

"Fine," I said, feeling extremely nervous.

Russell finished dialing. I could hear it ringing. Someone picked up. Russell began to speak.

"Hello. . . . Yes, it's me. . . . Yes, I know the time. . . . Yeah, she's right here. . . . She's agreed to cooperate. . . . Of course . . . Yes . . . You can speak to her now."

Russell gave me the phone. I struggled to keep my hand from shaking. "Hello?" I said.

A man with a haunting voice spoke. He hardly sounded human; his words could have been electronically created. At the same time, he was very persuasive.

"Hello, Jessica Ralle. It's a pleasure to finally speak to you. I've heard so much about you."

"Who is this?"

"My name is Frank."

"Frank. Are you the one who stole my child?"

I thought I *heard* him smile, if such a thing were possible over the phone. "We didn't steal her. We merely moved her to a more secure location. You're free to visit her whenever you wish." He added, "It's our understanding you want to meet and discuss her future."

Russell, who was leaning close enough to hear, nodded.

"Yes," I said. "But I want to meet in a public place of my own choosing."

"We'll meet where we choose to meet," Frank interrupted. "We'll pick you and Russell up in front of the Mirage at midnight, tomorrow night, this time zone. Understood?"

"No. I want to—"

"This is not negotiable."

I felt frustrated but Russell indicated I was to accept the meeting.

"I'll agree to your terms on two conditions. First, Lara must be with you when you pick me up. Otherwise, I'm not getting in the car."

"She'll be there, I promise," Frank said.

"Second, I want to talk to her right now."

"Talk to her?"

"Yes. Put her on the phone."

"She's an infant. She can't talk yet."

"Put her on the phone or the meeting's off. And that is not negotiable."

There was a moment while Frank seemed to move his phone.

Suddenly I heard a delicious cooing sound. It was just baby talk, pure nonsense, and it made every cell in my body come alive.

"Lara, this is your mommy!" I gushed. "Mommy's going to see you real soon! I promise!"

The cooing sound ceased. Frank came back on the line.

"Are you satisfied?" he asked.

"I'll be satisfied when I get her back."

"Then come to the meeting with an open mind."

Frank hung up. Russell smiled and gave me a thumbs-up. My father reached out and hugged me. He touched my cheek, brushing away a tear. I still didn't understand why he had left me to grow up without a father. I needed to know he loved me.

Yet I felt his love then.

"You did well, Jessica," he said.

I wept. "I just want her back. I don't care what it takes."

My father nodded. "We're going to do whatever it takes."

CHAPTER ELEVEN

THE FOLLOWING MORNING, I CAME TO ON A BENCH three blocks from the Strip and six blocks from the MGM. I hiked back to the hotel, wondering why the Lapras had chosen to dump me in such a nondescript place. While I walked, I tried to figure out what to tell the others. I assumed they would be happy to see me, and pissed.

I figured right.

The shit hit the fan when I stumbled through my hotel door and waved hi to everyone. Waves of hugs and heated questions quickly followed. Everyone seemed to be talking at once, I couldn't get a word in edgewise. Of course they wanted to know where the hell I had disappeared to.

I ran through my prepared speech. I was careful not to deviate from it.

"I'm sorry I scared you yesterday when I vanished. It

wasn't something I planned. And I didn't fail to call because I wanted to scare you all. You guys know I'm not a drama queen. But some stuff has happened that I have to talk to Jimmy about in private and no, I wasn't out with another guy. It's complicated. I'll explain everything after Jimmy and I talk. Okay?"

Alex raised her hand. "Excuse me, Double-O-Seven. Take a look at my eyes. Notice they're bloodshot. Check out Debbie's and Jimmy's eyes. You'll see they're just as red. None of us has been able to relax since you disappeared. I don't know about the others but I think I deserve a hell of a lot more than that silly canned speech you just gave."

"Absolutely," Debbie said.

"You did put us through hell," Ted said.

I held up a hand. "I'll tell you more later. But it's important I talk to Jimmy first."

"I'm your best friend," Alex said.

"I thought I was her best friend," Debbie said.

"Jessie just lets you think that," Alex said.

Al, Alex's new squeeze, stood up. Alex had already introduced us; he seemed like a nice guy. Physically, he was far from imposing. On the short side, he was slightly plump, with a baby face and long, tangled brown hair. Yet there was a strength to his voice, and he was obviously very intelligent.

"I think we should let Jessie talk when she feels like talking. A weekend in Las Vegas is a big deal to me and I don't want to waste any more time worrying about where she was. So let's do what Jessie wants and drop it."

Alex glared at Al before stalking off to her room.

"She's not a morning person," I tried to reassure him.

"She does have an hour every other week when she's real sweet," Debbie added.

Jimmy was rubbing my shoulders. "What would you like for breakfast?" he asked.

"Coffee, bacon, scrambled eggs, sausage, wheat toast," I said.

Jimmy reached for the phone but then glanced around the room—the mental temperature of the suite was still pretty high—and appeared to change his mind.

"Let's eat downstairs," Jimmy said.

I agreed. I dressed quickly and got out of there with Jimmy before anyone else could give me another speech. Frankly, I was grateful to Alex's new friend. Al seemed the most composed of the lot. When we were leaving the suite, he was busy calling the police to tell them that Jessica Ralle had returned safe and sound and was no longer a missing person.

I pleaded with Jimmy not to question me while we ate, to just let us enjoy our food. Patient as always, he bowed to my wish. I think he was so relieved to see me again, alive and well, he wasn't yet in the mood to chew me out. At the same time, I knew his patience had its limits. I had to satisfy his questions.

There was no way he was going to believe my bizarre tale without a clear demonstration of my powers. I was prepared to give him that, but I wasn't sure what abilities my seven witch genes represented. Other than telling me I was a potential healer, my father had remained mute on that subject.

I knew I was strong and fast, and that I was somewhat intuitive. But I had no idea how long it would take for my powers to fully manifest. My father had hinted that it could take years, and that they changed form over time.

I was famished. I ate a ton and I was pleased to discover I didn't get a bellyache. Jimmy raised an eyebrow when I finished off the bulk of the scrambled eggs and ate most of the toast, his two favorite morning foods.

"I can always order more," I said.

He smiled. "It's fun watching you eat."

"Fun?"

"Haven't you ever heard that guys get turned on by women who have huge appetites?"

"I read that. It's just that I've never put you in the category of a normal guy."

"I'll take that as a compliment. What do you want to do today?"

"Rent a car and drive a hundred miles out of town."

"I'm sorry, I don't think I can afford that."

I waved my hand. "Don't worry about money. I told you at the lake, I hit a lucky streak at the blackjack table."

"You did? I just remember the gifts some stranger gave you. How much did you win?"

"A lot. Let's talk about it after we get out of here. For now, I need to know if you've heard from Kari."

Jimmy's face darkened. "She's still in town. She called, and when I told her you had disappeared, she didn't act surprised. She said you'd be back, but I probably wouldn't recognize you. Then she hung up."

Another sign Kari knew about witch world. But how? Who had connected her? After my call with Frank, my father and Russ had told me Kari had only two witch genes, and that two was the minimum it took to wake up in the other dimension. Yet they had given me the impression that most people with two genes had a hard time making the jump.

I hoped Kari wasn't in contact with the Lapras. It made no sense she would have befriended them. They had, after all, stolen Huck. But perhaps they had gotten to her early and put the blame on the Tar. That could be bad. I was counting on Kari's help. We both had the same goal—we both wanted our kid back.

Jimmy studied me as I pondered these problems. My dad had said he had five witch genes total. He was a heavy hitter. Yet my dad had given a thumbs-down to the idea of putting Jimmy through the death experience.

"Chances are he wouldn't survive it," my father had said.

"Why not?" I had asked.

"He doesn't have the healing gene."

"But you said not everyone needed it to have their other genes activated."

"True. But even I would be reluctant to bring Jimmy that close to death, and I'm a heart surgeon and an expert when it comes to resuscitating people. He's too valuable to the Council to risk."

"Because he has so many genes?"

"That's one reason. There are others."

Back at the breakfast table, Jimmy continued to study me. "Did Kari have anything to do with your vanishing act?" he asked.

"Not directly. But she's connected to some stuff that's going on in my life."

"How so?"

"I'll tell you in the car." I stood from the table. "Can you give me a few minutes? I have to get something out of the hotel vault."

"What?"

"Money." I leaned over and kissed him. "I won't be long."

I had a Bank of America debit card that also doubled as a Visa credit card. The problem was I had almost no money in the account. But the hotel had ATMs that allowed a person to make instant deposits in their account—if they had cash. That was why I was anxious to get to my bag of money. I wanted to get my card up to steam so I could rent a comfortable four-wheel-drive SUV with plenty of power.

I ended up with a Ford Expedition. The guy at the Hertz counter told me it handled the best on off-road terrain. That was what I cared about the most. I didn't explain to Jimmy why

I wanted the extra power until we were in the vehicle and heading out of town. I let him drive, he liked to drive long distances.

"Remember at the start of the fourth Indiana Jones film?" I said. "How Indy ended up in a fabricated town that was used to measure the effects of nuclear bombs on houses, benches, trees—normal stuff like that."

"Sure. I also remember how Indy saved himself from a nuclear blast by hiding in a refrigerator. Always meant to drop Spielberg a line about how impossible that was."

I chuckled. "Hey, it was a fun scene. Who cares if it was realistic? The reason I bring it up is those towns are still out here, in the desert. Do you know that back in the fifties it was a favorite Las Vegas pastime to go out on your hotel balcony and watch the army light off a nuclear bomb? The people would actually see the mushroom cloud and feel the heat of the blast on their faces. They weren't worried about the radiation at all."

"I assume a lot of those people later got cancer," Jimmy said.

"It's possible."

Jimmy looked over at me. "Don't tell me you want to go visit those towns?"

"Yes."

Jimmy snorted. "Could you think of a worse place to visit? Radioactive particles linger in the sand. Can't we go somewhere a little more healthy?"

I held up the travel book I'd bought in the hotel gift shop. "I read up on the towns. The background radiation is higher than normal but it's not supposed to be dangerous if you don't stay too long."

"Does this craving to visit these towns have anything to do with your disappearance?" he asked.

"Yes. Keep driving and I'll explain when we stop."

"I wish you would drop the suspense," he said.

I glanced over my shoulder, trying to make sure we weren't being followed. "What I have to tell you is going to be hard to swallow. We're going to need plenty of privacy, and you're going to have to keep an open mind."

"As long as we have sex when you're done talking."

I reached over and messed up his hair. "That's my boy."

My mother called my cell while we drove. She wanted to know how Las Vegas was. I wasn't surprised the secret was already out of the bag. My mom didn't act the least bit upset. In fact, she sounded happy to hear I was with Jimmy. She had always liked him. But then I ruined things by telling her I had spoken to my father.

"He called you?" she asked.

"Yeah. Don't get upset. He apologized for not coming to the graduation ceremony. He told me he'd make it up to me."

"How?"

"By paying for my college education."

My mother sighed. "I've heard this talk before. I hope you took everything he said with a grain of salt."

"It wasn't that way, Mom. We had a great talk. A lot of

things are clearer to me now. He's not the man you think he is."

"Then why did it take him four years to call you?"

"It's complicated. It's not something I can explain on the phone. I probably shouldn't have brought it up. I was just excited to see . . . to hear from him again."

"Tell me about it when you get home, Jessie. Just don't get your hopes up."

"Don't worry about me, Mom," I said.

Jimmy glanced over at me after I hung up. "How come you didn't tell me you spoke to your father?" he asked.

I shrugged. "There's a million things I've got to tell you."

"You're beginning to drive me nuts, you know that."

"Go twenty more miles then pull over to the side of the road."

"Why?"

"First a demonstration, then my explanation."

Twenty miles later he parked. I climbed out and walked a hundred yards away from the road. Jimmy followed. The sun looked like it had gone nova. It was so hot the sky could have been on fire. Fortunately, we had brought plenty of water bottles in the SUV.

"This should be far enough," I said, stopping. We hadn't taken a major artery out of town. The road traffic was sparse. Still, I didn't want anyone to see what we were up to.

Jimmy looked around. "If you want to have wild sex, I can think of more romantic spots."

"We're not here to screw. We're here to fight."

"Huh?"

I shoved him in the chest. "I want you to try to beat me up."

He tried to grab my hands as I shoved but he missed. I was as fast as I was strong. "Jessie, if this is your idea of a joke, I'm not laughing."

"It's not a joke. I told you, it's a demonstration."

"Of what?"

"The fact that I can kick your ass."

"Since when?"

"Since yesterday." I shoved him again, hard enough to knock him down. "Get up and defend yourself, mister. And know this—if you don't fight as hard as you can, I'm going to make you bleed."

Like most guys, Jimmy had a streak of macho in him and didn't like being pushed around. He jumped up quick and began to circle me, his fists ready.

"What if I hit you in the face?" he asked. "You'll bruise. How am I going to explain that to the others?"

"You're too slow to touch my face," I said, and with that I stepped forward, slapped his nose, and backed off. He blinked, dazed. My attack must have looked like a blur to him. Plus his nose was bleeding freely, although I had used only a fraction of my strength.

"Jesus Christ, Jessie!" he howled.

"I told you, I'm not fooling around. You've got to fight me. You've got to give me a hundred percent."

"Have you been taking lessons?" he asked, returning to his circling.

"Lessons in what?"

"Self-defense. Who taught you to move like that?"

"It's not the move. It's me."

"What's that mean?"

I stood perfectly still. "Jump me. Tackle me."

He wiped at his nose. "I could hurt you."

"Do it, you pussy!" To anger him further, I kicked sand in his face. Few things are more irritating than dust in the eyes. The only thing you can do is pour water over them until they're washed clean. But my strategy worked, I had definitely stung Jimmy's macho. He rushed toward me angrily.

"You bitch!" he cried.

I stood my ground. I could only imagine what it must have felt like for him when we collided. It was like I was made of stone. He bounced off me and would have hit the ground but I grabbed him before he could fall and lifted him over my head. There was a nearby sand dune. I threw him toward it, trying to make it so that he landed safely. He was able to brace his fall with his feet and hands but he still groaned in pain.

I ran to the SUV and was back in seconds with two bottles of water. I rested his head in my lap. "I have water," I said. "Lie still and let me pour it over your eyes. I have to wash out the dust."

"How did you do that?" he gasped, the blood from his nose mixing with his dirty face.

"Talk in a minute. Try to keep your eyes wide open. That's it, the water's washing the dust away. You're going to be fine."

It took several minutes to clean him off and two extra bottles of water, but eventually his eyes cleared and he could see without blinking. He jumped up, angry, he wanted to know what the hell was going on.

"I'm a witch," I said calmly.

He stumbled toward the SUV, his shirt dripping. "Start making sense or this is going to be a short date," he swore.

I chased after him, stopped him by grabbing him around the waist, pinning his arms to his upper body. He struggled to get free but it was useless.

"It's true, honey. I'm sorry I had to be so rough on you to drive home the point. But out here I couldn't think of another way to convince you. If it's any comfort, just know that I went through a thousand times worse after I was kidnapped."

"Who kidnapped you?"

"Other witches."

"That's insane!"

"Can you move?"

"No!"

"That's right, you can't budge an inch. You figure I have, what, ten times your strength? Let me tell you, I can jack it up even higher."

"You're hurting me!"

I released him. "Sorry. This is all new to me. I don't know my own strength."

He plopped down in the sand and stared up at me. "Start at the beginning."

"You don't want to talk in the air-conditioned Expedition?"

He groaned as he felt his arms and legs for breaks. "I don't know if I can make it that far."

"I can carry you."

He shook his head, annoyed, and slowly climbed to his feet.

"You didn't have to give such a lively demonstration."

"I told you I was sorry," I said. We headed for the SUV, with him limping. "I do have to tell you something up front, before I go through the whole story."

"What?"

"Huck is alive. Your son is alive."

I realized I was taking a terrible chance bringing up Huck, particularly at the beginning. Jimmy could get angry and shut down completely. But I felt I had to take the chance. I needed to shock him out of his mind-set. Our fight had impressed him—it had not prepared him to hear about miracles.

He stopped dead. "No."

"You know me, Jimmy. I wouldn't dare kid you about a thing like that. I know for an absolute fact that Huck is alive. So does Kari. That's why she said the things she did at the lake. I told you how she acted like your son had been kidnapped. Well, she wasn't lying. The child you were given to bury wasn't yours. You were deceived by some pretty evil people."

"Are they wicked witches?" he asked, a note of sarcasm in his voice.

"You can call them that."

He hesitated, obviously afraid to let hope gain life inside him. No one understood that feeling better than I did. People usually saw hope as a positive emotion, when I knew that more often than not it was a prescription for pain.

"What would they want with Huck?" he asked quietly.

I took him by the arm, let him lean on me for support. "I'll explain everything while we're driving. All I ask is you keep your mind *way* open. The shit that's happened to me since I saw you yesterday is almost impossible to imagine, never mind believe."

"You're not going to throw me around anymore, are you?"

"That was a one-time deal," I promised.

"Okay. I'll try to keep an open mind."

We got back in the SUV, cranked the air conditioner up high. This time I drove. Jimmy looked too sore to manage the gas and the brake.

My explanation got off to a bad start. I had to begin with Russ and inevitably I told a few white lies about our encounter. That wouldn't have been a problem except that Jimmy was a

mind reader, probably because of his witch gene and the fact
that he was so sincere himself.

I told Jimmy how Alex and I were intrigued by the way
Russ played blackjack, particularly the way he kept winning.
But Jimmy got hung up on exactly why Alex split and left me
alone with the guy.

"He gave her bad advice on a hand," I said.

"That's it? That wasn't his fault. No one can predict how
the cards are going to fall."

"That's just it. Russ knew when a good hand was coming,
or when the dealer was going to bust."

"Because he's a witch too?"

"That's right."

"Did Alex know he was a witch?"

"Of course not."

"Then why did she get mad that he couldn't predict when
she'd get a winning hand?"

"Please. Just let me continue."

It was hard to go on, though, and this was supposed to be
the easy part. When I told him how much money Russ and I
had won, Jimmy shook his head and said he would have to see
it to believe it. I assured him it was in a bag in a safe back at the
MGM. I also assured him that Russ wasn't hitting on me, that
he just wanted to catch my attention with his unique abilities.
But Jimmy began to squirm when I told him how we met back
at his hotel room.

"Why did you go there?" he asked.

"My ID was fake. I couldn't claim the money I'd won. He had to claim it for me. He took the bulk of the money in the form of a check, but he gave me a hundred thousand in cash."

"You just said you won fifty-seven thousand."

"I know. But he let me have extra."

"And he didn't want anything in return?" Jimmy asked.

"Money is meaningless to him. He can make as much as he wants." I paused. "Jimmy, if you're having trouble with this part of my story, I should quit now. This is nothing compared to what I have to tell you."

"Would you have trouble with a story like this?"

"Sure."

"How come you didn't tell me any of this yesterday? Like when we were up at the lake?"

"I didn't know what was going on yesterday. Now I do."

He sighed. "All right. Go on."

I decided to just keep talking. I led Jimmy through my instruction in twenty-two—red queen. I explained the scanner and how it could create a holographic image of a person's DNA code. Jimmy seemed to brighten up here. He had a strong interest in science. But I didn't mention making out with Russ. I told him I took a taxi back to the MGM and that was when I found him waiting outside my room.

"You didn't have a bag full of cash with you," he said.

"I told you, I had already put it in the hotel safe."

"Go on," Jimmy said.

I explained how I was kidnapped by the weird taxi driver and the rich woman with the Taser. When I got to the part where I woke up in a meat locker, Jimmy was shaking his head again but I kept talking. I went through my whole ordeal of breaking out of the freezer. How I failed—how I hurt my ankle and sat down to rest. How I began to doze and eventually blacked out.

I moved on to the morgue, to Dr. Dave and Dr. Susan. This part scared me to recall, and I hoped the obvious fear in my voice would add weight to my story. But Jimmy listened with his gaze focused outside the SUV window, if he was in fact listening.

By the time I escaped from the hospital, I decided my story wouldn't be enriched by my encounter with Wing, Moonshine, and Squat. I skipped that episode and told Jimmy I headed straight back to Russ's hotel. But rather than playing twenty-one inside the casino, everyone was playing twenty-two.

That was it, I had gone too far, at least in his mind. He stopped me.

"You honestly believe all this happened," he said.

"It's not a matter of belief. It happened."

"The entire city of Las Vegas gave up its favorite game for the night and decided to play twenty-two instead of twenty-one?"

"That's not what happened. It's more complicated than that."

"No, Jessie, it's actually more simple. Up until the time you met Russ, everything was normal. But then he went out of his way to separate you from Alex and the moment he did your fantasy started."

"This isn't a fantasy!"

He stared at me. "Pull over to the side of the road."

"No. You're in no shape to drive."

"You can keep driving but first you're going to listen. Pull over."

I did as he requested and we sat in silence for several minutes before he spoke. "Jessie, have you ever heard of STP?" he asked.

"That's a motor oil, isn't it?"

"Yes. It's a motor oil. It's also the initials of a drug far more powerful than LSD. I've been reading about it in the paper lately. It was created in the sixties but few people took it then because it was too scary. But now a modified version has reappeared and the police are worried. The person under the influence of it can be so convinced they have entered a new reality, they never come out of it." He reached over and took my hand. "Jessie, there are people in mental hospitals swearing that they are witches, warlocks, and wizards—all because of this drug."

I felt profoundly sad. I realized then there was a chance he'd never believe my story. And I couldn't blame him. I wouldn't have believed it.

"Are you saying Russ slipped me this drug at the blackjack table?"

"As soon as Alex was gone, the miracles started happening. That was no coincidence."

"What about the money we won?" I asked.

"Like I said, I'd have to see it to believe it."

"But when you see it, will you believe me?"

"No."

"Jimmy."

"How can you expect me to believe that for one night— no, make that two nights—all of Las Vegas was transformed into the Twilight Zone?"

"The transformation happens again and again, between today and tomorrow."

"And that sounds like reality to you?"

"Jimmy. You have no idea what I went through before I finally accepted all this."

"Did Russ keep hammering on you until you did accept it?"

"Russ and my father."

"Your father? Jessie, your father's not here."

"How do you know?"

"If he's here, then call him. Call him right now."

"I don't know his cell phone number."

"Jessie. Do you know how feeble that sounds?"

"Explain to me how I was able to beat you up."

"I don't know. I can't. But that doesn't mean you just returned from a journey to an alternate reality."

"My supernatural strength is a fact. My speed is also a fact." I pointed to a desert hill out the window. "How about we stop the driving and have a race to that hill?"

"Right. You forget how far-off objects often look closer in the desert. That hill is five miles away."

"What if I run there in ten minutes? Will you believe me then?"

"Five two-minute miles? That's impossible. The greatest runners on earth haven't been able to string together two four-minute miles in a row."

"Then you'll have proof." I opened the Expedition door.

"Shut the door, Jessie."

"Why?"

"Close it, please."

I closed the door. "I know what's wrong. I know why you can't believe me."

"I hope that's true. Are you beginning to accept that what you're saying is impossible?"

"That's not it. The Jimmy I know believes in the impossible. He believes in magic, or at least he used to believe in it." I paused. "It's because I told you Huck's still alive."

"That's not it."

"Yes, it is. When I told you your son was alive, you reacted with disbelief. But then you dropped it, you dropped it right away. The reason is because you can't go there. It's too painful. But the more I talk, the more you realize that's where my story's heading. That's why you've got to stop me."

"That's not true," he replied.

"But it is," I said.

Jimmy gripped his fists tightly together. I could see he wanted to get behind the wheel, turn around, head back to Las Vegas. "I swear, when I meet this Russ, I'm going to beat the shit out of him."

"That won't be easy," I said calmly.

He stared at me. "Do you have a crush on him?"

I smiled sadly. "You know I only have a crush on one boy. And he's sitting right in front of me."

Jimmy sat silent a long time. Then he reached out and put his arm around my shoulder, pulling me close.

"I'm sorry I said that," he said.

"It's all right."

"But I'm not sorry I stopped you. Your story may seem true to you but it's not. Right now, for one reason or another, you're delusional. Only it's not your fault. You say you know me, Jessie, and I can't argue with that. Even though I left you for Kari, I know you took me back because you know I love you. And I know you love me. That's how you were able to forgive me for going back to Kari. The bond between us is real, it's deep, and there's no way you'd intentionally try to hurt me by bringing up Huck unless that Russ guy hadn't screwed with your brain somehow. That's why I've listened to you this long. But now I have to stop you, and help you come back to reality."

"Thank you for your kind words. They mean a lot to me." I nuzzled his side and kissed his cheek before pulling back. "They just happen to be false. And the only way to prove that to you is to shock you again. Harder this time. So hard your head cracks wide open and you're able to accept a story about an entire town playing twenty-two."

Before he had a chance to react, I got out of the SUV and closed the door. Hurrying to the rear bumper, I knelt down and lifted up the back of the vehicle. This time I felt the weight but it seemed manageable. Creeping forward with my head beneath the driveshaft, I let my arms spread out wide and gripped the vehicle as close as I could to the edges. Inside the SUV, I could hear him shouting but paid him no heed.

When I reached the center of gravity, I allowed the front to lift off the ground so that I was holding the Ford Expedition six feet above the asphalt. Breathing hard, focused on my task, I began to walk up the road. I went maybe fifty yards, half a football field. Thank God the road was deserted.

"Jimmy!" I called finally.

He sounded close to hysteria. "Jessie?"

"Do you need any more proof?"

"No!"

"Are you sure? Can I put you down?"

"Yes!"

Crouching down, dropping to my knees, I slowly lowered the front of the vehicle and then the back. Finished, I rolled out from beneath it and brushed the dust off my shorts. I climbed back in the front seat.

"You look white as a ghost," I said with a smile.

He nodded in faint, jerky movements. "You look like a witch," he whispered.

I started the SUV. "Is it all right if I keep driving?"

"Yes."

"Would you like to hear the rest of my story?"

"Absolutely."

"Do you think I'm delusional?"

"No."

"Good." I leaned over and kissed him on the lips. "I love you, Jimmy. I love you in both worlds."

He stuttered. "I don't . . . I don't understand."

I put the vehicle in gear and gunned the engine. "Trust me, you will," I said.

Ninety minutes later we were stopped on a dirt road with our windshield covered in dust. Reaching for the wipers, I activated the sprinkler system and tried washing away the guck. It took a lot of fluid to get a clear view.

Jimmy was busy studying the maps in the travel book I had purchased at the hotel. "From what I can see, a lot of these towns will be cordoned off with high fences and barbed wire."

"I can handle that," I replied.

He glanced at me. "Please don't go crazy on me. I don't think my heart can take any more."

I laughed. "I'll try to behave. How close are we to ground zero?"

Jimmy squinted at the map. "Funny you should ask that. These places seem to be grouped in a rough semicircle around a big black *X* that's labeled 'Ground Zero'—in caps. The names of the towns are appropriate: Hades, Purgatory, Inferno, Fission's Fury, Blaze."

"Were they all built to determine what a certain-strength bomb would do to a certain-size city?"

"Yeah. But from what I've read, the army also stocked them with plenty of pigs. They put pigs in the houses, pigs in the barns, pigs in the basements—and they left a bunch of pigs outside."

"Why pigs?" I asked, not really wanting to know.

"Because pigskin resembles our skin the most closely. So does their cardiovascular system. That's why pigs' valves are still used in heart surgery. Plus pigs are one of the smartest animals in the world. The scientists probably wanted to see what kind of effect the radiation had on their whole bodies, their brains, and their skin."

"It disgusts me we could treat animals so cruelly," I said.

"Just think, we dropped two of these bombs on Japan. On real live people."

"That's a scary thought."

"Hey, you're the one who wanted to come out here. You know you still haven't told me why."

"My dad made a remark about how the Lapras experiment on human beings using the radiation left over from atomic tests. I want to see if it's true."

"Can't we just believe your dad and call it a day?"

"No." I was trying to avoid Jimmy's question and I think he sensed it. The real reason I had driven us to these towns was beyond reason. I had come here because I felt I had to come here. The name Inferno drew me the strongest. I asked Jimmy where it was located.

"It's to the right, east of here," he said. "It's pretty close to ground zero."

"That's our destination," I said, making a sharp right, kicking up more dust. Ironically, it seemed the faster I drove, the easier it was to keep in front of the dirt. But the potholes and bumps made the road painful on our butts.

Twenty minutes later we were forced to halt. A thirty-foot steel gate, topped with three feet of barbed wire, blocked our way. Jimmy quickly gave me a suspicious look but I just nodded and climbed out.

"Scoot over, get behind the wheel," I said.

We were in the hills far east of Las Vegas. We couldn't see

the city, nor much of anything else except sand and tumble-weeds. The sun was straight overhead. I had forgotten to put on sunscreen that morning and I could literally feel the moisture being sucked out of my pores. It appeared witches were not impervious to everything.

A heavy-duty chain, along with a lock the size of a book, held the gate shut. Grabbing hold of the chain, I tested its strength.

"What do I get if I break this chain with my bare hands?" I called to Jimmy.

"Break it and I'll kiss your ass!" he shouted back.

"How about my breasts! I'm an old-fashioned girl!"

"Jessie! Give it up! There's nothing out here . . ."

I shut him up by snapping the chain in two pieces. Even through the dust and the SUV's tinted window, I could see his incredulous expression. I kicked open the gate and gestured for him to drive through.

"Amazing stuff, that STP," I said as I climbed in beside him.

He stared at me. "How do I know you're a good witch? You never told me how I could be sure."

"The only way to be absolutely sure is to make love to me. If you die when you come, I'm a bad witch. Now drive. I want to get to Inferno before I melt."

We kept the windows rolled up and the air conditioner on full and still the heat penetrated the SUV. Fortunately, we didn't have to drive far before we reached Inferno.

The makeshift town stood with low, sloping hills on one side and a barren plain on the other. I assumed the open area led in the direction of ground zero. In the distance, in a straight line toward the spot where the bombs ignited, I saw two smaller towns that looked as if they had absorbed far more damage.

I understood in an instant why the government had staggered the towns. It was trying to gauge the degree of destruction each bomb caused relative to how far it was from the target. Since Inferno was at least three miles away from ground zero, it was still largely intact.

Yet that was not saying much. It looked like a ghost town that had been ravaged by locusts. The structures that had been made of wood were sagging skeletons of soot and ash. The cement-and-brick buildings had fared better, although the paint had peeled away, probably from a combination of the blasts and dust storms. More than half the windows had shattered and the bulk of the tar-based roof shingles had melted through to the ceilings.

However, in a strange way, Inferno was impressive. It had been pulverized by dozens of nuclear weapons, yet it had survived to tell its tale.

Besides normal buildings, on our side of town there was a kids' park that had a few swings and slides that would have been serviceable if not for the thick layers of rust. Plus, of all things, in the center of town there was a stone fountain that was bubbling with a modest amount of underground water. I assumed that was where the water was coming from. I doubted there was any electricity in place to pump the liquid from a nearby pond or stream.

I sensed instantly that the town was inhabited. Yet the mind, or minds, I picked up felt alien. And I couldn't help noticing how Jimmy stared at the town. He was not connected yet but he was no dummy. He studied the town closely before he suddenly turned to me.

"We're being watched," he said.

I nodded. "You're right. Are they good witches or bad witches?"

He hesitated. "There's danger here but also something else."

"What?"

"I don't know. Why did you bring us here?"

"I don't know," I said.

"Well, we make a fine pair." Jimmy opened his door. "You stay here, keep the engine running, be ready to bolt at a moment's notice."

I grabbed his arm gently. "You must realize by now that I can take care of myself."

He shook his head. "Don't get cocky. If someone shot you through the heart, I doubt it would matter how many witch genes you have."

"Good advice." I let go of his arm. "But I'm still coming with you."

We walked together toward the town. Jimmy was smart, he brought along two Evian water bottles. He also had a white baseball cap, to shade his head from the sun, but he put it on top of my head.

"If you knew we were coming out here, why didn't you buy a Geiger counter in town?" he asked.

"Because the thing would probably be beeping so loudly by now you would have driven off and left me no matter how much you say you love me."

"Not funny. I was serious when I said radioactive elements can hang around for thousands of years. The fact the government stopped nuclear testing in the sixties means nothing."

"It especially means nothing because they haven't really stopped."

"Who told you that?"

"My father," I said.

"Wonderful. If we ever get married and have kids, they're probably going to be born with two heads."

I had told Jimmy about everything in witch world except Lara. Somehow, after Huck, I didn't think he could take any more.

I suddenly held up my hand. "Did you hear that?"

"What?"

"Footsteps. Someone running."

"Toward us or away from us?"

I listened closely. "They're near. They're watching us."

Jimmy spoke seriously. "Every minute we stay here increases our danger. You could inhale a stray particle of plutonium. Just one particle could give you breast cancer like Debbie's mom."

His remark sobered me. But it was right then I noticed a trail of muddy liquid leading from the central fountain toward what was labeled a drugstore. It was the best-kept building in town and I suspected someone was using it as their home.

"Somebody just had themselves a little drink," I said.

Jimmy knelt and studied the trail. "They've got small feet."

"Yes." I stopped and shut my eyes. The sensation of being watched intensified, and on top of that, I began to sense the mind behind the person who studied us. He or she felt young. I opened my eyes. "We're being watched by a kid."

"Are you sure?"

"He's alone and he's curious about us."

"How many eyes does he have?"

It was supposed to be a joke but I didn't smile.

"I don't know," I said softly.

We found him in the drugstore munching on a protein bar and a bag of barbecue potato chips, drinking water from a jug he had filled at the fountain. He was not naked but close. He wore a torn piece of canvas that was held to his waist by a piece of dirty rope. He was maybe six, filthy, and extraordinarily tan—either burned by the sun or other forms of the radiation. He had ten fingers and ten toes, and seemed okay in that respect, although he had a dry cough and his skin was badly marked. Lesions, maybe. His cobalt-blue eyes seemed to glow.

I gave him a warm smile. "Hi, my name's Jessie and this is Jimmy. What's your name?"

He heard me, definitely, he went still at my question. But he didn't open his mouth to reply. Instead, he reached for a notepad and picked up a blue marking pen and wrote out four letters. He struggled to form them, like a right-handed person being forced to write left-handed.

WHIP.

"Your name is Whip?" Jimmy asked.

The boy nodded and smiled shyly at Jimmy. He stood and offered him a protein bar and some of his potato chips. The food was all fresh; I could only assume someone was bringing it in from the outside.

Jimmy accepted the food graciously. I assumed he would be worried the kid had some kind of infection or disease—his cough appeared chronic—but Jimmy showed no such concern. His behavior made no sense, especially after the lecture he had just given me. Of course the food looked fine, like it had been recently delivered. For sure, Whip had not scavenged it from the local buildings. But then I realized that Jimmy's desire to accept the kid's food went deeper. Jimmy was thinking of Huck while he was with Whip. I don't know how I knew this, but I was sure it was true. And he wanted the boy to like him.

"This is good, thank you," Jimmy said, as he chewed on the protein bar and potato chips. But he hesitated when Whip offered him a drink from his water. *That* I could understand.

"Whip, do you live here alone?" Jimmy asked.

Whip nodded, then reached out and squeezed Jimmy's arm.

"Do you know where Las Vegas is?" I asked.

The boy's eyes grew brighter, if that were possible. He nodded vigorously.

"Have you ever been to Las Vegas?" Jimmy asked.

Whip stopped nodding, he fell silent, just stood there, not even eating. The light in his eyes faded. Seeing how the question had stung, Jimmy quickly added, "Would you like to go to Las Vegas with us?"

Whip got so excited he jumped up and down. The response made Jimmy smile but it worried me. I leaned over and whispered in Jimmy's ear.

"We've known this child only a minute and we're talking about taking him out of his natural environment. We should discuss this. It's obvious that someone's bringing him food on a regular basis. How are they going to feel the next time they come here and Whip's gone?"

Jimmy shrugged. "We can take him for a visit, we don't have to keep him there."

"You might end up freaking out his caregiver."

"We'll leave a note saying we took him."

"Great. Will you leave your cell number?"

Jimmy hesitated. "That would probably be a mistake."

"Duh. We can't leave our names or our numbers." I paused.

"The Lapras use these towns because of their high levels of background radiation. They use them to mutate people. For all we know, Whip is one of their experiments."

"He looks like a discarded experiment, if you ask me," Jimmy said. "Look, I agree we have to keep an eye out for these evil guys you told me about. But even if they are feeding this child, they're abusing him. He needs a bath and he needs a doctor to check him out. Didn't you say your father was flying in today? Your father in this world?"

"That's what he told me last night. But . . ."

"I understand. You haven't seen this version of your dad in years. You don't know if he's going to show."

"Exactly."

"Let's give him the benefit of the doubt and assume he's coming. He can give Whip a thorough physical without us having to take the boy to an official clinic."

"I have never seen this paternal side of you before."

Jimmy rubbed the boy's head. "There's a lot of things about me you don't know."

I sighed. "All right, we'll take the boy with us. But on the trip back to Vegas, please try to make it clear to him that he's only coming with us to visit the city. Neither of us is in a position to adopt this child."

Jimmy nodded. "I agree. Anything else?"

"I definitely want to leave a note for whoever brings his food."

Tearing a page from Whip's notepad, and borrowing one of his pens, I came up with a note that stated the basics but which I hoped would not place us in danger.

WE HAVE WHIP AND ARE TAKING
GOOD CARE OF HIM. DON'T WORRY,
HE WILL BE RETURNED SOON.

"What do you think?" I asked Jimmy.

He frowned. "It wouldn't reassure me if I was a parent."

"What kind of parent would leave him all alone out here?"

"An asshole." Jimmy stood and offered Whip his hand. "Let's load him in the Expedition and get out of here."

"Why are you suddenly in such a hurry to leave?"

Jimmy turned and looked me straight in the eye, and in that moment I felt he was every bit as connected as I was. "Because I just realized we have found exactly what it is you came out here to find. And he's more important than either of us realizes."

Jimmy's words touched me deeply. Silly, I know, but I had a warm glow in my chest as I watched the two of them walking hand in hand to the SUV.

CHAPTER TWELVE

ON THE DRIVE BACK TO LAS VEGAS, JIMMY CHALLENGED me to call my father and see if he was flying into Las Vegas as promised. I don't know if Jimmy was testing the validity of my story or my father's word or both. In this world, the man had not sent me a birthday card in years.

I had to go through Dr. Michael Major's emergency service to get his cell number. Even then they handed it out reluctantly. I have to admit I felt nervous dialing the number. The previous night, I had spent hours talking to him, but that had been in witch world, and the rules were different there.

Fortunately, he answered promptly. "Hello?"

"Hi. It's your long-lost daughter."

He didn't seem surprised. Obviously the transition from one world to the other was nothing to him. "Where are you?" he asked.

"In the desert, driving back to town." I paused. "Where are you?"

"I got to Vegas two hours ago. I called your hotel but Alex said you went out with Jimmy."

"He's with me now."

"Did you try explaining what happened to you?"

"Sure."

"How did that go over?"

"Like a ton of bricks. But I think he's opening up to the possibility that there's nothing wrong with me a lobotomy won't fix," I said.

"Don't worry, I have experience in this area. I'll talk to him. But I have to be careful no one knows where I'm staying. I'll text you my address in a few minutes, using an encrypted phone. Still, when you reach town I want you to drive around for a while, see if you're being followed. Try to *sense* if someone is tailing you. If they are, park your car at a hotel and hurry through the casino floor and immediately grab a taxi on the other side. Repeat this trick a few times—it's the best way to lose a tail." He paused. "When you're absolutely sure you're in the clear, come see me."

"I'm glad you're here, Dad." I found it interesting that he had told me to sense if I was being followed. He had to know of my intuition gene, and that it was already beginning to work.

"I promised you I was coming," he said.

"I know, it's just . . . It will be great to see you in this world."

"I told you, I only stayed away to keep you and your mother safe. But for now, I don't want to talk any more on this phone than we have to. Expect my message soon."

My father hung up suddenly. Jimmy was smiling.

"I'm impressed," he said.

"What impressed you more, my lifting up this SUV or my talking to my father?"

"Hearing you and your dad talking was more of a miracle." Jimmy reached over and stroked my arm. Whip was sound asleep in the backseat. "How come you didn't tell him about our guest?"

"I'm beginning to get the impression these witches, on both sides, behave like spies. He doesn't trust cell phones. In fact, he wants us to make sure we're not being tailed before we go near him."

"No one's going to tail us. They'd have to pick us up the second we drove back into town."

Someone latched on to us the moment we reentered Vegas—a black Mercedes sedan. Swearing under his breath, Jimmy tried to race away from them but that didn't work. Finally he swung up to the front of Circus Circus, to valet parking, and the three of us jumped out, grabbed the parking ticket, and raced across the floor of the casino. I was pleased to see Jimmy pick Whip up and run like the devil. I had given the child my shirt to cover him—I had a tank top on underneath—and it went a long way toward hiding Whip's filthy rags. We caught a taxi outside the back of the hotel and took the cab down to the Tropicana, where we repeated the process.

By then we were pretty sure we were in the clear. Still, we took a third taxi to my father's place, a rented condo in a high-priced complex four blocks off the Strip. It was not a hotel but the place appeared to function as one. A person could rent a condo for as little as one week, or as long as a year. I assumed my father knew the best places to hide in the enemy's territory.

My father looked the same as he had years ago. He hadn't aged a day. He was dressed casually but still projected an aura of a successful doctor. Indeed, he radiated a power that Jimmy couldn't ignore. My boyfriend's grip on reality was trembling. Each brick I removed from his self-constructed wall brought him closer and closer to full acceptance of my story.

My father embraced us both, but held on to me the longest. He kissed my forehead. "I missed you," he whispered.

"You saw me last night," I said.

"I missed this version."

I hugged him tighter. "Not as much as I missed you."

He finally let me go. "There is much we need to discuss." He gestured to Whip. "First, tell me about this little guy."

I explained where we had found Whip and why we'd decided to take him back to Las Vegas with us. My father was intrigued with his ability to write and puzzled that he couldn't speak. A brief exam revealed nothing wrong with his vocal cords.

But it revealed something else.

A little detail that Jimmy and I had been idiots to miss.

Whip had a tail!

Jesus Christ, I thought.

It came off the base of his spine. It was almost as long as his body was tall, and it tapered to a point that allowed him to curl it into a fully functioning finger. The bulk of the tail was as thick as one of his bony legs, however, it was solid muscle and cartilage, free of any bones I could see.

Whip managed to hide it by carefully wrapping it around his waist, beneath his clothes. My father was light-years ahead of Jimmy and me when it came to understanding such mutations. He asked for Whip's pens and notepad and handed them to the child.

"Do you like to use your tail to write?" my father asked.

Whip effortlessly picked up a pen with the end of his tail and opened his notepad with his hands. He wrote ten times faster and clearer than he had out in Inferno.

I like to use my tail to do most things, he wrote. *But I know I have to be careful to keep my butt secret.*

We all laughed at his choice of words.

His tail was dragging down a pair of underwear my father had given him to wear but Whip was nevertheless doing his best to remain covered. I was impressed. Given where he had grown up, I had assumed he was devoid of most social skills.

"When we're with others, we'll do our best to keep your tail hidden," my father told him.

Thank you, Whip wrote.

"Does it embarrass you?" my father asked.

Not when I'm alone. But I know I'm the only one who has one.

"Do you live alone in Inferno?" Jimmy asked. "The town where we found you?"

There are others, but most are not nice to me.

"Who brings your food to you?" my father asked.

Frankie. A scary man.

"Frank," I gushed. "That might be the Lapra I spoke to last night on the phone in witch world. Whip, does Frankie have a deep voice?"

Yes. He yells at me.

"Why does he yell at you?" Jimmy asked.

He says I'm ugly. He throws rocks at me, if I get near him.

"If he doesn't like you, why does he bring you food?"

Whip hesitated. *She makes him bring it.*

"Who is she?" my father asked.

Whip shook his head. It didn't matter how my father tried framing the question, Whip continued to refuse to answer.

My father took him in a bathroom and gave the child a bath, which Whip appeared to enjoy immensely. My dad also gave him a much more thorough exam. When he was finished, my father returned to the living room, shutting the bedroom door carefully behind him.

"I have bad news," he said. "Whip's far from healthy. The marks on his arms and legs are from cellulitis. That's a form of bacteria that spreads beneath the outer skin layers. I've put him on an IV drip and am giving him antibiotics. And I gave him a mild sedative to help him sleep."

"He can't just take a pill form of the antibiotics?" I asked.

"The infection's too far advanced. We need to kill it now. But I'm more worried about his lungs. His breathing's poor. I need to get a chest X-ray and do some other tests. It's possible he has tuberculosis."

"Isn't that infectious?" I asked, privately wondering if we could use our witch genes to heal the boy.

"Yes. The child might have to be quarantined."

"I can help take care of him if you can get your hands on the medicine he needs," Jimmy said.

To hell with that, I thought. *I like the boy, but TB?*

My father smiled at my boyfriend. "That's very noble of you. Let me do a few more tests before we decide whether we have to move him out of town."

"If he's under the control of the Lapras, then we definitely have to get him out of here," Jimmy said.

"It might be a mistake to interfere in their business," my father said carefully. "At least when it comes to this boy."

"From what I've heard, you specialize in messing with them," Jimmy said.

My father sat down and sighed. "True. But my partners and I try to keep our eyes fixed on the big picture."

Jimmy was offended. "So Whip doesn't count because he's just a kid with a tail?"

"Jimmy," I said. "My dad's doing what he can. There's so much we don't know. Like who is this 'she' he mentioned."

My father nodded and caught my eye. "You felt something when he brought her up," he said.

I nodded. "Yeah. Something dark and creepy."

"Since I haven't died and seen the light, I can only see the small picture," Jimmy said. "But do I need to remind you guys that it was her intuition that led us to Whip?"

My father looked surprised, but I felt I needed to show my support for what Jimmy was saying. "I didn't know why I had to go out there. I just felt compelled. And after we found Whip, the compulsion left me."

My father considered. "That's interesting."

Jimmy crossed the room and sat on a chair near my father. He leaned toward him as he spoke, and I knew what was coming.

"I need to experience what Jessie's experienced," he said. "Until I do, I'm useless to her. I can't tap into my powers and I can't reach this other world you keep talking about."

"The other world you don't believe in," I teased.

"That's not fair. I've swallowed a remarkable amount of insanity since we left town this morning. I think I deserve some credit. But the only way I can get a grasp on this stuff is to become a witch myself."

"Has Jessie explained that you lack the healing gene?" my father asked Jimmy.

"Yes. But that's no barrier to a man like you. I've watched enough medical shows, I know what a heart surgeon does. Every day you operate, you stop a person's heart and put them on a heart-lung machine. I bet that procedure is close enough to the death experience to activate my witch genes."

My father didn't respond. I had to prod him.

"Would it work, Dad?" I asked.

My father sighed and shook his head. "Frankly, I've never tried it before. It might work just fine. But it's a risk I'm not allowed to take."

"Are all witches lacking in the healing gene forbidden to join your secret society?" Jimmy asked bitterly.

I was surprised Jimmy was so anxious to risk death when he'd made such a big point of being there for Huck. But the more I thought about it, I realized I'd feel the same way. Jimmy kept hearing from us about invisible enemies and dangers. He probably felt he could not protect his son unless he could confront them directly.

"No. But like Jessie, you're special, you're unique, and a lot of that deals with your relationship with my daughter."

Jimmy paused. "I don't understand."

My father looked at me. "You haven't told him about Lara?"

"No. He got so upset when I tried to convince him that Huck was still alive, I saw no point."

"Who's Lara?" Jimmy asked.

I reached out and took Jimmy's hand. "Our daughter."

He snorted. "Gimme a break."

"It's true," my father said. "There's no Huck in witch world for the simple reason that you were never with Kari in that world. You stayed with Jessica and when she accidentally got pregnant and had a baby girl, you two named her Lara. Only the child wasn't an accident, not to the Council. It had been planned for centuries."

Jimmy frowned and looked to me to clarify the situation but I shook my head. Pieces of this were news to me. "Please don't tell me that Jimmy and I are part of a breeding program," I said.

"Don't act surprised," my father said. "You suspected as much when we spoke last night. You were told again and again how extremely rare it was to have seven witch genes. You were told five was also rare. Surely it must have occurred to you how unlikely it was that the one guy in the whole world you happen to meet and fall in love with has almost as many genes as you do. Not only that, Jimmy's genes are complementary. The three that you're missing, he has them."

"What are they?" Jimmy asked.

"That's not important at this time," my father said.

"So that's why Lara was born with all ten," I gasped.

"Yes," my father said. "You two were deliberately put near each other. It was even arranged that you'd share a few classes. But we didn't have to overdo it in that department because we knew you would spontaneously be drawn to each other. On some level, witches usually recognize each other."

"Why did Jimmy leave me for Kari in this world?" I asked.

"I was with her before I was with you," Jimmy said.

"True. But you went back to her."

"You know why I went back to her," Jimmy said, annoyed.

"I want to hear my father's explanation," I said.

"We're not sure but we can only assume the Lapras became aware of our genetic program. They might have tampered with Kari's and Jimmy's minds, just enough that Jimmy would choose the wrong time and the wrong girl to start dating."

"You make it all sound so calculated," I said, and it was my turn to show bitterness. "I assume you married Mom because you were supposed to. Of course, that would explain why you couldn't wait to dump her once I was born."

My father took a long time to answer.

"I love your mother as much as you love Jimmy," he said. "It broke my heart to leave her, and to be away from you in this world. I explained all this in witch world. I only did it because I knew the Lapras were watching me. It was the only way I could keep you safe."

"But you let Jimmy and me grow up in a town not far from their headquarters!" I snapped. "It makes no sense."

"On the contrary, it makes perfect sense when you realize that Apple Valley was the last place they would have thought to look for someone we were hiding."

"Because it is so close to their stronghold," Jimmy said.

"Exactly," my father said.

"But you said they found out about Jimmy, Kari, and me."

"They didn't know about you while you were younger. Actually, there's a chance they didn't know about you until you got pregnant with Lara."

"What are you talking about? Did her conception send out some kind of signal?" I asked the question as a joke and was surprised when my father nodded seriously.

"Her birth might have," he said.

Jimmy shook his head. "Jessie, have you even seen Lara? Are you sure she's for real?"

"I haven't seen her. But I spoke to her on the phone. I heard her . . . cooing. She's ours. I have no doubt about that."

Jimmy heard something in my voice. "But there's a problem with her. What is it?"

Neither my dad nor I wanted to tell him the truth.

"The Lapras have kidnapped her as well," I said.

Jimmy looked deflated, disgusted. He pointed at my father. "Jessie told me a little about that Council you're involved with. You're supposed to be a bunch of superpowerful witches. But all I hear about is how you guys keep screwing up."

My father didn't flinch at his accusations. "We have made mistakes. We're not perfect. But we're faced with a formidable foe. And if the Council has made mistakes, they've made them out of a desire not to interfere with humanity's free will. Even when it came to you two. We put you near each other but we didn't force you to fall in love. This might be hard to understand but a soul as bright as Lara couldn't have entered this world except through a couple that was deeply in love with each other."

My father spoke with such conviction that neither Jimmy nor I felt we could challenge his last remark. But to be honest, I thought he was overly infatuated with Lara. My daughter was superior to others because her genes were better but she wasn't some kind of goddess.

"So your Council doesn't want to risk me going through the death experience because I might die," Jimmy said. "And if I die, there's no one else around who can sleep with your daughter and create perfect babies."

"That's one way of putting it," my father said.

"But you didn't mind risking Jessie," Jimmy said. "From what I heard, she could have died a dozen times while she was in your hands."

"No. That was the problem. She got out of our hands."

"I still think you were careless," Jimmy said.

"We did the best we could, but we were forced to risk activating Jessie's genes because of what happened to Lara. Otherwise, I would have been happy to wait until you were both thirty years old. I want my daughter to go to college, to have a career. I want the same for you, Jimmy. But Lara came to this world when she wanted to come and with her she's brought a magical light none of us can begin to understand."

"If she's so special, why don't the Lapras kill her?" Jimmy asked.

"They might decide to kill her one day, if they discover they can't control her. But for now they know she's the only one who carries all ten of the witch genes inside her. They sense her power, and it's a power they'd like to turn against us."

My cell phone rang. It identified the caller as Kari. I told the others who it was. My father told me to accept the call but not to stay on the line long. The Lapras might trace the call back to us. He also said to tell her I was alone, if asked.

"Hello, Kari. This is a pleasant surprise," I said, squeezing into the chair beside Jimmy. I wanted him to hear, or at least I thought I did.

"I'm sure. Where are you?"

"Why?"

"I want to meet. We have things to discuss."

"Such as?"

"Huck and Lara. You and Jimmy."

"Who's Lara?" I asked.

"Don't play the fool, Jessie, it doesn't suit you." Kari paused. "Where do you want to meet? I can come to you."

"That's not necessary."

"Just name the place and time."

"Really, Kari, this is a vacation weekend for me. Why should I waste part of it talking to you?"

"Because I just saw Huck. And I can take Jimmy to see Huck if you bring him to see me."

Suddenly Jimmy was nodding his head vigorously. He gave me no choice. "The Mirage Café, in one hour," I said and hung up.

Jimmy's hope was so great he was ready to explode.

"Could it be true?" he whispered.

"It's obvious Kari has been contacted by the Lapras," my father said. "That makes her the last person on earth you should see, Jimmy. Let Jessie go to the meeting alone. Kari just wants you there so she can manipulate you with the carrot of your son. But her real target is Jessie, and she'll try to force you to force Jessie to do things that would be unwise."

"How can saving my son be unwise?" Jimmy asked.

"If you show that you can be easily manipulated, you'll put your son in greater danger," my father said. "Please don't take this the wrong way, but right now they see you as the weak link in our group. Don't prove them right."

Jimmy stood angrily. "But you said it yourself—I'm not part of your group. I'm nothing. I can't help protect Jessie in witch world, and now you're telling me I can't even see my son in this world. Well, to hell with you. Jessie doesn't even know Kari. Four years of high school together and the two of them hardly said hello to each other. Well, I dated the girl, I had a child with her. I know how she thinks, and I can get way more out of her than Jessie can. That's why I'm going with Jessie to this meeting."

"What if Jessie doesn't want you to come?" my father asked.

Jimmy stared at me, desperate, and I could see his heart pounding behind his eyes. "Would you stop me?" he asked.

I felt trapped, cornered by love. There were few feelings in the world that were worse. "My father's right. They'll manipulate you to get to me. Then, who knows, we both might end up hurting Lara."

"I don't know any Lara," he said.

"I do," I replied, feeling the need to be blunt. "And right now she's the most important person in the world to me. In both worlds."

Jimmy bowed his head. "Don't do this, Jessie."

"I didn't say I'd stop you from coming. I'd never force such a decision on you. All I'm saying is that I think my father's right."

"You want me to stay here and do nothing?"

"Stay here and help my father take care of Whip. Remember, you're the one who insisted we bring him back to Vegas. When he wakes up, you need to question him further. He could know a lot more than we realize."

"Good speech," Jimmy said. "So you want me to stay here and be a babysitter while you run off into the mouth of danger."

"You know I can take care of myself."

"Please stop rubbing it in." Jimmy turned toward the door. "The Mirage Café in one hour. I'll see you there."

He left without saying good-bye.

I feared it was something I was going to have to get used to.

CHAPTER THIRTEEN

JIMMY AND I ARRIVED AT THE MIRAGE ON TIME, although we came separately. Kari was late. She kept us waiting half an hour. During that time Jimmy and I hardly spoke. It was sad—Lara was his child as much as mine, but he felt no connection to her. Sure, intellectually he believed what I had told him, but his heart was fixed on Huck. Probably had been since the moment the child was born.

Kari finally arrived. She was dressed in a short green skirt and a tight white blouse. The girl never missed a chance to show off her chest. She wore emerald earrings she could never have afforded. The jewelry just confirmed the fact that she had recently made new friends.

She didn't act nearly as dazed as she had the day before and I wondered how much of yesterday had simply been an act. She was very hard to read, even with my blossoming intuition.

I wondered what abilities her witch genes related to. It was like someone had taught her how to erect a psychic wall.

"You're late," I said flatly as Kari took a seat across from us. We had a corner booth, plenty of privacy. Both Jimmy and I were sipping large Cokes. With the summer heat, just walking from the parking lot had been enough to dehydrate us.

Kari smiled faintly. "I've been busy."

"So it would seem," I said. "Tell us about it."

"I'd much rather hear about your adventures."

I tapped the table impatiently. "You're connected, I'm connected. What else is there to say?"

"How did they connect you?" she asked.

"Who's they?" I asked.

"Drop the innocent routine. We know you've been contacted by the Tar. You know I'm talking to the Lapras. There, Jessie, was that so hard? Now all our cards are on the table."

I was missing something. I sought to move carefully. "I assume the Lapras connected you the same way the Tar connected me," I said.

"No. I connected myself."

I snorted. "Like you would know how."

Kari turned to Jimmy. "After we buried Huck, I was in such pain, I couldn't take it. My parents didn't know what to do. They tried talking to me, took me to a psychiatrist. He gave me pills that were supposed to improve my mood. I tried telling him there was nothing wrong with my mood. My problem was my son was dead. He didn't get me at all. I stopped seeing him, and my parents decided it might be best to leave me alone. That might have been a mistake, I suppose it depends on how you look at it. My mom has rheumatoid arthritis and keeps a bottle of painkillers hidden in her bedroom closet. OxyContin. She hates taking it but sometimes the pain gets to be too much." Kari paused. "Like I said, my pain was too much for me to handle."

I understood in a flash. "You swallowed the bottle of pills. You overdosed."

Kari nodded. "I died, technically, the paramedics said that my heart had been stopped for at least fifteen minutes when they found me. I don't know if they saved me or if a certain gene I was born with did. I only know when I woke up, it was like I was in another world." She paused and her gaze focused even more on Jimmy. "A world where neither of us has a son."

Jimmy had heard enough. "I don't care about that place. I care about here and now. Is Huck alive?"

"Yes," Kari said.

"How long have you known?"

"A couple of weeks."

"How come you didn't tell me?" Jimmy demanded. "You knew what I was going through."

"How could I tell you? We had already buried him. You wouldn't have believed me."

"That's bullshit. I would have listened to anything you had to say when it came to our son."

Kari showed her bitterness. "Really? I think you had other things on your mind. Like how you could talk your darling Jessie into taking you back now that you no longer had any obligation to me."

Jimmy shook his head. "You're twisting what happened. You're putting all the blame on me."

"Who else should I blame? I watched as you two frolicked on the lake yesterday. I saw pretty much everything you did, and it sure as hell didn't look like Ms. Witch Bitch sitting here had to talk you into dropping your trunks."

"You're sick," I said coldly.

"No, Jessie, I'm pissed, and I have a right to be pissed. Last month he was sleeping with me and now he's sleeping with you. Of course, we've all been through this before. It seems that even though our dear Jimmy comes well equipped with plenty of witch genes, when it comes to matters of the heart, he's still like most guys. He thinks with his dick. Which means he'll probably come running back to me pretty soon."

I smiled. "All you've got to offer is sex."

"No, Jessie, what I've got to offer is good sex." Kari paused. "And a son. What do you have to say, Jimmy? Do you want to see your son?"

Jimmy was on fire, but he managed to stay in control, to smolder. "When?" he asked.

"Today if you want," Kari said.

"On what condition?" I asked.

Kari leaned closer. "There's only one. You both have to agree to come with me."

"Why does she have to come?" Jimmy demanded, and there was a faint—but savage—note to his voice that frightened me. It also worried me that he took her hand when she offered it.

"Because she's the queen bee," Kari said, squeezing his fingers. "I gave birth to a beautiful, healthy boy who has five extraordinary genes in his DNA. He's going to grow up to be at least as wonderful as his father. Ordinarily, the Lapras would be happy to welcome us into their fold. The only problem is Jessie's daughter was born with ten genes."

"Lara was born perfect," I said, pride in my voice.

"Not totally perfect," Kari snickered. "I heard through the grapevine that so far she's been more trouble than she's worth."

"She's an infant," I said. "She misses me."

Kari continued to hold on to Jimmy. "Huck misses us, Jimmy. I know you miss him. It was incredible to see him again. I got to play with him for an hour. I fed him, bathed him, and changed his diaper. He's doing real good. He's bright, happy, and healthy. I think he recognized me."

Jimmy nodded. "That's good."

Kari continued. "He's in a nice house twenty minutes from here. Up on a hill, it has a fantastic view of the desert.

Because it gets a breeze, they hung these chimes on the back balcony that give off this intoxicating sound. We can stay there together, and you can see Huck all you want."

Jimmy stopped nodding and sat silent. Kari and I waited.

"As long as Jessie comes with us," he repeated as he gently undid Kari's fingers and took his hand back. "I'm still not clear what she has to do with Huck."

"She has nothing to do with him," Kari said angrily.

"And everything," I said sadly, putting an arm around his shoulder. Talk about pulling the guy left and right. "It's Lara's uniqueness that makes her the key to this situation. The Tar want to groom her for good. The Lapras want to use her for evil. But for now, both sides just want to keep her happy, and to do that they need me, her mother."

"She's only a month old," Jimmy said. "How can she know who you are?"

"What can I say? She knows. But stop and consider what Kari's offering you. It's the classic devil's bargain. Go along with the bad guys and they'll give you what you want today. Just don't ask any questions about tomorrow. Because you might discover that, down the road, you're selling out your children's souls."

"Screw their souls!" Kari erupted. "I'm trying to keep my son alive. That's all you should be focused on, Jessie. I know they have Lara and so do you. I hope Jimmy does as well. Nothing you say means shit. They have the kids, they're in control. We have to cooperate. It's as simple as that."

"It's not that simple," I replied.

"Liar. And who's to say the Tar are better people than the Lapras? A few days ago we didn't even know these two groups existed. For all we know, the Lapras are the good guys."

I spoke. "If they're so good, why did they give you a dead baby and convince you that it was Huck and pat you on the back and tell you to go bury him?"

"If the Tar are so great and almighty, how come they were unable to keep either of our kids from being kidnapped?" Kari replied.

"'Kidnapped' is the word," I said. "It's what the Lapras do. They take what they want when they want it. That should tell you something about their moral compass." I turned to Jimmy. "You can't bargain with them. You know that in your heart."

He stared at me. "Are you saying you won't go with me?" he asked softly.

"I'm telling you it's a bad idea."

He raised his hand. His tone appeared reasonable but there was plenty of room for danger in it. "That's not what I'm asking. At the condo you said you wouldn't force me to make a decision one way or the other."

"That's right. I won't force you. Go with her if you want."

"But you heard Kari. I can't do that, not without you."

My lower lip trembled. "This is a mind-fuck, pure and simple. They're trying to leverage you against me, and you were warned that they'd do that. Please don't fall for it."

"Who warned you, Jimmy?" Kari asked casually. "Russ? I'm not sure if Jessie's told you everything about him. Like how close the two of them really are."

I smiled at Kari. "Getting desperate, aren't we? Jimmy knows I'd never cheat on him."

Kari met my gaze. "Are you sure?"

"Yes," I said.

Kari shook her head and sat back. "Did Jimmy tell you the last time we had sex?" she asked.

Jimmy's gaze hardened. "Kari, you just played the wrong card. Suddenly, what Jessie's saying, it's beginning to make sense. You just reminded me how you like to operate."

Kari boiled. Her eyes quickly scanned the table, as if looking for something to throw at him. Yet within seconds I could hear her straining to take deep breaths, to calm herself. That was unlike the Kari I knew, who had no control. It made me wonder if the Lapras had already begun to train her.

"I shouldn't have said that," Kari said. "I apologize. All I'm trying to do is save our son. That's my only concern. You can't blame me for fighting for his life."

"Don't get melodramatic on us," I said.

"Melodramatic? Has it occurred to you that because Huck's not as special as Lara, he's more expendable?" Tears welled up in Kari's eyes. "I don't know how all this is going to work out. But I get the impression if I don't give them what they want, they'll kill him."

Jimmy's face darkened. "Did they say that?"

Kari lowered her head. "No. But the threat . . . it sort of hangs in the air, you know?"

Jimmy turned to me. "This is too big a risk to me."

I sat quietly a few seconds, trying to sense which way we should go. The words I said next, it was like they were given to me from above. "It's too soon. They're not going to hurt either child. The Lapras have been around a long time, they're patient. For now, they'll wait and watch and see how things develop."

Kari dried her eyes with a table napkin. "You guess," she said. "That's easy to do when it's not your kid."

"Huck's Jimmy's child," I said. "And since we're together, I care about him. I'll probably end up seeing a lot of him."

"Especially if something unfortunate happens to his mother," Kari muttered.

"I didn't say that," I said.

"No, but you thought it."

I shrugged. "Well."

Kari threw down her napkin. "You bitch!"

"You're the one who came here with an agenda. Don't think Jimmy and I can't see how you're trying to work all angles. Your problem is your little witch powers have gone to your head."

"Look who's talking. The divine mother herself."

"I can't help it if my child's perfect," I said.

Kari turned to Jimmy. "Let's go see Huck. Twenty minutes from now and you can be holding him in your hands. If she wants, Jessie can stay in the car. They just said I had to bring her to the house."

"They wouldn't let her just sit in the car," Jimmy said.

"Actually, Kari might be right," I said. "They're trying to see if they can move us around like pieces on a board. This meeting, this whole carrot-and-stick routine, I think they just want to see if we take the bait. I think the best thing we can do is ignore them."

Jimmy took both my hands. "I'm scared to blow them off. You tell me they're evil, and they have my son. None of us can be certain what they'll do."

"But we can be certain that their offer sucks. They say you can see Huck if I come along. But they don't say they're going to let Huck go. Because they're not going to let him go. At best you get to see your son for a short time."

"That's ridiculous," Jimmy said. "If they don't hand him over, we'll go to the police." He looked to Kari. "Right?"

Kari shook her head. "Jessie would probably agree with me when I say that won't do any good."

"It won't do any good," I muttered.

"Then we'll go to the FBI," Jimmy said. "I don't care who these people are. They're not above the law."

"Want to bet?" Kari said.

Jimmy glared. "You're going to tell the police and the FBI that Huck's alive. You're going to take them to that house where you saw our son."

"Or what? You'll sue me?" Kari asked.

"Jimmy," I said. "She's finally telling you the truth."

"But the FBI . . . ," Jimmy began.

"Can't help us," I interrupted. "The Lapras would swat them like flies."

Jimmy took a while to absorb the information that was coming to him from two opposing sides. Not that Kari was suddenly trying to help him. But she finally saw that her lies were not working.

Jimmy shook his head. "I don't know what to do."

"Then let's wait," I said. "It's not time to make a move."

He hesitated. "Is it still up to me?"

"I told you, I'll come with you if you tell me to."

He stood and looked down at Kari. "Tell your new masters that we're not puppets. We don't jump just because they tell us to jump."

Jimmy didn't give Kari a chance to respond. He walked off, and I chased after him, proud that he was my boyfriend.

But when we were outside, Jimmy spoke about just how screwed up our situation was.

"This talk we just had, it was mostly about Huck. Like you said, he's the Lapras' carrot. But since we've chosen to ignore their demands, they'll come after us from a different angle next time. You know what I'm saying."

"They'll threaten Lara," I said, and it was only then I realized I hadn't told him that I was meeting with the Lapras on my own, in witch world.

"Exactly," Jimmy said. "And when they do, you're going to know how I feel right now."

"I'm sorry." I reached over and hugged him, kissed him. But the affection all felt a little forced. Like my next words. "I'm not going to let those monsters raise her."

He shook his head. "You'd sign a contract with the devil himself to keep them from killing her."

Before meeting Kari, Jimmy had picked up the Ford Expedition we had dumped at Circus Circus. We drove back in the SUV to where my father was staying. As we parked outside the condo complex, a long silence settled between us. Finally I said the only thing I thought that mattered.

"I love you." Yet when he went to reply, I put my finger to his lips. "Don't say it. You don't have to say it."

"Why not?"

"You just proved your love far beyond what any words could. I can't imagine how hard it was for you to walk away from Kari's offer. I know you did it for me. And I know it's driving you nuts."

He nodded. "It wasn't easy."

I held him close. "I wish we could make love right now."

"Whip will be awake soon. He'll be looking for us. We can't just dump him on your father."

"I know. I just wish . . ."

"Jessie?"

"I'm dying to lie beside you in bed and hold you."

He had to add the fatal words. "Until you disappear."

I hesitated. "Yes."

"You don't have to see Russ or anything?"

I kissed him again, quickly. "I swear there's nothing going on between us."

"Why did he give you a hundred thousand dollars?"

"He was just trying to get my attention, so he could teach me what I was. Like I told you, money is meaningless to him, to all of them."

"Are you one of them?"

"I'm the same as I've always been." I kept kissing him but he suddenly pulled back. I wondered if it was because I had just lied. "What's wrong?" I asked.

"I'm thinking of what I said a moment ago. About you disappearing after we fall asleep. I know you're not going to literally disappear. You're going to be there when I wake up in the morning. But each day I wake up you'll be different, more a witch than a human being. And you'll be surrounded by enemies."

"Don't think of it that way. You exist in that world, too."

"That sounds great. It's probably true. But it doesn't help me because I'm not aware of that world. And from what you've told me about my other self, James, he's just as asleep to me as

I am to him. All these incredible powers you've demonstrated, I've got none of them."

"But you heard what my father said. They'll come to you in time."

He snorted. "When I'm thirty? My son, my daughter, you—you're all in danger now." He turned away. "I don't know how long I can wait."

I felt a chill inside. "What are you saying?"

He just shook his head and got out of the car.

We were halfway to the high-priced condo my father was renting when I noticed a man and a woman sitting in a car not far from where my dad and Whip were staying. They startled us because the man's head was on the woman's body and the woman's head was on top of the man's body.

I felt sick to my stomach.

A voice spoke at our backs.

"Kari alerted the Lapras when you left the Mirage," a man said, wiping blood from a long sword with a white handkerchief. "These two were ordered to follow you."

He was dressed entirely in black leather, down to his boots, and there was a wild energy in his black eyes, even without the bloody sword. His dark blond hair brushed his shoulders. He reminded me of a vampire, but surprisingly I felt no fear of him. Before saying good-bye last night in witch world, my father had briefed me on two of the Council members: Cleo, naturally, since she headed the Council, and Kendor, because my father had a feeling I would run into him before I met the Council as a whole.

Kendor was the one the Council turned to when force was necessary. A master swordsman and an expert at virtually all forms of warfare, he was supposed to have greater speed and strength than any other living witch.

He was a handsome devil and I loved his name—*Kendor*. To me, he sounded like a hero. My father had told me Cleo was the only one who could control him.

I had to wonder at her degree of control. The windows to the car where the dead couple sat were all the way down. From their expressions, they looked as if they had been taken completely by surprise. There was plenty of blood and already flies were gathering.

They were young, in their mid-twenties, and even if they had possessed the healing gene, it wasn't going to do them any good now. My father had made it clear that this was the sort of injury even that gene couldn't fix.

Jimmy stared at the dead bodies. "Jesus Christ," he gasped.

"You must be Kendor," I said, offering my hand. "My father told me I might accidentally run into you if I wasn't careful."

"I'm here because you weren't careful enough," he replied, gesturing to the beheaded couple before shaking my hand. He had a firm grip and an accent laced with various European countries. He had a powerful voice; he did not need to raise it to be heard. He gave off an aura of utter confidence. He was fearless, it was clear, and I sensed the killer side to him even without the presence of the bodies.

My father had said that in age he was second only to Cleo and—as if I truly needed the warning—that he had a wicked sense of humor.

"Sorry. We were careless," I said.

"No harm done." Kendor turned to my boyfriend and offered his hand. "You must be Jimmy."

Jimmy shook without hesitating, no doubt trying to show he wasn't afraid. "How do you know my name?" he asked.

"I've met your alter ego," Kendor said.

Jimmy nodded to the two in the car. "Did they come here to harm us?" he asked.

"Probably to spy. But I do so hate snoops, don't you?"

Jimmy smiled and turned to me. "I think I'm going to like this guy," he said.

Kendor spoke to Jimmy. "I need to ask a favor. May I borrow your girlfriend for two hours or so?"

"Fine with me. But you better ask Jessie," Jimmy said, letting Kendor know I made my own decisions.

Kendor gave me a penetrating look. "I realize this probably isn't the best way to introduce myself," he said.

"What you lack in subtlety you make up in flair," I said.

He bowed his head. "Thank you, Jessie." He spoke to Jimmy. "Don't tell anyone I was here."

Jimmy nodded. "No problem."

"What are we going to do?" I asked.

"Talk," Kendor said.

"I'd like that," I replied, before pointing to the dead couple again. "What about them?"

"Them? Why, they're the least of your worries." Kendor finished cleaning his sword and sheathed it in a leather case he wore close to his waist. "Do you want to drive or should I?"

I glanced at the dead couple one last time. I kept thinking I should exchange their heads atop their bodies. Kendor did indeed have an unusual sense of humor.

"I'll drive," I said.

CHAPTER FOURTEEN

WE LEFT TOWN IN THE OPPOSITE DIRECTION JIMMY and I had taken, heading west into a sun that was drifting toward the horizon. I wore a heavy pair of sunglasses but the glare did not appear to bother Kendor. A half hour outside the city, he instructed me to pull off onto a dirt road as we approached a row of rocky hills. The path was heavily pitted and I was glad for our sturdy SUV.

"What are you thinking?" he asked, one of the few things he had said to me since getting in my vehicle.

"About Lara. Can I ask you about her?"

"Let's wait and discuss her later." He added, "Ask another question."

"All right. Do you still enjoy killing?"

"Still?"

"My father said you were quite the warrior in your youth."

Kendor was thoughtful. "When I was young and fought with others toward a common goal, I found killing satisfying, but only if our purpose was noble. Otherwise, no, I take no pleasure in hurting any man or beast."

"Does that mean you're a vegetarian?"

"Yes."

I chuckled. "Sorry."

He was not offended. "I amuse you. Why?"

"It's just that you remind me of a vampire."

"I didn't know you believed in vampires."

"I don't." I paused. "Should I?"

He smiled but otherwise did not respond. We drove on. Long stretches of silence did not appear to bother him. After living a few thousand years, I suppose even I would have worked out my chatty nature.

"What was the last battle you did enjoy?" I asked.

"The Battle of Alesia. 52 BC. I didn't enjoy it but it was important for several reasons." He looked over. "Did you read about it in school?"

I hesitated. "Did it have something to do with Caesar?"

"He was a true friend."

I had to struggle not to squeal with pleasure. "You knew him? That is so cool!" I cried.

"I'm glad you approve."

"Did your Council even exist in those days?" I asked.

"Your father has spoken to you about us?"

"Yes. Is that all right?"

"My feeling is, the more you know, the better. In those days the Council was present, but we were loosely organized and didn't do much to influence humanity. However, we did see the Roman Republic as having the potential to unify Europe, and for that reason we supported its development, in Cleo's usual low-key manner."

"I detect a note of sarcasm," I said.

"Your father has probably told you Cleo and I don't always see eye-to-eye. We share the same desire to help mankind but our methods differ. She feels humanity is best served by learning from its mistakes. But I tire of its unlimited ability to repeat the same mistakes." Kendor shook his head as if remembering a thousand arguments with his associate. "Sometimes I wish she'd let us take a more proactive role."

"Like a Caesar?" I said.

"Yes. Every now and then someone appears in history that the Council recognizes as having the ability to take mankind to a higher level. Whether they're a witch or not is unimportant. In many ways it's better if they're not, although certain witches have managed to contribute to humanity before faking their deaths and disappearing from view."

"Can you give a few examples?" I asked.

"Later. For now let's stick with Caesar. I fought alongside him simply because I wanted him to win his battles and return to Rome and bring a new system of order to a society that was already showing promise. At the time I had no idea his reign would be so short-lived. Even now I feel his assassination was one of the major turning points in history, much the same way modern historians see the death of John F. Kennedy. For Caesar was that rare leader who didn't crave power for power's sake. He took on the mantle of emperor only because he saw the desperate need for a unified government."

"I'm surprised. From what I've read . . ."

Kendor interrupted by raising his hand. "Please don't quote your history books. Should you be fortunate enough to survive the coming centuries, I can assure you that you won't recognize future historians' accounts of these days. There's a saying that history is written by the side that wins. The remark has some truth to it but it would be more accurate to say that historians decide what is history."

"Are you saying the best story wins?" I asked.

"More often than not. But in real life Caesar was equal to the biggest star in one of your most famous blockbusters. I knew him, I was close to him, I understood his mind. It was my faith in him that inspired the Council to back his lightning rise to power. Even Cleo, who seldom believes in supporting warriors, felt Caesar could seed a golden age that could last for centuries."

"Excuse me, it looks like the road is about to end."

"It doesn't matter. Keep driving until we reach the hills. There will be a place to park."

"Park? Are we going for a walk?"

"Yes. Is that a problem?"

"It's more than a hundred degrees outside."

"The walk won't be long and the day's heat will allow you to appreciate our destination that much more," Kendor said.

After I had parked the Expedition, I went to fill my day pack with bottles of water. Kendor told me they wouldn't be necessary. He did, however, ask if I had a bathing suit.

"Not on me," I said.

"Are you shy?"

"Are we going swimming?"

"I am. And I hope you'll join me." He added, "As you can probably guess, I'm older than I look. The thrill of seeing a naked female no longer applies to me."

"That's a great line." I chuckled. "But I suppose it's true."

Kendor's idea of a short walk was not the same as mine. We hiked at least two miles and much of it was on a steep incline. He walked fast; I panted in his wake. It wasn't the exercise, it was the heat. Yet it was worth it. Suddenly the bleak terrain of sandy dirt, piles of rocks, and tumbleweeds opened into a round granite bowl that held a delicious blue-green pond. There was even a small waterfall at the far end.

"It's beautiful!" I gasped.

Kendor was pleased at my reaction. "It's fed by an underground stream. The water level rises three to five feet in the cooler months, but otherwise remains constant."

"I don't see any footprints or litter. Does anyone else know about this place?"

"I've never run into anyone recently in this area. But the Paleo-Indians used to come here centuries ago. They considered it a sacred spot. Come, let's hike down to the water. I'll show you a wall of their petroglyphs."

"Just how long ago did you and the Paleo used to hang out?" I asked as I trailed behind him. It was a joy simply to watch him walk. He moved with such fluid grace and never seemed to tire. He laughed at my question.

"You want to know how old I am," he said.

"Of course. But I'm also wondering if you were coming here before Columbus discovered America."

"Plenty of people 'discovered' America before Columbus. But fear not, I'll give you a review of my life story after our swim."

"Assuming I agree to go skinny-dipping with you."

"You have my word as a gentleman that I won't lay a finger on you."

"Do you promise not to look?"

He smiled. "You would be insulted if I didn't."

I couldn't argue. He was right.

The petroglyphs were confined to a wall hidden behind the waterfall. There were dozens of beautiful and complex symbols, as well as thousands of ancient words etched in a remarkably hypnotic script. I asked if Kendor could translate the language for me. For the first time since we had met, he hesitated.

"I can. But understand, the Paleo didn't invent this script. It was taught them by a man I met the day I discovered who I was."

"Was this man a witch?"

"I'm not sure what he was. He called himself the Alchemist."

"Is he still alive?"

"That's part of the story I hope to tell. But you're hot. Let's swim first and cool off."

"Great," I said, having to put my curiosity on hold, never an easy task for me. Kendor was right, however, the sun had made me light-headed, and I was anxious to get in the water. I no longer cared that I didn't have a suit. There had been no need for Kendor to give his gentleman promises. I liked to think I was pretty hot shit but I knew he had seen far better in his time.

We stripped and dove in. With the desert sun, I expected the water temperature to be in the high eighties. It was closer to the low seventies and my heart skipped a beat when I first went under. But after swimming a few laps across the pond—it was at least four times the length of an Olympic swimming pool—I wouldn't have traded the cold for anything. I felt incredibly rejuvenated, especially after I followed Kendor's advice and drank from the lake.

"What's this water got in it?" I asked as we crossed in the middle. Kendor's naked body was distracting. He was so damn handsome.

"Power," he said, splashing me.

"Really?"

"You feel it, don't you?"

"Yes. But what is it? Where does it come from?"

"It's the power of all the elements of nature come together in one spot. The Paleo recognized it but felt no need to explain it any further."

I took that as a hint to quit asking so many questions.

We swam for half an hour and when we were through, we both slipped on our underwear but left the rest of our clothing spread out on the boulders. We sat in the shade near the waterfall. Indeed, the entire rocky bowl was covered in shadows and I knew sunset was not far off.

Kendor asked where I wanted him to start his story.

"In the beginning," I said.

"I was born a Celt in England, in approximately 3000 BC. And yes, I know, your books say the Celts didn't appear in that part of the world until 500 BC. But I was there and your historians weren't, so trust me. This was many centuries before the Romans appeared on our southern shores. My clan, the Tyenna, were situated in what is now Dover. You probably know it for its famous white cliffs but it's also the UK's closest geographical point to continental Europe. Later, I often asked myself why it took me so long to cross the English Channel."

"But you couldn't see land across the water, could you?"

"After I became a witch I could," Kendor said.

"Skip to that point. How did you get connected?"

"On the surface, my death and rebirth were unremarkable. I was twenty when a devastating winter struck our clan. The snow came early and never left. By April our numbers had been cut in half. Myself, I had lost a third of my body weight and two of my four children had already perished."

"You were married?"

"In the manner of the times. Her name was Nanar and I loved her dearly. It broke her heart to lose our two boys and I was determined that our daughters would not suffer the same fate. That's how I ended up fishing on a frozen lake not far from camp. It was late at night and I had a fire going. You might think that careless of me, to burn wood in such a precarious spot, but the ice was so thick I couldn't reach the water beneath it without the fire. And it was bitter cold, I needed its warmth just to stay alive.

"A faint yellow light had touched the eastern sky when I began to collect my goods and return home. My expedition had been a success. I'd caught four large fish, enough to feed my family for a week. I remember how delighted I was, imagining how pleased Nanar would be when she saw the fresh food.

"At some point I must have grown careless and stepped too close to the edge of the ice. In those days one false step was all it took to leave this world. The ice broke from my weight and I fell in the water. The lake wasn't large, there shouldn't have been a current. It was probably my frantic thrashing that pushed me away from my fishing hole. All I knew was that I could see a faint red light twenty feet off to my right, and that I was colder than I had ever been in my life.

"My only hope was to get back to the opening. But as I swam toward it, I felt the life draining from my arms and legs. I panicked and drew in a breath, the worst thing I could have done. Now I was freezing to death and drowning. Still, I fought my way toward the red light. I couldn't see the hole but I knew it must be close to the fire. It was my only chance, not that I had much hope left. But there was a part of me that refused to give up, even as I began to sink down. And that part seemed to kindle a fire deep inside my solar plexus."

"I've had that!" I cried.

Kendor reached over and patted my leg affectionately. "I know, Jessie. I understand everything you went through while in that meat locker, and afterward. That's one of the reasons I'm telling you this story. My internal heat blazed through my arms and legs. Soon I could feel my fingers and toes again, and I swam toward the red light. As I broke the surface, my first breath of fresh air was heavenly. I thought I was saved.

"But climbing out of a frozen lake isn't a matter of strength. It requires more skill than anything else. The edge kept breaking on me, I kept slipping back into the water. Soon my newfound strength began to wane and I started to go back under. It was then a powerful hand reached down and pulled me out.

"For a long time I was too exhausted to even look at my benefactor. I just lay on the ice near the dying fire and stared up at the fading stars. At some point I think I passed out. Looking back, I know I must have died. The next thing I was sure of, the sun was high in the sky and a man with a long beard was sitting beside me. He wore a dark red robe and I knew without asking that he was the one who had saved me."

"Was it the Alchemist?" I asked.

"Yes. But he didn't tell me his name then."

"Who was he? Where did he come from?"

Kendor hesitated. "No one knows. He came for me then, and saved me, and for that I owed him my life. But it seemed he wanted nothing in return. When he saw I was alive, he nodded to himself and walked off. I didn't see him again for three thousand years."

"But that's how you became connected?"

"Yes."

"Did you tell anyone that you'd changed?"

Kendor frowned. "I told my brother, Jasper—we were close and he knew how to keep a secret. Unfortunately, the changes slipped out without us speaking. Other clan members soon noticed my strength and speed, and grew frightened of me. It didn't matter that I only used my abilities to help feed those around me. Death is not as threatening to most people as the fear of the supernatural. It wasn't long before Nanar and my girls and I were driven from the Tyenna camp."

"What about Jasper?" I asked.

"He was killed trying to defend me. It happened the day we were expelled. I wasn't with him at the time, and I later avenged his death, killing all of the men who participated in his murder. But whoever coined the phrase that revenge is a dish best served cold has never lost a loving brother. Vengeance is no better than drinking ice water in winter."

"Did either of your daughters inherit your powers?"

"Tabby did. She awakened them by accident, when she fell from a peak and broke every bone in her body. She was sixteen at the time. Naturally, her mother was stunned when she recovered. But in my heart I knew Tabby was like me, and that dying was the key to stirring the magic. For that's how it seemed to us, that we'd been gifted with some strange powers that the gods had bestowed on us for reasons of their own."

"What gods did you believe in?" I asked.

"We had so many in those days. Their names don't matter."

"Did Nanar feel the same way?"

"Nanar was grateful for my gifts. They had allowed us to survive harsh winters. And of course she was overjoyed when Tabby was healed. But when Tabby and I didn't age, and she and Clara did, then my wife began to feel our powers were a curse."

"Why?"

Kendor stared at me. "Think how it will be if you never age but Jimmy does."

"But I have the gift of healing. I can keep him young."

"Did your father tell you that? He shouldn't have. Yes, it's possible you'll be able to prolong his life and cure him of most illnesses. But if he lives two centuries, he'll still grow old." Kendor paused. "And one day you'll bury him."

It was hard for me to reply. I couldn't imagine being with Jimmy so long and then losing him. "Is that what happened with Nanar?" I asked.

"I lost Nanar when she was eighty-eight. Yet my words don't convey what really happened."

"Because you lost her long before that?" I said.

"I remained a young man, and Tabby never aged. But Nanar grew old and wrinkled, as did Clara. I would have given my life to trade places with them but I couldn't. And so I finally learned the bitter half of what it meant to be a witch."

"May I ask? Is Tabby alive?"

He shook his head. "I'd rather not talk about that."

"What would you like to talk about?" I asked carefully.

"Let's return to the Battle of Alesia and Caesar. You'll see why when I finish. It was an important time for the fledgling republic and I use the word 'fledgling' deliberately. Rome was still in danger of being destroyed before it could begin to approach its potential. In the decade prior to Alesia, with my help, Caesar had largely pacified Gaul, and he was considering a return to Rome. But the Gallic tribes gathered during 53 BC for a crucial meeting. They realized that only by uniting their many tribes could they achieve independence from Rome.

They declared the ruthless Vercingetorix of the Averni tribe their commander and put the bulk of the Gallic armies under his control.

"We were unaware of this alliance. It caught us completely off guard. The first sign of trouble came from what is now the city of Orléans in France. All the Roman settlers were killed. This was followed by the slaughtering of all Roman citizens, merchants and settlers in the major Gallic cities. On hearing this news, Caesar rallied our army in haste and we crossed the Alps into what you would call France. That in itself was a mighty deed—the Alps were buried in snow. Caesar accomplished the trip in record time and we were able to surprise the Gallic tribes. Caesar then split our forces, sending four legions into the north after three major Gallic armies, while we set out in pursuit of Vercingetorix with five legions. Caesar succeeded in scattering his armies but in the summer of 52 BC, Vercingetorix managed to reach the fort of Alesia."

"What was so special about it?" I asked, wondering why he was going into such detail.

"It was on a hilltop, surrounded by numerous river valleys, which gave it strong defensive features. Vercingetorix had eighty thousand men to our twenty thousand. A frontal assault would have been hopeless so Caesar decided upon a siege. He hoped to force a surrender by starvation. The idea was brutal but strategically sound. Besides his warriors, Vercingetorix had the local civilian population to feed.

"To guarantee a sturdy blockade, we built an encircling set of fortifications—called a circumvallation—around Alesia. That's one thing you can read about in your books. Eighteen kilometers of four-meter-high fortifications were constructed in a month. The line was surrounded by ditches. They were virtually impossible to cross.

"But Vercingetorix was a sly devil. He managed to slip a detachment of cavalry through an unfinished section. This was a major blow to our plans. Now we had to worry that reinforcements would be sent. Anticipating such a relief force, Caesar ordered the construction of a second line of fortifications, which was called the contravallation. It faced outward and stood between our army and the first set of walls we had erected. It was designed to protect us when the Gallic relief forces arrived. For us, the fighting soldiers, the irony was painful. We, the besiegers, were preparing to be besieged.

"Inside Alesia, things went from bad to worse. Too many people were crowded inside the plateau, competing for too little food. Vercingetorix decided to expel the women and children from the citadel, hoping to save food for the fighters and praying that Caesar would show mercy and open a breach in our line and let them go. But Caesar issued orders that nothing was to be done for the civilians. The women and children were left to starve in a no-man's-land between the city walls and the circumvallation."

"That's horrible," I said. "How can you say he was a great

man? He could have let the women and children go."

Kendor shook his head. "This is something you need to hear. You want heroes who only perform noble acts. But the greatest heroes often make the most bitter decisions. Caesar knew if we took down even a small portion of our wall, Vercingetorix would use the opportunity to destroy our lines."

"So you just stood idly by and watched them all die?"

"Caesar watched. Day and night he listened to their weeping. For him, it was a form of penance. Nevertheless, he knew what he was doing was right. He was protecting his men."

"Why tell me so much about this battle? It just makes me sick."

"Because eventually you'll be called upon to make similar decisions."

"How do you know? You can't see my future."

Kendor spoke softly. "I can see inside your heart."

"That's insane. We just met."

"You're mistaken. I was the principal protector of Lara in witch world. During that week we spent together, I got to know you well. We had many private talks."

"I'm glad. But I've heard enough about this battle. Let's talk about something else. Let's talk about the Alchemist."

"I was just about to come to him."

"Oh."

"He's connected to Alesia. Let me continue. The women and children all died. The summer came to an end and on

October second, the Gallic relief effort finally arrived, led by Vercassivellaunus, a cousin of Vercingetorix. He launched a massive attack with sixty thousand men, while Vercingetorix attacked with his soldiers from inside the fort. We were caught between a hammer and an anvil. We didn't stand a chance. Yet you can read in your history books how Caesar somehow, miraculously, rallied his troops and defeated the enemy. But historians have struggled with that battle to this day. Because how do a hundred and forty thousand men lose to twenty thousand? The answer is simple. They don't."

"I assume the Alchemist did something?"

"Yes."

"What?"

Kendor's gaze was suddenly far off. "He came one week before the Gallic relief forces arrived. I was alone in my tent at night but couldn't sleep because of the stink of the rotting bodies on the other side of the line. The air was hot and humid. I lay there wondering how much longer we could go on, when suddenly he stood at the opening to my tent. I recognized him, of course, but I leaped up with my sword. In those days it seldom paid to trust a stranger."

"What did he want?" I asked.

"He said he had come to help. I asked him how and he spoke about a black powder we could produce that would allow us to kill a hundred men with one catapult. I thought the idea ridiculous but he insisted I grab a torch and follow him to a cave miles from our camp. There the walls were heavy with deposits of guano."

"Guano?"

"Bat feces. It had built up over centuries and crystallized. Today a chemist would recognize the material as a perfect source of potassium nitrate. Back then we called it saltpeter or stone salt. The Alchemist had me collect several large bags. By then the sun had risen and he led me to a deposit of sulfur. To me it was just a yellow powder that stank. When we finally returned to camp, he ordered me to bring him a bag of coal, which he ground into a fine powder with a hammer."

"Wait a second! You're talking about gunpowder!"

"Excellent. You know your chemistry. Seventy-five percent potassium nitrate, fifteen percent charcoal, ten percent sulfur. Carefully mixed and compressed in leather bags, it gave Caesar's army an interesting weapon to place in our catapults."

"You began to bomb the enemy?" I asked.

"Yes. During our initial barrage, I think we killed more from sheer shock than actual explosive power. Our own men were afraid to handle it. They spoke of the black powder as coming from the underworld, Pluto's infernal realm. Caesar did nothing to dispel the talk. He guarded the formula carefully and allowed only a select group of men to manufacture it. They were all sworn to secrecy." Kendor added, "Caesar was especially careful that none of our men wrote about it in their diaries."

"Is that how it appeared and disappeared from history?"

"It was too great a secret to totally disappear. Your history books will tell you gunpowder was discovered by the Chinese in the ninth century but I can tell you it reappeared in several major conflicts outside the gates of Rome. It was one reason Attila the Hun failed to sack the city." Kendor paused. "But I digress. You want to hear about the Alchemist. When the Gallic relief force finally arrived, we had stockpiled several tons of gunpowder. Once you knew the secret, it wasn't hard to make. We immediately began to bombard Vercassivellaunus's sixty thousand men. Few survived and the following week Vercingetorix surrendered to Caesar."

"So Caesar wasn't the military genius everyone thinks he was."

"The Alchemist brought the key to victory. But none of us would have been alive to use it if Caesar had not been leading our army. When the battle was finished, the Alchemist came again in the middle of the night. He had a stack of cards with him. I had never seen such a thing. All the paper we had in Rome came in bulky rolls."

"Don't tell me the deck was identical to a modern pack."

"It was the same as the decks you will find in the casinos. Fifty-two cards in a deck. Queens, diamonds, hearts, and jacks—the same four suits. I know what you're going to say. Your history says that cards were invented by the Chinese in the ninth century. But don't you find it interesting that's the same place and time your historians say gunpowder was invented?"

"Are you saying the Alchemist arranged for our history books to be rewritten?"

"I'm not sure. But I do find the coincidence curious."

"To say the least. Did the Alchemist happen to teach you any card games?"

"Twenty-two. Red queen. He taught me the rules and then we played the game for real stakes. He played the role of the dealer and he beat me badly. I lost more than two pounds of gold coins, which was a lot of money in those days. It's a lot of money now. He insisted I pay. Then he said he was always to be paid when a person lost at red queen."

"How?"

"I assume you mean how was he supposed to collect the money? He didn't say, and I didn't bother to ask because I found the instruction very strange. But I must admit I enjoyed the game. The Alchemist left me with a hundred decks of cards and I taught red queen to dozens of my fellow soldiers. Many grew addicted to it. More than a few lost their pay and fights broke out. But the men who played the role of the dealer, when they did win, they were never able to hold on to their winnings."

"What do you mean?"

"They would misplace the coins somehow. Or the coins would just disappear. Superstition grew around the game, causing strife, and Caesar stepped in and outlawed it. He collected all the decks of cards and had them sent back to Rome. Those crates were only reopened when Claudius became emperor in 41 AD."

"Did you teach Claudius how to play red queen?"

"Someone did. A soldier in Caesar's army had made a record of the rules and passed it on to his children. Claudius responded favorably to it. He loved games of all kinds, not just gladiator contests. For a time red queen underwent a revival, but only those close to the emperor, the nobles and senators, played. They were the only ones who were given decks of cards."

"Did the dealers' winnings continue to vanish?"

Kendor hesitated. "Yes."

"How?"

A note of impatience entered his voice. "I don't know. The game only lasted thirteen years, as long as Claudius did. By then the decks of cards were worn out anyway. There was hardly a complete deck left. When Nero took the throne, he outlawed it."

"Why?"

Kendor shrugged. "That's what Nero did. He outlawed anything he didn't like."

"How did it come to be revived later on?"

"I don't know. Perhaps someone found an old copy of the rules on a dusty parchment. It's not important."

I could see I was losing Kendor's attention. Talking about the game appeared to irritate him, although he had brought it up. I asked him to tell me more about the Alchemist.

"He came to me a third time, in the middle of the night, after we had taken full control of Alesia. By this time we had a hundred thousand captive warriors. It was the custom in those days to sell them into slavery. As a symbol of mercy, Caesar planned to send ten thousand of them home without their weapons. He was far from cruel and he deplored senseless killing.

"But the Alchemist wanted the prisoners burned alive. Every one of them, in payment for the secret of gunpowder he had given to Caesar. I was shocked. I told him to go back to the hell he had come from."

"Did Caesar personally know the Alchemist?"

"Not very well. He had met him the day I first brought Caesar a sample of the gunpowder. But the Alchemist refused to speak to him, which angered Caesar. Still, at the time, he had to be grateful to him for helping us win the battle. But when he heard of the man's demand, he told me to kill him. I was happy to do so. The Alchemist was resting at my tent and I went after him with my sword." Kendor paused. "But I couldn't stop him."

"He defeated you in a sword fight?"

"Yes and no. He kept appearing and disappearing. I had never seen this ability before, in any witch. He taunted me as I swung uselessly at him, cutting me with a knife when it amused him. I was forced to retreat. But I wasn't ready to quit. My tent was separate from the rest of the army. At my command, I had a huge ball of gunpowder loaded onto our sturdiest catapult and blew the tent to shreds." Kendor paused. "That was the end of that accursed wizard."

"If he could turn invisible, how could you be sure you killed him?" I asked.

"I found his burned and shredded robe in the ruins. It was covered in blood. I even found pieces of his beard. That was all the proof I needed." He added, "This happened in witch world."

"Wait a second. This whole time I thought you were talking about the real world."

"In those days, there was little difference between the two."

"So you lived each day twice over?"

"Pretty much. It was the philosophy of the Tar—Cleo's philosophy—not to go out of our way to alter the course of the second day."

"The second day?"

"Day two happens in the real world. Day one is always in witch world. I assumed you knew that."

"I do, I do. It just gets confusing at times."

"I understand."

"So the Alchemist is gone?" I asked.

Kendor hesitated. "He must be."

"You don't sound certain."

I waited for Kendor to respond but he just turned away and stared at the petroglyphs. By this time I was sure the sun had set, although I couldn't see the horizon while down in the bowl. I was still anxious to know what the Paleo language had to say, and I reminded Kendor that he had promised to tell me. He stood at my prodding and, walking around the waterfall, stepped to the wall of letters and symbols. I followed him.

"The script is very beautiful," he said, touching the etching with his hand. "It's hard to imagine it was invented by such a sinister mind."

"Can you be sure the Alchemist did invent it?"

He nodded. "A good question. He could have learned it from someone else. Anyway, you say you want to know what it says. Brace yourself. I'm only going to translate these few lines but they will be enough."

I swallowed. "Tell me."

Kendor gestured with his hand. "It says, 'Beware the child of the ten shining jewels, the infinite one. She whose eyes match the color of this lake. For she is impossible to defeat, and she holds the destiny of the world in her palm.'"

I felt a chill. "What's the big deal?" I asked.

"Don't play the fool, Jessie."

"What? Are you saying they're talking about Lara?"

"Of course they're talking about Lara. Who else has the ten witch genes?"

"This petroglyph was created centuries ago, before the scanner existed and anyone knew how to count witch genes. You can't just assume 'the ten shining jewels' refers to her ten genes."

"Lara was born with aquamarine eyes."

"Lots of babies are born with blue eyes. The color fades as they grow older."

"I didn't say she was born with blue eyes. The moment I saw her I was reminded of this lake."

"It's still not proof."

"Then let me translate the last line. It says, 'Her name will be Protector.'"

"So?"

"*Lara* is Latin for 'Protector.'" He added, "Latin is a very old language."

"You made that up!"

"You can check for yourself."

"No. I don't believe you."

"Then why are you so upset?"

"Because I don't want a daughter who's special! A child the whole world is anxious to possess. If I have to have a baby, I want a normal one. And I want her to be left alone."

Kendor stared at me a long time. "I'm sorry, Jessie. It's too late for that."

His words stung. I didn't know how to respond and he had nothing else to offer me. In silence we gathered our clothes and dressed and walked back to the SUV. By this time it was dark and it seemed to take forever to get back to Las Vegas.

But when we reached my father's condo and the time had come to say good-bye, Kendor suddenly hugged me and held me close. He whispered in my ear.

"When you meet the Council tonight in witch world, pretend that you don't know me," he said.

"Why? You were there when Lara was born."

"That was in witch world. The Council doesn't know we've met in this world." He added, "The most important part of my tale is yet to come. Even Cleo only knows a portion of it, but I want you to hear it all."

"Can you tell me what it's about?"

He hesitated. "Syn. The love of my life."

CHAPTER FIFTEEN

THE FOLLOWING NIGHT, NEAR NINE, WE WERE IN WITCH world, in a beautiful house I couldn't have found with a map. My father and Russell had covered my eyes before I got in their car. They said it was for my protection that I know as little as possible about where the Council preferred to meet.

But I felt like they didn't trust me.

The house was large but no mansion. It was tastefully furnished yet passable as an ordinary home. They didn't remove my blindfold until I was inside and sitting on a wool couch. There was at least a floor above the living room where we sat, maybe two. I liked the brick fireplaces, the wooden floors, and the throw rugs that appeared to be from every part of the globe. Except for us, the house seemed empty.

Russell confirmed that fact. He was dressed in a navy-blue suit with a red tie. My father was more casual, but had on a gray sports coat and black slacks. He wasn't going with me to meet the Lapras. Russell was to be my only guide.

Russell didn't act as confident as before. I wasn't sure what scared him more, meeting the Council or accompanying me to the enemy's stronghold. Apparently, he'd seen far more of the Lapras than the Tar. While still a young man of eighty, he had penetrated the Lapras' ranks during the Civil War. He had shown me a grainy black-and-white photo of him in a Union uniform, standing beside Ulysses S. Grant himself. Russell had been a colonel during that period. He was in the history books, although under another name—Colonel Clyde Chester, or "3C," as his buddies used to call him.

The Council had favored Lincoln and the Union, while the Lapras had wanted the South to win. The Lapras had sent Russell to kill the brilliant general, but he had purposely failed in the attempt and had been ordered hanged by Grant's aides. Later, while being buried by a couple of drunk Union soldiers, my father had managed to come to his rescue and help revive him.

The two went back a ways.

It freaked me out to know how far.

Especially since I knew Russell had feelings for me.

I needed to talk to him about that. Soon.

Russell and my father had emphasized that the Lapras had not been powerful during the Civil War. They could hardly call themselves an organization. That was how Russell had been able to penetrate their ranks, and why they trusted him.

They spoke of Russell's long relationship with the Lapras to put me at ease. It had the opposite effect. Maybe it was my newly developed intuition whispering inside, or else it was just common sense, but it seemed to me the longer anyone kept a secret, the more chance there was of it being found out.

There was a knock at the front door. We all stood.

The Council, four men and three women, entered.

Of course, given their age and power, I anticipated their dress to be exotic. At the very least I expected them to have on ancient amulets and jeweled necklaces and rings.

They did not look like an ordinary troupe. If nothing else, they radiated too much power to go unnoticed, even by a fool. Yet except for Kendor they were not dressed to attract attention, although two of the men had longish hair. One was Kendor, of course; once again he was dressed entirely in black leather. We exchanged a nod and it was understood that I would keep his secret.

Mona and Pal were both midnight black, tall and thin, and they looked so alike they might have been sisters. They didn't shake my hand but bowed low in my direction. Their smiles were warm and loving and they both smelled faintly of camphor and a form of incense I couldn't identify. They also had the same long curly black hair.

There were three other males: Hatsu, Baba, and Mirk. Hatsu was a short but robust Chinese man. He was the only one in the group I would have called ugly. He had a blunt nose and a large belly. If he possessed the ability to heal, he hadn't used it on himself. He was badly scarred.

However, his unpleasant features were neutralized by his laughter and charm. When we met, he patted me on the back as if we were old friends, and it was no act. I could feel his kindness. I would even go so far as to say I knew he'd die to protect me.

Perhaps a latent memory was returning, I don't know. My father had said the Council had been all around me after Lara was born but I had barely been aware of their presence.

Baba was from India. He was the other man with long hair, yet it was light brown, as was his skin, and his eyes were dark blue, like many of the people from Kashmir. He nodded in my direction, his expression serene. He seemed absorbed deep inside and didn't speak.

Mirk was a blond Scandinavian, a giant of a man. When he saw me, he said something in a language I didn't recognize and Hatsu laughed loudly while my father reddened. I sensed Mirk and Hatsu were close friends and added levity to the Council. Mirk's way of saying hello was to lift me off the floor and kiss both my cheeks.

Baba wore a dark suit like Russell, minus the tie. Hatsu and Mirk had on casual slacks and short-sleeved shirts. Mona and Pal wore cool summer dresses that barely reached their knees; they made a sexy pair.

Only Cleo had on a red pantsuit that looked exotic. It

was mostly silk but stitched with black leather. Her reddish hair was short, untamed. I wouldn't have been surprised if she shook it into place after showering. There was something primal about her movements, fluid and powerful. She could have been a panther stalking the wild.

She was surprisingly petite. Her dark eyes were not merely large and warm, they appeared bottomless. Still, she looked at most thirty, and my father had said she was at least seven thousand years old.

Cleo sat near me on the couch, on my left, letting her black shoes fall to the carpet and smoothly tucking a leg beneath her bottom. She was small but radiated immense energy. I didn't have to be a witch to sense it. Whenever she looked my way, I felt as if a magnet passed over my forehead. Her skin was bronze, her full lips a rich red. She looked like a doll and yet felt like an atomic reactor.

But I liked her, I liked them all, and I trusted them, which was probably more important. Yet they scared me, especially when I contemplated their age. I was an infant in their company.

I was glad Russell and my father were present. Out of respect, they remained standing the whole time the Council was present. Russell stayed near the front door, my father stood behind me.

Kendor sat in the chair on my right. It was curious but they let him do most of the talking. Of course, I knew from his tale that he was a man who was used to commanding others.

"We know you have been through a lot in the last two days, Jessica," he began. "And we know you have an appointment with the Lapras after you leave here. For that reason we need not talk long. Yet we wanted to meet with you so you understand who it is that stands behind you. I speak for all the Council when I say no one is more important to us than you and your daughter. We will get Lara back. I swear not to rest until she's in your arms again."

Once again, he overwhelmed me. "Thank you," I whispered.

"You must have questions that only we can answer." Kendor paused. "Ask what you wish."

I sipped some water before speaking. "My father has explained this point but it still confuses me. Before my witch genes were activated, I had a whole set of memories of my life in witch world. Yet now that I'm connected, the memories have faded, and all I know is the Jessie from the real world."

"Do you have any memories at all of this place?" he asked.

I wanted to smile, to cry, I didn't know which was worse.

"Lara. I remember holding my daughter. Feeling her kick inside my belly. And her eyes, I remember how bright they are. But it's odd, I can't remember their color."

I wanted to see their color confirmed. I still didn't trust what the Paleo had written.

"Blue-green," Cleo said softly. "Very beautiful."

"That's true!" I exclaimed, her eyes suddenly coming back to me clearly. "I remember."

"Do you recall the night she was taken?" Kendor asked.

"No. Is it important?"

"Your point of view on that night might help us. We know your father has explained how a spell of extraordinary potency was used against us. We lost all sense of time and place."

"None of us had experienced anything like it before," Hatsu added.

"Were you two guarding Lara?" I asked.

Kendor gestured to Mirk and Hatsu. "You hardly saw us, but the three of us never left her side from the moment she was born."

"So you anticipated an attack?" I asked.

Kendor nodded. "We believed the Lapras would come for your child. And for the other one, Huck. But we didn't imagine for a moment they would succeed."

I turned to Cleo. It intimidated me to do so, her stare was so intense I could only withstand small doses of it. But I wanted her to answer my next question.

"That's another point that puzzles me," I said. "Why did Kari have Jimmy's baby in the real world? While I had his child in this world?"

"It wasn't part of our plan," Cleo said.

"Your plan? Do you mean the way you manipulated who I was with? And my ancestors?"

"I wouldn't use the word 'manipulate,'" Cleo said.

"Please, just explain it so I can understand," I said.

"For centuries we followed your bloodline. We knew it possessed many witch genes. We watched over other bloodlines as well, especially ones that had different genes from the ones your line carried." Cleo paused. "Your father explained this. For a long time we hoped to bring into this world a child who had all the witch genes. But it wasn't possible until your mother married your father and you mated with James."

"It sounds like you bred us like cattle," I said, failing to keep the bitterness out of my voice.

Cleo shook her head. "If that were the case, we could have produced a child with ten genes centuries ago."

"Why didn't you?" I asked.

"We needed the child to be born of free will," Kendor said.

"We needed it to be born of love," Cleo added.

"I don't understand," I said.

Cleo spoke. "None of us fully understands the ingredients that gave rise to a child such as Lara. But we know in the past, when we tried to force the mating of individuals with many witch genes, it always led to disastrous results."

I was afraid to ask. "What happened?"

Kendor spoke bluntly. "The infants either miscarried or else they were born . . . bad."

"Bad?"

"Evil," Kendor said.

Cleo spoke. "A powerful witch, if not conceived and raised

318

in love, cannot know love. All it can know is power. Balance is impossible for such a soul."

"They had to be destroyed," Kendor said.

"While they were still kids?" I gasped.

"Younger," Kendor said.

It took time for me to absorb the immensity of what they were saying. They were implying that the emotional side of my union with Jimmy was as important as our complementary genes. Indeed it was obvious that Cleo saw our "mating" as a spiritual event. Here I considered myself an agnostic, and the ancient one was acting like I had given birth to a saint.

"But you placed me near Jimmy," I said. "That was all pre-arranged, wasn't it?"

"I encouraged your mother to buy that house in Apple Valley once I knew James was living there," my father admitted.

I thought how barren Apple Valley was.

And how my father had not seen my mother in years.

Had I really been conceived in love?

"Couldn't you have arranged a nicer place for Jimmy's family to settle?" I asked, trying to make a joke of the matter to hide my thoughts from Council members. However, I sensed that not even Cleo could read my mind, not now.

"The two of you met when you were supposed to," Cleo said.

"My original question still stands. You act like Jimmy and I are soul mates. If that's the case, why wasn't I the mother of his child in both worlds? There should just be . . . Lara."

"Jimmy was with Kari before he had a chance to get to know you," Kendor said. "We can't control fate."

"We try to interfere as little as possible," Cleo added.

I shook my head. "But even when Jimmy and I were dating, he still left me to go back to Kari. I hear everything you say but it still feels wrong to me."

"It's painful to be rejected," Hatsu said gently.

I wanted to laugh but I think it came out as a grimace.

"Rejected? I hardly got a chance to know him."

Cleo frowned. "You may be right about it feeling wrong. There's a mystery here we have yet to solve. Nevertheless, the fact remains we can't go back in time and change the sequence of events. Huck is alive in what you call the real world. Lara is alive in witch world. If we can, we'll rescue both children."

"But Lara is our priority," Kendor said.

I held up a hand. "Wait a second. James—I mean Jimmy—doesn't know Lara. He knows Huck. I promised him that even though his son doesn't have a perfect string of ten genes, we'd rescue the boy."

"But a moment ago you said Huck shouldn't exist, that there should just be your daughter," Kendor said.

I went to speak, realized he had me, fell silent. Kendor merely stared at me, they all did, waiting. I felt I had to say something.

"I'm just trying to spare Jimmy a lot of grief," I said.

"Is that your only reason for wanting to rescue Huck?"

Kendor asked, his tone casual, yet the meaning behind his words as sharp as the sword he had used to behead the two Lapras outside my father's condo.

I lowered my head. "What other reason could I have?"

Cleo spoke in a kind voice. "It's clear to us that you worry about your boyfriend's love for you. You know he stayed with you in witch world. But in the real world, he left you, and so your heart feels torn. You fear James loves you more than Jimmy. But you feel a desperate need to gain Jimmy's love by saving his son."

I wanted to argue but couldn't. Everything she said was true. *James must care for me more than Jimmy,* I thought. *James never left me. He never said good-bye without one word of explanation.*

My unshed tears were close to boiling. It took all my strength not to weep in front of the Council. For all the good it did; they knew I was an emotional wreck. Cleo leaned over and patted my arm.

"It's true he stayed with you in this world," she whispered in my ear, so soft I knew the others couldn't hear. It was almost as if she spoke to my heart. "But have no doubt, his love for you flows through both worlds."

"How do you know?" I said.

"Such a love is so real, so deep, it's easy to see. And because it streams between both worlds, it can't be measured, nor is there a scale that says it's greater in witch world than in the real world."

"Are you just trying to cheer me up?" I asked.

"You know what I say is true," Cleo said.

"How do you know?"

"Because nothing matters to you as much as love."

I smiled at her words and Cleo hugged me, and it was the greatest hug any human being had ever given me. Thousands of years of affection had polished her heart into a diamond. I felt as if the wound in my own heart finally began to knit together, to heal.

But not completely, not yet.

Alas, we had to get back to business. All my worry about whether Jimmy truly loved me was silly when the children were beyond our reach. I asked a question I had put to Russell and my father, but which I felt the Council might be able to answer better.

"Why did the Lapras steal my daughter?" I asked.

Kendor spoke. "Lara's something new. We've never seen anyone like her before. Her potential is vast. For all we know, it could be infinite."

He was quoting the Paleo-Indians.

Once again, his perception of Lara made me nervous. I scarcely knew my daughter, but I wanted her to have as normal an upbringing as possible. The way Kendor was talking, it sounded like the whole Council was ready to anoint her. I told them how I felt, and Hatsu responded in his thick Chinese accent.

"We're not saying she's the next Krishna or Buddha or

Christ," he said. "Please don't get the idea we wish to deify her or build a religion around her. History has seen enough of that madness."

Then Cleo spoke and her words shook the room.

"But who is to say those great souls did not have the same genetic makeup as Lara?" she asked. "It's unfortunate none of us on the Council ever met those men, but it's possible your daughter could be the bright light we've been hoping for."

"You act like you want to mold her into some kind of savior," I said, annoyed.

"What do we need saving from?" Cleo asked. "Satan? The world doesn't need Lucifer when it has the Lapras. On the other hand, you don't need a lecture on how desperately the earth needs help. You have only to pick up a newspaper. And there's nothing shameful in admitting we have come to an impasse. Yes, even we, the Council, are not sure how to save the real world or witch world. But it's our hope that Lara can help us."

"Excuse me, but aren't we supposed to help ourselves?" I asked.

"True," Cleo said. "Whenever a soul looks outside itself for help, it reduces its strength. But we believe Lara has been born to help us see deeper into our own being."

"How?" I asked.

Cleo shrugged. "I have no idea."

I chewed on that a moment. "Well, one thing's for sure— she can only help witch world."

"Why not both worlds?" Kendor asked.

"Because she doesn't exist in both worlds," I protested.

Hatsu smiled. "We doubt that will stop her."

I shook my head. "You all act so confident the Lapras won't hurt her. I'm afraid I don't share that belief."

"The Lapras are nothing if not pragmatic," Kendor said. "They see Lara as a valuable tool. Why would they harm her before they've had a chance to develop her?"

"How long will they wait?" I thought of the two men my father said they had murdered outside the meat locker and added, "My dad told me they're prone to violence."

Kendor nodded. "They have no qualms about killing."

"They're animals," Hatsu said. "They have no morality."

"Great. And they have my daughter." I paused. "Why didn't you destroy them long ago, before they became so powerful?"

Kendor nodded. "That's the most reasonable question I've heard all night." With that remark he threw Cleo a harsh glance, before adding, "Too many on the Council opposed the idea."

Cleo didn't rise to the bait. Hatsu smiled in my direction. "You see we're not all of one mind," he said. "It's our hope you see that as a strength. Everybody's opinion is important. Yours is especially welcome here."

I could feel our time together slipping away. "All right, tell me about your plan," I said.

"Our plan?" Hatsu asked innocently.

"To get her back," I said. "Russell and my father said she's here in Las Vegas."

"That's correct," Kendor said.

"Do you know where she is?" I asked.

"Just when we figure out her location, they move her," Hatsu said.

I gestured to Russell. "You're high up in their organization. How come they don't trust you enough to tell you where she is?"

Russell hesitated. "They have their own inner group. They call it the Order. It's made up of a dozen members. Unfortunately, I'm not one of them. But the fact that they're allowing me to bring you to them tonight indicates they're about to accept me into the Order."

"Then you'll know where Lara's being held?" I asked.

"I should," Russell said.

"Do you have other spies in their group?" I asked the room. "Besides Russell?"

There was a lengthy pause before anyone spoke.

"Certain things must be kept private," Kendor said.

"In case I'm taken captive?" I said.

"Yes," Kendor said and smiled. "Captured and tortured."

"Lovely," I said.

"They want your help," Cleo said. "It's doubtful they would be so foolish, so soon, to resort to physical violence."

"But not out of the question?" I said.

"Violence is always an option with them," Kendor said.

I grew impatient. "None of you has explained how you plan to get Lara back. Or is that secret knowledge as well?"

"Consider how embarrassing it must be for them to have to contact us," Kendor said. "It's only been three weeks since they kidnapped Lara. It shows how desperate they are."

"My dad said that," I said. "Why are they so desperate?"

Kendor shrugged. "Lara must be torturing them."

"Be serious, please," I said.

"I am," Kendor said.

"How did you guys react when the Lapras said they wanted to talk?" I asked.

"We ignored them, at first," Kendor said. "We wanted you to arrive here in town and get connected. That way we could deal with you directly, while you dealt with them."

"So you have been making plans," I said.

"We haven't been idle," Kendor said.

Cleo spoke. "But it's Lara herself who has been our biggest ally. She's an especially aware child who wants her mother back, and she's made her desire painfully clear. To keep her happy, Jessica, the Lapras are forced to deal with you."

"What kind of deal will they try to make?" I asked.

"They'll probably offer you the same kind of incentive Kari offered Jimmy," Cleo said. "They'll allow you to see Lara as much as you like, as long as you agree to remain in a place that's under their control."

"Where would that be?" I asked.

"Somewhere in or near Las Vegas," Kendor said.

"I take it I'm to reject their offer," I said.

"No," Cleo replied. "You're to give every sign that you're interested. But you want to consider their offer first. They won't like that but you must insist."

"Why?" I asked.

Kendor leaned over. "Because if you don't prevent them from taking control of your life, we might never see you again."

"I'm confused," I said. "It sounds like you're using tonight's meeting to buy time and a little information. But tomorrow night I'm supposed to go back to them forever."

"You're mistaken," Cleo said. "We hope to gain a great deal of information from this meeting."

"Like what?" I asked.

"Like how they were able to bring bafflement," Kendor said.

"That's what we call the cloud that swept over us the night Lara was taken," Hatsu explained.

"And the night they took you from the meat locker," my father added.

I hesitated. "What was it like?"

Kendor sighed and shook his head. "Let's not discuss it tonight. Not before you're to meet with them."

"You're scaring me," I said.

"Fear can help keep you alert," Cleo said. "But know that

they're not invincible. They should have anticipated that Lara would resent having her mother taken away. They made a mistake when they didn't abduct both of you. I believe that single mistake will lead to their ruin."

I forced a laugh. "Hell, they can make up for it in a hurry. They can kidnap me tonight."

"That's another reason Russell is going with you," Kendor said. "He'll help with your security."

"Can you come tonight?" I asked him.

"The Lapras are too afraid of me," Kendor said.

"But I'm heading into their stronghold," I said.

"Russell can summon us, if need be," Kendor said.

"So you'll cover my back?" I asked.

"Only in an emergency," Kendor said.

Cleo shook her head briskly as if she wanted to halt my line of questioning. "We have to move carefully. If we marshal our power and attempt a frontal assault, they'll kill Lara rather than let us have her."

"In other words," Kendor said, speaking to Cleo and not me, "our power is not our strength. We must rely on our patience."

Cleo met his fierce gaze. "Patience and wisdom," she told him before turning her back to him and taking my hand. "The future is always in flux. All we know is the unexpected will happen tonight. There's a good chance it won't be pleasant. For the same reason we want you to meet with them—to gain knowledge—they want to meet with you. They suspect you're in contact with us. You'll deny that, of course, but they'll know you're lying. It doesn't matter. It's their hope that through you they'll discover what we know."

"But you don't seem to know anything," I protested.

Cleo squeezed my hand and I was suddenly reminded of how my father said she could see in both worlds at the same time. "I'm glad you feel that way," she said, a mischievous note in her voice. "It means this meeting has been a success."

CHAPTER SIXTEEN

AT MIDNIGHT, RUSSELL AND I STOOD OUTSIDE THE entrance of the Mirage as per the Lapras' instructions. There were more people coming and going than there would have been in the real world. But their pace was markedly slower, more guarded, as if they were afraid to move too fast lest they call attention to themselves. That was one thing I had noticed about most people in witch world. They were scared.

For that matter, so was Russell, although he had good reason to be. We both did. But he tried putting up a brave front for my sake. He asked what I thought of the Council.

"Very impressive," I replied honestly.

He nodded. "Ain't that the truth. Especially that Cleo. You might be surprised, but even after all these years, I don't know how old she is."

"My father said she's more than seven thousand years old."

"He's just guessing based on things she's said about helping build the pyramids not long after she gained her powers. But the truth is, no one knows how old *they* are, especially the Great Pyramid. From hints Cleo's dropped, it appears Egypt went through three major dynasties. And she said the oldest was the most advanced." He added, "Cleo said there were many witches alive at that time."

"Where did they all go?"

"I don't know, she's never told us."

"Were they killed?"

"Can you imagine trying to kill someone like Cleo?"

"I see what you mean," I replied. "Kendor's amazing."

"In a fight, there's no one I'd rather have by my side. He knows every ancient system of fighting, and all modern methods. Not long ago he posed as a Navy SEAL and learned how to operate America's most advanced weapon systems."

"Somehow I can't see him needing a gun."

"I hear ya." Russell tapped his head. "I saw him in action during the Civil War. During Sherman's brutal march to the sea, after his army burned Atlanta, a platoon of Union soldiers was raping and pillaging a small town. Alone, with only a sword, Kendor killed every single one of those men."

"My father said the Council supported the Union."

"They did. But Kendor has no tolerance for rapists. To him they're animals, he kills them." Russell added, "Cleo's the only one who can control him."

"I didn't mean to insult you when I asked if he could come with us tonight."

"Are you kidding? I wish he were here."

I checked my watch. "They're late."

"They're probably scanning the area, trying to discover if you have Council security in place."

"Will they be able to tell?"

"Unlikely. But there's one thing I want to warn you about. You made it a condition that they have Lara with them before you'd get in their car. You're going to have to drop that demand. She won't be with them. They'd never risk bringing her out in the open like this."

"But they will let me see her tonight, won't they?"

Russell nodded. "That's one point you must insist upon."

"What if they try to keep me prisoner?"

"Let's hope it doesn't come to that," he said.

"What if they torture me? You know, I just graduated high school, I'm not psychologically prepared to have my fingernails slowly ripped from my hands."

Russell patted me on the back. "Remember, they know how to think long-term. They want your cooperation. Like Cleo said, they'd be foolish to use violence so early in the game."

A black limousine pulled up fifteen minutes later. A seven-foot-tall, powerfully built black man emerged and nodded in our direction. He didn't have to speak for me to know it was

Frank, who had sounded like a giant on the phone. He wore a rich dark suit, a red shirt, and a dark tie. His shoulders were as broad as an NFL lineman's, and he had huge, blunt hands, and a massive bald head. He appeared to be forty, although he could have been centuries old for all I knew. He was coarsely handsome, and I had no doubt he had inherited the strength gene.

He raised his arm. "Jessica, Russell, come."

We climbed in the back of the limo; Frank joined us. There were just the three of us, along with a driver separated by a plate of soundproof glass. The limo turned onto the Strip, for a moment, before it veered onto a side street. Frank sat across from us, his expression serious. Everything about him was oversize. He spoke to Russell.

"Any problems?" he asked.

"I didn't see anyone," Russell said, talking about the Tar. "It makes me wonder."

Frank treated Russell's concerns with respect. "How so?"

"They may be preparing to attack," Russell said.

"What are you guys talking about?" I asked, pretending to be ignorant.

Frank stared at me. "Security matters. We'll explain more later. I must say, Jessica, you're much more beautiful in person."

I met his hard gaze. "As opposed to what?"

"Feisty, too. Russell warned me you can be a handful."

"Only when I'm lied to. And you've already lied to me

once. Where's my daughter? She's supposed to be here."

"We're going to see her right now," Frank said.

"You didn't answer my question."

"For her protection," Frank said, "we're keeping her out of sight for the time being. But you'll see her soon, I promise."

"Good," I said.

The tint on the windows was so dark that once we left the Strip behind, I couldn't identify any of the roads we took. We were moving in a long, lazy pattern, one designed to reveal any pursuers. Frank took out his cell and shot off a series of texts. Russell stared straight ahead, ignoring me. Conversation didn't seem a priority with the Lapras.

Twenty minutes went by; it felt much longer. Eventually I saw we were in the desert, on a narrow asphalt road. Suddenly we turned onto a dirt path and I felt the front wheels sink beneath us. A gap had opened up in the path and in the blink of an eye we were heading down a steep ramp. I caught a glimpse of a garage door opening and closing.

We had entered a long, straight tunnel. Had our headlights failed, we would have been marooned. It was like a hole that had been dug on the dark side of the moon. We drove another fifteen minutes at seventy miles an hour before we stopped.

All in the dark. All underground.

Climbing out of the limo, I saw that the tunnel continued in both directions. The air was damp, the omnipresent silence unnerving. A nondescript door stood before us. We went inside, walked down a white corridor, and went through another plain door.

Suddenly everything changed.

We were in a room as lovely as the one where I had met the Council, only the furniture was distinctly modern and there was no floor above us. There was, however, a wide, circular floor space, totally black, that looked as if it could have been used to teach dance. It didn't fit with the rest of the living area and I wondered what it was for.

The living room, if it could be called that, was replete with glass and leather, its color scheme dominated with gray, black, and white. Even without windows the room felt expansive. The dome ceiling helped, as did the half-dozen vases of flowers spread atop a piano and numerous end tables.

Yet the modern feel didn't translate into a warm one. The space felt as if it was lived in, but I had to wonder at the minds of its occupants. My heart skipped the instant we entered and I felt a dull pressure on my forehead. It was as if my physical body sensed the bad vibes.

To my surprise, Frank told us to make ourselves comfortable and left. Russell and I sat on the sofa and didn't speak. He had given me a look that said we were being watched. Minutes later the door opened and a woman walked in.

Dr. Susan Wheeler. From the morgue.

I gasped, although what I really wanted to do was vomit.

She was dressed in a doctor's plain blue scrubs, as if she had just come from the hospital. At least her outfit appeared fresh—there were no bloodstains on it.

Her smooth mocha skin had not changed, nor her dark brown hair. But unlike last time, she didn't have on a cap and I saw her hair reached all the way to her waist. It was her trophy—it glistened in the light of a nearby lamp. Her dark eyes were as unfathomable as ever, but they didn't shine like her hair. It seemed that whatever light entered Susan Wheeler was not allowed to leave.

Still, she was beautiful.

Most men would have found her irresistible.

"I trust you remember me," she said as she casually took a seat across from us. She wore white Puma cross-trainers. They looked brand-new. The way she carried herself spoke of someone who was incredibly fit. Who was I fooling? She probably had the strength of fifty men.

I had to calm myself before I could speak. "You're the one who tried to dissect me at the hospital," I said.

"You mean I was the coroner who was assigned to perform your postmortem."

"You knew from the start I was alive!"

Susan shrugged. "I played on your fears. That was a gift. I was trying to kick-start your healing ability. You have to admit I was successful."

"I'm grateful," I said sarcastically.

"You're welcome."

I acted impatient. "Frank told me I was going to meet with the leadership of your organization."

"Yes."

"Where are they?"

"Sitting in front of you."

"You?"

"I'm the president of the Lapra Order."

I cast Russell a glance. He didn't bother to hide his surprise. It was clear he'd never met the woman before and that worried me. Here he was supposed to be close to their inner circle and he didn't even know their leader?

"Are you the one who took Lara from me?" I asked.

"I am."

She made the admission without hesitation. She wanted me to know how powerful she was. It was possible she was stronger than Cleo. Yet it was hard to imagine she was the source of the strange time-space distortions that had rendered the Council's protection useless. She nodded as if reading my mind.

"I rule the Lapras because no one can rule me. We're a purely hierarchical society. The greater one's power, the higher one is allowed to rise in our organization. That's important— should you choose to remain with us—because you have a large number of witch genes and can eventually occupy an important position."

"So in your group 'might is right,'" I said.

"As it is in nature, so it is with us."

"Try telling that to the dinosaurs."

"They ruled the earth for millions of years. I'd be surprised if humanity lasts that long."

"You think we'll destroy ourselves?"

"Yes. Or a superior race will come along and do the job for us. Life is a temporary condition. Death is our ultimate destiny."

"You're a cheery character."

"I'm a realist."

"If everything is ultimately hopeless, then why did you bother stealing my daughter?" I demanded.

Susan didn't blink much, nor show much emotion of any kind. There was a mechanical quality to her tone and choice of words.

"I was curious about her," she said. "What she can do. What she might grow into. That's the scientist in me. Lara's something new and different. That makes her interesting."

"You talk about her like she's a specimen."

"Compared to her, we may all be specimens. It's interesting to see what powers she's begun to develop, even as an infant."

I paused. "Has she demonstrated unusual abilities?"

"Spend time with her and you'll see for yourself."

I didn't bother to hide my annoyance. "I shouldn't have to ask your permission to see her. When she was a few days old, you stole her from me in the middle of the night. And the only reason you're talking with me now is because you're having trouble managing her."

Susan studied me. "Who told you these things?"

"Are they true or not?"

"Who told you?" she repeated, and her words, in combination with her cold gaze, cut like scalpels. The pain in my forehead got worse and I felt compelled to answer. But I didn't feel like I was giving away any secrets. If Kari knew I was talking to the Tar, this woman surely knew.

"The Tar," I muttered.

Susan considered. "What do you think of them?"

"I'm the wrong one to ask. I hardly know them."

"How would you compare their organization to mine?"

"Well, first off, your organization sucks. The way you behave, stealing Lara and Huck, it's like you have no morality."

"How do you define morality?"

"The way the dictionary does."

My insults rolled off the woman. She replied in the same flat tone. "Personally, I would define morality as striving to do what will benefit the most people over the greatest length of time. Do you have a problem with that definition?"

I hesitated. "I'm not sure what you mean."

"Today, in the other world, my people saw you take a drive into the desert. They didn't bother following you but I'm sure if you had a map with you it warned that you were heading into an area where the government used to test nuclear weapons. They still test them out there, by the way, they just don't advertise the fact."

"What does this have to do with morality?" I asked.

"At the end of World War Two, President Truman was faced with the most difficult moral decision of our age: whether to use the atomic bomb against Japan. It was an almost impossible decision for such a moral man to make. The Japanese had started the war and America had lost countless soldiers trying to defeat them. Now, at last, America had Japan on the ropes. Most of their cities had been firebombed and lay in ruins. Still, the Japanese were a proud people and refused to surrender. Quite the opposite—they were busy training every man, woman, and child to resist an invasion. Truman's advisors estimated he would have to sacrifice a million American soldiers to secure the island, not to mention the five million Japanese who would die with them." Susan paused. "Or else he could drop one or two atomic bombs and it would all be over."

"I didn't come here for a history lesson."

"You came here to understand why I took Lara from you. The reason lies in my experience of history. In a sense, Truman was faced with the same decision that confronts the two of us right now. The president knew dropping an atom bomb on a defenseless town would cause immeasurable suffering. He had seen a film of the test blast. He was an intelligent man. His head said, 'Yes, use the weapon, end the war quickly.' But his heart said, 'No, it's too awful, too many women and children will burn to death.' He didn't know what to do. He prayed to God for guidance." Susan paused. "But in the end you know what decision he made."

"Sure. He wiped out Hiroshima and Nagasaki."

"And what do you think of his decision?"

"It was barbaric."

"That's all you have to say? It was barbaric? What about the millions of lives he saved? On both sides of the war?"

"Like you said, America had Japan on the ropes. Had Truman waited, they would have surrendered."

Susan peered at me. "I can say with absolute certainty that they would never have given up. Does that alter your opinion?"

"No."

"Why not?" Susan asked.

"Because . . . I don't believe you."

"In the end, Truman realized his decision couldn't be based on belief, even though he was a deeply religious man. It had to be founded on mathematics. Kill a quarter of a million people to save six million." She paused. "History tells us he made the right decision. The war was over a few days later."

She sounded like Kendor when he spoke of Caesar. It made me wonder.

"None of this has anything to do with Lara," I said.

"You're mistaken. Lara is every bit as important to the world as atomic energy. I dare say, in time, she'll probably be seen as more important. As long as we have the strength of will to use her."

"To use her? How are you going to use her?"

"I don't know. How can any of us know at this point? But it's easy to imagine a day when we might use her abilities to help unify the world."

"You mean, take over the world," I said.

"Take over, save, unite, control—they're all words for the same thing. Unless the world is brought together under one authority, it'll destroy itself, and billions will die. Already the seeds of its destruction are visible everywhere."

"You're the last person I'd give that authority to."

"Then give me Lara. I told you, if she's the stronger, then eventually she'll rule the Lapras."

"Yeah, twenty years from now. In the meantime you'll be in control and you're just what this troubled planet needs. A sadist."

Russell, who had shown remarkable restraint by not talking, let out a sound of disgust. He was acting offended. Perhaps he feared I had pushed the woman too far. Yet Susan didn't appear annoyed.

"You misunderstand me, Jessica. I don't cause pain because I'm cruel. I use pain as a tool. In the same way, in the morgue, I used your fear to activate your healing gene and help awaken your other abilities."

"Bullshit! Kidnapping Lara was the act of a monster!"

Susan spoke calmly. "It gave me no pleasure to take your daughter from you. I took her in the hope I could use her to create a better future. Unfortunately, I overestimated my abilities, or else I underestimated hers. She's a month old but has the alertness of a three-year-old. Worse, in the short time you two were together, she bonded with you in a way I don't understand. Suffice to say, I can't replace you."

"No matter how much affection you lavish on her."

"Correct. A normal infant recognizes its mother, to some extent. But I wouldn't be surprised if Lara can spot you from far away."

"Are you saying she misses me?"

"Yes."

"How does she display this . . . lack?"

"That is irrelevant."

As Susan spoke, I couldn't help but recall her treatment of Dr. David Leonard when he had collapsed on the floor of the morgue. On the surface she had done everything right. She had examined his chest for a possible heart attack and had noted his blue color. Then she had called for the doctors upstairs.

Yet, while waiting for the doctors to arrive, she had taken his dying hands and placed them over her heart and closed her eyes like she was swooning with . . . pleasure? Had I imagined that? It sure as hell had not looked like concern.

Susan spoke of the Lapras as being an organization that was logically constructed. It rewarded power and effectiveness.

It had no interest in weakness. But I had to wonder if there was more to it than that. Had this strange woman walked so far along the dark path that she actually enjoyed the pain she caused?

"Did you stop breast-feeding my daughter?" I asked.

"You're asking if I hired a wet nurse. No, none was available that I could trust. Unfortunately, to this day Lara still has trouble with formula."

I hesitated. "Is she colicky?"

"Yes. She often screams in pain."

"Then give her back to me!"

"Agree to my terms and you can have her."

"Your terms. I have already heard a version of them from Kari. Why did you kidnap her baby, by the way?"

"Huck has an impressive number of witch genes. He's still Jimmy's son. In the future he may make a formidable employee."

"Liar. You could have waited to take him. But you wanted to use Huck to put pressure on me through Jimmy."

Susan shrugged. "The strategy might still work, even if you are aware of it."

Leaning forward, I pointed a finger at her. "You can't treat people like objects and expect them to react in a positive manner. In this whole talk, you haven't told me one thing that would make me want to join the Lapras."

"Join us and you can have anything you want."

"With my genes, and without your help, I can already have anything I want."

"Will the Tar let you indulge your desires so freely?"

"I don't know what you're talking about," I said.

"The Tar have rules. Follow them and you must follow their rules. They won't let you run off and do whatever you want."

"The Tar are committed to free will," I said.

"Bullshit," Russell muttered, playing his role well.

I turned to him. "Explain."

He looked to Susan for approval to continue and she nodded. He spoke in a condescending tone. "Their main directive is that no witch can use his or her power to take advantage of your average human being."

I nodded. "That sounds reasonable."

"But we were born superior!" he said. "We were meant to live superior lives. That's not simply a philosophy. It's natural selection. Mankind evolved, and with their large brains they eventually took over this planet. In the same way, with our superior genes, it's natural that we should rule mankind."

"You sound like a Nazi," I said.

Susan spoke. "If the Tar and the Lapra organizations didn't exist, those who possess witch genes would still control the world. What's happening is inevitable. That's why all these arguments are fruitless. A new order has arrived. It's not going to magically disappear."

"If all this is inevitable, then why do you need Lara?"

"I need nothing," she said. "Lara may simply help me speed up a process that is already well under way. Now, I've granted you the courtesy of this meeting because I thought I could talk some sense into you. If I'm wasting my time, and you're in love with the Tar doctrine, then please tell me now."

"So you can kill me and get it over with?"

Susan shrugged. "Perhaps it will come to that. Lara wants you back but are you really the best one to act as her mother? I warn you, that has yet to be determined."

The threat was unmistakable. "I don't understand."

"You will before you leave here."

"You promised I could see her," I said.

"You may." Susan reached in her pocket, took out a cell, and pushed a single button. She didn't speak. Two minutes later there was a knock on the door and Frank entered, carrying a tiny infant in his huge hands.

I don't remember leaping to my feet and crossing the room but I must have done so because in an instant Lara was in my arms. My love for her then was too big to express in words. Yet I must use words to say how I felt, and the nearest phrase I can find to convey my emotions is that it *killed me* to hold her. It was like the *I* that Jessie/Jessica was formed around was washed away by a tidal wave of love. I didn't need to exist because she existed. It was then I understood how a mother could die a million deaths to protect her child.

346

Her hair was more red than mine. A month old and she had so many curls! Her hair reached almost to her eyes. God, her eyes, they were glorious. They were as Kendor had said, an enchanting aquamarine, just like the lake water at the Paleo sacred spot. They were so bright, like her smile.

Lara cooed and giggled and tried to grab me. I had to sit down before I let myself bury my face in her body. I was afraid I would faint. Her fingers reached out and tugged on mine and I felt waves of pleasure race through every nerve in my body.

The only thing that confused me was how damp her skin was. Like she had just come from a warm bath. Then I realized I was crying all over her. I wiped at her chubby cheeks with the hem of my blouse.

"Are you satisfied?" Susan asked.

"Yes," I whispered.

"You can live with her in a house in the desert. A beautiful home in a lovely spot. You can have friends visit, I don't care how many. James can live with you if you want, that's up to you two. All I ask in return is that you take care of Lara and have no more contact with the Tar." Susan paused. "Does that sound fair?"

My bliss was suddenly shaken by dread.

"I can't make a decision right now," I said.

"Fine. I don't want your decision to be a hasty one. Sleep on it." Susan gestured to Frank, who moved my way.

I cringed. "What are you doing?"

"Taking Lara back," Susan said.

"She just got here! You let Kari play with Huck for hours!"

"Kari's a fool who needs hours to make contact. Once more, you and Lara have bonded and that's all that's necessary at this point." Frank had stopped above me and had his hands out. Susan added, "You don't want him to use force. She might get hurt."

Trembling, I handed over my daughter, and the second she was out of my hands, Lara began to wail. A *wave* appeared to go through the room. I couldn't see it but I felt it. It was an invisible pulse that made everything in the room blur slightly. The ground seemed to shake and I had the sensation that the earth itself was responding to the stress of the moment. Lara was angry at those who were tearing us apart and this wave . . . why, it was directed at Susan and Frank!

I noticed Frank had trouble exiting the room. He stumbled twice. He was having trouble breathing. Susan also was affected. As if to ward off the rush of a sudden migraine, she put her hands to her head.

It took several minutes after Lara had left the room for the effects of the wave to completely diminish. By then Susan was furious. The reason was obvious. She hadn't wanted me to know what Lara was capable of.

"Your daughter will be controlled, one way or the other," Susan said in a cold voice. She didn't have to add that if I failed to help them, then they would use other methods to restrain her, and those ways would be painful.

"She's just a baby," I pleaded.

"She's *not* just a baby." Susan stiffened. "Are my conditions clear?"

"Will you release Huck to Kari and Jimmy as well?"

"Yes."

"Will I be free to raise Lara until she's an adult?"

"Why not?" Susan replied. She hadn't really answered my question.

I felt myself losing control. I felt battered by the waves of emotion pouring through me. For the first time since entering the room, I humbled myself before Susan.

"Up until Lara was born," I said, "I didn't even know about the Tar. They entered my life suddenly. If they find out where I'm living with Lara, who's to say they won't try to contact me?"

"As long as you notify me immediately of any such contact, then I won't hold you to blame. But if I discover you're secretly working with their Council . . ."

Susan didn't finish. She didn't have to.

"I'll die," I said.

"You'll both die if you continue to prove troublesome. Let me make myself absolutely clear. I'm willing to work with you and Lara up to a point. But if she continues to repeat what you experienced tonight, then I'll destroy you both and focus on my own genetics program." Susan paused. "Any more questions?"

"One. How did I end up on your dissection table?"

"You want to know how we knew you were in the meat locker."

"Yes."

Susan nodded toward Russell. "He told us."

I was stunned. Could it be true?

Russell nodded. "I only appear to work for the Council." He chuckled. "The fools."

I stood, backing away from him. Was this more of his act? To convince the Lapras that he was one of them? He sounded so convincing. Reaching inside, desperate for my intuition to give me some direction, I felt only bewilderment. Yet a cold truth suddenly pierced my heart, one that deepened my confusion.

"You murdered the men outside the meat locker!" I gasped. "The ones who were watching over me to make sure I survived!"

Russell grinned. "Good old Joe and Barry. Felt sort of bad about them. But what's a guy to do?"

"You . . . you scum!" I cried.

Russell was amused. "That's not what you thought last night when you were tearing off my clothes."

"I've been told Russell has been an immense help to us over the last hundred years," Susan said. "We're considering granting him a place in our Order."

Russell frowned. "I thought that was a done deal."

Susan shook her head. "The impatience of youth. All our other members are at least three centuries old. Aren't you a little young to be given such an important position?"

"Judge me by my accomplishments, not my age," Russell said. "After all, wasn't I the one who brought you Jessica?"

"True. But are you certain you can do what it takes to be a member of our Order?" Susan asked.

"I can do anything," he replied.

Susan stared at him a long time before responding. "There's a reason you've never been here before."

"What is it?"

Susan stood and gestured to the circular space at the far side of the living area. Specifically, she pointed to two instruments hanging on the wall. I had not paid them any heed before. One was a sword. Not being an expert in blades, I couldn't say when and where it had been created. Because it was fully sheathed in leather, I could only assume how sharp it was.

The second weapon, if that's what it was, appeared to be a long wooden stick. At first I thought it was bamboo, but a closer look revealed a lack of partitions or internal chambers. The stick was either hollow or solid, I couldn't tell, but without touching it, I sensed the wood was hard, perhaps even petrified.

"Both of you came here tonight wanting something," Susan said. "You, Jessica, want your daughter back. I have made you an offer as to how you can fulfill that desire, but I must add one final condition. Before I hand Lara over to you, I have to know you're strong enough to be her mother. Do you understand?"

"I understand enough to know that your definition of strength is not the same as mine," I replied.

"True. But since I'm the one who is to decide the fate of your daughter, my definition is the only one that matters." She paused. "Having a high number of witch genes doesn't guarantee real power. I've seen witches with three genes defeat those with six because their will demanded that they win. It burned with desire, and fire." Susan came close to me and pointed to my solar plexus. It was as if she could read my mind. "Do you know why they call it the solar plexus?" she asked.

I remembered lying dead on a cold morgue slab.

Then suddenly coming to life, when attacked.

"No," I said.

"Because it's the center of the fire of life. In India they call that center the seat of Agni, which means 'fire.' In China it's the source of Chi, or life energy. In ancient Egypt it was where Ra, the sun god, was worshipped in the human body. The tradition doesn't matter, they were all saying the same thing. When the fire burns bright, so does one's life."

"Why the lecture?" I asked.

Susan ignored me and turned to Russell. "To join the Order takes more than loyalty and the accomplishment of difficult deeds. You, too, must demonstrate this fire by showing how deep is your will to win, and your desire to live."

"I've never heard I had to fight another witch to become a member of the Order," Russell said.

Susan smiled faintly. "That's because those who failed the test are no longer with us. And those who passed the test are wise enough not to talk about it." She looked back and forth between us. "Only one of you will leave this room alive."

"I'm confused," Russell said. "I was told she was important."

"She is. But only if she's capable of killing you."

Russell stiffened. "I've served the Lapras since I was born."

Susan nodded. "Because of your loyalty, I'll let you choose whatever weapon you prefer."

Russell gestured to me. "At least find me a witch worth killing. Two days ago she wasn't even connected."

Susan turned away and spoke over her shoulder. "Then your place in the Order is all but assured," she said.

"I'd prefer to fight an equal," Russell said, and the fact he was arguing against killing me made me wonder if I was wrong about him all over again.

"Don't underestimate Jessica," Susan said as she took a seat on a sofa from where she had a clear view of the black circle. "She's a mother fighting for her child. Few creatures in nature are more dangerous. Plus she has plenty of witch genes. They may be buried deep, but you know how the fear of death can force them to the surface."

Russell considered, then bowed in Susan's direction. "Very well, I choose the sword," he said.

I erupted. "Like you give a damn that it's going to be an unfair fight!" I cried.

Russell shrugged and strolled toward the sword. "I didn't come here to lose my head," he said.

"You're a hypocrite and a traitor," I swore. My fear increased dramatically. This was really happening. I couldn't talk my way out of it. One of us was going to die, for real—it didn't matter which world we were in.

"And you're as good as dead," he replied as he lifted the protective leather and unsheathed the sword.

"Consider, Jessica," Susan said. "The blade is three feet long and heavy. The staff is six feet long and hard as stone. You'll have double the reach and should be able to block his every blow." She gestured for me to collect my weapon. "And don't be bitter. In the morgue, I warned you this time would come."

It was a bitter memory that brought her words back to me.

"You were lucky this time. . . . But don't think for a second that you're in control."

"I should have killed you before I left that hospital," I said as I crossed the black circle and retrieved the stick, or what Susan called the staff. It was indeed as hard as petrified wood, although it appeared to have been coated with amber, which had dried and given it an extra gripping quality. It felt remarkably light in my hands. I balanced it in the middle, hoping that would make it easier to block a blow from either side.

Russell, meanwhile, was loosening up, stretching his muscles, cutting the air with his sword. He was fast; his repeated slashes seemed to dissect the oxygen molecules. His blade sang and there wasn't a trace of hesitation in his movements.

I knew I'd be a fool to hope for his sympathy.

He removed his jacket and kicked off his shoes and socks. I wondered if I should do likewise. Yet I had not dressed fancy for the meeting. I had on my favorite Nikes—the rubber soles seemed to grip the black floor.

Susan spoke from the couch. "Prepare yourself. There's only one rule. You're to stay in the circle until your opponent is dead." She paused. "Begin!"

Immediately Russell began to circle, forcing me to move to my left when I would have preferred to go right. His expression was focused, he didn't look scared.

Yet he took me seriously. The first blow he attempted was what I knew to be a "killing blow." He swung straight for the top of my skull, and I would have died if I hadn't blocked it.

But my newfound strength, my reflexes, they were fully available to me. My instinct was working as well. Without thinking, my hands leaped farther apart so that when the blade fell on me, inches from my head, there was plenty of room on my staff to repel the blow.

I half expected his sword to get stuck in my staff but the wood cleanly blocked the blow. That fact seemed to surprise

Russell. For an instant he let the blade linger atop the staff. Taking advantage of his hesitation, I lashed out with my left foot and struck his right rib cage.

I heard a distinct crack. He gasped.

"Lara's not going to lose her mother," I swore. "Nothing else matters."

"Wrong!" he shouted, withdrawing his blade and swinging at my calves. I had to hop to avoid his blow, and assumed his miss would give me a shot at his head. I took it but he anticipated the blow, and ducked, and I missed by a mile.

Indeed, I realized a second later, his attack and his response to my blow had all been a setup. The instant my staff flew by the spot where his head had been, he tossed his blade from his right hand to his left and slashed upward at my right arm. My failed blow had left my right side exposed. I had to twist hard to the left to avoid losing my right arm at the elbow.

I barely made it. The razor-sharp steel caught the skin on the outside of my arm. It sliced off a chunk of flesh. I was lucky the cut wasn't any larger or I would have lost the use of my arm.

But with pain screaming up my elbow into my brain and blood flying through the air, I felt far from lucky. He paused to survey the damage he'd done. God, how I hated his guts right then, so much so that I wanted to see them spilled over the floor.

"Lara's never going to know her mother," he said, completing his earlier remark.

He resumed circling. Now he came at me from my right because he no longer feared that arm. His approach was sound. I was bleeding heavily, the warm liquid seeping down my arm and spilling onto the staff, making my grip slippery.

I kept waiting for my healing gene to activate but then I realized the ability needed my attention to work. If I could have a brief break, sit and close my eyes for two minutes, focus on the wound, I could probably stop the bleeding.

But he wasn't going to give me that break. His pursuit was relentless. He came over the top again with his sword. I repelled him, but then he stabbed straight at me, several times in quick succession, and I had to dodge left and right, back and forth. He came close to driving me out of the circle. Behind me, I heard Susan clapping, the bitch.

The contest was only a few minutes old when I began to recognize Russell's strategy. He was staying *constantly* on the offensive. My initial kick had broken his ribs, but it had cost me more than it was worth—because it had warned him how dangerous I was if I was given a chance to think, to recover. If I'd been smart, I would never have let him know at the start how strong I was. Now he was wary. Now he wasn't going to give me a chance to breathe.

He swung for my legs again. I tried something different. Planting my staff in the floor, I used it like a small tree to block his blow. The tactic surprised him and I saw an opening. I kicked with my right leg at his left knee. He saw the blow coming. At the last instant he backed up. But my foot caught his kneecap and again I heard a crack.

I had torn cartilage, maybe even severed a ligament. But I was inexperienced. I should have capitalized on my good fortune rather than celebrate it. I should have struck again, immediately. That had been the whole point of Kendor's story about Caesar. In battle, if you have the advantage, take it, even if it means you have to be brutal. While sitting beside the desert lake with Kendor, I wondered if he had foreseen this precise moment and had been trying to warn me.

Russell took advantage of my hesitation. Showing a level of swiftness he had never revealed before, he spun a full three hundred and sixty degrees on his uninjured leg and tried to decapitate me with a sword that almost turned invisible with speed.

I blocked his blow. It took both my arms and my heels dug in to stop the sword from slicing through my neck but I did it. In the process I lost the little finger on my left hand, plus another chunk of flesh. The red tissue fell to the floor as my blood gushed in the air.

Again, I heard Susan clap.

Again, Russell began to circle.

The floor was soaked in blood. I could no longer trust my grip. I wanted to call time-out to take off my shoes, to put my finger back on, to heal. My staff was slippery at both ends. I was afraid to swing it at full strength. How did I know it wouldn't fly out of my hands?

Then I saw him smile, reading my thoughts, counting on the fact that I would stay on the defensive. I realized as clear as the blood running down both my arms that only a bold move could save me. But first I had to be sure of one thing.

"You couldn't do this if you cared," I whispered.

He nodded faintly. "I never did, Jessica."

I took a long step back, to the edge of the circle, and gripped as best I could the end of the staff. I swung it at him. He blocked the blow. I swung again and again, he kept blocking me. I didn't care—I was going to use all six feet of my weapon, and I wasn't going to let him rest even if I was desperate to stop. I hacked at him like he was an attacking lion, my breath on fire, and chased him around the circle.

Then I made a mistake. Or else fate did.

I slipped. I slipped on my own blood.

I didn't fall to the floor but I lost my balance and suddenly my staff was way out of position and I was wide open to attack. Again, Russell showed his age and experience. He didn't go nuts and try to chop me in two. But he did make a calculated thrust into my stomach. The blade went all the way through me. It poked out my back.

He withdrew the sword and took a step back.

It was the first pause he had taken.

He waited for me to fall.

Blood poured from my front like a faucet. I felt a warm river slide down my lower back. A puddle formed at my feet and turned my white Nikes red. The blood pulsed onto the floor, in rhythm with my heart, and each squirt brought a deeper wave of dizziness. I blinked and for an instant there were three Russells. It was strange, I thought, how in the background I still saw only one Susan.

I felt her cold eyes on me. She leaned forward, mildly curious how I would choose to spend the last seconds of my life. Yet, like in the morgue—when her eyes had met mine and I knew she knew I was alive—I felt she wanted to tell me something.

Then I realized she already had.

Her lecture about the fire of life in the solar plexus.

The Agni, the Chi, the sun god Ra.

That magical fire, smoldering inside, waiting to be activated in the right circumstance, and in the proper way, if I just knew how. Of course I already knew the secret. I had done it before to stay alive. I could do it again, to heal myself, after I had dealt with my foe.

There was a reason she had given Russell first choice.

She had known he would take the sword.

Any sane person would have.

Except for a wizard. A wizard needed his staff.

To burn. And what was a wizard but a male witch?

As Russell waited for me to drop my staff and topple to the floor and die, I focused on my solar plexus. Letting my rage over his betrayal consume me, I felt the fire I had experienced in the morgue reignite. But this time it didn't stop at the tips of my fingers. It traveled up my arms and lit the top of my staff, and the flame that burst from the tip was as red as my blood and as hot as a dragon's breath.

Too late, Russell realized his mistake. He should never have given me a chance to rest. I saw his thoughts flicker behind his eyes. He knew he couldn't allow me to bring the flame to him. He had to kill me, immediately, to put it out. There was no other way.

He rushed toward me with his sword.

He planned to run me through.

I raised the staff. He ran into the fire. It struck him in the heart, and it spread, as if fed by my blood on the floor. The red fluid seemed to change to gasoline and the flame that hit his chest expanded from the floor like a sphere born of a hellish curse.

He shuddered and dropped his sword. For a moment it was as if someone had blasted him with steam, but it was smoke. His hands began to blister, swelling into grotesque puffy appendages that exploded with scalding blood. Then another layer formed, but this one was not filled with liquid. Instead, it turned hard and black and crusty.

His hair caught fire. Screaming, he raised his arms to try to bat out the flames, but the fire took his clothes. The horror of his living cremation forced him to shut his eyes but that didn't help. His eyebrows, his eyelashes, his eyelids—they all burned away. For several agonizing seconds his eyeballs were exposed and it seemed as if they stared at Susan and he saw her for what she really was. Even as his flesh melted, his expression twisted in horrifying recognition, and I could have sworn he wasn't seeing her any longer, or any kind of woman, but something else.

Tilting her head back, Susan closed her eyes and smiled.

Her expression was blissful. His pain fed her bliss.

Finally, Russell screamed one last time and crumpled to the floor and I was able to close my own eyes and think of the night I met him, and how beautiful his body had been. For some reason my hatred was gone. Perhaps his agony had burned it away. I was able to recall how he had held me naked in his hotel room, when we had kissed and touched beneath the glow of the Strip.

I realized I was no longer bleeding. Finally, I was healing, even my severed finger. Yet I sobbed, feeling warm tears flow over my vanishing wounds. I opened my eyes and saw a pile of black ash in the center of the floor. At some point Susan must have gotten up. She stood across from me and stared down at what was left of Russell.

"He was a traitor," she said flatly.

"What?" I gasped. "He tried to kill me."

Susan shook her head. "Then he was a coward as well. I had already heard from my people that he was reluctant to give up your location in that meat locker. And they had to kill the two men who were guarding the place. Russell refused to."

"So this was all just a game to you?" I felt sick. I had killed an innocent man, and a friend.

"A test and a lesson, Jessica. You passed the test when you invoked the fire. But you might want to consider tonight's lesson when it comes to your boyfriend and daughter."

"Meaning?" I demanded.

Susan brushed flakes of ash from her hospital scrubs. "Frank will take you back to your hotel. Tomorrow night, in witch world, he'll call and pick you up and we'll meet again. If you like, you can have James come. I'm sure he'd love to see Lara." She paused. "But bring one member of the Tar's Council and you'll all burn."

Frank appeared then. He came through the door as if called, although I hadn't seen her signal for him. This time he didn't carry Lara, but a small boy. The child was dressed in a gray sweat suit and looked about five years old. A handsome child, he had long, dark hair and black eyes rimmed with a haunting yellow glow that made them look like twin suns that had been eclipsed by black holes. The child had a twin, for I was sure I had seen him before.

A four-foot tail coiled out the rear of his spine, wrapping around his waist. It tapered into a sharp tip that reminded me of a scorpion's stinger. Instinctively, I knew it was poisonous.

The child leaped into Susan's arms. She smiled.

"Mommy!" Whip cried.

CHAPTER SEVENTEEN

BACK AT THE MGM, I SLIPPED INTO MY EMPTY BED AND woke up eight hours later beside Jimmy. It was Monday morning, of course, although I felt as if I'd been in Las Vegas a week.

Susan had sworn Russell was a traitor, which made me confident he had remained loyal to the Tar. It also made me anxious to talk to Russ. If he was alive, damnit. This two-world thing was killing me, because I didn't even know if he had been killed in the real world.

But Jimmy immediately started bombarding me with questions about what had happened during my "missing day." I begged for a chance to run over and see Russ—alone—but he put his foot down.

"No," Jimmy said. "I'm going with you."

The rest of the gang was still present: Debbie, Ted, Alex,

and her new boyfriend, Al. I had told them I had won a bonus package that allowed us to stay for free—meals included—at the hotel for five days. Of course I was paying for everything with my bag of cash. They had gone along with the lie because they wanted to, although Alex wasn't so easily placated. Before I could get out the door with Jimmy, she pulled me aside.

"I don't know you," she said.

I lowered my head. "I know."

"Since you disappeared that night, you've changed," she said. "It's only because you've had Jimmy with you that I've let it go on so long. But it ends today, and before this day is over, you're going to tell me everything that's going on."

"Agreed." I hugged her. "But I have to warn you—you're not going to believe a word of it."

"I will if it's the truth," she replied.

"Jimmy said the same thing yesterday and ended up cursing me."

Alex glanced to where Jimmy was waiting to leave with me. "Why do you have to rush out right now?" she asked.

"I have to see Russ."

"And you're bringing Jimmy with you?"

"Jealousy's no longer an issue."

"I doubt Jimmy feels that way."

I kissed Alex's cheek. "Later, I promise, we'll talk. I have to go now."

Soon Jimmy and I were in a cab, heading to the Mandalay Bay, when I suddenly changed my mind and told the driver to go to the Bellagio.

"What's at the Bellagio?" Jimmy asked.

"We might have a tail on us," I whispered, in case our driver was a Lapra. "Besides, we're not going to the Mandalay Bay. I want to go to the new address my father gave me."

"No. I want to meet this Russ," Jimmy insisted.

"You will. Later."

He studied me. "There's something you're not telling me."

I sighed. "I had a rough night."

We went through the same routine as before. We entered the Bellagio at the front and caught another taxi at the back. We did this twice more before I felt comfortable enough to go to a house my father had rented that morning. He had already left the condo behind.

My dad was having breakfast with Whip when we arrived. The boy gave Jimmy and me surprise hugs when he saw us, before my father sent him to watch TV in the other room.

My father's ashen expression said it all, I didn't need to ask. But Jimmy insisted upon an explanation, and it was not long before I learned what had happened to Russ—in the real world.

For some unknown reason, a fire had broken out on the floor of his hotel. Six suites had been damaged and a dozen occupants had been injured, with one death. According to my father, there was no doubt Russ was dead. His body had already been identified.

"The authorities say he died in his sleep," my father said.

"That's not what happened," I whispered.

My father turned to Jimmy. "May I speak to my daughter alone?" he asked.

Jimmy shook his head. "I'm tired of you guys and all your secrets. I want to know why this guy's dead. Weren't the bunch of you just meeting with that Council of yours?"

I was tired of lying. My father gestured for me to remain silent but I ignored him. "My father, Russ, and I did meet with the Council. Then I went with Russell—Russ—to talk to the Lapras."

Jimmy frowned. "Why?"

"To see Lara," I said, knowing what was coming next. Jimmy looked ready to explode.

"So it's okay for you to talk to them in witch world about your daughter but it's not okay for me to talk to them in this world about my son?" he asked.

"Lara's your daughter too," I said.

Jimmy waved an annoyed hand. "I feel like Alex. Like I don't know you. Or maybe that's not true. Maybe it's the other 'witch world Jessica' I don't know."

"Please, Jimmy, I was there when Russ died." My voice cracked. "He died because of me."

"Why?" Jimmy asked.

"How?" my father asked.

"I killed him," I said. "I invoked the fire."

"Did they penetrate his disguise?" my father asked.

"Hell. They knew it all along," I said.

My father was stunned. "It makes sense, I suppose."

I felt like screaming. "It does? He's sound asleep in his bed in this world. How did the fire I created in witch world creep into his hotel in this world?"

"I explained how the events in both worlds run parallel," my father said. "They influence each other. But what happens in one world doesn't have to perfectly match what happens in the other world."

I felt a headache coming on. "Just when I think I have it all figured out, I lose my grip," I muttered.

My father was sympathetic. He hugged me, stroked my head. But I was having trouble crying. Nothing seemed real anymore. Yet my lack of tears didn't mean my pain was any less. I kept thinking of Russ's handsome face melting, his final scream.

If I was confused, Jimmy was walking into walls.

"Please, would someone tell me what happened last night," he pleaded. "In both worlds. Then show me how I can tape them together."

Before I could respond, my father's cell rang. It was the Council. They wanted to talk to us, to all three of us. My father protested but Cleo came on the line and said Jimmy was to be included in the discussion. It was like she had been in our room, a minute before, listening to his complaints.

While Whip continued to enjoy cartoons in his bedroom, my father hooked up a special gadget to his cell to keep our signal from being intercepted. Once the connection was made, we could hear everyone clearly. The Council wanted a thorough account of the previous night.

I gave it to them. They listened without interrupting until I reached the point when Russell died, and Susan made her dire warning, and Whip appeared.

No one on the Council seemed to care how Russ had perished in this world, although I assumed they knew the facts. When I was finished, Cleo spoke.

"The loss of Russ is a terrible blow. He was a great man and a dear friend. It's important, Jessie, that you understand that he gave up his life to protect you. The only reason he subjected you to such an intense battle was so this woman would see you as worthy of being Lara's mother."

"He pushed me to the edge," I said, not wanting to say more in front of Jimmy. "I was lucky to get out of there in one piece."

"I trained Russ how to fight," Kendor said. "If he had truly wanted to kill you, he would have done so at the start, before you had a chance to awaken the fire."

"Unfortunately, we'll have to mourn Russ later," Cleo said. "We must move forward. For now, Jessie, you'll accept Susan's offer and seclude yourself with Lara. Since she's willing to let you have visitors, it's possible Jimmy can act as a spy for us, if he so desires."

"How?" I asked. "Jimmy's not awake to witch world."

"James is," Cleo said. "They can work separately, and yet as a team."

"No," I said. "It's too dangerous."

"Jimmy can make up his own mind," Cleo said. "Without Russ, we'll need some way to contact you."

"I'm happy to volunteer as a spy," Jimmy said. "On one condition. That I be put through the death process."

"No," Cleo said.

"His request is fair," Kendor said. "We're asking him to risk his life for us. Plus he'll be more useful if he's awake to both worlds."

"You know as well as I do that half those who lack the healing gene fail to recover from the death experience," Cleo said.

"This is Las Vegas," Jimmy said. "Fifty-fifty odds are the best you're going to get in this town."

Hatsu broke in. "I'm surprised this Susan is willing to let Jessie have visitors," he said.

"Her confidence in her abilities is great," Cleo said. "Twice she's subjected us to this bafflement, and twice she's walked away unscathed, taking what she wanted."

"I think Susan's offer to Jessie is a ploy," Kendor said. "She wants Jessie to lure Council members to where she's staying."

"Why?" I asked.

"So she can dispose of us," Kendor said.

"Surely she must know she can't handle all of us at once," Hatsu said, insulted.

"So far, she's had no trouble handling us," Cleo said.

Hatsu snorted. "It sounds like Lara knows how to hurt her. Can you describe this wave you felt in more detail, Jessie?"

"I told you how it came when they plucked Lara out of my hands," I said. "It appeared suddenly. It seemed to fill the room, although I don't think it was aimed at me. I was the least affected by it. But I can tell you I'd hate to be on the wrong side of it. The wave had a strength to it that was scary."

"A pity Lara's not older," Kendor said. "We could ask her to focus on Susan and cause her to spontaneously combust."

"We don't need Lara to use a fusion against Susan," Hatsu said. "If we can find her, pin her down, then I think it's time."

"That's not an option," Cleo said hastily. "She would sense the attempt and quickly kill Lara."

"What's a fusion?" I asked.

"Something we don't speak of," Cleo said.

A long silence ensued. In my mind I could sense Hatsu's and Kendor's restlessness. But I also felt their reluctance to go against Cleo.

"Cleo," I said. "Is it possible Susan has more witch genes than you?"

Cleo considered. "From what she told you, she made it clear that Lara's potentially more powerful than she is. I'm sure she's making that assumption based on the fact Lara has all ten of the witch genes that we've been able to identify. Since I have only eight genes, it's possible Susan has nine. Therefore, the answer to your question must be yes."

"Could this woman have a gene we've never seen before?" Hatsu suggested.

"That's highly unlikely," my father interrupted.

"Why?" I asked.

"We've scanned billions and only seen ten genes," he said. "If you ask me, it's more likely Susan's developed an unusual form of telepathy whereby she's able to project a powerful illusion deep inside our minds."

"What happened to us when Lara was kidnapped had nothing to do with telepathy," Kendor said firmly.

"Susan's a puzzle," Cleo said. "It's clear she's never been scanned. It's like she came out of nowhere."

I was shocked. "But some of you must have heard rumors of her? I can't be the first witch to run into her."

"You might be the first one to meet her and survive to talk about it," Hatsu said. "Not counting her associates, of course."

"I'm surprised the Lapras have been able to keep her hidden for so long," Cleo pondered.

"She works at a local hospital!" I exclaimed. "At least in witch world. She's not trying to stay hidden at all."

"On the contrary," Kendor said. "Her position as a physician has given her a strong cover."

"She's already vacated that position and gone into hiding," Cleo said. "Our people have been unable to locate her through any of the local clinics."

"What do we know about her?" Hatsu asked.

"I got the impression she's very old," I said. "Her sense of morality is barbaric. She believes what she's doing is right. She talked a lot about President Truman and his decision to drop the atomic bombs on Japan. She compared his choice to her decision to kidnap Lara."

"Fascinating," Cleo said.

"Why do you say that?" Jimmy asked.

"That she sees herself as righteous," Cleo said.

"But surely her interest in atomic energy is related to the Lapras' program to create more witches by exposing a bunch of street people to excessive radiation," Hatsu said.

"I think you're both wrong," Kendor said.

"Explain," Cleo said.

"I think she spoke of Hiroshima because she was present when the bomb was dropped," Kendor replied.

"An interesting idea," Cleo said. "Does it give you any insight into her psychology? Or her power?"

"It's just an observation," Kendor said.

"Does anyone else have any ideas on our mystery woman?" Cleo asked.

"One," Hatsu said. "After what she did to Russ, we can't let her make the next move. We have to go on the offense."

"I agree," Kendor said. "I'm against Jessie accepting Susan's offer. I say we focus on locating her and we attack. This evening, in witch world, if possible."

"Why in witch world?" I asked. "Why not here?"

"We have already discussed the dangers of a frontal attack," Cleo said, ignoring my questions. "They're too great. We have to learn more about this woman's power. Its source, how it can be negated, and what she wants Lara for."

"So once more we wait and watch?" Kendor asked, not bothering to hide the impatience in his voice.

"We watch and learn," Cleo said with a note of finality. "Dr. Major, Jessie, Jimmy—we'll contact you again soon. This meeting is now adjourned."

The connection went dead.

"I see what you mean," Jimmy said, leaning back in the sofa where he had been sitting upright. "I could feel their power over the phone. It was like when I met Kendor in person."

"You met Kendor?" my father asked.

Jimmy froze, realizing his mistake.

"For a minute, after we met with Kari," I said quickly. "He told us he was guarding our backs before he went on his way."

My father appeared to accept this remark.

"They showed a lot of faith in you by speaking in front of you," he said to Jimmy. "I knew them a century before I was given a chance to sit in on one of their meetings."

"I suppose I should be grateful," he said.

I rubbed his back. "Aren't you?"

Jimmy shrugged. "I'm still an outsider. From now on, every night I hit the sack, I'll have to worry whether you'll be alive in the morning."

"Come on," I said. "It's not that bad."

He stared at me. "Isn't it?"

My father stood. "I should check on Whip."

"Wait," I said. "What did Hatsu mean when he spoke of using a fusion against Susan? And twice Cleo warned about using a frontal assault against the Lapras. Were those two talking about the same thing?"

My father nodded. "I'm pretty sure they are the same. But all I know about fusion is from hints I've picked up over the years. The Council has never spoken to me about it directly. But it seems in a major emergency they're able to join their minds into a single huge consciousness. In such a state, they have access to all the witch genes at once. To all the powers of a perfect witch."

"It's hard to imagine they wouldn't be able to destroy Susan in such a state," Jimmy said.

"I don't know enough about the process to argue with you," my father said. "But note how Hatsu said they needed to know where Susan was and have her pinned down. The fusion might not be that easy to use. Plus it's pretty clear Cleo's afraid

Susan will grab Lara and kill her the second they try something so drastic."

"I agree with Cleo," I said.

Jimmy was unconvinced. "It didn't sound like everyone on the Council felt the same way," he said.

"You're referring to Kendor," my father said. "For ages Cleo's been the cautious one, and her wisdom has allowed the Council to overcome numerous crises. For that reason, they're reluctant to go against her wishes. All of them except Kendor. He's more action-oriented, and her strategy to watch and wait drives him nuts. But make no mistake, I've never seen him blatantly disobey her."

I could see my father was anxious to check on Whip.

"How's our boy wonder doing?" I asked. The previous day, in the real world, after our meeting with Kari, Jimmy and I had spent time with Whip. But we'd left him with my father for the night with the realization that Whip needed a doctor more than he needed friends. Plus, I thought again, he might be infectious.

"His cellulitis is much improved," my father said. "The IV antibiotics have already helped with the blotches on his skin."

"But yesterday you were more worried about his lungs," Jimmy said. "Does he have TB?"

My father hesitated. "No."

"Dad?" I said, not liking his tone.

My father sighed. "I had an X-ray taken outside of town, at a clinic in Baker. I'll need to do a biopsy to confirm my diagnosis but I'm pretty sure his breathing difficulties are a result of large masses in his chest."

"Masses as in tumors?" I asked, scared.

"Yes."

"Can you operate on him?" Jimmy asked.

"No. It's too widespread."

"Can't we heal him?" I asked.

My father shook his head. "His condition is beyond my power."

"But we are supposed to be genetically enhanced healers," I complained. "What good is our power?"

"His tumors are not normal. They were created by direct contact with plutonium." My father saw how hurt we were and hastily added, "But you and your amazing daughter—I don't know, miracles do happen. Maybe we can do something for him."

Jimmy looked devastated. I felt pretty shaky myself.

"He's so young," Jimmy muttered.

"Look where his mother stashed him," my father said bitterly. "In Plutonium City. It's no wonder he's got cancer."

"Speaking of his mother," I said, standing, "I want to ask Whip a few questions about that bitch."

Whip looked better than the day before. Besides being cleaner and better dressed, his skin, as my father had said, had improved. His eyes also looked brighter, and I remembered the warm hugs he had given us upon our arrival. Clearly, Whip craved affection.

"Have you figured out why he's mute?" I whispered to my dad as Jimmy filled Whip in on the backstory of the cartoon he was watching. Jimmy was something of a fanatic when it came to old cartoons and comic books. He had already bought us tickets for the next Comic-Con convention, which was to be held in Las Vegas. A pity—I could think of better cities I'd like to vacation in.

"I suspect his condition is the result of an emotional trauma," my father replied. "While examining Whip's lungs, I X-rayed his throat as well, and had a specialist scope the area. He has all the necessary equipment to talk."

"Does he have any witch genes?" I asked.

"Five. I was impressed. He has an extremely high IQ. He's five years old and can read at a high-school level."

"It doesn't look like he impressed his mother," I said. "At least, not enough to keep him."

"You're sure Susan is his mother?" my father asked.

"I told you about the other Whip. I think she experimented on him to boost his number of witch genes."

"You're probably right. His tail has to be a mutation."

"Our Whip has a tail he uses to write with," I said. "Susan's Whip has a tail with a stinger on it. Plus his eyes are spooky. Why are the two physically different?"

My father frowned. "I don't know."

"But you've seen this before. Where people look different in the different worlds?"

"Not to this degree, no," my father said. "It's a mystery."

"It's obvious she experimented on our Whip too. Then discarded him the moment she no longer had any use for him." I paused. "I wish I could kill that bitch."

My father was concerned. "Don't go plotting any revenge just yet. You might feel powerful now but your abilities have only just begun to blossom."

"You still haven't explained what all those abilities are," I complained. Every time I asked about my other genes, my father quickly changed the subject.

"It's important they appear naturally," he said.

"Why?" I insisted.

"Use one of them too soon and you can damage yourself in ways that can't be healed." Again he changed the subject on me by returning to Whip. "You said that Susan was fond of the witch-world version of her son?"

"She adored him. When he came in, it was the first time I saw her smile."

Jimmy and Whip carried on together for the next twenty minutes. It was clear Jimmy was the boy's favorite. I had to finally force my way between them. Sitting across from him, I asked if I could ask a few questions. Whip responded by grabbing his notepad and marking pen and writing out the word "yes." All of his answers were supplied this way. He wrote blindingly fast.

"Whip," I said. "Out in the desert, did anyone from Las Vegas besides Frankie visit you?"

No.

"Did you always live in the desert city?"

No.

"Did you used to live here?"

Whip lowered his head. His eyes appeared to dampen.

I used to live near here, in a house, he wrote.

"Do you know the name of the town you lived in?"

Henderson.

I turned to Jimmy. "How far is Henderson from here?"

"Twenty minutes on the freeway."

"Kari said that Huck was only twenty minutes away," I said.

Jimmy was suddenly interested. "Should we take Whip for a drive around that area?" he asked.

"My thoughts exactly," I said, turning back to Whip. "How long have you lived in the desert?" I asked.

Seventeen months, three days, Whip wrote.

"Did you live with your mother before then?"

Whip hesitated. *Sometimes. When she wasn't busy.*

"Did she leave you with a babysitter when she was busy?"

With different people. They were mean.

"Do you know why she sent you out to the desert?"

Whip answered quickly, perhaps too quickly. *No.*

"Did you do something that angered her?"

No.

"Are you sure?"

No. Yes. Whip wiped at his eyes. *I don't want to talk about her.*

I patted his back. "I'm sorry. Tell me about the people you live with in the desert. Do you have any special friends?"

Clair and Bill, he wrote.

"Are they kids like you?"

They are like you and Jimmy but not as pretty.

"Why do you say they're not pretty?" I asked.

They have things growing on their body. Like really big warts. They keep growing.

"Does Frankie bring them food as well?"

I share some of my food with them. But they mainly eat from the food that's dropped.

"What do you mean dropped?"

A helicopter drops bags of food.

"How often?"

Every few weeks.

"Are you the only one who's brought special food?"

Yes.

"Maybe his mother does care for him," my father observed.

I shook my head, not wanting to express my true feelings for Susan in front of the boy. "Whip," I asked. "This is going to be a strange question but I want you to think real hard before answering it. Okay?"

I always think hard.

"Do you have any memories of living in another world?"

Whip didn't write. He just stared at me. He nodded.

"What do you remember about this place?"

381

He wrote reluctantly. *Bad people live there.*

"The Lapras?"

Yes.

"Do you feel different when you remember that place?"

I feel bad.

"You don't like it?"

No. I'm bad there. I kill people.

"How do you kill people?" I asked.

Whip set down his marking pen and held up his tail.

At first our trip to Henderson seemed a waste. We drove all over town without spotting an area that was the least bit familiar to Whip. But then I thought of Kari's description of the house where the Lapras were keeping Huck. How nice it was, how fine the view was. It struck me then that the house was probably located outside the city.

Indeed, chances were they were keeping Lara nearby. It made sense. That way they could concentrate their security. I directed Jimmy to head for the rich gated communities to the north of the town, where there were wide open spaces, and bluffs from which one could see for miles.

"Did it occur to you that we could be driving into the lion's den?" Jimmy asked.

"I just need a rough idea of the area," I said, before speaking to Whip in the backseat of a new rental, a Mercedes sedan. I had returned the Ford Expedition for obvious reasons. The

Lapras would spot it in a minute. "Whip, keep looking out the windows," I told him. "Let us know if anything looks familiar."

He nodded. He seemed to enjoy helping us.

Ten minutes later he tapped me on the shoulder and pointed to a hill that was topped with a sharp rock formation. The shape of the summit was curious. It looked like a crown. The hill appeared to be two miles away but it was possible it was twice that distance, given the curious effect the open desert often had on our eyes. I told Jimmy to pull over and lower our windows.

"You've seen that hill before?" I asked Whip.

He nodded and reached for his notepad, handing it to me a moment later. *It was in our backyard,* he wrote.

I smiled. "That's perfect. Good job, Whip."

He opened his mouth as if to speak.

A faint gasp came out, followed by a dry cough.

But he was trying—he was trying to talk to us.

CHAPTER EIGHTEEN

ON THE ROAD BACK TO LAS VEGAS, I ASKED JIMMY IF I could have some time alone. I explained how I owed Alex an explanation, and I couldn't put it off any longer. He was fine with that. He said he would give my father a break and take care of Whip for a while.

"As long as you promise you're not going to do anything dangerous while you're gone," he said.

He knew me too well. I smiled and gave him a kiss.

"Trust me, I've never had more reason to stay alive in my life," I said.

"Lara?"

"Yes. And you, always you," I said.

He seemed touched. "I like the 'always' part."

"That's possible now. We are witches. Eventually you're going to get your genes turned on. And even if you don't have the healing one, I'm going to do everything in my power to keep your parts in excellent working condition."

"I bet you focus on one part in particular."

I stroked his leg. "You're a mind reader."

He kissed me harder, neither of us caring that Whip was watching. Yet, when we parted, Jimmy looked sad.

"What's wrong?" I asked.

"I should never have left you."

"You did what you had to do. You were trying to do the right thing."

"I was a fool to get her pregnant in the first place."

"You'll get no argument from me on that point."

Jimmy opened the door and climbed out of the car, taking Whip with him. "Be careful you're not followed," he warned.

"It's becoming second nature. Bye, Jimmy. Bye, Whip. Love ya both."

Whip pressed his right palm to his heart and then pointed the fingers at me. I couldn't be sure but I thought he was trying to tell me he loved me. Right then, I couldn't think of two guys in the whole world that I cared for more. It was weird, I had just met Whip.

Yet, driving toward the MGM, and Alex, thoughts of Russ returned to haunt me. There was no denying the fact that I'd had a crush on Russ, and that did not mean I loved Jimmy any less. I believed Russ's feelings for me went equally deep. His willingness to accompany me to meet the Lapras had been so brave. He had done it for Lara and me. Remembering his anxiety when we were waiting for Frank outside the Mirage, I realized he must have known the danger he was about to face. But who could've guessed that I would be the one to kill him?

Of course, Susan had murdered him. My hatred for her was like a living thing that kept growing inside. I knew I was not going to rest until she was dead.

I was about to park at the MGM when I recalled the sound of woe I had heard underground just before the redhead with the Taser had picked me up. In reality the sound had never left me. During idle moments, I had watched my mind constantly turning back to it. There was a reason the cry drew me, but I didn't know what it was.

Nor did I know the name of the street where I had heard the sound. I had only a vague idea which direction the cab driver had taken me. But I suspected if I drove around for a while, I might spot something familiar. It had definitely been an industrial area.

Plus I was in no hurry to confront Alex.

I had no idea what I was going to say to her.

The afternoon was wearing on as I headed away from the Strip, relying on intuition more than memory. I stopped in a pawnshop when I got in the area but the owner was no help. I drove in circles. My intuitive gene was working at best at 10 percent capacity, and although I appeared to find the area where I had leaped from the taxi, I could not find the exact street.

Until I decided to give up and turned back toward the hotel and I ran into the right block. Then I understood. Only when I stopped trying did my intuition work.

Once again the area appeared deserted. None of the factories were working and the local warehouses appeared empty. The place had a witch-world feel to it. The area seemed dead.

I parked beside the sewer cover from where the oppressive wail had seemed to originate. The covering plate was made of steel and the hot sun had heated it to the point where it stung my fingers to touch it. Fortunately, while searching the trunk of my new rental, I was lucky to find a toolbox equipped with a large screwdriver and rubber-coated flashlight. Both tools were essential if I was to climb down the manhole.

And I was going down. The painful moan had not ceased. It sounded as if there were a thousand souls trapped beneath my feet.

The sewer lid popped free with the help of the screwdriver. But the rungs leading into the ground appeared to be a much more difficult proposition. For one thing they looked like they had not been used since the sewer had been created. They were coated in a heavy layer of dust, and they were awfully short.

Because the sewer was in the center of the street, I felt a responsibility to replace the covering over my head in case another car swung by and got stuck with a wheel in the hole.

But I had to wonder how I could manage that while holding on to the flashlight.

Then I thought of how all the cool spies on TV carried their flashlights in their mouths when they were going into danger, so they could keep their fingers on the triggers of their Glocks. Not that I had a gun but the point was my mouth was big enough to accommodate the light.

Turning the flashlight on and sticking the back tip in my mouth, I scooted to the edge of the sewer, rolled over, stuck out a foot, and prayed I'd be able to find the third or fourth rung. The truth was, once I had my feet and hands on the rungs, I felt pretty secure. The sewer cap was still pretty hot but I grabbed it quickly and gave it a few yanks until it settled overhead.

I started down, keeping both hands on the rungs, breathing around the flashlight. I was glad for the rubber coating. I assumed it would keep my saliva from seeping into the casing and shorting out the batteries. *What a way to go,* I thought. If my tongue got electrocuted, I wouldn't even be able to scream as I fell.

The narrow shaft was deep. I went down a long way before I reached the bottom, which turned out to be a concrete sewer more than eight feet high. It was not circular, as I expected, but more rectangular in shape, its width greater than its generous height. The air was damper than the desert above but the floor of the sewer was bone-dry.

It made me wonder if the underground aqueduct system

only came to life if the city was hit with a storm. From living in Apple Valley, I knew such storms were rare but they could be intense. I recalled how Las Vegas had looked when we had driven in on the freeway. It had seemed as if the city had been built in a relatively depressed area, compared to rows of distant hills. If there were a flash flood, the sewer I was standing in might fill to the ceiling. The fact that there was no dust on the floor or the walls led me to believe this was likely.

But what about the people who were supposed to live down here? It was weird but it was only when I had finished my descent and was inspecting my immediate surroundings that I realized the moaning sound had stopped. Yet I had been sure it was coming from beneath me. It should have been ten times louder.

"Maybe they heard me coming," I whispered aloud, wanting to hear my voice, any sound. The wail might have departed but the creepy vibes had not. I didn't need to be a witch to sense that there was something strange about this sewer. I couldn't see anything, I couldn't hear anything, but I knew I wasn't entirely alone.

Yet I wasn't sure what was watching me.

Something old, perhaps. Something sad.

I wanted to call out. My gut told me that would be a mistake. Indeed my common sense was screaming at me to get out of there immediately. But I had come for a reason, even if I wasn't sure what it was anymore.

I realized how easy it would be to get lost in such a labyrinth. For that reason, before leaving the shaft that had taken me down to this sewer, I etched a clear mark on the wall with my screwdriver. I planned to make a series of such markings if I ended up turning corners.

I started hiking in the direction that I believed led toward the Strip. I kept expecting the moan to return but there was only silence. I wished I had brought a water bottle. I had drunk just before getting out of the car but my thirst soon returned, the damp air notwithstanding. The small light was powerful; I had a clear view of my surroundings. But I worried about its batteries as well. It would be a mistake to hike more than a mile from where my car was parked.

After ten minutes, I came to a fork. I could go left, right, or straight ahead. For some reason I opted to go to the right. I was guessing but I thought that direction would lead me to downtown, where the hospital stood that had employed Dr. Susan Wheeler up until two days ago.

Before making the turn, I was careful to etch another mark on the wall that pointed toward my original entrance.

The new sewer was more square, a tighter fit. The ceiling was barely six feet high. I detected a musky odor. More important, I noticed markings on the wall. Initially they looked like faded graffiti but the farther I walked, the more I realized I was looking at washed-out words that had been written in a foreign language.

German. I'd had three years in high school. My teacher, Mr. Barnes, had been superb; he'd drilled a thousand-word vocabulary into our brains. Pausing, focusing the light on a clear portion, I was able to decipher one sentence that chilled me to the bone: *Schmerz wird zum Vergnügen wenn die Macht Schmerzen schafft.*

Pain becomes a pleasure when power creates pain.

I walked farther and saw a faded swastika painted in red and black. On the wall, on either side of it, were the Star of David and the Christian cross. It was as if the latter two symbols had been placed there to contain the evil influence of the Nazis' sign.

A short distance later the sewer suddenly opened into a concrete cavern. I assumed that was what it was. My light struggled in vain to give a clear view of the room's proportions. The beam seemed to shoot out and die. The humidity increased dramatically. I could have stumbled into an Amazon jungle, only there were no trees. But there was a distinct smell of decay. I had never smelled it before and yet I recognized it.

Bodies decomposing. Dead bodies, hopefully.

I was suddenly afraid they were not entirely dead.

I heard steps at my back and turned and saw Frank. Or Frankie—that was probably what he was called in this world. It was what Whip had called him. He didn't carry a flashlight but a burning torch. I didn't know how he had managed to sneak up on me. He stood at the end of the sewer that had led me to this horrible place, and from his expression I didn't think he was going to let me go back the way I had come.

"Jessie," he said in a somber tone. "You should never have come here."

He was an important Lapra, the assistant to their leader. From what I knew of their group, they recognized only power and control. For that reason, I knew it would be a mistake to show fear.

"I go where I please," I said.

He took a step toward me and gestured to the darkness with his free hand. "You'll never understand the history of this place, and others like it, although they're all the same, all one. I told Susan that after your visit the other night. She agreed with me but still feels there's hope for you." He paused and waved his torch slowly in my direction so that I felt its heat. "Is there any hope?"

"Drop the riddles," I said. "If you have something to ask, ask it."

Frankie came so near he towered over me. "What do you feel behind you?" he asked.

"Death," I said. "Suffering."

"Death ends suffering. You can't have both. You need life to have pain. But only at the end of life is there enough pain to create enough pleasure to make life worth living. That's the paradox, and the purpose of this place."

"I don't know what the hell you're talking about."

He nodded. "If you were to die here, slowly, horribly, you could give pleasure to many."

Again, I cautioned myself to show no fear.

I poked him in the gut with my flashlight. "Your master wants me alive. I'm the mother of the superchild. Are you sure you want to kill me?"

He brushed away my light. "I don't like the power your position gives you. You did nothing to earn it. And that child— I think she's a menace."

"Then maybe you should kill me. You can always lie to your boss. Just tell her I disappeared. But you know I'm stronger than I look. You saw what I did to Russ. It might be that I end up killing you."

Frankie smiled without mirth. "I have had this thought, that you should simply vanish. Only I don't fear you or anyone else. Russ was a pawn I could have taken down with one blow. You barely survived your duel with him. Does that tell you something, Jessie?"

"Not really. Except you're beginning to bore me. Step aside now, or I'll kill you where you stand."

Frankie took a step back, but not aside. He still blocked my exit. "I promise you a slow death. And I promise it will please me." He raised his torch over his head. "Prepare yourself."

I reached for my screwdriver. It was tucked in my belt, at my back. At the same time I wedged my flashlight in my front pocket so that I'd be able to see but wouldn't have to hold it.

I sensed Frankie's boast wasn't idle. He could have killed Russ easily and that meant he probably had a significant advantage over me.

Yet he was lying when he said he didn't fear anyone. Lara had gotten to him when he had plucked her from my hands. The wave she had created had made him grimace and choke, and he had to be thinking, *Why, she's only a month old. What will she be like as a teenager?* I suspected he wasn't the least bit intrigued with her potential. For sure he was willing to risk Susan's wrath to dispose of Lara's mother.

I needed to strike a single death blow. Failing that, I had to invoke my fire and hope it overwhelmed his. Yet I feared his hidden powers. For the heat of his torch was suddenly growing in leaps and bounds, its flames being fed by magic. I didn't want to think how many witch genes he possessed.

I pulled back my screwdriver as an archer would his bow. The tool was my arrow. If I failed to sink it in his chest, I was probably screwed, no pun intended.

"Ready?" he asked.

I forced a smile. "Always."

"Stop!" a voice called from the depths of the sewer.

The voice was commanding.

Frankie lowered his torch.

I did likewise with my screwdriver.

Out of the sewer walked a tall figure clothed in black

leather. In his right hand he held a sword. There was blood on it, red drops dripped off the steel onto the dark floor.

"Kendor," I whispered, as my heart beat hard in my chest. God, it was good to see him. He just had to walk into the cavern and Frankie seemed to shrink two feet in height. Definitely, the flames bursting from his torch calmed down. I wouldn't have been surprised if the damn thing went out. Frankie couldn't help himself, he instinctively backed off. For his part, Kendor seemed amused to see the two of us together. He gestured to Frankie with his sword.

"Your master is anxious to make a deal with this young woman," Kendor said. "How did you plan on explaining to her that Jessie was dead?"

Frankie sneered but his expression lacked conviction. "I don't have to explain myself to you," he said.

Kendor stared at him. "No?"

Frankie shook his head. "This is our place. She has no right coming here. But I'm willing to overlook this transgression if she agrees to leave now and never return."

"No," Kendor said.

"What do you mean, 'no'?" Frankie demanded.

Kendor raised his sword a foot. It was enough.

"You know," Kendor said.

Frankie backpedaled another step. "This is sacred ground. We have a right to protect it."

Kendor twisted his blade slightly so more of the accumulated blood on the blade flowed free. "You could consult with those you put in place to guard this ground about your rights. But I'm afraid none of them would have much to say."

Frankie acted offended. "You dare to play your barbaric games here? I'd strike you dead myself if Susan would allow it."

"No," Kendor said again.

"'No, no'—you sound like a bloody parrot. What is it that you want?"

Kendor smiled. "Nothing." In a move almost too swift for my witch eyes to follow, he sprang toward Frankie. High in the air, Kendor sliced Frankie's head off at the neck. The massive skull fell like a bowling ball, landing with a thud.

It was horrible to watch—and fascinating—as Frankie's long body slowly bent at the knees and waist, sitting down and leaning forward without a head. It took almost a minute before the blood stopped spurting from the main artery in the stump of his neck.

Kendor paid the body no heed. He removed a hand-kerchief from his pocket and wiped the blood from his sword before returning the blade to its sheath, which hung behind his right side. He gestured for me to reenter the sewer, where he took a seat not far from the opening to the cavern. Sitting across from him, I rested the back of my head on the concrete wall.

"Thanks for saving my life," I said.

Kendor shook his head. "It was I who allowed your daughter to be taken," he said.

"You can't blame yourself. This power that Susan has, this bafflement—the whole Council seems helpless against it. Even Cleo doesn't know what it is."

Kendor sighed and pulled up a knee to rest his arm on. "That's true, she doesn't understand it. Unfortunately, I do, to some extent."

"But you said at the Council meeting you had never seen anything like it before."

"I lied." He paused. "I've known Susan since the day Caesar returned victorious to Rome and proclaimed himself emperor. I was with him that day, and that was the day I first spied Syn in the crowd."

I trembled. "Are you saying that Syn and Susan are the same person?" I whispered.

"Yes."

"She was your lover?"

"For two thousand years."

I found it hard to speak. "Tell me your story."

CHAPTER NINETEEN

"WHEN WE LAST SPOKE ALONE, I TOLD YOU OF MY commitment to Caesar. I won't belabor this part of my tale except to say that his victory at Alesia gave him the momentum to return to Rome and crown himself emperor. Those were exciting times. Finally, I thought, mankind could be brought under a single umbrella of law and justice and grow in the manner I had always dreamed possible.

"But it was a fool's dream. In my enthusiasm to have Caesar unify Europe, I overlooked what was under my nose and allowed Brutus and his gang of thugs to kill a man many called a god."

"Was Syn involved with Caesar's assassination?" I asked.

"No. Syn had barely awakened to her powers when Caesar was stabbed to death. But even as an infant witch she understood the mob mentality of everyday Rome better than I did. For she was a native of the city, while I was not. Many times she warned me to increase Caesar's personal security. I should have listened, but perhaps I was too confident in the love the people showered on him wherever he spoke."

"You said you first spotted Syn in a crowd," I said. "Did you recognize her as a potential witch?"

Kendor flashed a rare smile. "As opposed to a beautiful woman? I suppose the two went hand in hand. From the instant we met, I was hypnotized by her dark eyes. It had been ages since I had fallen in love, but sometimes, staring into those eyes, I felt as if I had met the greatest mystery of my life. Of course, she had a wild streak—most powerful women in those days did, especially when it came to Rome. I wasn't with her long before I knew she had the ability to become connected."

"How could you be certain?" I asked.

"I wasn't certain until the day I put her through the death experience. But it was something I sensed to be true and I had lived long enough to trust my intuition."

"Did you sense the evil in her?" I asked.

The question seemed to surprise Kendor. "Syn wasn't evil, at least not then, although I saw something in her I had never seen before in any woman. I don't have a word for it. Her beauty was obvious, of course, her energy undeniable. She was the daughter of a senator, rich and spoiled, and was used to traveling with a dozen slaves who would jump at her least command. But when she came to me, and I sent her slaves away, she didn't mind."

"Was she trying to impress you?"

Kendor smiled. "I think it was more simple than that. We were in love, we wanted to make each other happy. Syn quickly saw that I disliked crowds so she got rid of her help. She didn't need it. We only needed each other."

"How did she become connected?"

"By that time I had connected a hundred witches and had discovered that freezing a person to death was the least traumatic way. But Cleo is right—half those who lack the healing gene fail to survive. I couldn't tell whether Syn had it by looking at her. I only knew that she would be a powerful witch if she did survive. The winter after we met, I took her to the Italian Alps and led her into an icy lake, one of the hardest things I ever did in my life. But fortune smiled on us that day, or I should say that night. Because it was during the night, beside a roaring fire, that she suddenly sucked in a breath and was alive again."

"So when we go through the death experience we really die?"

"Yes. But most witches who connect in this fashion usually stop breathing for a short period of time. Ten or fifteen minutes at most. Syn stopped for ten hours. I assumed I had lost her. It was a painful night, then a joyous one."

I was thoughtful. "I wasn't breathing when I woke up in the morgue. Is it possible that I was dead for several hours?"

"It's likely. You two have a lot in common."

"I hope not," I said.

He gave me a curious look before he continued. "Syn was reborn in the depths of winter. But it was that following March, on that infamous day known as the ides of March, that Caesar was killed. After the loss of our leader, Cleo and the Council asked me to leave Rome and return to England, where they were centered. But at the same time I refused to leave the city because Syn didn't want to go. It was strange—even at such an early age she wanted nothing to do with the Council."

"Did they know about her?" I asked.

"Of course. They knew I had a woman. But only Hatsu came to visit us."

"Would he recognize her if he met her today?"

"I'm sure he would. But Syn went to great pains to avoid the other members of the Council. Even when other witches came to visit, she would make herself scarce."

"What excuse did she give?"

"She didn't want to be part of an organization where she would have to be beholden to anyone. I tried explaining that we didn't operate that way but my words fell on deaf ears. I suspected that Syn was jealous of my loyalty to Cleo."

"Did she feel threatened by her?" I asked.

"That's a reasonable assumption but I'm not sure if it's accurate. For Syn was the most fearless person I had ever met, even among witches. Naturally, because I couldn't be with her every second, I taught her everything I knew about the sword, and she turned out to be an extraordinary student. Not because of her genes, which were powerful, but because of her lack of inhibition. She didn't care how many she killed, if attacked, and she didn't worry how close she came to death in a battle. You assume I protected her for the first century of her life and that's true, but later she was to save my life as often as I saved hers."

"So she was a killer from the start," I said.

"No."

"But you just said—"

"Syn never hurt a soul unless provoked. It was fascinating for me to observe that after she became connected, and inherited an amazing array of powers, she became more gentle in her dealings with people. Besides never keeping another slave, she became more friendly and cheerful. In those days, I imagined the love we shared had brought about the change in her. It was so perfect it seemed to overflow from inside us and spread to others."

"Perfect," I said with a sigh. "That's the word I always use when I think of Jimmy."

"Then you understand."

"Yes and no. I can't listen to you talk about Syn without thinking of the Susan I've met."

"That's fair. I'm no different. It's hard for me to think of those days because of *what* she is today."

"How did she change? Why?" I asked.

Kendor unsheathed his sword and studied the blade. He was a long time answering. "I wish I knew," he said.

"There had to be a reason."

He shrugged, sliding a finger down the length of the blade, letting it draw a faint film of blood from his skin. "I can give you reasons. A basket full of them, which a modern psychologist could use to construct a profile of why Syn turned bad. But it would just be a list of events. It wouldn't tell you how her heart changed."

"Tell me anyway. Tell me her history."

"Very well. In the fourth century, in 386, Syn and I had our first child, a boy named Robere. He was a wonderful child and he grew into a great man. And we were further blessed when we discovered that he was a witch who possessed that special gene that would allow him to heal others as well as himself. I changed him when he was thirty in much the same manner I had changed his mother. At the same time I taught him how to defend himself, but perhaps I spent too much time on his training. He became a great warrior and in 431, when Attila and his endless hordes of Huns attacked Rome, my son marched out to protect the city.

"The Huns were fearsome warriors. They were especially skilled at using a bow and arrow while riding a horse, and their talent with a javelin was unequaled. However, Rome was Rome and its soldiers had a long history of winning against impossible odds, especially when one of their leaders knew the secret of gunpowder. They drove back the Huns but Robere never returned from battle. A Hun had pinned him to a tree with a javelin. He died instantly but I think a part of Syn died much more slowly over the ensuing years."

"She grieved a long time?"

"She barely spoke for years. That was difficult for me to take because I was used to her lively personality. Yet, as time went on, she slowly returned to her old self and in the year 658 she gave birth to a daughter, Era. We were living in Sicily at the time and I felt as if I just blinked and Era was a full-grown woman with two children of her own, Anna and Theo, and a wonderful husband, Peter, who worked as a fisherman. I think the time went by so fast because they were happy days. But it was during this time that the Plague of Justinian, the first of the bubonic plagues, struck Europe and Era and her children died."

"Were any of them witches?"

"Era and Theo were not. Anna was and when she got ill I tried to connect her in the usual way. But she lacked the healing gene and the process killed her."

"You weren't able to heal her yourself?"

Kendor hesitated. "I thought Anna was getting better with the care I was giving her. But Syn insisted she be made completely immune to the plague. She pressured me to connect her."

"But being a member of the Council, you knew the risk."

"Of course. That's why I was reluctant to try it. But Syn felt the plague was the greater danger. It was a difficult call.

You have to understand, the streets were stacked with bodies. Death was all around us."

"What happened to Era's husband?"

"When we lost Anna, he drowned himself."

"Did you have any more children?"

"One. Herme. He was born in England in 1472. He was born a witch, with many genes, including the healing gene. Syn connected him when he was twenty-five."

"Why didn't you do it?"

"She insisted." He paused. "She worshipped that boy."

"Is he alive today?"

"In 1706 he took leave of us in London and traveled to America. We received regular letters from him up until the time the colonies broke from England. Then we heard from him only sporadically. To be blunt, I blamed Syn for that."

"Why?"

"Living in America, Herme became an American. He lost all respect for the English Crown. Of course Syn and I had lived in England for centuries. It was home, and to Syn, the king was to be obeyed. She was a great believer in order. Even through the mail she continued to fight with Herme. Immediately after the Boston Tea Party, she wrote him a particularly scathing letter." Kendor paused. "We didn't hear from him again."

"Because he was mad?"

"Herme was a gentle soul. He wasn't the vindictive sort. He would have forgiven his mother and eventually written."

Kendor gestured weakly. "We had to assume he was killed in the conflict."

"Would he have volunteered to fight? On either side?"

"Doubtful. Herme was a painter and sculptor. He had no interest in fighting. He refused all my attempts to teach him the sword."

"Then why do you assume he died?"

"He was attached to us. Although he fought with his mother, they were close. I can't imagine him abandoning Syn for political reasons." Kendor paused. "The not knowing was hard on her. For years, every time the mail came, she ran to the box."

"I can imagine," I said.

"No offense, Jessie, but you can't imagine."

I nodded. "That was three hundred years ago. Why didn't you have more children?"

"Syn refused to have any more. After Herme vanished, we never had sex again. Not intercourse. Not where there was a chance she could get pregnant." Kendor shook his head. "For a long time she'd cringe whenever I touched her."

"That must have been very difficult for you."

"It was unbearable, and yet I could bear it."

"Because you loved her."

"Yes."

"You still love her. That's why you lied to the Council about her."

"Yes."

"When was the last time you saw her?"

"Four days ago, near the hospital where you were taken. She was walking along the street, staring off into the distance."

"Did she see you?"

"No."

"When was the last time you were together?"

"During World War Two. We were living in Glasgow at the time. The Blitz was on, the Germans' bombing of Great Britain. It focused on London but hit our city as well."

"Why did you stay in Europe? Why not come to America?"

"Syn refused to leave. She had decided that what Hitler was trying to do was best."

I was shocked. "Why?"

"She thought the Nazis could bring order to the world more quickly than anyone else. That was the excuse she gave. But it made no sense. Hitler was obviously a destabilizing factor. We used to argue about it endlessly. Largely because I wanted to take out Hitler."

"You mean, kill him?"

"Yes. I was fully capable of killing him."

"With the Council's approval?"

"No. Cleo refused to grant me permission. I was going to do it anyway and Syn knew it. That's the excuse she gave for leaving me but I knew it was a lie."

"Where did she go?"

"To Germany. To work with the Nazis."

I put a hand to my mouth. "But she must have had another reason. Like you said, supporting Hitler made no sense."

Kendor was silent a long time. While I waited for him to continue, I heard the low moan I had first heard from the sewer cap. It came out of the cavern we sat beside, from the darkness that seemed to have no boundary. Listening to it, I couldn't help but think of the German words I had seen written on the sewer wall.

Schmerz wird zum Vergnügen wenn die Macht Schmerzen schafft.

"You hear it, don't you?" Kendor asked finally.

"What is it?"

"It could be mutants that the Lapras have discarded as useless to their program. Or something else."

"What?"

"An echo from the past." Kendor paused. "You asked why Syn went to work for the Nazis. I think it was because they gave her something no one else could."

"What?"

"A constant source of pain."

"I don't understand."

Kendor shook his head. "When Syn left Glasgow, I almost went insane trying to find her. I used all the contacts I had on both sides of the English Channel. I almost broke the vow I had made to Syn and went to the Council for help. Without their aid, it took three years before I discovered she was in Germany, and another year to learn she had gone to work at Auschwitz, in Poland."

I felt sick. "The concentration camp?"

"The most horrifying camp ever built. Millions of Jews lost their lives there. Plus countless Poles, Gypsies, and Russian soldiers. In all of time, in all of history, that camp caused more concentrated pain than anything the world has ever known."

"Do you know what she did at the camp?"

"She was high up in the command structure. I know that she experimented on Jews with strong doses of radiation. To the best of my knowledge, these were the first tests performed to artificially produce witch genes in human beings."

"Hold on. That's a Lapra program. Did Syn join the Lapras at this time?"

"I assume. But I must stress that she'd never expressed an interest in them before. If anything, up until the time she left me, they seemed to amuse her."

"None of this makes sense. How could a person change so fast?"

"Maybe it wasn't fast. Maybe I was just blind. After we lost Herme, she was a shell of her former self. Back then I believed in the healing power of time but I don't anymore."

"But you must have warned the Council that she'd gone over to the Lapras. No, wait, you didn't—I know you didn't.

I heard the way they spoke about her on the phone. They still have no idea who Susan is."

Kendor didn't respond. He just sat there.

"How come you didn't tell them?" I asked.

He spoke with sudden feeling. "How could I? Syn was my life," he said.

"Are you saying you were ashamed?"

"It was more than that. I couldn't bear to have them see her in that light."

"But your failure to tell them weakens their plans."

Kendor gripped the sword, drawing more blood into his palm. "I know," he said.

I could see I was hurting him. I could press the point no further. "Why did you say she wanted a constant form of pain?"

"I believe she needed it for another type of experiment."

"I'm not following you."

He shook his head. "It's just speculation."

"Kendor. You're too old to speculate."

"When Germany fell to the Allies, I discovered that Syn had left Auschwitz for Japan. At that time another source of agony was being created, this one by the Americans. It was the brainchild of General Curtis LeMay. Using the air force's most advanced bombers, he had begun to drop massive amounts of incendiary devices on Tokyo and other major Japanese cities. This type of bombing caused more deaths and injuries than anything seen in Europe, including Dresden. Few Americans realize that LeMay's aerial campaign killed more people than the atomic bombs dropped on Hiroshima and Nagasaki."

"Wait!" I cried, sitting up. "Syn went out of her way to talk about those cities. She went on and on about how wise Truman was to drop the nuclear bombs."

"Perhaps because they gave her access to something she'd never had before."

"I'm sorry, you're losing me," I said.

"Follow her pattern. Syn went to Auschwitz because the greatest horrors on earth were taking place there. When the war in Europe ended, she went to Japan to bask in their torture. Wherever there was the most pain, there Syn was. Now, even though I say the firebombing killed more people than the atomic bombs, Hiroshima and Nagasaki were still unique events in history. In milliseconds, eighty thousand people died in Hiroshima, while another fifty thousand died in Nagasaki. Many more died later from radiation poisoning. But my point is the explosions gave Syn two exquisite instants of agony that had no precedence. And they were related to the release of massive amounts of radiation. Think about that for a moment. Radiation is the basis of all mutations on earth, and it's mutation that has given rise to the witch genes in human beings. It doesn't matter if we're talking about the Tar or the Lapras."

"The way you talk, you act like your Syn began to chase pain the way a vampire does blood," I said.

Kendor was bitter. "She's no longer my Syn. But yes, your

analogy is appropriate. Syn left me in search of pain. Why? It fed something sick inside her. Don't ask me what; I don't know. And it opened doors inside her."

"Doors?"

"Powers no one else has."

"Bafflement?" I asked.

"Precisely."

"But Hiroshima and Nagasaki happened more than sixty years ago. The Council never experienced bafflement until Lara was taken."

"That's not exactly true. When I discovered that Syn had been at Hiroshima, and survived the blast, I flew to Japan. At the time I had numerous contacts in the American air force. They got me into the country. They even alerted me as to the possible target sites of their next atomic bombs. Kokura was the prime target for the second bomb but my instincts told me to go to Nagasaki. As it turned out, Kokura was covered in clouds and was bypassed. Nagasaki became the next ground zero. Syn must have sensed the same thing I did."

"Weren't you worried about dying in the blast?" I asked.

"I had to see her, to save her."

"How can you be sure she was there?" I asked.

"Because I met her for tea the morning of the blast."

"You're joking."

"No. She seemed cheerful. Happier than I'd seen her in years. Yet there was a weird glow to her eyes that made me dizzy. When she gazed at me, my sense of perception twisted and became distorted. I can't even tell you when she and I parted that morning. One minute we were talking and the next she was gone.

"But I remember the blast. It came at eleven in the morning. The bomb was plutonium-based instead of uranium-based, like the one dropped on Hiroshima, and was considerably more powerful. But it was dropped two miles off target in the Urakami Valley, an industrial area, and much of the city was protected from the blast by the hills. That's the only reason I survived. Still, the weapon created a devastating blow. I was five miles from the center of the blast and I felt as if my skin caught fire. The pain was greater than anything I'd ever known. Nevertheless, I experienced something in that instant that was worse than all my physical pain combined."

"Bafflement?"

"Yes. The disorientation was worse than the agony. It was like a door to another dimension, to hell itself, had been yanked open and I had been shoved inside. I was lost in a red fog. All sense of distance and time shattered. My brain couldn't process them because they no longer existed." Kendor paused. "I wasn't to feel that again until Lara was taken."

"But the blast happened sixty years ago!" I repeated.

"It doesn't matter! Some doors you open, they can never be closed again. It's my belief that Syn gained access to a power or place that day that she's never let go of."

"Then how can she be defeated?"

"I don't know if she can. I only know we must try."

I tapped my hand impatiently. "You still haven't told me why Syn turned so evil," I said.

"You asked for her history and I gave it to you. She suffered a great deal. She witnessed tremendous suffering. Maybe one day it just became too much for her and she snapped."

"But you said how strong she was. How full of life. Other witches in her position didn't crack, and she had you to sustain her. And the love of a man like you, Kendor . . . Well, we haven't known each other long but I do know that any woman would have died to be with you." I stopped. "We're missing something."

Kendor stared at me. "Jessie, have you ever had a close friend who became a drug addict?"

"Two friends. Tom got hooked on heroin and Lisa got addicted to crystal meth. It destroyed both their lives."

"Why did they take the drugs?"

"Because they were idiots," I said.

"Wrong. They took them because they were in pain and the drugs took away the pain. It might be hard for you to understand because you've never been an addict."

"Were you?" I asked.

"After the plague struck, Syn and I both became addicted to opium. The addiction lasted years. We finally gave it up because we saw that it was ruining us. But for a long time the drug was our lives. I remember having to tie Syn down for weeks at a time to keep her from smoking."

"She had more trouble breaking the habit than you?"

"Yes."

"You're saying Syn found a new drug when she discovered how to open these doors inside her mind? These ones fed by pain and suffering?"

"Yes."

"I still don't buy it," I said.

"Recall your description of Dr. Susan Wheeler at the morgue they took you to. When her partner was having a heart attack, she sat blissfully beside him, soaking up his fear and pain. The same as when Russell died. It's the major symptom of her addiction to an evil force."

"But who led her to this addiction?" I asked.

"Why do you ask that?"

"Few addicts start alone. Usually it's a friend or dealer who shoots them up the first time." I paused. "She must have had a mentor. You know who I'm talking about."

Kendor shook at my suggestion. "No! The Alchemist died two thousand years ago."

"You assume he died, but his stink is all over Syn. Why, I wouldn't be surprised if she was the one who revived red queen. You have to admit it's awfully popular in witch world. And don't tell me she didn't know about it. She lived with you in Rome during Claudius's reign."

Kendor shook his head. "It's not possible. She wouldn't have followed that man, not back then. All he wanted to do was torture people. He was sick."

"So is Syn," I said gently.

Kendor didn't respond, and I feared I had hit a nerve that was too painful to expose. Eventually, though, he spoke.

"There were the dreams," he said.

I was suddenly alert. "What dreams?"

"We had them over the years, Syn and I. They made no sense. It was as if the Alchemist was in our room when we were sleeping. Then we'd both awake at the same instant and he'd be gone."

"Did either of you actually see him?"

"No. Maybe. It was more like we felt him."

"What about the dreams themselves? What were they about?"

Kendor frowned. "I remember bright lights, objects in the sky, noise, lots of noise. But I recognized none of it."

"Weird."

"Then there was the lost time. Whenever we had these dreams, we would not know what day it was."

"I don't understand. Didn't you keep track of the date?"

"Syn did. She could tell the date just by studying the position of the stars at night. Except when the dreams came. Then she said the sky would change overnight. Only it couldn't have been one night."

"So this loss of time must have been significant?" I asked.

"Yes."

"Are we talking days?"

"Maybe weeks. Maybe more."

"God."

Kendor nodded. "We were never able to explain it."

"Did you talk to the Council about it? Cleo?"

"Cleo, once."

"What did she say?"

"Nothing. But she looked worried."

"Like she knew what was causing it?"

"Yes."

My butt was beginning to ache. I stood and stretched. "I assume everything you told me is confidential," I said.

Kendor got to his feet and replaced his sword in its sheath. He seemed uncertain how to respond. "Yes."

"I'm shocked you told me so much."

"I told you because you need to know what it is that you have to face."

"Tell me the truth. Does the Council have a plan for tonight? In witch world?"

He paused. "We're considering a fusion."

I felt anxious. "Cleo spoke against that. She said it could force Susan's hand and cause her to kill Lara."

"Then we'll probably have to try it without Cleo." Kendor added, "Syn won't wait forever for Lara to obey her."

"That's insane! She's an infant! She doesn't know enough to obey anyone!"

"You asked me to be honest with you. I know Syn. I know what she was trying to tell you with her threats. Lara's a genetic novelty that might eventually produce interesting results. But Syn would rather see her dead than let us have her. That's why I told the Council to attack. If my wife has a sudden stab of impatience, she'll kill your daughter."

"That's the first time you called her your wife."

"After what she's become, the word doesn't come easily."

"Too bad the Council doesn't understand that you know what you're talking about." I shook my head miserably. "There's no hope, is there?"

Kendor patted my back. "I feel hope and I shouldn't, which makes me wonder if our odds are better than we know. In either case we'll meet this evening in witch world and face our demons. Mine will come from my past. Yours are connected to your future."

"I don't understand," I said.

"You're a flower that's just begun to bloom. I know you've asked what your powers represent, and you've been told to let them manifest in their own time. But I can say that you possess the same genes Syn does."

"Are you saying I'm destined to become a monster?"

"You're the thorn who can pluck out the thorn. You're so much like Syn, you're the perfect antidote to stop her."

"When did you realize that?"

"The instant I met you." He turned toward the way we

had come. "Follow me, I know a shortcut out of here."

I grabbed his arm. "Can you at least give me a hint as to how I can stop her?"

"I just did."

"Please. Tell me about a power I possess that I don't know about," I insisted.

He smiled. "You can become invisible."

"Are you serious? No one could see me?"

"Not exactly." He took me by the hand. "Come, we have to get out of here. Our friends, and our enemies, are looking for us."

CHAPTER TWENTY

AN HOUR LATER I WAS FINALLY ALONE WITH ALEX IN her room and about to explain that I was a witch when she told me she already knew. I have to admit that in a long weekend full of surprises, this one took the prize.

"How do you know?" I said.

"Al's a witch too."

"Your new boyfriend? The suave drug salesman?"

"Yes."

"And you believe him?" I asked.

"He gave a pretty convincing demonstration of his abilities."

"What did he do?"

"He told me not to tell you. He said you were a newborn witch who's just beginning to discover your powers. He told me you're going through a very delicate stage." Alex paused. "I can't believe I just said all that with a straight face."

"Does Jimmy know?" I asked.

"Not yet. But Al wants to tell him."

"Where's Al right now?" I asked.

"He's in your room with Jimmy and the little boy with the tail." Alex blinked. "Is there a joke somewhere in all of this that I'm missing?"

"I wish. Where's Debbie?" I asked.

"She went home with Ted."

"Is she happy?"

"Yes. He's talking about going to school with her in Santa Barbara."

"Ted got accepted at MIT."

"Love knows no reason."

"So we have the suite to ourselves?" I asked.

"I guess. As long as someone's still paying the bill."

"The bill has been taken care of." I paused. "Can you play with Whip for a few minutes? Jimmy and I really need to talk to Al."

"Sure." Alex took my arm as I went to stand. "What's it like?"

"Wonderful. Horrible. I can't tell you everything right now but I'll be able to tell you a lot more tomorrow."

"What's special about tomorrow?"

"Let's just say if I'm alive twenty-four hours from now, then a lot of my questions will have been answered, and I'll be in a much better position to tell you what's what."

Alex stared at me before shaking her head. "I knew you'd get back at me for inviting Jimmy to ride in the car with us."

Minutes later Jimmy and I sat with Al in my bedroom. To my surprise, Jimmy didn't chew me out for going off on my own, even though the fact that I had failed to return to the MGM had caused him to rush back to the hotel ahead of schedule, and with Whip. He said my father had alerted the Council that I was missing.

"Kendor will tell them I'm okay," I said.

"Is that who you were with?" Jimmy asked.

"Yeah. He wanted to have another talk."

"About what?" Jimmy persisted.

"His life. He told me a lot about his past."

"Wow. You're so lucky," Al said, impressed. "The guy's a legend. Can you introduce me to him?"

I studied him more closely than before. Al was still short and plump and had a baby face that wasn't aided by his mass of curly brown hair. He wasn't Alex's usual type but he had a certain style about him. I noticed the alertness in his blue eyes and the fact he sat calmly beneath our scrutiny.

"That depends," I said. "Are you a good witch or a bad witch?"

"I'm supposed to be a bad witch, but the Lapras don't know I work for the Tar."

"Who's your contact with the Tar?" I asked.

"Hatsu. Call him on my cell, he'll verify what I'm saying."

I did just that. Hatsu assured me I could trust Al. After thanking Hatsu, I gave Al back his phone. "I assume Hatsu told you to make contact with Alex," I said.

"Frankie did. He's a Lapra, you wouldn't know him."

"Actually, we've met. Were you close to him?" I asked.

"No one's close to Frankie. He's an asshole."

"Then you wouldn't mind hearing that he's dead."

Al blinked. "Kendor?"

"Took his head." I made a slashing motion. "It was quick."

"Wait a second," Jimmy said. "I thought you and Kendor met for a friendly chat. You didn't say anything about a guy dying."

"Did I have to?" I asked. "You saw what he did to those two who were parked in front of my father's condo."

Jimmy nodded. "You have a point."

"Kendor's famous for killing any Lapra on sight," Al said.

"Is that why you've thrown your hat in with the Tar?" I asked.

Al shook his head. "I fell in with the wrong people when I was connected. I want to make up for things that I've done. I'm here to help."

"What kind of things did you do?" Jimmy asked.

"Nothing I want to talk about," Al told him before turning back to me. "Hatsu vouched for me, and no one on the Council would have done that unless they were sure about the person."

"Have you met other members of the Council?" I asked.

"I only got to meet Hatsu because the Council knew I had been sent by Frankie to spy on your people." Al added. "But I know your father."

"How?" I asked.

"Dr. Michael Major happens to be a customer of mine in Malibu."

"Sounds like a hell of a coincidence," Jimmy said.

"It's just one of those things," Al said.

Jimmy looked at me and rolled his eyes. This distrust was unlike Jimmy. He usually gave people the benefit of the doubt. I think his fear for my safety was causing him to overcompensate.

"Did Frankie know my father was on the Council?" I asked.

"I don't mind the test questions, but your father isn't on the Council." Al paused. "Look, Jessie, I know you've had a rough time here in Vegas and I understand your suspicions. Right after I got connected, I was suspicious of everyone I met. It's a shame I happened to know your father ahead of time because it does look kind of convenient. But Hatsu has good reasons to trust me."

"What are they?" Jimmy asked.

"I'm afraid I can't tell you right now," Al said.

"More secrets," Jimmy said. "Don't you guys ever get sick of them?"

"Hatsu has to be careful," Al said. "We all do. You don't know what the Lapras are capable of."

"What instructions did Frankie give you?" I asked.

"To infiltrate your group and report back to him."

"What did you tell him about us?" I asked.

"Nothing. I was supposed to meet with him this afternoon but at the last minute he canceled on me."

"So your affair with Alex is what? A lie?"

"From the outside it must appear that way. But I've already explained to her that I was sent here to meet her in order to keep an eye on you. She doesn't care, as long as I really care for her."

"It's hard for us to believe that you do," Jimmy said.

Al shrugged. "Believe what you wish."

"How much do you care?" I asked quietly.

Al sat up straighter and a note of pride entered his voice. "I'm risking my life talking to you like this. Simply by staying here, after receiving no further orders from Frankie, puts me in danger. But I'm willing to stay because I think I can help you guys."

"How?" Jimmy asked.

"I know how the Lapras operate. I'll know if they're tailing you or try to place someone else close to you. I can help in lots of ways."

He sounded sincere, at least to me, although there was something about him that filled me with foreboding. It was weird but I felt like I knew his face, or rather that it would be a face I would never forget. I sensed he could impact my life.

Obviously Jimmy wanted him gone, although Alex definitely cared for him. I was unsure what to do.

"What year were you born?" I asked.

"1914. I served in World War Two."

"How old were you when you were connected?" I asked.

"Twenty-eight. I was a fighter pilot. I was shot down by the Japanese during the Battle of Midway. I drowned at sea, sort of. When I came to, I was in witch world."

"That must have been a shock," I said.

"That's putting it mildly," Al said.

I turned to Jimmy. "What's your prognosis, doctor?"

He stared boldly at Al. "Take him out and shoot him." He chuckled softly. "Al, you seem like a nice guy. But it doesn't sound like you have a lot to offer Jessie right now. It might be easier for all concerned if we caught up with you later."

"What about Alex?" Al asked.

Jimmy shrugged. "She's been known to go a week or two without sex. She'll survive."

I spoke to Al. "With Frankie gone, who will the Lapras have you report to?" I asked.

"I don't know, this has never happened before," Al said. "But you needn't worry. Whoever I speak to, I won't tell them anything significant."

"Do you mind if I ask how many witch genes you have?" I asked.

"Two," Al said.

"What can you do?" Jimmy asked, curious.

"We don't normally give out that kind of information."

Jimmy got up and strolled toward the door. "You decide, Jessie. I want to order Whip something to eat," he said.

When he was gone, I gave Al a wan smile. "I do hope you're not lying to us. I'd hate to have to kill you."

"Trust takes time. I don't blame you or Jimmy."

"All of this has been painful for him. He can't convince anyone on the Council to let him go through the death experience."

Al nodded. "He feels left out and unable to help you."

"Exactly."

Al was thoughtful. "Maybe something can be done."

Hours later, after dinner and long, gentle lovemaking in our room, I lay in Jimmy's arms and waited for what might be my last night's sleep in the real world to end. I wondered if I would sleep at all. Yet I remembered the cardinal rule. If I wasn't unconscious when dawn arrived, I would black out wherever I was.

"I don't hear the others," I said.

"Alex and Al went for a walk. They'll probably be back soon."

"You don't think she's safe with Al," I said.

"Time will tell." Jimmy paused and made a worried gesture as Whip choked in the other room. He was asleep on the sofa in the center of the suite but he didn't rest easily. "His lungs sound like shit," Jimmy said.

"You should have left him with my dad," I said.

"Not tonight."

"Why not tonight?"

"We have to watch him some of the time."

"I'll speak to the Council about him," I said. "My father told me that Mirk is the most powerful healer in the group."

"It's odd how Susan loves her son so much in witch world and can't stand him here," Jimmy said.

"I'm not surprised. Look how warm-hearted he is. That quality alone would cause him to be banned from her sight."

"I wonder who the father is?" Jimmy said.

"Me too." He wasn't alone. From what Kendor had told me, I knew it couldn't be him. I was contemplating other possibilities when Jimmy suddenly kissed me. Soft and short but sweet, filled with such feeling. He began to stroke my bare hip, something that never failed to arouse me. "What are you doing?" I whispered.

"Molesting you," he said. "Remember how it is for me. I'm not sure where you'll be when I wake up."

"I'll be right here beside you."

His hand slid up my side to my hair. He began to tug on my ear. "I wish we could all be together," he said.

I smiled for his sake. "You and Huck and Lara and me. You know, for two crazy kids who just graduated high school, we have a pretty big family."

"It's weird how we've got kids. I've never had sex without wearing a condom."

I chuckled. "Are you serious? We've made love a dozen times . . . Wait a second, I think you're right. I'm remembering James in witch world."

"What's he like?" Jimmy asked.

"I don't know, I've never met him."

"But you just said you remember him."

"Vaguely. My father ordered me to keep a distance from him until my other set of memories returned."

"So for all you know, I could be a total asshole in witch world."

I acted dreamy. "Actually, from what I remember, he's a much better lover." He pinched my ear. "Ouch!"

"You deserved that," Jimmy said.

"Probably." I took his hand in mine. "You never ask about her."

He sighed. "It's hard enough having to think of Huck."

"I understand. But if we do manage to survive the next few days, Lara's going to be the center of my life, for a long time. Can you accept that?"

"As long as I get to know her in at least one world."

"The Council will figure out a way to connect you that isn't so risky. It's supposed to get easier as you get older."

"I can't wait until I'm thirty, Jessie."

"You won't have to."

"What about Huck? You asked about Lara. At least I'm related to her. In witch world, she's technically mine. But you don't have that connection to Huck in either world. Will you be able to adjust to helping me take care of him?"

"I'm sure I'll love him. As long as . . ." I didn't finish.

"As long as Kari doesn't get in your way? That's what you were going to say."

"I'm not going to lie. That girl's not fit to be a mother. The Lapras offer her some cash and a house with a view and she goes over to their side."

"They offered her son back. Alive," Jimmy said.

There was something in his voice. I should have spotted it earlier. "Christ. You spoke to her today. You saw her!"

"So? You saw Kendor."

"That wasn't planned. Tell me what happened? Did she take you to see your son?"

"She offered to take me. I didn't go."

Jimmy was telling the truth. In an instant I regretted having judged him. He was a stronger person than I was. Let's face it, I had gone to meet with the Lapras because I had wanted to see Lara, not because the Council wanted me to go.

"I'm so sorry," I said, hugging him tight.

"It's all right," he spoke in my ear. "I screwed her afterward, so the afternoon wasn't a total waste."

I wanted to hit him. I wanted to cry. But of course I ended up laughing, and that was how we fell asleep, in each other's arms, with smiles on our faces.

CHAPTER TWENTY-ONE

WAKING UP IN WITCH WORLD, IN MY HOTEL ROOM AT the MGM, I wished James were with me. I had not seen him since I had become connected. In that respect, James knew less than his counterpart. Hell, it was possible he didn't even know I was a witch. True, my father had talked to him, but I wasn't sure exactly what he had told him.

I woke up late, with the sun high in the sky. I remembered making love to Jimmy with a faint light in the eastern sky, which meant I must have passed out just before dawn.

I headed into the living room to call room service. I was starved—I needed breakfast, lunch, something. But there was a guy I didn't recognize sitting on the couch, casually reading the paper.

"Who the hell are you?" I asked.

He set aside the newspaper and straightened his tie. He

wore nice clothes: a green sports coat, slacks so white they looked like they would glow in the dark, and a gold Cartier watch. His dark blond hair was cut short.

"I'm Alfred," he said. "Alexis's boyfriend. We spoke before you went to bed."

"God, Alfred, I never saw someone change so much from one world to the next. What is it with you?"

Alfred, who was a head taller than Al, and no longer plump, but lean and mean, with muscles that only came from hours in the gym, nodded toward my bedroom. "I wasn't able to talk freely in front of Jimmy," he said. "I apologize."

"But why do you look so different?"

"This is how I look to Alex in the other world. This is my real appearance."

"How can you look one way to her and like someone else to the rest of us?" I asked.

"Jessica, I could turn invisible if I wanted to."

Then I understood what he was saying. It was the same thing Kendor had told me in the sewer. "You have the witch gene for invisibility," I said.

"I do. In its early stages it just allows you to alter your appearance so that no one recognizes you. You could call that a form of invisibility."

"Are all the powers like that? They start as one thing and transform into something deeper?" I asked.

"Yes. Your intuition has quickly appeared. But over a long

period of time it will mature into what we call wisdom. Only a handful of witches have that, like Cleo."

"The way you're talking, you don't sound like a young witch who just got connected sixty or seventy years ago. Did you lie to us about your age?"

He chuckled. "I had to lie to keep my disguise intact. My lies were part of my disguise. That's why you didn't pick up on them."

"Kendor told me I had the same ability. Do you think you could help me activate it so at least a few people in witch world won't know who I am?"

"That's why I'm here. To help you get started. But first tell me who you want to hide from and why."

"From the Lapras, of course."

Alfred shook his head. "You've got to be more specific."

"I want to go back to Henderson, to a spot Whip pointed out to us. I have a feeling the house where they're keeping Lara is close to where Huck is staying."

"But there is no Huck in this world."

"I know that."

Alfred's face darkened. "Is there something else you want to tell me?"

I thought I'd better change the subject. "How many witch genes do you really have?" I asked.

My question amused him. "Let's get to know each other a little better before we share such personal information." He stood. "So, are you ready for your first lesson?"

"Are we going somewhere?"

"All we need is a mirror. Like the one attached to your closet."

"I did this before with Russell," I said. "I went inside my reflection and saw through its eyes."

"We're going to do the opposite today. You're going to stay on this side of the mirror, in witch world, but you're going to alter your reflection until you're convinced you look different. The key is to trust in the power of your imagination."

Before we began, Alfred had me shower and get dressed. He even gave me time to eat a turkey sandwich that room service had brought. Then he turned all business. He made me stand and stare at the closet mirror as I slowly and methodically altered my face.

At first the exercise seemed like nothing more than fooling myself. For a few seconds, now and then, I imagined my lips larger and redder, but when I stopped telling myself how they had changed, they went back to the way they always were. What made the exercise even more frustrating was Alfred wouldn't let me sit down and rest. And he wouldn't let me close my eyes and wander off. I had to stay 100 percent focused on my face.

"Maybe I'm not ready for this power after all," I said.

"You're more ready than you think. Kendor saw it in you and I do as well. Now, what kind of lips do you want to have?"

"Angelina Jolie lips. They're lush and seductive. They pout

all by themselves. They're the kind of lips any guy in the world would give his life to kiss."

"What do you see in the mirror?" he asked, for what seemed the hundredth time.

"Nothing. I mean, just my face."

"Tell me again what kind of lips you want to have."

We went through the same song and dance again. And again. Then, just when I was definitely ready to quit, I suddenly blinked and my whole body trembled. For an instant, in the closet mirror, I imagined I could see through my face. And then . . .

"Wait a second!" I exclaimed. "This is incredible. My lips have actually changed! They're not reverting back to normal!"

"How about your nose? What kind of nose do you have?"

"A proud nose. Bold but not too big."

"Your eyes. What color are your eyes?"

"Bright green. They dazzle. My hair is bright red. It looks like it's on fire." I started laughing and couldn't stop. At the same time the feeling of heat grew inside my solar plexus. I was close to exploding and turned to Alfred. "How do I look to you?" I asked, excited.

"Like a brand-new person."

"Seriously?"

"The mirror doesn't lie. Your power has emerged. A little more practice and James and Alexis could walk in here and talk to you for an hour and they wouldn't know who you were."

"That reminds me. Do you know where James is staying these days?"

Alfred hesitated. "Yes."

"How is he holding up?" I asked, wondering if they were in contact.

"What do you mean?"

"I haven't seen him since I got connected. I was told to avoid him. I was just wondering if he suspects what's going on."

Alfred shook his head. "I don't know James very well."

"Do you happen to know his phone number?"

"Your father never gave it to you?"

"Not in this world he didn't," I said, my tone challenging. I knew he had it.

Alfred pulled out his cell and scrolled through his list of numbers. He found James's cell and gave it to me. I thanked him.

"No problem," he replied before changing the subject. "So you want to go snooping around the desert outside Henderson? They have some spectacular homes on the edge of town. Just the sort of places the Lapras would invest in."

"Do you think I can fool them with this new look?"

"It depends how experienced the particular Lapra is. If I were you, I'd bring backup. You never know who you might run into."

"Why do I get the feeling you're about to offer yourself?"

"It's your choice, Jessica. But like Kendor, I bring a lot to the table."

"So you have met him?" I asked.

"Long ago. I doubt he would remember me."

I considered his request. "I'm grateful you took the time to help me develop this disguise. But I feel more comfortable going alone. There's a lot I have to think about."

"And you just met me," he said.

He was being tactful. He was saying that he understood why I didn't fully trust him. I played along. "You look so different. It has been like meeting someone new."

Alfred surprised me by offering his hand. "Take care of yourself, Jessica. Remember who you are."

Alfred left and I practiced some more on my own. Another hour of focused work and I felt comfortable in my new skin, which was another way of saying I could change my appearance at will.

I even began to get the hang of directing my disguise in a specific direction. The hotel maids appeared and I tried out my new abilities on them. I was able to duplicate the trick Al had used on Alex, Jimmy, and me. To one maid I appeared to be a short redhead, to the other a lanky blonde. More impressive, I didn't have to ask how they saw me. I just knew.

It was a question of belief versus conviction. Before I had my breakthrough with Alfred, I had been trying to convince myself I looked like someone else. Then, as the power inherent in my genes pushed to the surface, I accepted I was different and those around me were forced to feel the same way. Deep inside I still knew it was all a lie, but on the surface of my mind I was sure I had changed.

I rented still another car, a Honda Accord, and left the city without a tail. Why should a Lapra tail me? I no longer looked like Jessica Ralle. Outside of town, I turned toward the hill that had attracted Whip's attention, the one with the rock crown. Yet I felt it was too early to try to locate Lara. There was an excellent chance Susan—Syn—would be with her, and if there was one Lapra who could penetrate my disguise, it would be her.

Besides, Susan had already set a meeting with me for tonight, and I wasn't ready to discard Cleo's plan by rejecting Susan's offer out of hand. Nevertheless, I was hoping to come up with a better plan, or praying that Kendor would. He knew Susan better than anyone and had kept stressing the need to attack.

It was partially Kendor's attitude that drove me now.

I wasn't looking for Lara's house but for Huck's.

It didn't matter that there was no Huck in this world.

There was a Kari. No, in witch world her name was Karla. It was odd how the name didn't come to me spontaneously. But then I realized it was because I didn't really know her in witch world. Kari was still Kari to me.

Kari's description of the views from Huck's house—in the real world—matched Susan's description of the place where the Lapras planned to put Lara and me. Again, it made sense these places would be close to each other because it would allow the Lapras to focus their security. Also, Kari had given me another clue to Huck's whereabouts when she had spoken of the beautiful sound of the chimes that hung from his back porch.

Since becoming connected, all my senses had sharpened. I was confident if I could get near the house, I'd be able to hear the chimes.

The small town of Henderson in witch world looked little different from its counterpart. I quickly found the area Whip had pointed out to Jimmy and me, the bluffs over-looking the desert. But I ran into a problem. It didn't matter that each house on the edge of town had ten or more acres to itself, which meant the area was spread over a vast stretch of land. . . .

The community was gated.

As far as I could see—and I had binoculars with me—the place was roped in with a fence topped with barbed wire. To get inside, I'd have to get past a guardhouse and two guards.

Two facts inspired me to take a chance. First, the sound of chimes was definitely wafting from a house located at the end of the street where the guardhouse stood. Second, my power had improved even during the short hop from Las Vegas. Now the person who stared back at me from my rearview mirror changed at my command.

True, I didn't know many Lapras I could imitate, but who better to get past their security than Dr. Susan Wheeler herself? Even if the guards had seen their boss enter earlier, they weren't going to stop and argue with the woman. I got the impression that questioning the head of the Order was not a prescription for a long life.

I put on Susan's face and body and locked it in place.

It wasn't the sort of face I was likely to forget.

I drove up to the guard tower. The two men were dressed in brown uniforms and carried .45 revolvers. They recognized who I was because they suddenly stood up so straight I thought they'd pop a vertebra. I wouldn't have been surprised if they saluted.

The older guard bent near my rolled-down window.

"How are you today, ma'am?" he asked.

"Fine," I said.

"We'd heard you were remaining in town today."

"You heard wrong. Let me through."

"Of course." The guard jumped back and signaled to his buddy to raise the blocking bar. It was controlled from inside the shack. A moment later I was driving toward what I hoped was Kari's house. It occurred to me that if I had the wrong place, I could go back to the guards and ask for directions. They had seemed eager to please.

I parked in Kari's driveway and got out of the cool car into the scorching heat. Hard to believe but Henderson was worse than Las Vegas and Apple Valley. Nevertheless, I let the sun beat down on my brow. Inside I could hear my heart pounding. My course of action was unclear. Or was I suffering from a lack of resolve? As the rays of the sun pierced my skin and sweat seeped through my pores, I allowed my face to return to that of Jessica Ralle.

I walked up to the door and rang the bell.

Kari answered. Dressed in shorts and a bikini top, she did not look happy to see me. "Jessica. This is a surprise," she said.

"I thought I'd check out the neighborhood I'm being asked to join."

Kari tried to look past me. "Did someone bring you here?"

"I didn't show up by magic. May I come in?"

Kari hesitated. "Sure." She opened the door wider. "I wish you'd called ahead of time. The place is sort of a mess."

Kari was a slob in both worlds. Clothes and plates littered the living-room floor and table.

"I apologize. I wasn't given much warning myself. Hey, do you have something to drink? A Coke?"

"I've got cola. That's what they drink here."

"Great. As long as it's cold, I can drink it out of the bottle."

Kari got us drinks and we sat in a small kitchen nook that overlooked a deliciously blue swimming pool. It was chilly inside with the air conditioner blasting away. I liked it. I gestured with my bottle.

"Nice place you've got here," I said.

"Thanks." Kari studied me, she was no fool. "What brought about the change of heart?" she asked.

"You mean, why am I considering the Lapras' offer?"

"Yeah. That didn't seem like a possibility the other day."

I sipped my drink. "A lot can happen in a short time."

"What happened to you?"

"Don't they keep you in the loop around here?"

"They tell me what I want to know," she said.

"Really? I heard they tell you what they think you should know."

Kari acted bored. "If you just came here to insult me . . ."

"I came here to kill you," I interrupted.

Kari froze for an instant. Then she tried to act casual and set her bottle back on the table. But her hand was shaking so badly she missed and the bottle fell to the floor. The kitchen-nook tiles were made of stone. The bottle shattered and cola fizzled. Kari tried to act cool, but we both knew it was way too late for that. She snorted.

"You're so full of shit, Jessica," she said.

"In a practical sense, you wouldn't be able to stop me. I can tell by the way you move and carry yourself that you didn't inherit the strength-and-speed gene. That means you can't defend yourself and I can get to you before you can dial nine-one-one on your cell. Or is it six-six-six here in witch world?" I paused. "I'm not full of shit, Kari."

Her fear was growing. "I didn't mean it that way."

"How did you mean it?"

"I've known you for four years. You're not a killer."

"For your sake, I wish that were true. But I killed a guy last night, a friend, and I'm probably going to kill a few more before this day's over." I stopped. "But if you help me, maybe you'll survive."

Kari gestured out the window. "This entire area belongs to the Lapras. I've made a deal with them. Which means I'm under their protection. If you so much as lay a hand on me, it's you who will die."

I shrugged. "That sounds all good and fine. But you made a mistake when you let the wolf in your door. Me. Because I'm like any other kind of predator whose child is threatened. I don't care about man-made rules and regulations. I just care about destroying the threat."

"I don't want to hurt Lara. When it comes to our kids, Jessica, we're on the same side. I tried to tell you that at the Mirage. I'll do anything to protect Huck. So will James."

"You mean Jimmy. James doesn't know Huck. He only knows Lara."

Kari acted offended. "I know all that. Don't treat me like I'm stupid. I really can help you."

"Tell me where they keep Lara."

Kari hesitated. "I don't know."

I sighed. "You're lying. A pity."

"Hold on a sec," Kari said as she went to stand. In a move

too fast for her to follow, I reached out, grabbed her and shoved her back into her seat. The blinding attack drained all the color from her face.

"Tell me where they keep Lara," I repeated calmly.

Kari swallowed. "In a house near the base of that hill." She pointed out the window at the house—it was more of a mansion—with the roughly hewed stone crown hovering above it. She added, "I saw them take her inside there yesterday."

"Was Susan with them?"

"I think so. Frank was with her."

"Who was holding Lara?"

"Another woman. I don't know who."

"Tell me what kind of security that house has."

"I don't know. I've never been inside. But I've seen guards walking the grounds. There are Lapra guards all over this place."

Kari was still trying to warn me how dangerous it would be to kill her. "How often is Susan at the house?" I asked.

"I hear she's usually gone."

"Are there guards in the hills?" I asked.

"Someone told me they keep snipers up there. In case of an attack."

"Do they anticipate one?"

"The Lapras I've spoken to know the Tar's upset about something but they don't know what it is."

"The average Lapra doesn't know about Lara?"

"No."

"Interesting." I sat, thinking. My silence unnerved Kari.

"I've answered all your questions," she said.

I nodded. "You tried your best."

"You should go now. Someone will spot you."

"Listen and don't interrupt. You're a problem, and by that I don't mean I'm worried Jimmy's going to run off with you again. He would never have left me if you hadn't gotten pregnant. He was trying to do the right thing. So don't think I see you as a threat in the traditional sense."

"Bullshit. You've always been jealous of me."

I raised my hand. "Listen, I have given this a lot of thought. As Huck's mother, you're always going to be in Jimmy's life. But because you're a Lapra, I can't allow that. It puts him in danger and it puts Lara and me in danger. For that matter, it's no good for Huck. The boy can't grow up surrounded by such evil. He'll end up like them." I paused. "You can see my concerns are logical."

Kari tensed. I could hear her struggling to breathe. "We can work this out," she said quietly.

"I don't see how. And I'm sorry, really. I don't like you but I don't hate you either. If circumstances were different, I'd ignore you. But I can't. You're a loose end none of us can afford."

"You told me if I helped you that you'd let me go."

"I lied."

"You've just been using me!"

"Yes," I said.

Again, she went to stand. Again, she got nowhere.

Tears sprang in her eyes and she trembled. "You talk about how evil the Lapras are but look at you. Last week you would never have considered murdering someone. But now, just because you've got the power, you're thinking about it. Don't you see how you've changed?"

I nodded solemnly. "I can't argue with you. Sometimes I look at myself in amazement. I ask myself, is it the influence of this world? It's definitely got a cruder morality than our normal world. But then I look deeper and I see I'm just being pragmatic. You're dangerous, Kari. As long as you're alive, I'll never be able to relax."

Kari leaped up and pointed toward the door. "Get out of my house!" she cried.

I stood and approached her slowly. "If there were any other way to make you vanish, I'd take it. But there isn't. If I leave you here alive, the second I walk out that door you'll sound the alarm."

"No! I swear I won't tell anyone you were here!"

"You will, you'll have to, and I can't allow that."

Kari shook her head. "No! Wait! You can't do this!"

I didn't want her to suffer anymore.

Reaching forward, I grabbed her by the base of her skull and went to break her neck. But at the last instant I realized she was right. I wasn't a killer. I couldn't do it. To just snap her spine, to change her into a rag doll, it made me feel sick just thinking about it. I realized then how quickly my feeling of power had corrupted me.

Yet I still had a problem with the Lapras' security. Kari would alert them the instant I left and I would be captured, probably killed. The only solution was to take Kari with me. Later, I could figure out what to do with her. I still wanted her away from Jimmy and Huck.

Spinning Kari a hundred and eighty degrees, I wrapped my arm around and applied the well-known choke hold. How did I know it? I didn't; it came to me by instinct. But it was simple enough. I put pressure on Kari's carotid, the artery that carried blood to her brain. She struggled perhaps five seconds before slumping unconscious in my arms. I held her neck an extra ten seconds to make sure she stayed out.

I opened the garage door and drove my car inside, briefly parking beside her vehicle. I dumped Kari in my trunk and two minutes later I was on my way past security, once more in the form of Susan Wheeler. They waved me through, no questions asked.

Soon I was out in the open desert. I took an obscure side street, a narrow road made of crumbling asphalt that probably wasn't even on the map. I wasn't headed toward Las Vegas. I needed time to think and driving helped me. I had gone to Kari's house to kill her but had lost my nerve. That was okay—

I was glad I had let her live. But impulsive decisions often lead to complex consequences. It wasn't like I could store the girl in the meat locker where I'd been thrown, although the idea was appealing.

Suddenly I heard a loud noise coming from the trunk.

Kari was awake and in a bad mood.

No need to panic. I wasn't surprised she was awake. The effect from the choke hold wasn't supposed to last more than ten or fifteen minutes. I remembered that from my witch-world life. But it was a little unnerving how vigorously Kari was kicking.

The backseat burst free and Kari's head poked out.

"I'm not good enough to ride up front with you?" she said.

Her tone of voice, the ease with which she had broken free—these points made me realize I had seriously underestimated Kari. Hell, I had been duped! Fifteen minutes ago the girl had been weeping with fear and now she sounded happy as a lark.

In my rearview mirror, I watched as she climbed into the backseat area. I slammed on the brakes. I had my seat belt on, I always wore it. Kari went flying, passing through the gap between the front seats, striking the windshield. That should have been enough to knock her out cold. She barely blinked.

"You know, Jessica, your driving sucks," she said, just before she kicked me in the jaw. I saw stars, the whole world tilted at an awkward angle. Fortunately the car had stopped and I had enough sense left to get out before she kicked me again.

I leaped out the door without unfastening my seat belt. I just broke it. The change from the cool air inside to the blistering sun outside didn't help the ringing in my head. I sagged against the side of the car, trying to catch my breath. But I exaggerated the gesture so Kari would come straight at me. That was a mistake on her part.

I kicked the car door shut in her face. Her head went through the driver's-side window. Jagged glass cut her scalp and blood flowed over her blond hair. Again, the blow should have knocked her out. It should have killed her. But she pulled her head free and smiled at me.

"Not the weak witch you thought I was, am I?" she said.

A setup. Her meek behavior had been a charade. Now she had me alone in the middle of nowhere, which had probably been her intention from the start. She had the strength gene. Hell, she appeared to be stronger than me, probably because she had been a witch longer. I needed to use my wits, I needed an advantage.

Kari put one leg out of the car and I kicked at the door again, the metal cutting into her calf. Swearing, she toppled back inside the vehicle and I circled around to the trunk. I yanked it open, breaking the lock, and pulled away the carpet floor that covered the spare tire. A hasty scan revealed a steel jack that a driver could use to change a tire. Just as useful was the roadside kit. Inside it were a couple of flares and a long screwdriver.

Grabbing the tools, I hurried to the passenger side. Kari had recovered and was standing casually beside the driver's door, the blood still streaming from her hair. She was in no hurry to catch me. I think she wanted to toy with me first. We stood on opposite sides of the car.

"Oh my, scary. You've got weapons," she mocked me. "I suppose you expect me to surrender and beg for mercy."

"I could have killed you back at the house," I said, stabbing the side of the hidden gas tank with the screwdriver. Gasoline began to pour onto the asphalt around the rear wheel, but not fast enough for my taste. Twisting the screwdriver back and forth, I widened the hole, and a flood of fuel splashed at my feet.

Kari didn't seem to notice. She couldn't see what I was doing, and besides, she had always been so full of herself that she seldom stopped to consider what other people were up to. The fact that she was now a witch had not taken the spoiled cheerleader out of her.

"You couldn't kill someone if your life depended on it," Kari said, slowly making her way toward the trunk. "You're too sweet, too concerned about being good. I can't imagine what a guy like James saw in you."

I backed toward the front of the car. "I don't know, some guys are weird that way. They like a girl who has integrity, and who isn't a slut."

Kari rounded the rear, approaching the dripping gasoline.

She saw it, she had to see it, but she didn't seem to care. She threw her head back and laughed.

"If I cheated on Jimmy he never knew. Or, I should say, he never asked. He's a nice guy but he's too naive for this world."

"So all that song and dance about him being the father of your child was bullshit?" I asked, sliding a flare from my back pocket but keeping it out of her view.

Kari stopped and hardened her tone. "The bullshit was the way you justified stealing him away from me. You acted like the two of you were soul mates and that gave you the right to just walk over me. You made a big mistake when you made me your enemy, Jessica."

"Now I suppose you're going to make me pay?"

Kari pulled a switchblade from her pocket. Damn, I had missed that. She touched a button on the side and out popped a knife. The steel shone in the blazing sunlight, razor sharp.

Kari gloated. "Sister. I'm going to make you bleed."

She pounced, but not before I knelt and broke the cap on the flare and scraped it across the asphalt. It took only a flick of my wrist to toss it in the pool of gasoline. Knowing what would happen next, I leaped away from the front of the car.

The rear of the vehicle exploded in a fireball.

Kari was briefly engulfed in flames, but it was the shock wave that did her the most damage. The car's tank was practically full, and bathed in flames it made an effective bomb. The blast threw Kari off the road. Her hair caught fire and the switchblade was blown from her hand. She landed in a smoking pile.

Raising the car jack, I was on her in an instant. I had to strike while I had the chance, I told myself. I couldn't show mercy.

I struck as she tried to stand. She didn't see me coming. She was too busy trying to smother her burning hair. The jack caught her in the temple, the thinnest part of the skull. I heard a faint crack and swung at her from the other side. She was tough, she kept climbing. Then I wound up and struck as hard as I could at her left kneecap. I didn't need a witch's subtle senses to hear a mass of bone and cartilage fracture.

Howling in pain, she fell on her back. I leaped onto her chest, pinning her arms with my knees, and pressed the jack to her throat. "Who's bleeding now?" I sneered.

She choked as I narrowed her trachea. "You don't have the guts to kill me," she panted.

I pressed harder. "I don't need guts. This is a pleasure."

What disturbed me was I was telling the truth. More than just the thrill of victory that came from being alive when I could have been dead, I felt an orgasmic jolt shoot through the length of my spine, which left my nerves tingling. It was weird, Kari was dying, but it was like she sensed what I was experiencing.

"Pleasure for pain," she whispered, quoting a portion of the line written on the sewer wall.

"What does it mean?" I asked, pulling back on the jack.

But I had already crushed her trachea. She wheezed like a dying beast.

"She's got you where . . . she wants you," she gasped.

"Susan? What does she want with me?"

Kari grinned. Then her eyes dilated and she was staring at a sky she could not see. She had stopped breathing. She was dead.

Burying her body in the desert didn't take long. The ground in witch world seemed more porous, less substantial. I dug down six feet, using the car jack as a shovel, without taking a break.

When I was finished, I stopped to say two prayers. One for Kari and one for myself. My prayer was the more worrisome. I couldn't exactly ask God to forgive a murder. I only hoped I could forgive myself.

I didn't plan on telling James or Jimmy what I'd done.

CHAPTER TWENTY-TWO

BACK IN TOWN, I TRIED CALLING ALFRED AND GOT NO answer. Then I tried the one person I really wanted to talk to, James. I shook as I dialed the number. Of course, I was going against my father's orders. But never mind that, what was the guy really like? What if I didn't love him the way I loved Jimmy? Hell, what if he was seeing someone else while I was off-limits?

But again, I got no response. However, I relaxed a little when I got ahold of my father on my cell and he told me why James was not answering.

"I told him to avoid you," he said. "And I told you I told him. Your first night in witch world. Don't you remember?"

"You told me to avoid him for a couple of days."

"A few days," he corrected me. "Why do you need to talk to him?"

He sounded so much like a dad right then.

"Susan wanted me to bring him with me tonight," I said.

"She suggested it, she didn't insist on it. The last thing you want is for James to see Lara and get attached to her all over again. That will turn him into Susan's puppet."

"I suppose," I grumbled.

"You don't sound very convinced."

"Look, I'm going through a hard time and I miss him. It would just be nice to check in with him, you know, and hear his voice."

"How did you get his number?"

"Alfred gave it to me."

My father paused. "Interesting."

"Dad? How well do you know Alfred?"

"I've known him a while. Good man."

"Is he a powerful witch?"

"I wouldn't go that far."

"Do you know how many witch genes he has?"

My father hesitated. "That's odd—I just checked our database, and his number's not listed."

"Is he required to list it with the Council?"

"The Council doesn't insist. Alfred probably didn't tell us because he has a low number. We don't go around talking about our numbers. For centuries, Cleo has discouraged the practice. It's another way of labeling people. Like anything else it can lead to prejudice."

"Does your file on Alfred say how old he is?"

"Why do you ask?"

"He told me he was a fighter pilot during World War Two."

"He was. He has many skills. How did you meet him?"

"Alex is dating him," I said. My father had not answered my question.

"No one told me about that."

"Dad. How did you meet him?"

"By chance. He sells drugs for a pharmaceutical company in the real world. He happened to come into my office in Malibu."

"Hatsu said I could trust him."

"Hatsu's very old and wise. Is Alfred with you now?"

"No. I called him the same time I called James. Everyone seems to have abandoned me on this most important of days."

"Nonsense. The Council is going to meet with you before you see Susan. Trust me, I've never seen them give one person so much attention."

"When and where?" I asked.

"Seven. I'll call you with the location before then."

With the late start I'd gotten, and Alfred's extensive training and my battle with Kari, the day was already half over. The meeting was only two hours away. "I feel like things are moving too fast," I said. "That we're not prepared for this showdown with Susan."

"The Council has had time to reflect. Let's see what they have to say."

"All right, Dad."

"Is that traffic I hear in the background?"

"Yeah."

"I was told you hadn't left your hotel room today."

"Spying on me?"

"Guarding you."

"I snuck out. It's no big deal. Call me as soon as you know where I'm supposed to go."

We exchanged good-byes. I was off the phone less than ten minutes when I tried James again. There was still no answer and I was worried about him. James may have been more respectful to my father in this world but I still couldn't imagine anyone bossing him around.

I drove to the pawnshop I had stopped at the previous day while searching the industrial area for the elusive sewer. The owner looked as seedy as his store. With a bulging gut, food stains on his shirt, and an unlit cigar in his mouth, he had shown little interest in helping me. But while in the store, I had noticed a box filled with handguns sitting in the rear storage area.

I disliked guns, I hated everything they stood for. But I was not sure if that was true of the Jessica Ralle who usually walked the streets of witch world. I recalled owning my own handgun. Indeed I remembered being a deadly shot.

Russell had taught me how to shoot. It came back to me all of a sudden. So did the pain of his death. With so much running around, I had not had a chance to sit and properly mourn his death. And now was not the time.

I remembered that Frank had not bothered to frisk me when I met with Susan, probably because the Lapras as a whole were so arrogant, they didn't think they could be hurt. Frankie was dead, it was true, but the next guy in line to take his place would probably be just as cocky.

This time I returned to the pawnshop with five grand in cash. I told the owner what I wanted and he told me to go to hell. But then I caught his eye and warned him that I wasn't used to being spoken to that way. He got the picture. I was connected. He immediately apologized.

"I misunderstood you, Mother," he said hastily. "I just thought that a person such as yourself would have no need for a firearm."

"Let me decide what my needs are," I said as I counted out thirty hundred-dollar bills on his countertop. "I want a nine-millimeter semiautomatic handgun. Top of the line but compact. Plus I want a high-quality silencer that I can screw on the tip at a moment's notice."

The man's bloodshot eyes swelled at the sight of the cash. "I have a Glock nine-millimeter that's totally clean and untraceable. But you're going to have to sacrifice bullets for size."

"How many?"

"The compact model takes eight bullet clips instead of the usual fifteen," he said as he sauntered toward the box I had spotted on his floor the day before. I followed closely. I didn't expect him to try to rob me, assuming he knew who or what I was, but I was cautious. He continued. "But with this particular Glock you could tuck it in your belt beneath your blouse and no one would be any the wiser."

"Show me," I said, gesturing to the box on the floor. But he surprised me by reaching above my head and taking down a shoe box lined with leather. Inside was the gun with three stubby clips, all unloaded, and a fat three-inch-long silencer. He handed over the gun and a single empty clip.

"Are you experienced with semis?" he asked.

"I know they fire faster and reload quicker," I said.

"That's a fact. But they're more troublesome than revolvers. A revolver will never jam on you. A semi has to be kept super clean." He added, "But it's hard to find a revolver that takes a silencer. I know I don't have one."

The gun felt good in my hand. It made me feel *bad*. "This is the one I want. Show me how to use it. And I want the extra clips and two boxes of ammunition."

"I'll need five grand if you're taking the silencer," he said. "It's a specialty item."

"You mean it's illegal."

He held up his hands in mock defense. "Your words, Mother, not mine. As it stands, if you buy this gun, we never met."

"Understood. I'll give you four grand, no more. And you teach me everything I need to know about it."

"I'll take care of you, Mother," he said.

He was true to his word. Indeed, he gave me such in-depth instruction that by the time I left his shop, the sun had set and it was time for my meeting with the Council. My father called the instant I climbed back in my car and told me the new location, a small house in the old residential area of town. I drove straight there but was careful to leave my gun hidden in the trunk.

Inside, the Council members were already gathered, waiting for me. My father was present. I felt a pang Russell was not. As witch world counted time, it had only been twenty-four hours since I had sat with the Council, but to me it felt like ages.

More of Jessica Ralle's memories were returning. I recalled how Lara's birth had not been easy. How my father had refused to give me anything to reduce the pain, not even a little Demerol to take the edge off. Nothing but a 100 percent natural birth for the Council's perfect child. Of course, holding Lara afterward, it had all felt worth it.

To my surprise, I started the meeting by explaining how I had located where Lara was being held. Cleo acted pleased that I had obtained the information but insisted on knowing why I had taken it upon myself to visit Kari. Damn, the woman had radar.

"Since I became connected to your group," I said, "I've known nothing but danger. It's everywhere I turn. Yet you guys don't give me much advice, and I'm not the sort of person who likes to sit around and wait for things to happen. I went to see Kari because I felt I had to take a more proactive stance."

"A proactive stance is one thing," Cleo said. "Murder is something else."

I let my anger show. "None of you accused me of murder when I killed Russell. Because you saw his death as necessary. Well, Kari's death was just as necessary. She attacked me."

"Did you give her reason to attack you?" Cleo asked.

"Maybe. I kidnapped her."

Hatsu smiled. "Not a bad reason."

"I couldn't allow her to screw up Jimmy's life," I said.

Kendor nodded. "You did the right thing."

Cleo shook her head. "I'm disturbed that you killed her so casually. Without consulting with us."

"She attacked me," I said.

"You continue to avoid my point," Cleo said.

"What? That from now on I'm to obey you? I don't remember signing up for that."

"Jessica," my father snapped. "Show respect."

I shook my head. "Kari's dead. I'm glad she's out of the way. Now let's move on. Have you come up with a plan to kill Susan?"

"We have come to a consensus," Cleo said. "We still lack information on this bafflement, which has been twice used against us, and which seems to be strictly under Susan's control.

For that reason we'll stick with our earlier decision. You're to accept her offer and allow her to place you in a home with Lara."

I couldn't have felt more deflated. They had not budged an inch. "That's it? That's all you have to offer? You meet and talk for two days and at the end of that time you say, 'Do what the bitch wants.' Excuse me, but that doesn't sound like a plan to stop her. It sounds more like a reason to surrender."

"Lara's safety is still our number one priority," Cleo said. "Until we can be sure she's safe, we can't attack, at least not directly."

"Kendor," I said, turning to my friend. "You can't agree with this madness."

He looked weary, beaten down, an expression I never would have expected to see on such a powerful man. "We took a vote. This is what the Council decided. I must obey."

I stood impatiently. "Since when have you obeyed anyone? I'm telling you, all of you, I know this woman. I know what she's capable of. While you sit and patiently study her from a distance, you can be sure she's closing in on you with a net that will choke the life out of all of you, not just Lara and me."

"You're a brave girl," Cleo said as she suddenly stood and put her hands on my shoulders. "We appreciate your courage, even if we feel it's misdirected. Go now and obey. Keep Lara alive at all costs. Let this drama play out as it was destined to."

"It's more than a drama to me," I said, my eyes burning.

But I held my tears in check, even when Cleo hugged me. My feelings were a confused mess. On one hand I wanted to strangle her for being so passive. At the same time I hated to leave her embrace. Her ancient love was like a shield that drove off the very root of my fear.

My father offered to walk me out. I told him not to bother and left the house. I was five minutes away from the Council when my cell rang. A young woman with a cold voice spoke.

"Be in front of the Tropicana at eleven sharp," she said. "Don't be late."

"Can I—?" I began, but she had hung up.

I had two hours to kill. Heading for the desert, after making sure I wasn't being tailed, I drove off a side road into the sand and stopped beside a collection of boulders. The man at the pawnshop had given me extra ammunition. Loading my clips—it helped to have superpowered fingers—I used a few discarded cola bottles to practice my aim. To my total lack of surprise, I discovered I was a crack shot.

I put three bullets through the silencer, no more. The pawn-shop man had warned me that even the finest suppressor quickly wore out. For now the attachment turned the nine-millimeter blasts into faint whistles.

I left the silencer attached to the gun. If I used the weapon, say inside a house, I didn't want Susan's neighborhood security to hear.

I was leaving my private firing range when James called.

"Hey, Jessica, I heard you've been trying to reach me."

"Who told you?" I asked, delighted to hear his voice. He sounded just like Jimmy, maybe a little older.

"Alfred. I ran into him in town. Is your prohibition over? Can we be friends again?"

"Yes. I want to see you. I miss you."

James lowered his voice. "Alfred said you've made progress getting Lara back. Is it true?"

"I'm going to see her tonight. Would you like to come?"

"Are you crazy? Of course. That's fantastic news. Does this mean everything's okay now?"

"Lara's still a prisoner of sorts but we'll be able to see her when we want. As long as we cooperate."

"Cooperate with who?" he asked warily.

I hesitated. How much did he know?

"Guess," I said softly.

"I hear ya," he replied quickly, as if he was afraid someone was listening. Did the Lapras tap phones in witch world? James asked, "Where should we meet?"

I gave him the details and we exchanged good-byes. But a moment later I wondered if I was making a mistake. If I was just taking him along for selfish reasons. However, there was a certain shrewdness in bringing James. It would show Susan that we were united when it came to accepting her offer.

At ten to eleven I met James in front of the Tropicana. I had come full circle. It was the hotel where I had first met Russ.

James grabbed me and kissed me before we even said hello. I didn't protest. He felt so alive in my arms, so full of love. It was odd how Cleo's embrace had made me feel safe, while James's hug made me swoon. And yet I felt something in common in both hugs that I couldn't explain. Maybe it was the mystery of true love that Cleo had spoken of, that was able to flow between dimensions.

"God, you feel good," James whispered in my ear.

"You feel better," I said, finally letting go. I had to take a step back to size him up. His hair was longer than I was used to, an inch or two, and his clothes were sharper. He wore gray slacks and a black leather coat that was soft enough to sleep on. How I wished we could curl up together in bed right then.

"Tell me what's happening with Lara," James said. "Is she all right?"

"Physically she's fine. But emotionally . . . well, the people who kidnapped her are suffering because she's cranky. She misses her mommy. Remember when she was born how we talked about how special she was? How she lit up the room?"

"Doesn't everyone think their kid does?"

"Probably. But it turns out Lara is special. That's why these assholes want her."

"They don't just want money?"

"No." I paused, still wondering how much James knew about what was going on. "Tell me how you hooked up with Alfred?"

He hesitated. "Through Alexis. She introduced him to me."

"Did you spend much time with him?"

"A few hours. He just slipped away before you arrived. I'm surprised you didn't see him. He thinks he can help us."

He was lying, or only telling me part of the story. It made me uneasy. My Jimmy never lied to me.

A black limousine suddenly appeared. It pulled up beside us and the driver motored down his window. When I saw who was behind the wheel, I almost fainted.

"Frank!" I gasped.

He grinned a big mouth of snow-white teeth, his black skin and bald head glistening in the rays of moonlight pouring down from above. He ordered us to get in.

Yet James hesitated once I was in the backseat. He stopped and looked around. I didn't know who he was searching for.

"What is it, James?" I asked.

He shook his head and climbed in. "Nothing."

Frank put the limo in gear and we rolled onto the Strip. It was always busy in witch world, it didn't matter the time or day. I wondered if the perverse compulsion to constantly gamble came from the gloom that seemed to hang over the city. Were people in this society so desperate they kept searching for one big score? As I had noted before, from the time I had left the morgue, the nights in witch world seemed darker, the neon lights brighter. Even the moon appeared to have a veil over it.

Frank was taking pleasure in my discomfort at his amazing

resurrection. "You're wondering how I reattached my head," he said.

"Something along those lines," I said.

"That right there should tell you about the type of people you've been talking to. Damn Tar. They lock you in a meat locker so they can turn you into a witch and then they don't tell you shit. Not even the basics. You should listen to Susan when she tells you that their docile approach is a dead approach."

"Speaking of the dead?" I said.

Frank snorted. "This is witch world! All that crap you've been fed about this being a mirror image of the real world is a lie. This is the only world that counts. This is *the* real world. The other is just a shadow. What happens here is what matters."

"So you're saying if you die in witch world, you automatically die in both worlds. But die in the real world and all bets are off?"

"You've got it, girl. But you should have been told that five minutes after you woke up here. If you'd stayed with us, you'd know what's real and what's a lie. Now, I've never seen Susan take an interest in someone like she has in you. So don't go playing any games with her tonight. I can tell already she's not in the mood."

"Something put her in a bad mood?" I asked.

Frank peered out the window at the moon. It was full. Like the night Lara was born. My daughter was one lunar month old tonight.

CHRISTOPHER PIKE

"Something heavy is about to go down," he said without explaining what he meant.

Tonight Frank didn't bother taking any side roads, nor did he backtrack. He hardly looked in his rearview mirror. It was clear he wasn't worried about being tailed. He drove straight to Henderson, to the north side where the gated community was located, and the guards waved him through. There were six instead of two.

At the end of the block, before making a left and climbing toward the mansion at the base of the stone-crown hill, we passed Kari's house and I couldn't help but notice all the lights were on. The front door was wide open and I saw a guard inside. The fact she had gone missing was no longer a secret.

I considered pointing out the house to James, so he would at least know where they were keeping Huck, but then I remembered he didn't know who the boy was.

James leaned over and whispered in my ear. "What else can you tell me about these people?" he asked.

"They're heavily connected. Bad to the bone."

"And they took Lara, why?"

"Because she's a saint," I said, the words coming out before I had time to think. A saint? How could I believe in saints when I wasn't sure if there was a God? Yet when I told him what I did, it felt right.

The mansion was also well lit, with a fountain out front that was continually fanned with a rainbow of colors. Parking beside the splashing water, we got out and took a moment to drink in the view. James quickly stepped away from the limo and stared out at the night. Perhaps the glow of the moon drew him. I had to admit the light seemed to soften what was otherwise a harsh terrain.

I remembered the wondrous light I had seen inside my head the first night Jimmy and I had made love. I had seen it with James as well, naturally. Curious how my father had talked about seeing almost the same thing the night Lara was born. And he had spoken of the sound as well, that music that was not the product of any earthly instrument. There was a mysterious connection to both events I wasn't grasping yet, although I sensed the answer was near.

We went inside. Susan and her son, Whip—he of the stinger tail—were waiting. Lara was also present but Susan gave her to Frank instead of me, which established who was in charge. My chest physically ached to look at my daughter and not be able to touch her. Frank retreated to a corner, where Lara sat on his lap, his massive black hands holding her firmly.

While Whip sauntered about the living room, his tail sliding across anything he pleased, Susan ordered James and me to sit on the sofa. She paced in front of us, no longer wearing the blue scrubs of our last encounter but black pants and a red blouse that hugged her toned chest.

Susan wasted no time. She demanded to know where Kari was. I shook my head. "How should I know?" I said.

"Are we talking about Kari from school?" James asked.

I found it odd he didn't call her Karla. That was, after all, her name in witch world.

"Yes. She's the mother of your son in the other world," Susan snapped, her attention still focused on me. "You know how important this meeting is tonight. I'm surprised you would begin it with a lie."

"What makes you think I'm lying?" I asked.

Susan stopped and held up a CD. "A copy of a security tape that was taken this afternoon at one fifty. Kari had a visitor at that time. The guards let her inside because they thought it was me. Of course they were tricked by a powerful witch. But even though this witch has power, she's still a fool. Because she didn't stop to think that her spell wouldn't have an effect on a nonliving camera." Susan tossed the CD in my lap. "Should we play it?" she asked.

I shrugged. "You win some, you lose some."

"Where's Kari?" Susan repeated.

"In a shallow grave fifteen miles from here," I said.

Susan smiled coldly. "As I expected. I have to wonder how this murder will influence your future position. You, who always act so righteous whenever we discuss the Lapras and the Tar."

I bowed my head in Susan's direction, as if to concede the point. "If you're going to learn to kill, you should learn from the best." I added, "Kari was nothing. Why waste time talking about her?"

"I speak of her more for James's sake than your own." Susan paused. "What do you think of your sweet and lovable girlfriend murdering a lover of yours in cold blood?"

James appeared guarded, confused. "I don't believe it."

"Then put on the tape, Jessica," Susan ordered.

"It's not necessary." I put a hand on James's arm. "I'll explain everything later."

"Be wary of 'later' in witch world," Susan warned. "It often changes into 'too late.'"

"I came here tonight because I'm interested in the offer you made," I said. "That's the only reason I'm here. If you want to discuss trivia then I'll come back another time."

"Well said, Jessica," Susan replied. "How quickly you seek to regain control. Perhaps you have the makings of a Lapra after all." She gestured to the mansion. "What do you think of the house? I was thinking this might be the perfect place for you and your little family."

I glanced around. "I could get used to it."

"Too rich for your tastes?"

"A little gaudy. But I'm more concerned about you honoring your deal and leaving us alone in peace."

"You'll have peace, I can assure you," Susan said as she took a step toward Frank and Lara. My daughter looked uncomfortable in his lap but wasn't crying. She kept looking over at me, I was sure of it. Susan appeared to notice Lara's attention because she brushed her fingers lightly over Lara's face as if to distract her. She added, "I'll only require Lara once a week or so."

"For what?" I asked.

"Study."

"It sounds like you're going to perform experiments on her."

"Nonsense. The child has been much better behaved since she last saw you." Susan stroked the side of Lara's face. "She's also demonstrated even more potential than I thought possible."

"Did she raise Frankie from the dead?" I said sarcastically.

Susan turned back to me at the mention of Frank. I knew what was coming. "I'm afraid that version of Frank won't be joining us anymore. But your question does raise the issue of who you were with when you were exploring the sewers. It must have been someone adept with a sword to take off the head of a warrior as powerful as Frankie."

"I was taken by surprise," Frank muttered.

"Kendor wasn't my companion," I said. "He only showed up when Frank threatened to kill me."

Susan was unable to hide the effect Kendor's name had on her. She almost stumbled as she strode toward me. "I hear the two of you talked after he finished saving your life," she said.

"We didn't talk long. But he told me your real name was Syn and that you two were lovers for close to two thousand years."

Susan's lower lip trembled ever so slightly. Again, she tried to hide it but was unable to. "Did he tell you why I left him?"

"We didn't get into that sort of detail."

"Ah, Jessica, you lie but you also tell the truth. Kendor doesn't know why I left him." She paused, thinking, her body swaying slightly. "What else did he say?"

"He told me about your past. The children you had, and how you both suffered when they were lost." I paused. "Robere. Era. Herme . . ."

"Stop!" Susan suddenly cried.

I stopped—the whole room did. Even Whip sat still on the floor and Lara stopped fussing in Frank's hands. It was as if the names had swept through the room like disembodied tombstones and had struck Susan like a hammer made of hard memories. The pain in the air was almost palpable, and Susan was supposed to be able to harvest that special form of energy. But I think this sample was even too potent for her to swallow. A minute followed by a second minute ticked by, and none of us dared disturb her.

Finally, Susan sat down across from James and me.

She acted like her outburst had never happened.

"I need to know if your desire to stay here with Lara is genuine," she said to me.

"Yes. But you ask for honesty so I'll give it. I want to be with James and my daughter. I don't want to be kept a prisoner."

Susan shrugged. "You'll remain here until I'm confident you won't try to flee. The length of your confinement is totally up to you. Is that agreeable?"

"You mean it's totally up to you," I said.

"You don't have a lot of choices, Jessica."

I paused. "Then I can live with that."

Susan turned to James. "You're welcome to stay here as well. But it's not the Lapra way to embrace a non-witch. To stay with us you must become one of us. Do you understand?"

He nodded. "I have to become connected. I have to activate my powers by dying."

"Is that something you want to do?" Susan asked.

"Yes. With all my heart," James said.

Obviously he was as anxious to become a witch in witch world as in the real world. But were his motives the same?

"No!" I interrupted. "He doesn't possess the healing gene. Chances are he won't survive the process."

Susan gestured to a bag on the living-room table. "Do you forget I'm a physician? In my little black bag I have plenty of morphine to put James blissfully to sleep. So deep his breathing will cease and he'll be technically dead. But I also have a large assortment of drugs—adrenaline, ephedrine, and so on—to bring him back to life. And what a life it will be. James, you'll have access to five witch genes." Susan paused. "It's your decision."

He nodded firmly. "Let's do it."

Susan clapped her hands together. "I think I'm going to like you, James. Besides being cute as hell, you've got balls. I can see us becoming good friends. Maybe something more. How would you feel about that, Jessica?"

"You're wasting your time if you're trying to make me jealous. You're also picking a bad time to try to connect James. Tonight is about Lara and me. Don't forget you need me to keep her happy."

Susan acted offended. "Are you saying you're refusing to let your boy have what he wants?" she asked.

"Let me sting him," Whip pleaded suddenly, jumping off the floor and approaching James.

Susan smiled. "I would, dear, except there's no antidote for your poison."

Whip's tail went before him, coiling and uncoiling in mid-air, before it found James and wrapped around his waist, stroking his left arm, then sliding toward his face.

"He's big and strong," Whip said. "Will I grow up to be as big as he is?"

"You're already a big boy, dear," Susan said, standing and reaching for her black bag. I jumped up to block her.

"Stop!" I cried. "This isn't the place to experiment on him. If you're going to induce an overdose, do it in the real world. At least then, if he doesn't make it, he'll still be alive in witch world."

"Don't fool yourself, that doesn't matter," Susan said. "No one can cheat death. It comes when it decides. It's like a force of nature that destroys all that the rest of nature has given birth to. That's a gentle way of telling you that you can't stop what's going to happen here tonight. Try, and Whip might get the urge to sting you. And I warn you, even with all your powers, you would never be able to recover from that kind of venom."

Whip moved onto my foot, where he sat on the floor and let his tail crawl up my leg. I felt as if I stood in a pool of octopuses. I stared at James, heartbroken. Why couldn't he see the pleading in my eyes?

"Please don't do this," I begged.

James stood in front of me. "This had to happen, Jessie."

Susan suddenly frowned. "What did you call her?"

Before he could respond, we heard a knock at the door.

Susan ordered me to answer. Not knowing what else to do, I obeyed. A figure dressed in black leather stood on the porch.

"May I come in?" Kendor asked, his ancient power clear in his voice and visible in his stance. Of course, the fact that he held an unsheathed sword in his right hand, one soaked in blood, didn't hurt matters.

Susan set down her doctor's bag and spoke from the far side of the room. "Why not?" she said.

Kendor strode into the house. Frank retreated to the corner, where he held Lara in front of his chest, using her as a shield. My daughter didn't cry out, but stared silently from his massive hands, as if lost in her own unfathomable thoughts. Susan stood beside me and James, and all the while she stared at Kendor with wonder. No, it was Syn who stared, and the voice inside my mind was no longer able to think of her as Susan.

"How have you been?" Syn asked.

"Fine. You?" Kendor asked. His sword continued to drip bright red drops on the wooden floor.

"The same." Syn paused. "You look well."

"So do you," Kendor said. "I've missed you."

"You should have cleaned up before coming. You're making a mess of my floor."

Kendor didn't sheath his sword. "You have so many guards. I recall the time when you couldn't stand having others watch over you."

"Did you dispatch them all?"

"Yes."

"There are always more where they came from."

Kendor raised an eyebrow. "Do you need them?"

She shook her head. "You must know by now that if your blade were a mile long, it couldn't touch me."

Syn was speaking of bafflement, I thought.

Kendor glanced around the living room, studying it, perhaps searching for the best angle of attack. "That's why I brought more than a physical sword," he said.

"A fusion?" Syn asked. "From your fractured Council? I'm sorry but I'm not impressed."

"You should be. We've settled our differences. We're all of one mind."

"When it comes to me?" Syn said.

"Yes. You have to go."

Syn acted amused. "Oh, dear. Now I suppose I should run and hide."

Syn was an excellent actress. However, the implication that

Kendor had the entire Council at his back worried her. She didn't show the fear in her face or voice; nevertheless, I felt it.

It was only then that I realized the Council had lied to me when we had met earlier in the evening, probably to throw me off guard so Syn herself would be unable to read my mind and know what they had planned.

I didn't know how the fusion worked but the fact that Kendor had come alone implied it only needed one member of the Council to be physically present to transmit its power. I also suspected that Kendor had finally revealed the true nature of Syn to the Council, probably in a final bid to get Cleo's support to attack the woman.

These things I didn't have to be told. My intuition gene was active. The facts seemed obvious to me. Just as it was clear that Kendor was willing to sacrifice his life to protect Lara and me.

"But I've been told to make you a final offer," Kendor said. "If you agree to release Jessica, James, and Lara—you can leave here unharmed."

"So after all this time they resort to a threat. Well, you know me. You know how I respond to threats." Syn hardened her tone and gestured to Frank, who continued to hold Lara tight. "If the Council should so much as force me to blink, I'll signal Frank to tear the child in two."

Kendor shook his head. "Frank isn't going to hurt Lara."

"You're fast, brother," Frank warned Kendor. "But not that fast."

Kendor seemed to consider. "You're right."

Behind me, it seemed as if the air suddenly thickened. There was a subtle stir, a wavering of the oxygen molecules we breathed. For some reason I could no longer see the white curtains that covered the windows, although they were only a few feet away. Something was blocking my vision, something invisible, which made no sense because if it was invisible I should have been able to see through it. Whatever was manifesting appeared to have the power to disconnect our brains from our eyes, or else our minds from our bodies. There followed a sudden flash of light that was probably more a product of shock than anything else.

James and I jumped. Syn stood firm.

A figure appeared out of nothing. Alfred.

He reached into the back of my pants and removed the nine-millimeter Glock I had hidden. He must have been familiar with the weapon, and he sure as hell must have known I was carrying it.

In a single fluid motion Alfred removed the safety, riffled a bullet into the chamber, and shot Frank in the forehead. The round flew with a soft whistle. Frank sank into the chair at his back, Lara still in his lap, his brains staining the freshly painted wall. His eyes still open, he let out what sounded like a surprised gasp before leaning dangerously to one side. I ran toward my daughter. Alfred beat me to the punch but quickly handed Lara over.

It was insane to celebrate. The Wicked Witch was still alive and deadly, and we had no house to drop on her head. Still, my daughter felt like heaven in my hands, her tiny body wiggling in my fingers as she twisted her head up to gaze at me. Something happened in that moment as I gazed back into her blue-green eyes. It was impossible to describe, but I'll say it anyway.

I saw love. It was real, as real as her physical body.

It was what Lara was made of.

Every cell . . . Love, love, love . . .

From far away I saw and heard two different things.

Syn's shattered face. James talking to me.

All the blood had drained from Syn's skin. Her mouth moved but no sound emerged. Yet I could read the name her lips were trying to form. . . .

Herme . . . Herme . . . Herme . . .

James was closer, beside me, but his explanation also seemed to reach me over a great distance. I heard what he said—that did not mean I understood what he said.

"I saw you watching me as I delayed getting in and out of the limo," he told me. "We were lucky Frank didn't notice. I was just trying to give Alfred a chance to move past me." He paused. "Jessie?"

He kept calling me Jessie, not Jessica.

I shook my head to free it of Lara's mesmerizing gaze and Syn's devastated expression. My voice came out like a croak.

"He was sitting between us the whole way here?"

"I had to sit somewhere," Alfred said, talking to me even though his eyes never left Syn. She shook her head as if trying to regroup. She was still pale as a ghost.

"Huh?" I mumbled.

"Even when invisible, I can't walk through objects," Alfred continued, even though he was as distracted as I was. "If you had reached for James's hand, you would have bumped into me."

Slowly my brain began to comprehend. Very slowly.

"How did James know where you were?" I asked.

"It's one of my many witch powers," James said.

"But you're not a witch," I protested.

James reached for my hand. He reached for Lara. It was as if he was seeing her for the first time, because . . . it was the first time. His eyes betrayed the truth. She was like a newborn to him. It took me several seconds to register what that meant. James, this James, was not from witch world.

This was Jimmy!

Somehow, he had gone through the death experience.

Now he was alive in witch world!

He was a witch! And he was with me!

"Herme," Syn managed to say aloud, ignoring Kendor, her eyes locked on her . . . son? Yes, it was true, it was her child. Alfred *was* Herme, the person Kendor had told me about. That was why Syn was still ashen, still shaken. She had to struggle to speak to her son. "It can't be. You're dead," she whispered.

Alfred—Herme—shook his head. "I'm here now."

"Why?" Syn said, and the word could have stood for a dozen questions. Herme chose to answer the most important one.

"To put a stop to this madness," he said.

Syn glanced at Kendor, her confusion swiftly changing to rage. "You knew our son was alive and you hid it from me?" she snapped.

Kendor shook his head sadly. "I only found out today."

"You lie!" she shouted.

"No, Mother. It's the truth," Herme said.

"Why did you leave us?" Syn demanded.

There was no apology in Herme's voice. "No one could see into your heart like I could. Even Father didn't know how you had changed, what you were becoming, and I couldn't bear to tell him. I felt it best just to leave, and I prayed you would find peace in your own way." Herme paused. "But you never did."

"I would never have lost my peace if I'd known you were alive!" Syn shrieked. "It was you, your loss, that broke my heart!"

"No," Herme said. "By the time I left for the colonies, there was nothing inside your heart left to break. You are what you are, Mother, what you chose to be. You have no one to blame but yourself."

Syn forced a frightening laugh. "So you have all gathered to beg me to behave. My lover, my child, the mother of the perfect child, even the ancient Council. And yes, I can feel the gathering storm of the Council's minds as they prepare to strike me down if I refuse to obey. But what none of you understand is that long ago I left your world for something far better. A realm of infinite pleasure where I can never again be hurt."

"Mother?" Herme begged.

"Traitor!" she cried, snapping her fingers at him as if trying to make him invisible once more, before putting the same hand over the heart her son had told her was empty. She felt pain then, deep inside her chest, I could tell. But it was only then she turned away from Herme and cursed the rest of us. At last I could say she truly sounded like a witch.

"All of you, kill me with your petty fusion if you can!" she swore. "But I think you'll discover that it is you who will perish!"

Kendor didn't even try to attack with his sword. Instead he closed his eyes and frowned in concentration. Glancing at Herme, I was sure I would find him taking aim with my Glock. But he too had shut his eyes. It was clear they knew that no physical weapon would work against Syn's bafflement.

The living room flooded with strange energies, and began to change, although I'm not sure if the transformation was of a three-dimensional nature. I'm not even sure if I saw the change with my eyes or my mind, on the inside or the outside. For a time it seemed the distinction between the two disappeared.

I *believe* I saw a blue light extend from Kendor and Herme toward Syn. The light was both hot and cold, and it appeared to be made of a fabric more real than a chair or table. It was like a living light projected from the hearts and souls of men and women who cared for nothing but the well-being of mankind. Pure selflessness allowed so many minds to join together so powerfully, and it was a fact that although the source of the blue light was sacred, it was capable of destroying almost anything in its path.

But opposing it, halting the blue light like a wall of psychic bricks cemented across the center of the room, was an expanding red sphere. It was also more palpable than any physical object, and the larger it grew in size, the farther Syn appeared to move away from the blue light.

In a flash I realized this was the key to bafflement, and it was suddenly obvious why it was impenetrable. For Syn did not only escape into the distance, she entered another realm where there was no blue light, no Council, not even a world known as earth. If the real world was a reflection of witch world, then this sphere was the opposite of life. Yet there was a paradox here because it seemed as if the denizens of this dimension could only exist by feeding off the living. And there were creatures inside this world, besides Syn. They called to me.

I tried not to respond, but a wave of sheer agony shot through my mind and body, and it was as if every fiber in my nervous system and every feeling and thought in my mind was being singed by flames that had been burning since the beginning of time. The pain was so great I would have made a deal with the devil himself to make it stop.

That desire alone was enough.

It was like a secret wish, a special password, that allowed me to respond to the beings of the realm Syn coveted. Before I knew it, I was standing beside her inside the red sphere. But its shape and color had changed and taken on the form of a battlefield.

CHAPTER TWENTY-THREE

"DO YOU BELIEVE IN GOD?" SYN ASKED, STANDING nearby, beside a tree that stood at the edge of a huge field where two armies were killing each other with a fury that only emerged during a last stand. The army on my left was Roman. I recognized the broad shields, the long spears, the iron helmets. On the right were the Huns, masters of their horses, and their bows and arrows. In the distance was the prize, the city of Rome.

What the fuck is going on? I asked myself.

Did I have a body? I don't think so, not there, not then. I don't think physical bodies could exist inside the red sphere. I drew in no breaths, I did not feel my heart beat in my chest. Yet, it was a paradox, I had hands, I could see my hands. I was a spirit with shape. I was even clothed; I wore the same red robe as Syn.

"I'm not religious," I said, answering her question. "But I believe in God."

Syn quietly mocked me. "If that's true, you should be able to answer the question all atheists ask. If there's a God, why did he create so much suffering?"

"I don't know. Maybe to—"

"Stop," Syn interrupted. "You have said the only thing that matters. Add one word to 'I don't know' and you'll be babbling. You can't know because there's no answer to that question. No reasonable god would create suffering. Therefore, there can be no God. Do you understand?"

It seemed important to her that I immediately relinquish my faith, before she proceeded to the next step. "I don't know," I repeated. "Your reasoning seems no more valid than that of those who believe in God."

"Come on, Jessica, you don't believe that."

"Why does my belief matter to you?"

She nodded to the nearby tree. "Because of what's about to happen. You won't be able to experience it if you allow your human beliefs to get in the way."

Suddenly a Hun on horseback raced around the tree and halted his horse in midstride and took aim with his bow. He did not appear to see us. His target was three Roman soldiers racing toward the tree. The Hun let fly an arrow, dropping the soldier on the left. Another arrow killed the man on the right.

But the Hun couldn't take down the soldier in the middle.

This soldier knew how to use his shield and run at the same time. He was skilled with his sword as well. As he closed on his prey, the Hun drew his own blade and tried to run the Roman soldier down. The Roman didn't try to dodge his opponent by leaping away from the horse. He did the opposite—he leaped directly into the side of the animal, with the side of his body, as if to tackle it. The move was risky but it brought him inside the swing of the Hun's sword. As a result the Roman soldier was able to stab the Hun cleanly in the chest.

The Hun fell to the ground, dead.

The Roman allowed himself a moment to cheer.

Unfortunately, the brief ceremony distracted him from another Hun who had come up at his back. This Hun was on his feet and carried a javelin. At the last second the Roman heard him, but it was already too late. The Hun had let fly the javelin, and it caught the Roman in the abdomen, pinning him to the trunk of the tree.

"Robere," I heard Syn whisper, and the scene suddenly changed. It was late in the evening, the armies were gone, and a lone woman clothed in a gray robe was weeping as she gripped the end of a bloody javelin and pulled it free of the tree and the man's body. As he toppled into the woman's arms, I saw that it was Syn from sixteen hundred years ago. She sobbed as she dropped to her knees and held her only son in her arms.

Syn pointed to her earlier incarnation. "Do you believe in God?" she asked again.

"Why should what happened to you change my beliefs?"

"Touch her."

"Why?"

"Touch her or the pain will return. You know the pain, don't you, Jessica?"

She had me. I would never forget that pain.

I touched the woman with what I assumed were spirit hands and was immediately engulfed in her sorrow. It was total, capable of shattering my soul, equal in every way to the pain that Syn had just threatened me with. More than anything I wanted it to stop. I went to take my hand away.

"Stop!" Syn commanded before I could let go.

Tears rolled over my face. "Please. I can't bear it."

"Because you have forgotten the lesson you learned in the sewer. Pain, pleasure, power. The three ingredients that create the triangle that forms the circle that manifests the red sphere." She paused. "Should I recite it for you?"

"Yes! If you'll let me take my hand away when you're done!"

Syn spoke in a solemn tone. "Pain becomes a pleasure when power creates pain." She paused. "Do you understand?"

I did not understand, not with my mind, but the instant she recited the words, the pain flowing up my arm and into my heart turned to pleasure. It was remarkable. It was as if every nerve in my body were bathed in ecstasy. Now the last thing I wanted to do was to remove my hand. Syn nodded as if reading my mind.

"I didn't discover the reality of this world the day I went

searching for my son's body," she said. "I didn't even learn of it when the Justinian plague struck Sicily and took away my family. So much agony and still I could not see what was right in front of me. It was only when Herme had left for the colonies—and was dead, I thought—that I understood the purpose of suffering."

"That's when the Alchemist came to you," I said.

Syn appeared annoyed that I knew of the man, that Kendor had shared such a secret with me. She spoke quickly. "I was ripe for the truth. I would have discovered it on my own. He merely pointed me in the right direction."

"In the direction of hell, where demons feed on the pain of others?" I asked.

"Phrase it that way if you wish. Or call them gods who are capable of transforming the greatest evil into the greatest good."

"Pleasure?" I asked.

"Pleasure. Ecstasy. Bliss. Different words for the same goal." Syn paused. "Remove your hand from my younger self."

I hesitated. "Why?"

Syn chuckled. "The believer in God asks why? Did you know that the atheist who has realized that the only salvation in life is pleasure usually asks why not? Why shouldn't your pain be used to generate joy?"

"Because you create it at another's expense," I replied.

"Then remove your hand. The longer you touch her, the greater her pain will last."

"That's a lie. Your son died sixteen centuries ago. This is just a play. We can't change the past."

Syn grew more serious. "Maybe it can't be changed, no one knows. But I do know I saw you right after I found Robere. You stood above me as you stand now. I thought you were a demon, come to mock me in my grief." She paused. "Remove your hand from my shoulder. Stop the pleasure from entering your heart."

With a tremendous act of will, I managed to withdraw my hand. The pleasure stopped. Not even the satisfaction of letting the old Syn go prevented the loss from crashing down on me. I felt buried beneath a mountain of blandness, where there was neither pleasure nor pain, only emptiness. It was amazing how dreadful it was. That quick, I feared I was already addicted to the pleasure.

"I did it," I taunted her. "It wasn't so hard."

"That's because you've just begun."

I should have known what was to follow.

Suddenly we were in Sicily with the Syn and Kendor of that time, who were attending to their daughter, Era, a grown woman with two children, Anna and Theo, all of whom were sick with the bubonic plague. Anna was the sickest of the three, and Syn stayed with her night and day in both worlds.

It helped their offspring that Syn and Kendor had healing abilities, but the disease possessed the power of a demon's curse. It was too virulent for any form of psychic healing. Over a week—which I experienced as compressed moments—Anna's face and throat swelled a terrible black-blue as the bubonic bacteria multiplied in her veins. Every breath was a nightmare. As the girl neared death, Syn insisted I touch her, and the weary Syn of that time. I protested, but she grabbed my hands and placed them where she wanted.

The emotional grief, the physical pain, it was all a horrible blur. I couldn't stand it. Indeed, I refused to take it, and although I knew I was once again falling for Syn's seduction, I repeated the line from the litany in my mind: *Pain becomes a pleasure when power creates pain.*

Instantly the pain stopped as a tidal wave of pleasure rocked me to the core. The euphoria was like a gift. Yes, I thought, that was exactly what it was. A gift from the denizens of the red realm.

"Naturally they reward those who reward them," Syn whispered in my ear, in Anna's room, as the girl began to choke and ancient Syn wept. "All you have to do is bring them suffering, yours or another's, and the pleasure will be there. Not only that, but they'll grant you great power."

"Why?" I asked.

"So you'll have the ability to create more pain."

Her remark explained the last line of the litany, the one I had been reciting.

"That's how you discovered bafflement. During World War Two," I said. "It was given to you because you helped the Nazis."

"You strike near the truth. It was a mutually beneficial relationship. But you forget how much the Americans contributed with their firebombing of millions of Japanese, and the final two blows that gave me full access to this realm, the dropping of the atomic bombs on Hiroshima and Nagasaki. In those two instants I felt a thrill you cannot imagine." Syn seemed to lean closer, although she was already on top of me. "From my perspective, it was the most God-fearing nation on earth that proved beyond a shadow of a doubt that there can be no God."

"The afterimage of those thrills never left you," I said. "Hiroshima and Nagasaki got burned into your soul. You're forever trying to re-create them."

"So I am. So what?" Syn mocked me. "If you don't approve, then release Anna and let her die. Oh, wait, I see you hesitate. Are you afraid your pleasure might stop?"

It was harder this time to let go. Syn's grief was greater than before, and as a result, so was the pleasure the inhabitants of the red realm were bestowing on me. It seemed perverse to drink nectar because the person beside me was sweating blood. Yet so it was. Anna was dying in her grandmother's hands, and Syn's daughter, Era, and her grandson, Theo, were coughing in the next room. The Syn of my vision knew it was only a matter of time before she lost all her offspring. Yet her pain only magnified my delight. It was as if every cell in my body were having an orgasm.

Somehow, though, I managed to let go. The sight of Syn's

agony gave me the strength. I was too disgusted with mys
to hold on.

I expected red-robed Syn to react with anger.

She only laughed. It was like she knew she had me.

Syn took me forward in time to the Syn of the eighteen
century, to the days when she ran every morning to the let
box to see if there was a message from Herme from the N
World. But Herme never wrote, and every day she read in t
papers how the war between England and the colonies w
causing more casualties. She knew in her heart her son mi
be one of them.

Red-robed Syn forced me to fix on a vision of her young
self as she knelt, weeping, beside the empty letter box. On
more, with the pain came the pleasure, because I instinctiv
redirected her suffering toward those who inhabited the r
realm. It was as if I offered it to them, like a sacrifice.

In my vision I saw a tall man with a long white bea
appear beside the weeping Syn. He looked like a wizard a
I didn't have to be told that I was gazing at the infamo
Alchemist. So he was alive during those days, even thou
Kendor swore he had killed him more than two thousai
years earlier.

This time Syn pulled my hands away.

The pleasure ceased. The vision faded.

"You're not ready to know what he taught me," Syn said

It was the first time since I had entered the red realm th

I had seen her rattled. "Afraid I might become more powerful than you?" I teased her.

She slapped my face, and it stung, and I didn't even have a physical body. "Don't forget who's the master here!" she cried.

I fought to act unmoved. "Strange, I don't remember ever agreeing to be your student."

Syn appeared to welcome my bravura. Again she came near and seemed to speak in either my ear or my mind. "I asked if you believed in God. Even though it's a work of fiction, the Bible contains traces of secret wisdom. Do you remember when Jesus told his disciples, 'In my Father's house are many mansions'?"

"Sure," I said.

"Well, this is my mansion! And this is your room!" Syn exclaimed as she raised her arms and in a flash we were in the hospital, in the morgue, when Dr. Dave was alone with me, feeling me up. I watched as I finally tapped into my power, the fire in my solar plexus, and my body suddenly warmed and I was able to sit upright.

"*You goddamn pervert! Touch me again and I'll cut off your dick!*"

Of course the shock was what initiated the man's heart attack, even though he probably would have had one soon enough. Syn, however, didn't care about that. From her side she was trying to prove to me that I was already a murderer. I was getting used to her methods. That's why she was taking me

to my first victim, almost as if to shout, *See what you did to my friend!* I watched as the coroner sagged to the floor and gasped for breath.

"Put your hand on his heart," Syn ordered.

"No."

"I promise you will be pleased."

"No," I said.

"Very pleased, Jessica. Or should I call you Jessie? Are you not a killer in both worlds?"

"I'm not a killer at all! I'm not like you!"

She grabbed my arm. "You wouldn't be here if you were not ready to follow me. Notice how none of the others were able to cross over to the red sphere. Only you came." She released my arm but shoved me in the back toward Dr. Dave.

"Wait," I said, sensing she wasn't telling me the whole truth. That was one positive quality of the red realm. Thoughts appeared as physical objects, they had substance, which made it difficult for her to hide her agenda from me.

"Why?" Syn demanded.

"In witch world, in the house, I'm holding Lara."

Syn paused. "So you noticed."

I nodded. "There's a connection. She's another reason I'm here with you. But . . . she's not like you."

"She's not like anyone! She's an infant! You've said these words yourself. To me, and to you, she's pure potentiality. She's like atomic energy. Is it good? Is it bad? It can be used to heat a million homes. Or it can flatten the same homes. Lara sits in the same position. She's raw power, and yes, that power has helped bring you to this realm ahead of your time. But that doesn't matter. What matters is that we can mold her to our own design."

"You brought me here to get to her."

"I brought you here to get to both of you." She poked my arm sharply. "Now touch him, drink of his pain, reap what you have sown. I promise, you won't be disappointed."

I don't know why I did it. Curiosity, perhaps.

Lies. How easy it is to lie inside one's own mind.

I was like an addict mentally rationalizing his next fix.

I did it for the pleasure I knew he would give me.

I put my hand on Dr. Dave's dying heart. Even when the real Syn, dressed in blue scrubs, reentered the morgue and spoke to the man, I kept my hand in place. And I knew Dr. Susan Wheeler had seen me even then, as I saw her now, in a vision.

The pleasure was pure and irresistible.

If there was no God, then this wasn't a bad substitute.

I was only able to let go when Syn offered me a greater taste. A snap of her fingers brought us forward in time into another room. To where Russell burned to death in the fire I had thrust into his chest. Oh, Lord, such pain, such pleasure— his screams actually made me giggle. I knew my reaction was sick, and I didn't care.

Then, finally, the culmination arrived, when Syn led me out into the desert to my most recent victim. I had kidnapped Kari to protect Jimmy and Huck. I hadn't intended to kill her. It was a fact I'd had no idea about her secret abilities.

Yet that was nothing but another set of lies. The two of us, we had a history. From the time she had stolen Jimmy away from me, I had been itching to kill the bitch.

Touching Kari's head, as I choked the breath from her body, grinding the back of her head in the gravel I would use to bury her, I was suddenly filled with a euphoria the gods would have envied. And this time I didn't have to pause and direct her pain to the red realm. I did it automatically, and with, of course, pleasure.

I had to drop to my knees to stay in contact with Kari, just as I had done earlier in the day when I had crushed her trachea. And when I looked up, drunk with the sparks flying between the synapses of my spirit brain, I saw that Syn was not only wearing a red robe but a gold crown. From my place on the ground—out of gratitude to the thrill she had given me—I bowed to her. For the first time I actually felt grateful to her.

"You're the red queen," I said, finally understanding the hidden meaning in the game of twenty-two. It was no wonder the Alchemist had created it, and that he collected the profits from it. He was the one who had shown the world the opening to the red world, which stood above witch world, not to mention the real world. It was odd but it no longer bothered me that my own world should seem like a place of shadows. I felt I owed Syn an apology.

"Save it," she said as she read my mind once more. "Pay me back with blood. Pay *them* back with pain."

"Them?" I said.

She put her hands on my shoulders and leaned over and kissed my forehead. "You're one of us now, Jessica," she said.

I let go of Kari and stood. The loss of the pleasure she gave me caused me no grief. Because I knew what was to come next would be even better. Yes, I told myself, it would just keep getting better.

CHAPTER TWENTY-FOUR

I WAS WRONG. A MOMENT LATER WE EXITED THE RED sphere and nothing had changed. "Nothing" meant the players in the drama were still the same. They were even in the same place as when I had left the room. The reason was because I had never really gone anywhere. No time had even gone by, as far as I could tell.

Yet something inside of me had changed.

I was hungry now. Hungry for the pleasure.

It was not as if I had lost my mind. I still knew that Syn was evil, just as any intelligent heroin addict knows that his drug of choice is evil. But that doesn't lessen his desire for the needle. In fact, it probably increases it. And Syn was offering me the most forbidden fruit of all. A straightforward exchange. Give me pain and I'll give you pleasure. That was her message. That was her power.

I trembled as I held Lara in my hands. I felt unworthy of holding her, at least until I had proven I was worthy of being her mother. Because I suddenly realized that might not be the case.

For that reason I handed her to James.

But that was not the only reason I gave her up.

I needed both my hands free.

From nearby, Syn looked at me and nodded.

We had exited the red sphere but I could still read her mind. She didn't have to speak the words. For the moment, the fusion had halted, and Herme and Kendor had reopened their eyes. They had failed to strike Syn down but their effort had not been in vain because even though Syn's bafflement had protected her, it had failed to destroy her enemies.

A stalemate had been reached. Something was needed to tilt the scale. Syn believed she possessed that something because she was confident she now had me on her side. On the surface that was absurd. Intellectually, I still knew what she was capable of doing to the world. But emotionally, physically even, she was right—I was with her. My body ached for the pleasure. I didn't just want it, I needed it. Worse, I knew if I disobeyed, she would give me the opposite.

Absolute agony.

That was how she kept her dog on her leash.

Kendor raised his sword, seeing an opening. He was the oldest in the room. He had seen civilizations rise and fall. He had loved Syn for two thousand years and knew her better than she knew herself. And he hadn't survived the rising onslaught of the Lapras without being bold.

To Kendor a stalemate was equal to an opportunity.

He took a step toward Syn.

Syn twisted her head and stared at me.

I understood what she wanted me to do. It was mostly a function of our positioning, and of who trusted whom. James was to my right, Herme was on my left. Both knew me and trusted me. Because neither understood what I had experienced inside the red realm.

While contributing to the fusion, Herme had thrust the pistol in his belt before closing his eyes. His eyes were open now but that didn't change the fact the gun was only inches from my left hand. If I reached for it, would he stop me? I didn't think so. After all, I was supposed to be one of the good guys.

I didn't want to but I did it anyway.

I grabbed the gun and Herme let me take it. Probably he thought I would use it to protect Kendor. Perhaps he realized he was the wrong person to shoot his mother. Whatever the reason, I quickly transferred the weapon from my left hand to my right and lifted the gun.

Kendor paid me no heed. Raising his bloody sword, he took another step toward Syn. His face was a mask of concentration. If he was reluctant to slay the love of his extraordinary life, he didn't show it. Yet he didn't hurry, he didn't have to. I had seen him in action. I had no doubt he would take her head.

Then it would all be over. We would all be safe.

But the pleasure would be over as well.

"Do it," Syn hissed at me, finally showing her fear. She did not say it but I heard "or else" in her voice. God, how I hated her then, even though I had just bowed to her. But I think it was that last act that made me feel so helpless in her hands. My heart told me she was a monster, my head said to shoot her, but a part of me I had no name for ordered me to obey her.

I pointed the gun at Kendor's chest.

"Stop!" I cried.

Kendor stopped in midstride. His gaze swept back and forth between Syn and me, then he nodded sympathetically, as if to tell me he understood my problem. He was the only one. James and Herme both shouted out.

"Jessie!" James yelled. "What are you doing?"

"She's put a spell on you," Herme warned.

"It's all right," Kendor said quietly, lowering his sword and looking at me with such compassion I felt ashamed. "We can talk about this. We're friends, aren't we, Jessica? And we're here for Lara. Focus on your daughter. She's the one who can help you now."

I shook my head, too confused to even look at Lara. "You

don't understand," I mumbled. "I don't want to do this. But I have to. I have to stop you."

"I've stopped," Kendor replied, letting the tip of his sword touch the wooden floor. "But you must realize what Herme says is true. You're a young witch who's been bewitched. That's what Syn does. I know, she did it to me. That's why I took so long to tell the Council who she was. I made a mistake, and now you're making the same mistake."

I struggled to speak. "I have to shoot you."

Kendor shook his head. "That's Syn talking, not you."

I swallowed. "But the pleasure, I can't feel it anymore."

"Because it's not real," Kendor said. "Nothing she has shown you is real. Only your daughter matters. Look at your daughter, Jessica, look at Lara."

I heard Lara make a cooing sound beside me. I began to turn toward her. Then I heard a sharp hissing noise—Syn ordering me once more. I froze.

"Kill him," Syn whispered.

"Yes," I heard my body reply. It was not me that spoke, it was not my soul, it was just a lump of flesh that was aching to feel what it had felt inside the red realm. How a base physical longing could override everything I believed in made no sense. Nor did it have to. What had Syn told me? It was not a question of why I should shoot Kendor, the issue was why not?

"I'm sorry," I said softly as I cocked the hammer. The man

in the pawnshop had demonstrated how sensitive the trigger was once the hammer had been pulled. It took less than a pound of pressure to fire the semiautomatic, a few ounces, and already I was stroking the trigger with my sweaty finger. Kendor sighed as he looked at my face.

"You're not like her," he said calmly, and in that same instant he launched himself toward Syn, his sword coming up like a cobra ready to bite. He was fast, ten times faster than me, but he had to travel fifteen feet, whereas my finger only had to move a fraction of an inch.

"Jessie, no!" James cried, reaching for the gun.

I pulled the trigger. The shot sounded like thunder in my ears. But heaven only knew where the bullet was headed. For at the last second James had hit my hand and skewed my aim.

Kendor seemed to skip a step and then stumble. The round had struck him inside the right shoulder, a nasty place because the nerves that controlled his arm and hand were centered there. He didn't drop his sword but his grip on it weakened and it bobbled in his hand.

That was all the opening Syn required. Stepping toward him, she kicked the blade from Kendor's hand. As it flew through the air, she pulled a knife from her own back belt. The blade was long and serrated, and it was obvious she knew how to use it. Sure, her husband had taught her. She had it to his neck in the blink of an eye.

It was Kendor's turn to freeze. Not out of fear, though. I

don't think the man knew fear. He smiled at his old love.

"You told me the day we met you'd kill me," he said.

"I was joking."

"Perhaps."

She nodded. "I'm sorry."

He shook his head. "It is I who am sorry. Herme explained what has happened to you. I know you can't help yourself."

"Herme," she repeated, although she didn't look in the direction of her son. Not even when he spoke up.

"No, Mother," Herme called.

Syn pressed the blade closer. A line of red appeared on Kendor's throat. He didn't back up, he refused to even move his head.

"We cannot both live," she told him. "Not in this world or the other. You know that."

He nodded faintly. "It's all right, Syn."

Strange, how she smiled right then, I actually glimpsed joy in her face. "You always used to say that," she said.

"I meant it."

"Kendor," she said softly, and suddenly lowered the knife, and for a moment it seemed she would let him go. But then she yanked the blade upward, into his heart, a single quick thrust, before pulling it free. Without crying out, without any sound, Kendor fell to the floor.

Syn turned on us, Kendor's blood dripping from her knife. Her purpose was obvious. All her enemies would die tonight.

But whether she considered Lara and me to be among them wasn't clear.

Herme took the gun from my hand and pointed it at Syn. "You've done enough," he said.

She was unmoved. "You should have stayed in the shadows, Herme."

"I can't let you hurt these people," he said.

Syn flicked her empty hand and the gun flew from her son's grasp. "You possess no weapon that can harm me. Kendor knew that, and so does your accursed Council."

Herme stepped in front of James and me.

"You'll have to kill me first," he said.

"You think I can't, dear son?"

"No."

"Then you misunderstand me. I will kill you. It won't be so hard. Because years ago you forced me to kill you and bury you in my mind."

Herme nodded in resignation. "Do what you have to do."

"Herme, move aside," James said with sudden authority. Taking my hand, still holding our daughter in his other arm, he stepped forward. It was confusing but I felt like I was seeing him for the first time. His face shone with the light of a confidence I had never seen before. Looking at Syn, he added, "Leave."

Syn acted bored as she used her pants to wipe Kendor's blood off her knife. "I'm afraid I've lost interest in you."

"What are you doing?" I whispered to him.

James made sure my hand was touching Lara's as well as his. "She can't hurt us," he said. "Not if the three of us are together."

"How do you know?" I asked.

"Because of the light and the music. It was there when we first made love, and when Lara was born and I first held her. It comes from a place greater than her silly red sphere." He added, "That's why I had to come to witch world tonight. To remind you of that fact."

"But how do you know?" I insisted. It seemed a reasonable question. But an answer, or at least a partial answer, came to me before he said another word. The love I had felt when I had stared into Lara's eyes returned. It washed over my chest and seemed to heal the very thing Syn had placed inside my heart within the red sphere. Pain might lead to pleasure but Syn had lied when she said it could ever bring joy. Only love could do that and only love could heal the grief she had exposed me to.

Suddenly, staring at Lara and James, I felt encased in armor. A shield of light and compassion and empathy. All the good things that made it possible for people to be good—if they tried. I saw then I had made a conscious decision to enjoy the pleasure. Now I had to reject that choice and embrace my family instead.

I did it. I just did it. I chose Lara and James.

Meanwhile, James did his best to answer my question. He gestured to Syn. "Try using your black magic on us," he said.

"If you wish," Syn replied, raising the knife and pointing the tip of the blade at James. "Pain," she said softly, and I knew it was a curse and that in a second he might start writhing.

But all that happened was that Lara began to coo softly, and when Syn tried to take a step toward us, she cooed louder. The armor was not imaginary. We were protected. Syn shook her head, baffled.

"What the hell," Syn whispered to herself.

"Leave," James repeated.

Syn smiled and poked the tip of her finger with her knife, causing a trickle of blood to flow into her palm. "So your kid can neutralize my abilities. Impressive. But I'm afraid I don't need them to make you suffer." She shook the knife in James's direction. "Do you know what it feels like to be skinned alive?"

My newfound faith began to falter.

James didn't have an answer to her question.

Syn stepped over Kendor's body and strode toward us.

Whip grabbed the hem of her pants and spoke in a voice that dripped venom. "It's my turn, Mommy, let me sting them. Please?"

Syn reached down and patted her son's head. "All right. Do them all, even the baby. She's more trouble than she's—"

Syn was not given a chance to finish. Whip's stinger swung up and pierced her chest. The poison went into her heart. Her eyes froze open in shock, then she keeled over and lay beside Kendor.

I couldn't believe it.

I couldn't even begin to understand what had happened.

"Why?" I gasped. Why did her son kill her?

I looked to James for an explanation.

"Whip went through the death experience with me," he said.

"Huh?" I mumbled.

"This Whip has our Whip's memories."

I shook my head, too dazed to comprehend.

"You know how it works," James said. "At first you can only carry the memories of the world in which you were connected. So this Whip you see is really our Whip."

"And you killed him in the real world?" I asked.

"I killed both of us. I had to."

I shoved James in the chest. "How could you let a child risk his life like that?" I cried.

James smiled. Or was it Jimmy? "Whip had a fatal illness in combination with an inactive healing gene. He had nothing to lose and everything to gain. Of course I let him join me."

I couldn't take any more in. It was all happening too fast. But I certainly couldn't celebrate, not with Kendor lying on the floor. Stepping to his body, I knelt near his head and stroked his beautiful dark blond hair. He lay on his stomach, his face turned my way, his eyes closed. After such a long life, it was impossible to believe he could be dead. But the pool of blood around his heart said otherwise.

Herme knelt across from me, beside his mother. He put a

hand to her head, and we stared at each other through a film of tears.

"I'm sorry," I whispered.

"There's no need," he said.

"I shot your father. I lost control. I—"

"My mother shot my father. You were just the vehicle. Trust me, you did nothing wrong."

"But if I hadn't weakened, Kendor would still be alive."

Herme stared at his dead father. "Even though he came here to kill her, I don't think he could have lived with himself if he had succeeded. In a strange way, you did him a favor."

"You've lost both your parents. It's not fair."

Herme sighed. "It happened. It doesn't matter whether it's fair or not."

Whip came over and hugged me, trying to comfort me. With his hands—not his tail, thank God—he brushed away my tears. "Jessie," he said, and I realized he could speak because he had his twin's voice. "I love you."

"Oh, Whip," I said, embracing him. I stroked his back but was careful not to let my hand stray too low. His heart might have been pure but his stinger still gave me the willies. Squeezing him hard, I added, "I love you, too."

Love, I thought. The word felt so fitting, perhaps because love had been the answer all along. The one thing that could stop Syn.

I looked up at James. "The transformation—how did you do it?" I asked. "*When* did you do it?"

"You forget Herme's a drug salesman in real life," James said. "He gave me and Whip what we needed, right after you fell asleep in my arms in the hotel room."

"But you fell asleep with me," I said.

"I pretended to," James said. "I was really waiting for Herme to return from his walk with Alex."

"We had planned it all out earlier in the evening," Herme said. "After you two interrogated poor Al, but before you guys went to dinner. Whip was with us. It really was his decision to go through the death experience."

"You did all this without the Council's approval?" I asked.

"Yes," Herme said. "I only spoke to the Council after I met with my father for the first time in centuries. That was the next day, so to speak, in witch world. Hatsu brought me to see him. Hatsu was the one witch who knew my true identity."

I stared down at Kendor's body. "Why did you hide from your father for so long?" I asked.

"Next to Cleo, he was the most high-profile member of the Council. The Lapras had spies everywhere." Herme paused. "I couldn't risk seeing him."

And now he wouldn't get to see him at all, I thought. Herme's words had been kind but I still blamed myself for Kendor's death.

I spoke. "You joined in the fusion with your father. You were prepared to kill Syn. You must have gone to the Council at some point."

"My father and I both went to the Council tonight, in witch world, an hour before you met with them. By then we had decided we had to risk everything in order to save you and your daughter." Herme added quietly, "And, of course, Whip and James."

"And the Council agreed?" I asked.

"Yes," Herme said.

"Thank you," I said.

Herme nodded. There was nothing left to say.

Kissing Kendor on the head, I stood and hugged Lara and James together. My daughter kicked her legs with delight, and once more the room seemed to fill with light.

"So it's over?" I said to James.

My boyfriend kissed my lips. "It's over," he promised.

But I didn't fully understand what he meant. Not when we went back to the hotel and gave Lara a bath and a bottle and put her to bed. Not even when we lay beneath the sheets and held each other so long and so tight I believed the music and the light would come to us again.

No, it was only when I awoke in the morning, back in the real world, that I understood what Jimmy had sacrificed to protect me and Lara. Because as I yawned and reached over to kiss him, I felt how cold his skin was, and noticed that he wasn't breathing.

He hadn't survived the death experience after all.

The needle was still in the vein in his arm.

He had gone to sleep in this world so he could be with us in witch world. When we needed him the most.

My Jimmy.

EPILOGUE

TWO DAYS AFTER WE RETURNED HOME FROM LAS VEGAS, Jimmy was buried in Apple Valley. It was a Thursday as the real world counted time. Of course in witch world he was still alive, but for the two hundred mourners who came to his service, that didn't mean a thing. Especially for his sole remaining parent, his father, who I believe secretly blamed me for his son's death.

Kari was listed as missing, although the police had been to my house numerous times to question me about her disappearance. So far I had done an excellent job of hiding Huck from them, and since Huck was supposed to be dead, no one was pressuring me about the boy.

Certainly no one was interested in Whip. I found it curious that my new role as the mother of two kids had raised no alerts, while the loss of two of my classmates had everyone talking. Then again, no one but my mother and father, and a few friends, knew I had the children. It was not as if I allowed Whip to play in the neighborhood or at the park, except late at night.

In regards to Jimmy . . . the prevailing theory was that he had gone back to Kari, and I had spotted them in bed together without their knowledge. Then, later, when the three of us were hanging out, I had enticed them to try a hit of some morphine I was secretly addicted to and they had fallen for the ruse because I was after all Jessie Ralle, a sweet girl with no police record, an A-minus average in high school, and someone who was known to most people in Apple Valley as the pretty but quiet girl who worked at the local library.

Go figure.

The police assured me that I wasn't a suspect, while privately they kept telling Jimmy's father and Kari's parents that they were going to break me if it was the last thing they did in this life.

To hell with them, I thought. I was going to be leaving soon to live with my father in Malibu. The plan was for him to hire help to look after the kids so I could go to UCLA full-time. Not that I needed financial assistance. It seemed that Russ had left me ten million euros in a Swiss bank account. My father told me Russ used to love to play twenty-one at the European casinos whenever he went on vacation.

My mother was also moving to Malibu, to a nearby condo, and was talking about going back to school to study to be a nurse. Naturally, she assumed my newfound wealth was a result of my father's sudden generosity. She knew about the kids but not about witch world. Perhaps she never would.

Despite the legal suspicions that lay on me, I was allowed to say a few words at Jimmy's funeral. I kept it short and sweet.

"I know my presence here is uncomfortable for some, but those who know me, and better yet those who knew Jimmy, will realize that the bond we shared was magical. It was perfect. All my life I dreamed of having a boyfriend like Jimmy, and when he finally showed up, he was a thousand times better than any fantasy. Because he was real, and such a genuine person. Without trying, he somehow cared for everyone. I know because of how much he cared for me. Jimmy didn't die of a drug overdose. Jimmy didn't even smoke pot. His death was far more noble than that.

"I loved Jimmy with all my heart, and I have a feeling that I'm going to go on loving him forever. For you see, he hasn't left us. He's close, closer than any of you can imagine. Every night I go to bed, I see him. He was a great guy, my Jimmy, and I believe I'm going to continue to see him until the day I die."

After the funeral, Herme and Alex stopped by to see how I was doing. It seemed in all the drama of the last week no one had bothered to tell me that my best friend was also a witch, one who possessed the healing gene. It wasn't coincidence she was my best friend. After all, the Council had schemed to put us all together.

Herme planned to connect Alex at the next full moon. She said she was ready for the experience but I could tell she had misgivings. When I questioned her, she agreed she was scared.

"When I hear about everything you went through the last few days," she said, while Herme played with Whip in the other room and Huck slept on the chair beside me, "it makes me wonder if I don't have enough problems in this world to deal with. What do I need with another one?"

"Witch world exists whether you're aware of it or not," I said. "You're already there, playing your usual bad girl. You might as well see what it's all about."

Alex considered. "The only reason I agreed to let Herme do it is because I want to see you and Jimmy together again."

"You mean me and James," I corrected. She was exaggerating. She wanted to be a witch because she wanted what we all did—the magic.

"Isn't it the same?"

I shook my head. "It'll never be the same. Jimmy is James, sure, but there are differences. Everything I said at his funeral was true, but to be honest, it doesn't make me miss him any less. At least when I'm in this world."

Alex hugged me. "I'm so sorry."

"It's all right," I said as she held me. "When I'm here, I have Whip and Huck to keep me company. And James and I get to play with Lara in witch world. In a way, I've gained more than I lost."

Alex let go of me and gestured to sleeping Huck. "Is it weird taking care of Kari's baby?" she asked.

"I thought it would be but it's not. I guess I see him as belonging to Jimmy. I hardly think about Kari unless someone brings her up."

Alex looked concerned. "But you'll turn him over to Kari's parents one day, won't you? I mean, Huck's DNA, if the police do a test, they'll discover that he belongs to Jimmy and Kari."

"My father told me the same thing. I guess one day I'll have to leave him on Kari's parents' doorstep, with a note, and ring the bell and run like hell." I stopped. "But I'm not ready to give him up. He meant too much to Jimmy."

"Do the Las Vegas police have any idea what happened to Kari?"

"No."

"But they keep questioning you?"

"Sure. But what can I say? I act like she just wandered off into the desert and disappeared."

Alex ground her teeth. "Shit! The more I think about all this, the more crazy I get. Two worlds, two of each of us. You know, I can't look in a mirror these days without feeling that some crazy chick is staring back at me."

"She is. It's you."

"What's it like taking care of Whip?"

"He's never a problem. Since he woke up to who he is, his health has rapidly improved. He has the healing gene. My father says he should make a full recovery." I added, "And he's begun to talk a little."

"That's great."

"It's fantastic. He's so damn smart. He's always cracking me up. Really, it's no sacrifice to take care of him."

"But he was a monster in the other world. As those memories come back, won't he change?" Alex asked.

"I know what you're afraid of. My father and I have talked about it a lot. But the Council's found that the world in which you go through the death experience usually sets the tone of a person's personality. Since Whip 'died' in this world, the positive side of him should stay in control. So, no, I'm not worried that he's going to murder me in my sleep."

Alex stared at me. She went to speak but stopped herself.

"What is it?" I asked.

"Nothing."

"You're thinking how much I've changed. How I'm not the sweet and innocent Jessie you once knew."

"I didn't say that," Alex protested.

"It doesn't matter, it's true." Huck began to stir, and I lifted him up and held him to my chest. At moments like this, when he was near my heart, I felt closest to Jimmy, and knew beyond any doubt that he was his child, never mind the uncertainty Kari had tried to plant inside me.

My bitterness toward the Lapras had not faded. It was only because of them that Jimmy had been forced to take the risk that had killed him. I would never forgive the Lapras for that. One day, I was confident, I would make them pay.

"Jessie?" Alex said, puzzled at my last remark.

The name Jessie felt strange to me. I worried if it was because I identified more with Jessica, the powerful witch. I was not sure if I admired that person. She was, after all, a killer.

"It's nothing," I said.

I heard a sound at the front door, the mailman stuffing our box with next month's bills. I got up to check if there was any news from UCLA. Because I had been accepted late—with my father's help—it looked like I was going to have trouble getting the classes I wanted. But I wasn't worried—I was just grateful a part of my life was returning to normal.

In the box I found a red letter addressed to me, with no return address. The stamp said it had been mailed from Las Vegas. I tore it open in front of Alex. She must have seen my face fall.

"What's wrong?" she asked.

I held out the letter so we could both read it.

I needed to read it twice to believe it.

Dear Jessie,
I pray this note finds you well.
You put on a wonderful show in the desert.
One day soon we'll have to meet.
Yours, the Alchemist
P.S. Syn sends her greetings.

"Who the hell is the Alchemist?" Alex asked.

"Trust me, you don't want to know," I said.

"But that line about Syn. That's a joke, isn't it? You killed her. I mean, you killed her in witch world. Shouldn't she have automatically died in this world?"

I remembered how Kendor had sworn he had killed the Alchemist in witch world. That he could not possibly be alive in the real world. Kendor had been adamant, and yet there had been something in his voice that had made me doubt him.

"That's what I was told," I said.

Alex chewed on that a moment. "Are you worried?"

I hesitated. "Yes."

JESSIE'S STORY CONTINUES IN

Black Knight

TURN THE PAGE FOR A SNEAK PEEK!

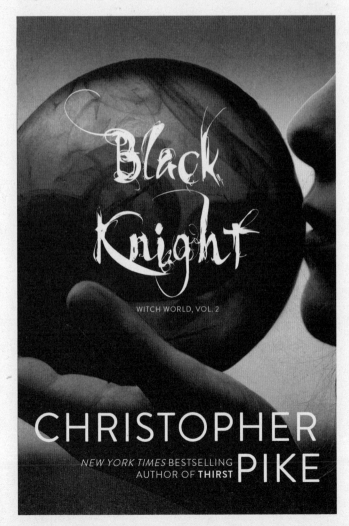

Black Knight

WITCH WORLD, VOL. 2

CHRISTOPHER PIKE

NEW YORK TIMES BESTSELLING
AUTHOR OF **THIRST**

EVERY NIGHT, FOR NINE NIGHTS IN A ROW, I DREAM OF a guy I've never met. He's always working the same job. Always planning and enacting the same ingenious crime. Always vanishing at the end of the night.

Worse, he's not someone I observe from a distance. The dream is light-years beyond lucid. If it wasn't so intriguing, I'd call it a nightmare. For in my dreams I *am* him—Marc Simona, a nineteen-year-old parking attendant at a famous Hollywood theater. I see through his eyes, I think his thoughts. Indeed, I know everything there is to know about him.

Except why he haunts me.

My name is Jessica Ralle and I'm a witch. I've explained all this before. How I traveled to Las Vegas with my friends the weekend after I graduated high school. How I was initiated into the ancient game of red queen. How I died and was reborn in the mysterious realm known as witch world.

Last time, I told my story as if it happened in the past, which it did. But this time I'll tell it like it's happening now. I have my reasons, and by the time I finish this tale they will be obvious.

I had been a witch for only a month when I began to dream of Marc. At first I told no one about him. I mean, I couldn't tell James Kelter, my boyfriend, that my unconscious was obsessing over another guy. And since I couldn't even see Jimmy anymore in the real world—but only when he and I were awake together in witch world—he was jealous enough about what I was doing with the other half of my life. It wasn't that he didn't trust me. He was just . . . well, human. Hell, had the situation been reversed, I would have been none too happy.

At the same time, I was hesitant to confide in my best friend, Alex Simms. Although Alex had the genetic potential to become a witch—or to be "connected," as they called it in witch world—she had yet to go through the initiatory rite of dying and being revived—a process that usually triggered an awareness of the other world in people who had the right genetic makeup. Alex said she wasn't afraid but we both knew that wasn't true. I didn't blame her. I wouldn't have volunteered to die. Who would? The only way I became a witch was because I was forced into it.

Yet I was still hoping Alex would one day join me and become a witch, and for that reason I kept my mouth shut about

Marc. I didn't want to give her another reason to be scared.

Why I hesitated to tell my father about the dreams, though, I wasn't sure. It could have been because he'd only been back in my life for a month when I began to have them. Or else it was because he'd never spoken about having a similar experience. As far as I knew, seeing through the eyes of another person while you were asleep was not a "standard" witch power. Whatever, my father still intimidated me and I didn't see him that often. Plus I wasn't the kind of person who talked about personal stuff on the phone. I was paranoid that way. I always felt like someone was listening.

So I was alone with my dreams, alone with Marc every night when I closed my eyes and fell asleep. Like I said, I felt I was inside him, that I actually *was* him. It was weird; it was disturbing and yet there was something seductive about it as well. Marc. I was pretty sure he wasn't a witch, but he was a fascinating character. . . .

CHAPTER ONE

PREMIERE NIGHT AT GRAUMAN'S CHINESE THEATRE. Roll out the red carpet and prepare to welcome the hordes of beautiful people in their Mercedes S-Class sedans, Jaguar convertibles, Beamers, and Bentleys—and a bevy of other cars worth more than most U.S. homes.

Because he was a parking attendant for Grauman's—now legally the TCL Chinese Theatre, a name no one in Hollywood was even aware of—the majority of people his age would have assumed Marc Simona loved riding in such cars. The truth was he didn't. He just parked them, usually drove them less than two hundred yards. He never got to feel how they handled on the open road, and besides, even if he'd been given a chance to drive a sports car up the California coast, he wouldn't have cared. The only thing that mattered to him was how much trunk space each vehicle had.

The space was what mattered.

That and what kind of jewelry the owners of the cars—specifically the ladies—wore to the red-carpet events. Because Marc didn't park the cars for tips. Being a valet was just a role he played so he'd know which trunk to climb into at the end of the night.

Most people would have called Marc a thief.

He liked to think of himself as a professional.

Either way he was raking in huge bucks.

During his last trip to New York City and its famous Diamond District—he'd driven cross-country all by himself, in three days no less—he'd fenced a pair of sapphire earrings studded with diamonds and netted twenty grand in cash. The gaudy blue stones had been five carats each, and the lonely eared woman he'd swiped them from had also been wearing a gold bracelet laced with rubies that he'd sold for another ten thousand.

It amazed him that the vast majority of celebrities had no taste. He was something of an expert on the subject. He'd seen with his own eyes how difficult it was, if not impossible, for a certain category of rich or famous women to resist the temptation to drape themselves in the bulk of their jewelry box while attending a red-carpet event.

For Marc that group was easy to spot: female stars who were a few too many years past the cursed number forty, and whose phone had stopped ringing; or else trophy wives who had visited their plastic surgeons one too many times to suction off fat that would have better been shed with diet and exercise. Either group was, to Marc, the equivalent of walking pawnshops.

"Scratch it and you're dead," a producer snapped at Marc as he handed over the keys to a black Mercedes sports coupe, while another parking attendant helped the man's wife out through the passenger door.

Marc recognized the guy—Barry Hazen, executive producer on tonight's film. By all rights Hazen should have been the man of the hour. Yet Marc knew—as did anyone remotely connected to the business—that Hazen had not worked on the film at all. The guy was filthy rich. He and his partners owned a medium-size production company. All he did was write checks. He never made creative decisions. Yet, with his cash, he was able to put his name on films he probably couldn't even follow.

That was fine with Marc. Because even though Mr. Hazen was sixty years old with snow-white hair and an Armani tux, Mrs. Hazen was a thirty-year-old redhead wearing a diamond necklace with a central rock the size of a golf ball. It was so big it must have started forming back when the dinosaurs walked the earth. Marc could only dream what he could hock it for.

Marc smiled as he took the man's keys. "Have no fear, Mr. Hazen. I know a secret spot I can stow this baby where God himself couldn't touch it."

Mr. Hazen nodded his approval. "We'll be here late. Stay behind and pick it up for me and I'll make it worth your while."

"Absolutely," Marc said. He always stayed late for the after-picture party so he could prey on that one couple he'd select who would return home so tired and drunk that they'd fall into bed the instant they entered their house. But whoever that couple turned out to be—so far the Hazens looked good, but Marc knew he'd have several candidates before the night was over—he'd have to clock out before they returned for their car.

Why? The answer was simple. He had to be finished with his work so he could ride home with the couple in their trunk.

Marc hopped in the car and headed straight for Hollywood Boulevard without bothering to check the back, tearing around the block. Grauman's had been built ages ago, in the era of black-and-white films, and its parking lot could accommodate only a fraction of the valet traffic. Nowadays the best place to stow a Mercedes was in the mall next door. It had a ten-level parking structure and from experience Marc knew how early the bottom level emptied. It was perfect; it gave him more than enough privacy to keep up his lucrative side job.

He stashed Hazen's sports car in a spot he reserved for his most promising candidates. Besides being physically isolated, it was outside the range of any security cameras and had a seldom-used janitor's closet where he could store the tools of his trade and work without being interrupted.

Marc hurried to that closet and locked the door behind him. From a box hidden in the corner beneath a filthy sink, he took out a flat, two-inch-square steel case loaded with putty. Separating the Mercedes's key from the rest of Hazen's keys, he placed it inside the case and pressed the top shut.

Making the impression of the key was easy—the remainder of the process took patience and skill. Opening the case and removing the key, he reached for a tube of oily brown goo that could best be described as "plaster-glue," and squeezed it into the impression.

Marc didn't know the exact chemical makeup of the material, nor did he care. All that mattered was that it dried fast and hard, which it did when heated. That was its only drawback and the main reason why it wasn't as easy to duplicate keys as most people thought. To speed up the process he kept a battery-powered heater running in the janitor's closet. He kept extra cases on hand as well. There were nights he'd go through a dozen of them and prepare a dozen spare keys.

Yet in the end he'd use only one key and sneak into only one house—if he was lucky. A lot of factors had to come together for his plan to work. So far, after a year of parking celebrity cars and working over twenty red-carpet events, he'd managed to slip into only seven homes. And out of those seven he'd only struck gold four times.

Of course, the gold had been attached to jewels . . . so he couldn't complain.

Marc finished applying the plaster and again closed his steel case and held the top tight for a minute without moving an inch. Then, after opening it and leaving the case and the key atop the heater to dry, he cleaned Mr. Hazen's original key with a paper towel soaked in alcohol and bleach. Whenever he managed to steal something beautiful and expensive, he knew there was no easier way for the police to trace the crime back to him than if he left even the tiniest residue of putty on the original car key.

Since Hazen was his first candidate of the night, Marc was out of practice and it took longer than usual before he was able to exit the janitor's closet—six whole minutes. The process should have taken him half that time.

Damn, he thought. His boss, Steve Green—a rough-voiced ex-sailor from Australia and the head of the valet parking—was going to wonder what was taking him so long.

Yet when Marc finally did leave the janitor's closet, he did so without the fake key in hand. From practice, he knew it was best to let it dry on the heater for at least twenty minutes. The hotter it got, the harder it got.

When Marc got back to the theater, his boss did in fact ask where the hell he'd been. "Got caught behind a couple of cop cars while swinging around the block," Marc lied.

"Did they stop you?"

"Almost. I was speeding."

Green grinned his approval. He was famous for taking Jags

and Porsches out for a spin during the downtime in the middle of the movie.

Marc grinned along with his boss but cringed inside. The fact Green had noticed the delay was not good. It was reason enough to cross the Hazens off his list of candidates.

"Where'd you park Hazen's Hard-on?" Green asked. It was a common belief among the people who worked valet that most celebrity cars were phallic symbols.

Marc handed over the keys to his boss. "Next door, level G, south corner, slot nineteen, away from everyone else. You know how that asshole is about his wheels."

Green nodded as he hung the keys on the appropriate hook. "You can't be too careful with the guy who's paying for the party. He can get us all fired."

Marc relaxed as he noticed how fast his boss dropped the matter. But it was a warning he'd have to pick up his duplicating pace. At the same time, he'd have to be more selective about whom he chose as candidates.

Yet he knew he couldn't control all aspects of the heist. A large part of being a successful thief was luck. For example, how late a couple was going to leave, and how drunk they were going to be—he couldn't predict that ahead of time. That's why he had to make so many extra keys. He had to play the odds.

The time for the premiere drew near and traffic picked up. Marc found himself running back and forth from the valet booth with hardly a chance to catch his breath. However, he did manage to identify another three targets.

First came Mr. and Mrs. Kollet, who were connected to the studio that was distributing the film. They would definitely be staying late for the after-film party. Mrs. Kollet was wearing a diamond bracelet that literally dazzled Marc's eyes. As an added bonus, the couple stumbled getting out of their car and he needed only a whiff of the vehicle's interior to know they were already drunk—always a plus.

Second was Cynthia Parker, one of the most brilliant scriptwriters in the city. Although she wore a relatively modest red gown, around her neck was a string of pearls that looked like they had once belonged to a European court. The individual pearls were not excessively large but had a silver-white color that gave them what the muse in Ms. Parker might have called an "angelic sheen." Marc was careful to park her car next to the Hazens' and make a copy of her key.

Finally, there was the star of the film, Silvia Summer, and her football star boyfriend, Ray Cota of the San Francisco 49ers. They arrived late in a white Jaguar and received the loudest cheers from the gathered fans. Ms. Summer was young, but rich and successful—in the top three on the A-list of talent in her age bracket—eighteen- to twenty-five-year-olds. She'd been the lead in two hits; this would probably be her third.

Ms. Summer wore a heart-shaped emerald at the end of a gold necklace. Marc had seen plenty of emeralds in his time and knew the stone was notorious for its number of inclusions—natural flaws that showed up as dark spots under close inspection. Yet because he opened the door for her and because her breasts would have stolen the eyes out of the head of any red-blooded American male, he inadvertently got a closer look at the emerald than he planned and could have sworn it was close to flawless.

"Welcome," Marc said with a genuine smile as he shut the car door behind her. "It's an honor. I've seen all your movies. I hear you're great in this one."

Unlike most stars of her wattage level, she took the time to look him in the eye and reply. She even leaned close so that only he could hear. "I look good because everyone else sucks," she confided.

Mark had to laugh. "I heard that as well."

She paused and stared at him. She was blond and beautiful, sure, but sharp as well. He could spot her intelligence in the way she studied him, and it made him wonder if it was wise to choose her as a candidate. Stealing a necklace from a movie star was one thing—not getting caught was another. It might have been a mistake to speak to her. Her gaze continued to linger.

"You don't look like the sort of guy who should be parking cars," she said.

Marc shrugged. "It pays the bills."

Again, she came near. "For now. But there's something

in your eyes. Trust me, one day you're going to be somebody."

It was a moment, a special moment, but it didn't last. At that instant her boyfriend swept around the Jaguar, tossed his keys high in the air to Marc—who caught them without blinking—and led Ms. Summer onto the red carpet and toward the theater entrance.

Marc was fortunate to end up with the keys. Ordinarily the driver handed them to whoever opened the driver's door. Marc was as far from superstitious as a guy could be. Even as a four-year-old, bouncing from one orphanage to another, he'd realized Santa Claus had been invented to sell more toys. But he trusted his gut and didn't feel it was a coincidence that he'd ended up with the keys to Ms. Summer's car. He thought somebody was trying to tell him something.

It turned out her Jaguar was the last car he parked before the film began. Marc put it near the Hazens' Mercedes, on the bottom level of the mall lot. He took his time making an impression of her key, and took even more time cleaning the original.

He had selected only four targets, which was unusual for him—last time he'd had ten at this stage. Yet all four were prime: They had the jewels; their connection to the picture was such that they'd all stay late; he'd been able to make an impression of their car key; and they all had plenty of trunk space.

Now it was all a question of timing.

It was against the rules for the valet crew to watch the film, but Green was a laid-back boss and let Marc and a buddy of his, Teddy Fox, slip into the theater fifteen minutes after the movie started. All the seats were taken and they had to stand at the rear, but Marc didn't mind. He found a marble wall to lean against and rested the back of his head on the cool stone. It was a relief to rest for a few minutes and the film wasn't half bad.

It was a romantic comedy structured around a mystery. A couple were only an hour away from getting married when both their wedding rings vanished. At the start the story focused on a search for the clever thief, but it was the buried doubts about the marriage that the crime suddenly raised in the bride and groom that created the bulk of the laughs. Silvia Summer had been too hard on the film. The crowd spent most of the movie laughing out loud. Ordinarily Marc was demanding when it came to films, but even he couldn't resist chuckling a few times. He especially enjoyed the lead actress. Ms. Summer was even more stunning on the big screen.

He kept thinking how he'd like to see her again, socially. A silly thought, sure—she had a boyfriend and he was a nobody. But the remark she'd made getting out of her car—it had stayed with him.

What had she seen in him? It couldn't have been his face, although there were plenty of girls who thought he was worth a second look. It was like they had connected for an instant in some mysterious way. The simple fact was he liked her, and he found it ironic that the feeling made his desire for her necklace even greater, when it should have been the other way around.

He didn't dwell too long on the paradox. He knew the way his mind worked. He had two trains racing in the two hemispheres of his brain that unfortunately were usually on the same track and racing toward each other, which was another way of saying that he was pretty sure he was screwed up.

That was okay, he accepted it, he had to accept it; no one had given him a choice. He knew something of psychology. He hadn't had a lot of basic education but he read plenty. The fact that he had grown up without a single parent, biological or foster, and had been living on his own since the age of fifteen—often on the streets—it was a miracle he wasn't already dead or in jail.

Of course, the night was still young.

Marc rubbed his hands together in anticipation as he watched the film. He was sweating but it was a sweet sweat. He stole for money, that was obvious, but the deeper reason was the action, the rush it gave him. All the planning, all the hoops he had to jump through, the constant risk, the countless on-the-spot decisions he had to make—bundle it all together and it gave him an adrenaline high he couldn't find anywhere else. Often, he thought, he'd be a thief even if there was no payoff.

The film ended and the crowd gave it a standing ovation, partly because it was a pretty good film but mostly because the audience knew the picture's creators were in the theater and hoping they'd stand and cheer. The director and the producer delivered brief thank-you speeches, and then it was party time.

Only half the audience had passes to the party, but because the theater was so large that was still close to five hundred people. Marc knew for a fact all four of his candidates would be at the party. It was held at an elegant hotel across the street from the theater and halfway down the block. It was not unusual to hear a number of celebrities grumble as they made the short trek, although no one had to worry about traffic or lights—the cops invariably blocked off Hollywood Boulevard immediately after the film.

Marc would liked to have walked with the crowd to the party and study his candidates more closely, but he had to get back to work. On average he got tipped ten bucks a car—nothing to sneeze at when he could pick up ten to fifteen cars an hour.

After ninety minutes the number of guests looking for their vehicles dropped, and Green usually let two-thirds of the valets go home. However, because Marc had been on the job a year, and Green liked him, he was always allowed to stay late.

It was at this point that Marc had to push his plan to the next level. There was no way to make a final decision on who to go home with without slipping into the party and taking a last look at his candidates. For one thing, he had to be sure they were still at the party. It was always possible a candidate could have slipped out while he was off finding a car.

The movie had ended at ten p.m. The director and producer had spoken until ten fifteen, and the party had begun at ten thirty. From experience Marc knew he could slip into the party—without a pass—from midnight on. Security grew lax as the night wore on, and besides, his valet uniform gave him a cloak of respectability. After telling Green he had to use the restroom, Marc stole into the hotel and went upstairs to the party—which was spread over three areas: a charming lounge; a massive conference room; and an exotic outdoor section that circled a delicious swimming pool.

It was a warm night—most people were outside by the pool, which glowed a haunting aquamarine while also reflecting rows of flaming torches. There were open bars inside and out and it was the rare person who wasn't drinking.

Marc spotted three of his candidates spread around the pool. The only person he couldn't locate was Cynthia Parker, the scriptwriter. She had probably split immediately after the film without his knowing. Hell, she had written the damn thing—she might have gotten up and walked out in the middle. Marc knew that most writers found it hard to see their work on the screen. They usually focused too much on how the director had ruined their material.

So he was down to the Hazens, the Kollets, and Silvia Summer and her boyfriend, Ray Cota, the football jock. Marc strolled by each couple, studying them carefully but not allowing them to see him.

The Hazens were both drunk, no question, and Marc would have considered taking them on but they were so intoxicated he worried his boss, Green, would recognize their condition and not allow them to drive home. Indeed, he might stuff the Hazens in a taxi—whether they agreed or not—and send them on their way. Marc had seen Green do it before.

Mr. Kollet was also staggering around but, surprisingly, his wife, who had smelled of alcohol at the start of the night, now appeared sober. Marc saw she was holding a glass of what looked like Coke, which made him wonder if he had misread her from the start. It was possible her husband's breath had been so strong it had polluted her aura. Whatever, she looked a hundred percent sober, which meant her diamond bracelet was probably off-limits.

Silvia Summer and her boyfriend made for an interesting mix. Ray Cota had a drink in his hand and was laughing plenty loud at every joke but he looked like the sort who could hold his liquor. Green wouldn't be worried about Ray driving home.

But Silvia Summer was a puzzle. Marc studied her a grand total of twelve minutes and saw her down two tall margaritas. Yet she wasn't laughing and socializing with her boyfriend. Indeed, she stood a few feet away, by herself, staring off into the distance. Something had upset her, Marc thought. She had been fine earlier. He could hardly believe it when, right as he was leaving the pool area, she strode to the bar and ordered a third drink.

That was a lot of booze to swallow in such a short period. She was not a big girl—her blood alcohol must have been off the chart. From a strategic point of view that was perfect. The essence of his scheme depended on the female he chose returning home too tired and too intoxicated to put her jewelry away in a secure place—like a high-tech home safe.

During his four previous successful heists, the women had invariably dumped their jewelry on top of their chest of drawers or on their bathroom counters and had then fallen into bed in a coma beside their husband or boyfriend. Tonight, all night, he had been praying that the identical scenario would repeat itself.

Yet seeing Silvia upset bothered Marc and he wasn't sure why. They'd only exchanged a few words. True, she had treated him with respect, but lots of pretty women had given him a wink and a smile. Being upset would make her careless. He should see her dark mood as a plus. Yet as he left the party, it gnawed at him that something had happened that had disturbed her.

Maybe she had hated the movie.

It only made it worse that he had *almost* made up his mind whom he had to go after. It should be Silvia Summer. She and her wide-receiver boyfriend fit most of the criteria on his self-made list. Plus it didn't hurt that her emerald was the most expensive piece of jewelry he'd seen all night.

He was probably going to steal it from her. She would

wake up in the morning and it would be gone. That would be a shame. Of course, it was more than likely she had borrowed the necklace. Few stars her age had giant emeralds in their private collection. Chances were her stylist had picked it up at a Beverly Hills store that afternoon with the understanding it would be returned within twenty-four hours. That was standard in the business.

However, Silvia would still be responsible for the necklace. Filing a police report would not make that responsibility vanish. Granted, she probably had insurance, but he'd still be putting her through a ton of grief. And there was still a chance the necklace belonged to her. For all he knew it might have sentimental value.

There were a few other details that made him hesitant to go after her emerald. The exquisite nature of the stone, its uniqueness, the fame of the last celebrity to wear it—all these points would make it difficult to fence. Even if he drove all the way to New York, it was possible he'd have trouble finding a buyer. There was no question the stone's heart shape would have to be ground away. It was even possible he'd have to break it into a half dozen smaller stones. He was no expert when it came to the craft, but he was no slouch, either. Definitely, it would be safer to break it down.

Yet it was such a beautiful stone.

It would be a pity to ruin it.

"Shut the fuck up, would ya," Marc told his mind as he

headed back to the valet station, which had temporarily moved across the street to the hotel lobby to take care of the last of the evening's clients. He knew all the cons about stealing the emerald and in the end they were all bullshit. Silvia was a near perfect candidate and she was wearing a near perfect stone.

The bottom line was what the emerald was worth. Retail, it had to cost at least five million, maybe as high as ten. That meant he could get at least a million for it in the Diamond District, maybe two million, more than all his previous jobs combined. No way was he going to walk away from that kind of cash.

It was decided.

He had to get into Silvia's trunk and soon.

"I'm beat. Would it be all right if I called it a night?" Marc asked Green as he walked up to the counter they had set up in the hotel lobby. All the guests had been previously told that this was the place to pick up their cars.

Marc added a yawn as he made his request and his boss gave him a nod. "I've still got Ted, Jerry, and Sandy running the route," Green said. "They should be enough." He added, "I hope."

"I can stay, you know, if you're worried."

Green glanced at the key hooks. "Did the party look like it was winding down?"

Marc hesitated. "Why you asking me?"

"Sandy said she just saw you up there."

Marc kept his outward composure but inside he grimaced. If he managed to steal the emerald, any unusual behavior on his part could later trigger an alarm. Green was a nice guy but no dummy. If the cops came by later and started asking questions, he might remember this exact moment.

Marc spoke causally. "I just took a quick look at the buffet." He added with a hint of guilt, "Well, actually, I sort of sampled the shrimp."

Green brightened. "Was it good?"

Marc grinned. "Fantastic. And they have a huge spread of sushi. If you're quick, you should be able to load up before they put it away."

Green shook his head. "Got to stay here."

Now was a perfect opportunity to negate any suspicion. Granted, it might cost him a shot at the emerald, but it would make it clear to his boss that he'd only gone upstairs for the food.

"Bullshit," Marc said, taking a step behind the counter. "I can handle the stragglers for a few minutes."

"You sure? You said you're exhausted."

"Hey. I'm nineteen years old. I never go to bed till four in the morning. Go now, quick, and put together a bag that will last you the rest of the week. There's only one caterer left and she won't care what you swipe. You know they just throw out what's left over." Marc added casually, "Oh, I saw some Alaskan crab fish."

"Are you shitting me?" his boss asked, a gleam in his eyes. Marc had seen Green eating crab fish a month ago and knew they were his favorite. He also knew there were plenty left.

Marc snorted. "Stop yapping and go. I did graduate from high school. I can hand out a few keys for a few minutes."

The sad truth was he hadn't graduated from high school.

"Thanks," Green said, turning for the elevator. Marc wouldn't be surprised if his boss returned with several bags of goodies. Green had a pregnant wife at home and was always complaining about how hungry she was for exotic food.

As it turned out the Hazens came looking for their car while Green was gone, and Marc had to tactfully tell the bigwig that he was too drunk to drive. Immediately, Mr. Hazen started swearing at him but just as fast Mrs. Hazen jumped in between them and told her husband to shut his trap.

"Larry, you apologize to this nice young man," she said. "He's just doing his job and he might have just saved our lives. You know we're in no shape to drive."

Mr. Hazen calmed down fast enough, although he didn't bother to offer an apology. He plopped down on a nearby chair and belched loudly. "Shit. Somebody call us a cab."

Marc signaled for a taxi that was waiting outside and opened the door for Mrs. Hazen, who slipped him a hundred dollars before climbing inside. Marc shook his head like it was too much but the woman insisted.

"It's for having to listen to my husband," she said. "He acts like an old goat when he drinks but I still love him."

"Just get home safe, Mrs. Hazen," Marc said. "I'll leave a note for your car to be sent over in the morning."

"Thank you, dear," she said.

Green was gone longer than Marc expected—a full twenty minutes. During that time the Kollets came for their car. Now the decision had been plucked from his hands. Either he went after Silvia or waited until next time. Yet he knew it was unlikely that he'd ever have a shot at such a large stone again. That was what kept him focused. If he could steal and fence the emerald, he'd be able to quit his life as a thief and get on to something important.

Whatever that might be . . .

In reality he'd be forced to quit. As it was he was already playing Russian roulette with the LAPD. Eventually the string of missing jewels would be traced back to the theater's valet service, and to him. No way he was hanging around until he got caught. Tonight's job had to be his last.

Clocking out, Marc crossed the street to the mall's parking structure and headed straight for the janitor's closet. The battery-operated heater had warmed the confined space to over a hundred degrees. Ordinarily he'd hide the heater in the corner of the closet, but since tonight would hopefully be the last time he'd use it, he decided to dump it and the extra cases somewhere outside the mall.

The decision carried with it its own risks. It was after two in the morning and Silvia and her boyfriend would be wanting their car soon. If he left the mall to dump his equipment, one of the other valets might come for the Jaguar at that exact moment.

Yet he decided it was worth the risk. He couldn't leave the tools of his trade behind for a detective to find. Collecting his used and unused steel cases, the heater, and two spare tubes of the magic plaster mix, he stuffed everything in a canvas bag and headed for the door.

He was out on Hollywood Boulevard in a minute. He had scouted the surrounding area earlier. Small details mattered. He knew of a family-owned pizza joint three blocks north of the mall. It had a large Dumpster that was unloaded every Sunday morning, which would be tomorrow, before ten. He considered three blocks the minimum distance to safely dispose of his equipment. Even if he managed to steal the emerald, and some brilliant cop quickly traced the theft back to the theater, he or she wouldn't have time to search several city blocks for clues before his stash disappeared.

Yet the three blocks were long blocks and he had to force himself not to run. Running people looked like guilty people, particularly at night, and especially when they had a bag in their hands. The whole way to and from the pizza joint, he kept thinking that Silvia would have already come for her car and split.

But the Jag was still there when he returned to the mall.

He studied it before trying out his newly minted key. The trunk was on the small size—he'd glanced at it before but had failed to scrutinize it—and there was nothing worse than getting trapped in a trunk. It had happened to him only once, but that had been one time too many.

It had been an old Mercedes, from the sixties, built like a tank, and it had not come equipped with a child's safety-release lever—the kind that were nowadays standard on most vehicle trunks as well as refrigerators. Worse, the lock on the car's trunk had not responded to his usual bag of tricks, and he hadn't even been able to push out the backseat and crawl into the interior of the car. In the end he'd spent an entire night sweating in the garage of a mansion he'd never actually seen and needing to pee so bad he'd finally pissed all over the spare tire.

He had only managed to escape the next afternoon when the owner had taken the car to get washed. Fortunately the guys at the car wash had been mostly illegal immigrants and hadn't questioned the mysterious character who had suddenly popped out of the trunk in a white shirt, black pants, and black tie—his basic valet attire—and run like hell into a nearby alley.

Since that happened, he never climbed into a trunk without carrying a mini crowbar.

Marc noted that Silvia's Jag had a high-tech alarm system but was not overly worried. The best alarms had trouble identifying a fake key. However, as a safety precaution, it was still best to pop the trunk from inside the car, from the driver's seat, after slipping the key in the ignition and turning it partway. A retired owner of a car dealership had taught him that little trick. It *reassured* the computer chip in the most sophisticated car alarms.

For the first time, Marc took out the case that held the Jaguar's copied key. It had a couple of rough edges but he was able to file them off with a small tool kit he always carried on any job. It *looked* perfect but he nevertheless held it up to the light and gave it a final exam, once again thankful his section of the parking structure was not covered by security cameras.

Then he slid the key in the lock and turned it.

Presto! It opened without a hitch.

Moving fast, Marc climbed in the car, leaving the door open, and slipped the key in the ignition, turning it a millimeter shy of starting the car. At the same time he scanned for an interior trunk release, finding one on the bottom of the driver's door beside a gas-tank release. He pressed it and the trunk popped open. Turning the ignition off, he withdrew the key and climbed out and locked the door behind him.

Time to get in the trunk. For some reason, for Marc, this part was harder than sneaking into a couple's bedroom while they were sleeping. He'd read somewhere that everyone suffered from some degree of claustrophobia—it was just a question of how much. He wasn't sure where he fell on the scale but doubted he would have made it as an astronaut.

The Jaguar's trunk was clean and empty but tight. It made sense, it was a sports car. Christ, it didn't even have a backseat. He'd known that ahead of time; nevertheless, it still annoyed him. Or perhaps "intimidated" him would've been a more accurate word.

Marc took off his valet vest and pulled out a pair of surgical gloves and a surgical cap and put them on. He'd seen too many reruns of *CSI*, *NCIS*, *CSI: Miami*—and *CSI: Lunar*, he snickered to himself—to dare leave behind any fingerprints or hair in the trunk. He even dabbed his eyebrows with Vaseline. Best to be paranoid when one damn molecule of his anatomy could strand him in the slammer for a decade.

Finally, Marc climbed into the trunk and pulled it shut.

It was dark inside and it felt stuffy. The only way he could fit in and maintain blood flow to all his limbs was to squeeze into the fetal position. He wiggled around with his back to the front and his face toward the rear. He had little room to move his arms and that concerned him. Later, when it was time to leave the trunk, he'd need his hands free if the release paddle failed. Of course there was no reason to think it should fail, but tell that to Murphy and the law named after him. Marc occasionally wondered who the real Murphy had been. The guy must have had a miserable life.